IN WALKED TROUBLE

DANA HAWKINS

Ebook ISBN: 978-1-80508-207-1
Paperback ISBN: 978-1-80508-209-5

Cover design: Leah Jacobs-Gordon
Cover images: Shutterstock

Published by Storm Publishing.
For further information, visit:
www.stormpublishing.co

ALSO BY DANA HAWKINS

Not in the Plan

To my forever. You are the pomegranate in my Cosmo, the lemon in my Lemon Drop, the strawberry in my daiquiri. You make everything brighter and my life complete. I love you.

ONE

DRINK SPECIAL: SUGAR-RIMMED MORNING WITH TWO SHOTS OF BITTERS

Today was the day. Today was absolutely, hands down, without a doubt, *the day*.

A text message asking Remi James to come in early for her shift to chat about a few changes popped up on her cell from her boss, Gabriella, at exactly 9:09 a.m. Already a numerology omen. Not that Remi believed in that kind of stuff. But her roommate, Ben, did, and some of his insufferable optimism had rubbed off on her these last seven years.

Gabriella ended the text with a smiley face. Gabriella didn't *do* smiley faces.

Remi tapped her feet into the pea-green-and-brown cracked linoleum floor in her and Ben's tiny kitchen and refrained from jumping up and down. A micro-squeal slipped from her lips, and she snapped her mouth shut.

Ben glanced up and cocked a perfectly groomed eyebrow.

"What?" She tossed up a hand. "What are you looking at?" *Okay, fine.* Maybe she was being a little suspicious. She didn't do smiles either—unless the potential of a tip from one of her bar patrons existed, of course.

But today, just like Gabriella's text, she was smiling.

He cleared his throat with a not-so-subtle *eh-hem*. "Did you just almost dance?"

"No." She shoved her phone in her pajamas pocket and poured herself a cup of coffee.

He crossed his golden-brown arms, and flashed a dimpled grin. "Nope. I distinctly saw foot shimmy action. Spill it, Remington. Or I'm gonna call the hospital and have you involuntarily admitted for a full MRI."

She rolled her eyes. "Less than six months of being a nurse and you drop words like 'MRI' on the daily. It's annoying."

"You know, that's a super common word."

She picked up a frayed-edged pillow from the couch and threw it at him. "Nobody likes you."

He shoved the pillow behind his head. "That's not what I heard in the bedroom with my last girlfriend. And boyfriend."

"Gross." The last thing she wanted to think about was the type of sex her roommate—who was like her brother—had with anyone. The paper-thin walls in their two-bedroom apartment were enough to make her frequently want to gouge out her ear canals with a rusty butterfly switchblade.

As he rose from the flamingo-pink couch they found next to the dumpster when they first moved in seven years ago, the single remaining spring squeaked. He grabbed his rainbow sasquatch mug from the coffee table and joined her in the kitchen. "You find another loan officer?"

She shook her head and swiped a dark, curly chunk of hair that fell in front of her eyes. Pretty sure she had gone through every home loan officer in all of Seattle and dipped into a fair chunk of Western Washington. She had half a mind to cross the border into Vancouver to see if a Canadian banker would take pity. After a year of living off ramen noodles, mac 'n' cheese, and bananas, armed with more savings than she ever dreamed possible, she visited a home loan officer. And then another, and another. After begging, pleading, and even dropping a swear word or two—which did not help her cause—they all came back with the bottom line: she needed more savings, or a salaried position.

And today she'd get one of them. Because *today was the day*.

She blew into the mug and sipped. "Gabriella wants me to come in early for my shift."

"So?"

"So? *So?*" she asked. "She never asks that. She doesn't want to pay extra hourly wages for us to come in early."

He twisted his mouth as he rinsed his cup.

Although Ben had never worked at his aunt Gabriella's bar, Remi knew he understood Gabriella was as frugal as they came. "I'm getting the promotion." She grabbed the towel hanging from the stove and dried his dishes. "I feel it down to my burgundy, chipped toenail polish. It's comin', grasshopper."

He reached for a box of cereal and dug out a handful of dry corn flakes. "Did she say that?"

"I already told you what she said."

He leaned against the sink. "Well, you've kissed Gabriella's ass enough over the years that your lips are probably numb."

She narrowed her eyes. "Let's call it ass dusting. I have some pride left."

"I just don't want you to get your hopes up and have them crushed," he said between crunches. "Maybe she needs to talk to you about health codes or wants help with the menu or something."

Remi loved Ben, of course. He was as close to a family member as she had. But right now, Remi needed *insufferably optimistic Ben*, not *practical nature Ben* who made her want to drop-kick him in the liver. "Do not kill my buzz. Please don't do this."

He popped another handful of cereal in his mouth and returned the box to the cabinet. "It's just sometimes you read into things—"

"Ben. Stop."

"Okay, okay. I'm done. Lo siento, mi pequeña bootie-butt."
He squeezed her on the shoulder.

"I hate it when you call me that."

"No, you don't." He hip bumped her on his way to the bathroom, knowing damn well he could defuse any situation with
her by using his native tongue.

She bit back her grin and cracked open the window. The
misty Seattle air carried a trace of fresh laundry from the mat
two buildings down. Normally, by this time in the year, she was
fully over the rain. The heavy gray clouds that felt like a protective blanket in the fall lost their magic by May. But today, she
welcomed the cover.

When Remi had started at Nueve's, a moderately upscale
Puerto Rican bar and restaurant in downtown Seattle, four
years ago, she had one goal—become the head bartender. She
kept her salty attitude in check, a begrudging smile on her face,
and worked her way up from prep to day bartender, to night
bartender, and now to senior. She'd earned the title of Head
Bartender, *dammit*. And finally, it was hers.

Mist drifted through the window. She slammed it shut and
hand-washed the remaining dishes. She hung a mug back on the
hook next to the sunflower-yellow fridge that was probably built
with a combo of lead, resin, and formaldehyde, and waited for
Ben to finish in the bathroom.

Once his bedroom door closed in the distance, she stepped
into the shower and double-checked that no loose tiles were
scattered across the floor. Last week, she'd cut her toe on the
edge of a chunk that had detached. She almost called the landlord to replace it but refrained. After that *one little incident* on
the stairs last month which really wasn't her fault this time, that
resulted in a broken railing, a broken pinkie (not hers), and the
third threat of eviction in a year, she was not so sure that the
landlord would move swiftly to fix anything.

The heated water of the shower calmed her excitement and nerves, and she whistled.

Whistled. Remi didn't whistle.

Knuckles rapped against the door. *Ugh.* Top requirement for their new home: two bathrooms. "No," she yelled as she rinsed the conditioner from her hair. "Didn't you already pee? Use the kitchen sink if you still gotta go."

"That's disgusting," he shouted through the door. "Heading out for a run. Be back in an hour."

After a full body scrub and a twenty-minute hair-diffusing process, she flopped on her bed and pulled out her laptop. Carefully opening it, she sent a quick thankful prayer to the electronic gods that a decade after the Seattle high school district gave kids like her a free laptop, this baby still ran.

Two bedrooms, one bath. *Nope, need more bathrooms.* Next. Three bedrooms, two baths, south side. *Nope, too expensive.* Next. Two beds, one-and-a-half bath. *Nope, not residential enough.* She scrolled through the local listings and scribbled notes down about houses she liked. Then she froze. Right in front of her lay her future via a quaint, mid-century brick bungalow nestled directly in the University of Washington "U District." She scanned the details—three bedrooms, one-and-a-half bath, pink-tiled bathroom, cement basement, and original hardwood floors.

It. Was. Perfect.

Rolling her neck, she made her way into the kitchen and reached for her relaxation stack. She lined up bottles of vodka, gin, vermouth, liqueurs, and other staples across the burnt-orange ceramic counter, and visualized herself doing this in her new home. Next, she laid out bitters, basil, mint, oranges, lemons, lime, sparkling sodas, and miniature juice bottles. She sniffed each one, in different orders, and arranged them like a boozy puzzle. Maybe mixing three-quarters of vodka with a one-eighth of orange liqueur and one-eighth of elderflower liqueur could work. What if she warmed fresh-squeezed orange juice in a pan and added smashed basil with a touch of fine sugar?

Lost in her trance, Remi transformed into a mixology scientist. Her cheeks puckered at the scent of the freshly squeezed lime she added to the glass. In her alcohol-free mixing glass, she layered lavender syrup with club soda, grated a bit of orange zest on top, and sipped. The sweet tang hit her tongue, and she rolled the liquid in her mouth. Nope, not enough orange. She squeezed a bit more of the citrus and a teaspoon of vanilla.

"Uck." The drink only needed a kiss of vanilla, and the added teaspoon turned it into a vanilla tsunami.

In her booze tunnel, as Ben called it, she barely heard him come in until the metallic sound of keys hitting the counter next to her almost made her knock over her glass. "Dude. Really? I swear to God sometimes I want to pluck your lungs out through your eyeballs. You scared the crap out of me."

He snatched the keys and flipped them in his fingers. "You literally suck the fun out of life. You're like the opposite of a life straw. You're a death draw." He grabbed milk from the fridge, sniffed it, and then drank from the carton.

She didn't even bother chiding him.

The scent of muddled cucumber filled the room. She added a small measure of vodka and orange liqueur, shook, then double-strained into a glass. Two lemon zest swipes were added on top. She held the drink to her nose and inhaled. The burn of the booze was subtle, almost like a fog settling on top of a more powerful, colorful scent.

She handed the glass to Ben. "I need a sip test."

He put the milk back in the fridge and wiped his upper lip with the back of his hand. "It's barely after noon."

"It's happy hour somewhere. Come on. I think this might be good." Did being a bartender who didn't drink have some disadvantages? Perhaps. But to her, sobriety was a superpower.

Focusing on the smells and mixer pairings allowed her to be creative with accompaniments she may have otherwise ignored.

Ben rinsed his mouth with water, then brought the glass to his lips. He took a small sip and handed it back.

"Well?" she asked.

"Good stuff."

Satisfied, she grinned.

Ben was fiercely honest, sometimes to a brutal fault. So, when he said something was good, he meant it. He hung his jacket in the closet and moved toward the hall. "Gonna hop in the shower. If you're gone before I get out, kick some juicy bootie today."

"Thanks." She put away her loot and checked the time. One hour left before she could start the rest of her life.

Remi turned the car engine off in the Nueve's parking lot and pulled down the sunshade to check her face in the mirror. Nueve's was one of the few restaurants downtown that had free parking for employees. It was like hitting the employment lottery, especially being so close to Pike Place Market. Now, if only her car that was made in the same year Gwen Stefani released "Hollaback Girl" didn't croak, everything would be good.

She strutted across the parking lot. The rare afternoon sun peeked through the buildings and hit her vampire pale skin. Feeling lighter than she had in forever, she contemplated jumping on the light post and swinging herself Tarzan-style into the entrance. In the kitchen, a cloud of fried pork, garlic, and soup base led her to Gabriella's tiny office in the back.

But when she turned the corner and saw Gabriella laughing with a woman who looked about her own age or a bit younger, she froze. Because it was not just any laugh—it was a hefty laugh. A *familiar* laugh. The laugh Remi thought Gabriella reserved for only her, because they were tight.

Not only was she laughing, but this woman was also sitting in *her* chair. With *her* Gabriella.

And they were so preoccupied with how apparently hilarious this woman was that neither even noticed Remi standing there. Finally, she knocked on the open door.

"Remi! Come in." Gabriella brushed her fingers through her gray waves, a new chic bob that Remi was still getting used to after seeing her for four years with a braid down her back. "This is Maya. Maya, Remi. Maya's going to be joining us on the team."

Remi scanned Maya. She was literally the opposite of her. Remi had nearly black, curly hair tamed only by buckets of cream and a very specific conditioner. Maya's hair was so blond and straight it looked like it could shatter. Remi's dark eyes were a stark contrast to Maya's, a Caribbean-water turquoise that probably had a specific name, but Remi didn't care to know. Unlike Remi's thick thighs, round belly and muscles that could carry two cases of beer at once, Maya's endless legs and long, lean arms looked so unstable that if Remi blew hard enough, she'd fall over.

And then Maya stood, and *of course*. Remi would have to step on her tiptoes to meet her eyes.

Note to self: Wear heels tomorrow.

"Maya?" *She probably spells it My-ah.*

Maya nodded, her posture so straight she looked like she was ready for a runway.

Remi had the urge to square up her shoulders. "How's it going?" she asked, because that was what polite people were supposed to say. But really, she wanted to ask her why she was in her manager's office, sitting like she owned the place, with absolutely no sense of nerves flashing across her flawlessly chiseled face and excruciatingly perfect button nose. Remi supposed she should shake her hand, but she didn't.

"Nice to meet you," Maya said with a wide, perfectly straight-toothed grin. "I've heard a lot about you. Sounds like you have some impressive skills."

"Thanks. Wish I could say the same. Never heard of you."

Gabriella flashed Remi a death glare.

Remi swallowed the *what?* settling on the tip of her tongue.

Gabriella folded the bifocals hanging from the gold chain around her neck. "Maya's an old family friend. Known her since she was in diapers."

The sharp pang of jealousy jabbed deeper than it should at a simple statement. So Gabriella and Snow Princess had history. *Cool, cool.*

Maya tugged on the cross-body purse strapped across her chest. "Should I tell her the story of you spiking my baby bottle with blackberry whiskey to make my cough go away?"

"Oh, Dios mío, your mom is such a liar." Gabriella leaned back in the chair. "I would've never done that to a baby. Now, there *may* have been a time when you were four or five that I told your mom to do it to get you to sleep, but she ignored me."

"Was that before or after I threw up from eating the entire chocolate bunny I stole from your purse?" Maya laughed.

Gabriella laughed.

Remi remained silent.

"So, Remi." Gabriella spun her chair and faced her. "I wanted you to come early for your shift so we can talk about some exciting news."

Finally. Remi's chest lifted. *Maybe this won't be so bad.* She needed to let go of every single mommy, daddy, and green alien issue she had and refocus. Maya might be the new day bartender. They'd been looking to hire a replacement after the other bartender left last week.

She looked at Maya, who offered a soft smile. An annoying,

picture-perfect smile. Her mouth drew Remi in, and *Jesus*, what a pair of lips. Plump, full, smooth, and a delicate shade of pink.

F me.

Gabriella had zero tolerance for workplace drama and sub-arctic tundra tolerance for workplace relationships. *Second note to self: Do not hit on the day bartender.*

Not that Remi would. Her job was too important. She'd never violate Gabriella's trust and had no intention of making anyone feel uncomfortable with unwanted flirting. Never mind that this woman gave off exactly zero queer vibes, so it wouldn't be an issue, anyway.

Remi glanced between Maya and Gabriella, and neither moved. The silence went from awkward, to heavy, to so thick she almost choked. Getting her promotion in front of a Snow Princess audience was not how Remi pictured her afternoon, but whatever. She'd waited four years for this and would take the news in almost any form.

"Remi, Maya will be your new co-bartender for the summer," Gabriella said.

Did she just brace herself? Gabriella was the toughest woman Remi had ever known. Came from Puerto Rico with a suitcase and a dream. Widowed at forty. Last month single-handedly broke up a bar fight between two longshoremen.

And she just braced herself.

"She's got a ton of experience, is less of a pain in the ass than you, and I think you two are going to be amazing together," Gabriella added.

Co? No, she must've misspoken. As a native Spanish speaker, Gabriella sometimes flipped words. Surely, she didn't mean Remi had to roll with a partner now. Remi stared at Gabriella, completely ignoring the other woman. "You mean my second."

Gabriella straightened her back and crossed her arms.

Oh God. The power stance.

"No, your *co*." Gabriella laid her palms flat on the desk. "I'm testing out a new model, having two senior bartenders on at the same time. Orders are taking take too long the usual way, and my profits are dipping."

"Seniors?" Remi studied Maya. "You look like you're two days over being legally able to drink."

Maya lifted a delicate eyebrow. "I'm twenty-three."

"Cool, so you've been bartending for what, two years?" Remi snapped.

"Five, actually."

"How is that even possible?" Remi barely registered the harshness of her tone. A slow burn trickled from her gut and seeped into her cheeks, and she flipped her gaze back to Gabriella. "But what about lead? We've been talking about that for months."

Gabriella dipped her chin and took a breath. "We can discuss that later, but right now, you two will be co-bartenders. Remi, you'll train Maya."

But the house! The listing said it was going on the market in thirty days. She needed this more than she needed anything in her life. Houses don't leave—once you have one, it is there forever. Her dream, her life, was slipping through her fingertips. If Gabriella didn't promote her, she wouldn't get the house, and then everything would be ruined. She exhaled through her teeth. "Is that position still available?" She cursed her voice for cracking.

Gabriella sighed. "As of this moment, no."

"What? *No?*" Four plus years of work for a promotion that no longer existed? Remi felt her cheeks flame. "If there's no position available, what's the incentive for working harder?" *If she says a sense of personal accomplishment, I'm out.*

"I'm glad you asked." A grin spread on Gabriella. "I'm putting forth a onetime cash bonus for my top bar employee. If profits increase by twenty-five percent this month..." She scribbled on a piece of paper with a Sharpie, then turned the paper around. "You take home this."

Remi swallowed at the amount—enough to tip her over the edge to qualify for the home loan. She glanced at Maya, who held an expression that could only be classified as "Oh. My. God."

Gabriella set down the paper and folded her hands. "I think some friendly competition is just what the doctor ordered." Her voice was calm and collected.

Remi was not. She opened her mouth to protest, and Gabriella held up one hand.

Beside her, Maya stood with her posture so firm that Remi was fully convinced she was either part royalty or trying her hardest to intimidate her. *She thinks she can scare me? Puh-lease.* Remi had eight years of foster care in five different homes under her thrift-store belt. She spent three summers picking grapes in Yakima with the sun, bugs, and field mice. A few summers back, she was part of the janitorial crew at Coachella.

Princess Snow Face had nothing on her.

"Remi."

Gabriella gave her that stern mom look that Remi normally pretended to hate, while it secretly filled a hollowness. But today, Remi actually hated it.

"You're gonna play nice, right?"

Gabriella added a sharp, annoying enunciation to "right." Remi had a choice. Cooperate, show Gabriella she could be a professional, and secure her rightfully earned bonus. If she did this, she could qualify for the home, start living her life, and officially bury her past.

Or, she could tell them all to shove it, stomp out of Nueve's jobless, and keep whatever shred of dignity she had left.

The bonus won.

She flashed her most forced smile and shook Maya's hand with the strength of a pit bull ripping open a bacon package.

Maya didn't even flinch.

And now, Remi double-dog hated her. "Of course." Remi masked her gritted teeth. "Welcome to the team."

With absolutely no amount of intimidation or nerves, Maya vise-gripped Remi's hand. "Glad to be here."

A burn filled Remi's belly. *My-ah* was going down.

TWO

DRINK SPECIAL: BEST FRIEND BOURBON
WITH A WELCOME HOME CHASER

Oh my God, she's the most intimidating person I've ever met.

Maya's toes grazed the pavement as she speed-walked down the alley. *Shoulders straight, head high. Shoulders straight, head high.* A half block away, she double-checked no one was watching and leaned against the brick wall.

What a crap show. Her entire body cramped from clenching so tightly from the interaction with Remi. Pinching the bridge of her nose, she exhaled an hour-long worth of trapped air.

The hum of electric city busses on wires and honking traffic created a temporary, nostalgic reprieve. She'd missed so many things about Seattle when she moved to Minnesota. The briny crab smell from the Puget Sound mixed with the evergreen trees, the mild temperature, the Olympics peeking out from the clouds while Rainier waved from the south.

Her phone pinged. She dug it out of her purse and saw the sender of the email: "University of Minnesota Master of Nursing Program Admissions." She stared at the words as tunnel vision developed. The people walking past her with hoodies snugged over their ears and bike riders whizzing by blurred in the background. Her trembling fingers hovered over the scroll tab. She had to read it and accept her fate. But knowing her entire life was on this screen made her want to puke.

She gripped the phone in her palm, then selected Face-Time. As soon as the call connected, Maya blurted out, "The graduate admissions office sent me an email."

"And?" her best friend, Sophie, asked. After a long pause, she exhaled. "You didn't open it, did you?"

Avoidance was Maya's next best friend, and Sophie knew the drill. When they had dated as freshmen in high school, which was so weird to think about now, Maya didn't answer her phone and ate in the library for two weeks to avoid the dreaded, yet inevitable, breakup conversation. She couldn't stomach looking at the face of someone she disappointed. "Did you see your barber today?"

Sophie ran a flattened hand across her buzzed head. "Freshly shaved just like my—nope. Stop distracting me. You've got to read the email."

She shook out her trembling hand. Everything she had gone through, all the promises she'd made—to herself, to *him*—the years her mother spent worrying, all led to the contents of this Calibri-fonted email. Acid built in her stomach, and she breathed through a sharp metallic taste. "I can't, Soph. What if they've denied me?"

"Then we figure it out." Sophie brought a mug to her lips. "How about you read it out loud? Or forward to me and I'll read it for you."

The brick wall dug into her back, and she switched positions. "No. I can do this. Hang on." She flipped off FaceTime, opened the email, and took an unsteady breath. "Dear Maya Marek. We are pleased to inform you that you have been accepted into the fall master's program—"

"Accepted!" Sophie clapped her hands. "You effing did it!"

Maya's heart thumped so ferociously that she almost dropped the phone. She scanned the email again. And one more time, reading each word as slowly as she could. "Accepted. I can't... I didn't think I would." She continued reading, ignoring the honking city street in the background. Bursts of memories flashed by—crying in the library, study sessions, colored highlighters over textbooks. She actually did it. *He'd be so proud.*

"Please see the attachment for the cost associated with the program, and the offered financial aid package. Congratulations, and looking forward to having you join us in the fall." She scrolled through all the information. "Oh, God."

"What? What is it?" Sophie asked.

Her breath ripped from her lungs. She flipped FaceTime back on to see her friend. "They denied the scholarship and financial aid."

Sophie lowered her mug. "I don't understand. Why?"

"Because I'm considered a dependent on my mom, and my mom's promotion last year pushed me over the aid threshold."

Sophie scrunched her nose. "You haven't asked your mom for money since your sixteenth birthday."

Maya kneaded a knuckle into her temple. "I know, but it's complicated. It's based on age, not on the money given to you by your parent."

Sophie's mouth twisted. Forgoing college to start work immediately, Sophie never dealt with issues like mid-terms and financial aid. And in less than five years after graduating high school, she made more money at a creative agency than Maya would dream about making as a nurse for several years.

"Do I have this right?" Sophie said. "We've got a good news, bad news sitch here. Good news, you got accepted! Right?"

"Yes, but bad news is that I don't have the money for it."

"How much is that?"

Maya sighed and kicked a small rock down a gutter. "About the cost of a new car."

Sophie slow whistled. "Yikes." She propped the phone up on the desk and reached to tie her hiking boots. "You moved back home for the summer to save on rent, so that should help, right?"

That's what Maya told everyone. She loved her family. She loved her friend. But she wasn't ready to share the real reason why she returned to Seattle with them, yet. "Yeah, it does. A little."

"And I hate to point this out, but there's the money your dad—"

"No." Maya already knew what Sophie was going to say, and she refused to even entertain the idea. When her father passed, he left everything to Maya's mom, sister, and her. The money for her and Harper was supposed to go into a college fund, but Maya refused to touch hers and instead bequeathed it to Harper. The medical bills and insulin costs Harper would have for the rest of her life were beyond unfair, and Maya needed to level out the playing field.

"Okay." Sophie shook her head. "Sorry. It's a ton of money, but we can do this. Didn't you meet with Gabriella about the bar job today? That pays really well, right?"

Maya exhaled. "Yes, it does. And she told me and the other bartender there's a cash bonus at the end of the month for the top employee."

"What? That's awesome. See! You got this." Sophie threw a jacket on and grabbed her keys. "There's hope on the muddy, gray horizon. You're an amazing bartender."

"You've never once seen me bartend."

Sophie laughed. "Well, that's because you left me in Seattle and moved to the frozen abyss of Minnesota. Seriously, besides being close to your grandparents, why would anyone want to live there?"

She dug the heel of her magenta Converse into the brick. "Because people are nice, the lakes are beautiful, the cost of living is cheaper, and I like having more seasons than just rain and wildfire smoke."

"Fair." Sophie grabbed the phone from the counter and walked out her apartment door. "How are you doing with everything else?"

The metro bus Maya was supposed to hop on zoomed past. *Crap.* She walked to the edge of the alley and slumped down on the green recycled-plastic bus stop bench to wait for the next one. "I don't want to be here."

Maya peeked up to make sure her mother hadn't somehow appeared in the alley and overheard her gut-punching revelation.

Sophie's lip piercing dipped as she frowned. "I know, but it's nice having you back in the city, and you know your mom loves having you home."

"That's not what I meant. Of course it's good to be home, but I want to be back in school. I'm already so delayed."

"Why do you do this to yourself?"

Maya rested her arms on her leg. "Because I was in college for five years and only have a four-year degree."

Sophie's eyes narrowed. "You know that happens to a ton of people, right?"

Of course she knew this. She had to lighten up on her credit load for a few semesters because of her bar shifts, and now she was behind. Every day she was a hamster on a wheel, running, chasing, flailing, and never catching up.

The phone bounced as Sophie walked down the stairs. "How's Harper today?"

"Surprised I'm not asking you with how much time you spend with them." Maya's tone was sarcastic, but she was deeply grateful Sophie had stayed close to her family all these years.

Sophie shrugged. "Whatever. Your mom hooks me up with food."

Maya grinned. Her mom was, in fact, the queen of comfort casserole. "My sister's a freaking champ. How does a kid her age manage her diabetes and still succeed in annoying me within my first week back home? If I was a quarter as tough as her, I'd take over the world."

Half of Maya's heart was left in Minnesota. Half had always been in Seattle. And she knew she'd end up back here. But not like this, not just waiting for time to pass so she could continue her studies.

Harper and her mom welcomed her back with open, squishy bear hugs, but the reality was Maya living here severely broke Harper's routine. She had been a day over seven years old when Maya left for college, and most of Harper's life comprised of just her and their mom. And Maya came back and screwed it up. No matter how excited her mom claimed to be to have Maya home for the summer, her presence was a burden.

She said goodbye to Sophie, watched a sea of luxury electric cars silently drive by, and cranked her neck to check if the approaching bus was hers.

Three months. Ninety days. Then she could return to U of M for her master's degree. Prove herself worthy and receive a spirit wink from her dad. She could do anything for three months—joining a traveling circus act, working on a farm in eastern Minnesota, or a repeat of her last, disastrous relationship.

When Gabriella told her about this summer bartending gig, she failed to mention Maya would be working next to a smoke show with the darkest, most sultry eyes she'd seen in forever. No matter how irritated the words flying from her soft, pouty mouth were, nor how much Maya wanted to crouch under the table and hide from her invasive stare, Remi reeked of womanhood and sexiness. *Damn.* She shook her head to remove the thought.

This was business. She may be a pushover in certain aspects

of her life, but when it came to her degree and family, she took no prisoners. No way would she let smokey eyes, a raspy voice, and killer curves knock her off her game.

The bonus was hers. She needed this money for grad school, or she couldn't go. And not going was not an option.

Ms. Soft Pouty Mouth had better prepare herself.

THREE

Remi's thighs burned. Her arms flamed, and her muscles begged her to stop. Sweat droplets rolled down her neck, and she furrowed her eyes at her nemesis. She raised her aching clenched fists and shielded her face. Exhaling a breath, she squeezed her core, rotated on the ball of her foot, and punched. And again. And again.

"Dude, hold up. Water break. My arms are killing me." Ben dropped his grip from the punching bag. "Give me a second."

Remi lowered her fists and swiped her arm across her forehead to catch the remaining moisture. She bounced back and forth on her feet to keep up her heart rate for a bit before giving up and flopping on the bench. Inhaling, she tried to soften her breathing. The raggedy gym smelled like sticky plastic mats and dried-up sweat, but it held a certain charm. A few *Rocky* posters were slapped on the cracked-paint wall and a clear case holding bronzed mitts from when the owner won a championship in the '80s hung next to it. The gym was cheap, near their apartment, and they'd been going here since they moved in.

"We've only been going like forty minutes," she complained.

He pushed his palm into his shoulder and lifted it with a grimace. "I know. But I seriously underestimated how hard it was doing a puppet show with every single pediatric patient yesterday. Pretty sure I tore my rotator cuff."

"Beauty before pain, always." She couldn't help but feel pride in Ben's transformation over the years. When she met him at thirteen in a foster home, he was a pissed-off, skinny Puerto Rican kid who swore at their foster parents in Spanish and ignored her for the first week. But by week two, they'd become close and stayed in contact even after the courts granted his abuelita custody. Remi was always a little jealous of Ben. Even though his family was dysfunctional, he had a solid support system with his best friend, Charlie, a woman who ran a successful coffee shop, and his aunt Gabriella.

"You better stop hitting it so hard, Rem-a-lem. You're not gonna be able to work your full shift tonight."

"Pfft. I've done worse. Just working off some tension." Or *trying* to work off tension. Her entire body refused to release. After sizing up her competition yesterday, she came home determined, on fire, and... terrified.

"Seriously, what fire bug crawled up your ass?" He ran a towel over his glistening forehead and tossed it back in his gym bag. "Wait. Are you dating?"

She scrunched her mouth. "What? No."

"I mean, I know I've been gone more than normal, but—"

"Seriously. What the hell? Why'd you even ask me that?" She shot a look at him, then stood to stretch and angle herself to avoid his gaze. The question wasn't totally unfair. She had a very strict breakup routine. Melody, Emma, Skylar, all followed the same pattern. Remi would hit the gym—hard—for a week, pick up an extra shift, and look for a replacement. And never, ever cry.

Ben would swoop in, her Puerto Rican Knight in Shining Armor, force her to eat arroz con gandules, Doritos, and chocolate, and attempt some heartfelt conversation about why she sabotaged relationships (she didn't).

Until Violet came into her world. Fire and sass and perfection—until she wasn't. For six months, equal amounts of screaming and screwing filled Remi's world. A release before a release and *my God...* when it was good, it was *So. Goddamn. Good.* And when it was bad, it was the depths-of-Satan's-breath bad. When Violet took a job in Atlanta last year—without talking to Remi about the decision, without seeing if Remi wanted to join, without so much as a wave from the airport—Ben was relieved. And Remi almost cried. The gut-punching, familiar message that Remi wasn't even worthy of an afterthought gnawed at her insides. She worked out so hard she nearly passed out, and yet the memory of Violet wouldn't release. Until finally, the breakup fog lifted, and she promised never to open up like that again.

Ben grabbed a sports drink from his bag. "Is this about yesterday?"

When she got home last night after her shift, all she had said was, "Didn't get the job, met the new co-bartender, don't want to talk about it." Now she gulped water and wiped the moisture from her upper lip. "I just don't think me and this chick are going to work out."

He raised an eyebrow. "Since when do you call women chicks?"

She breathed out as the vision of Maya's wide smile and apple cheekbones filled her head and knotted her stomach. "I know. I don't. God. It's just, she better not slow me down, I swear to God. I'm giving her two days to get fully trained in, but I expect with all her *experience* she better be ready."

He slammed back a hefty gulp. "That's a little rough, right? Normally, you love training in the newbies."

She refused to make eye contact. "And she's so willowy. No way can she carry a case by herself. I bet she does it half at a time like an amateur, and hell if I'm helping. Gabriella should have thought of that before she hired her. She probably has some dickhead boyfriend named Channing or Tate with the IQ of a frog who'll come in with baby T-shirts and stupid muscles and watch to make sure she doesn't get hit on."

Ben's dark brown eyes grew wide.

"What?" she snapped.

He let out a quick puff of air through his nose and shook his head. "Did she seem like a crappy person to you?"

She wrapped her arm across her chest to stretch. She didn't want to think if Maya may or may not be a good person. Thinking of everything she currently despised about her was much easier. "I don't know. I mean, she seemed tight with Gabriella."

"Who's a pretty good judge of character, right?"

She shrugged.

He pushed his thumb into his shoulder and rubbed in a circle. "You don't normally judge people."

She planted her ankles into the mat and stretched her calf. "What do you mean? Judging is my favorite pastime."

He winced as he dug his knuckle deep into his arm and continued massaging. "No, judging racists or homophobes is your favorite pastime. Not judging new co-workers."

Damn him and his wisdom. He was right. But she kept her face neutral so he wouldn't know she agreed. Her phone beeped, showing an alert. She reached across him into her bag and read the notification. "No way! A new open house popped up in Renton for this afternoon. I can make it there before my shift."

"Did you set up phone alerts for open houses now?" He stood from the bench and stared down. "Why do you do this to yourself? We can't afford it, yet. Can you just wait a few years until I pay off some of my student loans?"

Her chest tightened. "You know I can't. And it's not just a

few years. Your student loans are going to be with you for like twenty years. And I *can* afford it. I just need the loan."

"Seriously, though, you're verging on borderline obsession. What's your deal with needing this right now? We've got time. I'm not going anywhere, you're not going anywhere, we—"

"I need this!" She didn't cry. Ever. But her chin began an unfamiliar twitch.

For years, she had a void, an itch, that she couldn't quite scratch, and couldn't identify the cure. Until she went to her first open house, and it clicked. Everything she'd been missing in her life, the sense of family and stability, was represented in the realtor magazine outside her favorite coffee shop. She wanted, *needed,* to own a home. Then the rest of her life could begin.

He gripped her shoulder and nodded. "Okay, okay. I got you."

They sparred for twenty more minutes when he called it. "All right, Sugar Ray Remi. Let's get those gloves off and head home."

She checked her watch. Even though the fire in her needed smothering, she had to save some strength for work. From here on out, she'd bring her A game every night to Nueve's. Nothing would stop her from taking down Maya.

Two hours later, she took a right off of I-5 and headed into Renton. Passing Jimi Hendrix's gravestone on the left, she pumped "Purple Haze" through the speakers in homage. She trekked into the neighborhood filled with gigantic pine and maple trees, old growth, and single-car-garage, mid-century homes. She parked a block away, knowing that realtors could be an elitist bunch. If they took one look at her car, they'd treat her as if she couldn't afford the home.

Her heart was set on the home she saw yesterday in the U

District, but it was always good to keep her options open. Maybe other people wouldn't want to buy their first home near the campus. Frat parties, loud noises, and traffic could be a nightmare. But to her, it was heaven—not too far from work, architectural masterpieces on every corner, a cotton candy field of cherry blossoms lining the streets in the spring, and the best, cheapest food in the city.

Open houses provided a glimpse into what life was like for other people. For *normal* people, with *normal* families and *normal* childhoods. Usually, the homeowner removed pictures of their family or personal effects. But once in a while, she'd hit the jackpot and see a few displayed. She'd stroll through the rooms picturing a dad folding laundry while the mom cooked. Or two dads getting ready to take their daughter bike riding and adjusting helmets near the coat closet. Or a single mom laughing while making cupcakes with her children.

Remi took her shoes off in the entryway, put on the disposable slippers, and tiptoed into the living room. She scanned the crack in the brick fireplace, the paint-chipped wood windows, and the weathered front door, and pictured her and Ben watching a movie in the living room.

"Hey there, welcome. Here's the info sheet on the home." The realtor handed her a piece of paper. "Look around and let me know if you have questions. First-time home buyer?"

She hated they always asked that question. Like she reeked of inferiority. She refused to believe it was because she was barely pushing twenty-five and the average home buyer's age was in their thirties.

"Yes." She straightened her back. "I've been living downtown for work, but ready to move to a place that is quieter."

"What is it you do?"

"Investment banking." Last week, she said she worked at a local tech company. This weekend she'd say she was a consultant. She'd never forget the way a realtor made her feel last year that she was "just a bartender." Her face had screamed red that day. She had stumbled on her comeback and left a few minutes later as the woman in her pencil skirt and blazer gave her a sad frown.

The home was a clear fixer-upper. Fabric softener scent mixed with mildew and old paneling spread throughout the home. Floorboards creaked with every footstep and had hefty gouges missing. The petite floral wallpaper in the living room and kitchen was ripped in multiple places. One of the closet doors was missing, and the marigold kitchen sink was, well, marigold.

Not only did the work *not* scare her, but her adrenaline pumped. Over the last year, she gorged on every home renovation show available. With enough time and grit, she could transform any area into something beautiful. She could spend her days renovating and her nights working.

She could do this. She *would* do this.

She moved into the primary bedroom and pushed her foot into the blue carpet, assessing if original hardwood floors existed under the fabric. The nightstand held a photo of a gray-haired couple on a cruise ship. She visualized coming home from a trip with a partner and unpacking while reminiscing about the midnight chocolate buffet.

The main bathroom was down the hallway. *Whoa.* A cluster of seashells projectile vomited in the tiny room. Wallpaper, soap containers, towels, and the shower curtain all contained seashells. She studied the space and wondered what would happen if she ripped out the tub and replaced it with a standing waterfall shower and large gray tiles.

After viewing each room, she thanked the realtor for their time and made her way back to her car. Bumping over a few potholes on her way up I-5 toward downtown, she tried to exhale all the nerves of the first shift with Maya. She wanted a home *so effing bad.* And she should probably stop torturing herself with open houses, because every time she went to one, her chest ached.

She needed this bonus. More importantly, she needed to start her life.

Once she rolled into Nueve's parking lot, she rested her head on the back of the seat. She dug out one of her gazillion tinted lip balms—her emotional support product, as Ben called it—swiped it across her lips, then made her way to the alley entrance.

The chill in the air sprung goose bumps across her arms. She stepped into the steamy kitchen, and sounds erupted—clanking pots and pans, line cooks barking orders, food plates being arranged on trays.

The schedule taped on the outside of Gabriella's office door made her belly sink. Sadly, *My-ah* spelled her name "Maya" and now she'd needed to think of something else annoying to hold on to. She pushed her fist into her chin to crack her neck and exhaled.

"Afternoon." A silky voice sounded behind her.

Remi stiffened her shoulders. A deep, warm scent, almost like honeysuckle and cinnamon, reached her nose. She turned to face her opponent. "Hey. Welcome to day one."

Maya smiled. A big, picture-perfect smile on a heart-shaped face.

Her teeth were too white. If she smiled wide and the sun was out, she was going to blind Remi, and she couldn't afford an eye doctor. She mentally added this to her long list of grievances she'd be sure to bring up to Gabriella.

"Thanks. Really excited to learn from you." Maya stuffed a bag into the locker.

Remi didn't know Maya well enough to tell if her tone was genuine. She decided to believe she was blowing smoke. "I'll keep it easy on you for day one." Condescension laced her tone more than intended.

"Pretty sure I can handle this." Maya winked.

A wink. *Really*. Did she think this was a game? She looked like she had absolutely no nerves for her first day, and now Remi wanted to squirt her sparkly green eye with the soda gun. But just one eye because she wasn't a total monster.

Would it kill her to be a little nervous? Sure, Maya had experience, but *still*. She didn't know anyone, didn't know where the products were, and didn't know the regulars. Remi's first day here, her knees quivered under black work pants. She shoved her hands in her pocket to keep from shaking, skip-jogged like a kid trying to keep up with their faster sibling, and frantically scribbled in her notepad.

"Cool." Remi tossed her bag into the locker and picked up speed. "Let's go into the kitchen and meet the pit crew. We've got Luigi over—"

"We're good. I popped in this morning to meet everyone and brought them Top Pot doughnuts."

She what? Remi froze and stared. God, she had a face that begged to be smashed with a pie.

Maya lifted her brow. "You know, first day and all. Want to make a good impression."

And that hint of condescension Remi flung earlier just ricocheted and smacked her right in the head. Why hadn't she thought of doing something like that on her first day? "Huh. Well, I guess that makes it easier."

Remi pushed through the swinging doors with Maya a step behind and nodded at the daytime bartender. "The crowd right now is to be expected for a Tuesday at three p.m. in May."

Maya glanced around. "So, hardly anyone."

Remi nodded. "Happy hour's not gonna start for another hour. Then we'll get some businesspeople, maybe a few college kids who want a change of pace from the U District, and some date-night folks."

A handful of people sat in the tall, dark leather booths, with their food and drinks nestled on top of the wrought-iron tables with deep, cherry wood tops. The shades were open and brighter during the day but would be closed in a half hour to create a darker, more atmospheric mood. Remi always liked being here when the hostess closed the blinds. The motion was like a changing of the guards, a sign for the magic to start. The mirrored wall with various rums and top-level liquors would sparkle like holiday lights when the room darkened and the warm lights turned on.

"The recipe book said the piña colada was the number one selling drink. Is that still accurate?" Maya ran her fingers across the rail, inspecting each bottle.

"Yeah. We use the globe glasses for those with a brown sugar rim. The up-charge is using the whole pineapple, so we push that when we can." Remi grabbed a towel from the hook. "Did Gabriella give you a recipe book yesterday?"

"She emailed it to me last week when she told me about this job."

Remi's stomach felt like Maya had kicked her with a dusty hiking boot. Gabriella sought her out? She just assumed Maya had reached out needing a job. Maya didn't have to sweat through Gabriella's "audition"? *Unbelievable.* "Ah." Remi ran a towel across the bar and kept her voice cool as her chest grew hot. "So, you didn't even apply for this job?"

"No, she called and let me know she had an open position." Maya's eyes focused on the top-shelf rum. She picked up a bottle and sniffed. "Seemed like a great opportunity. Such a beautiful place."

"Sure is." Remi forced a grin and flipped open the garnish container to check the supply. Bartending competitors were like bloodhounds. They'd smell insecurity and pounce. Remi refused to allow Maya to know she felt like throwing the ice bucket through the window.

"She said you were great to work with," Maya added, a hint of doubt laced in her voice.

If Maya thought her perfect cheekbones and charming tone were going to melt her frozen heart, she was dead wrong. "Another one is the almond colada." Remi purposely ignored Maya's obvious attempts at sympathy. "We use house-infused almond rum."

Maya nodded. She opened each cooler and her eyes traveled slowly across the contents. "Sounds delicious. Have you thought of adding a splash of condensed milk to that drink?"

No. "Yeah, I thought about it but didn't have time to test it out. We can try that on our next tasting night."

Remi spent the next hour going through the bar's contents, as she stressed the importance of maintaining order. Left to right, rum, vodka, gin, whiskey, orange liqueur, and tequila. Behind them on the display were all top-shelf liquors, mostly rum. The tray station had sliced pineapples, oranges, lemons, limes, olives, and cherries.

She pointed out the muddler and strainers, and what soda and juices were in the soda gun. She opened coolers, rattled off the names of the bottled and tapped beers, and showed her the location of the garnishes' back stock.

Maya slid across the bar floor like a pro, clearly comfortable in her element. She asked if they ever changed up the Bloody Mary's garnishes, the house rules on comping drinks, and if Gabriella allowed flaming fire shots.

"Why does Gabriella only stay open until ten?" Maya asked as she looked through the dry-stock cabinet with straws, coasters, and napkins.

"She says nothing good ever happens after ten." Remi wiped down the bottle toppers. "But between us, I think she's just sick of people's crap by then."

Maya lifted her chin in acknowledgment.

"So, Gabriella says you're only training for three days?"

Remi tossed one of the sugar-crusted bottle toppers in the sink and reached for a fresh one in the cabinet. "Then you're on the floor on your own?"

"Yes, that's right." Maya put a squirt of each juice in a shot glass and tasted. Her jaw worked in a circle like she was wine tasting.

A bit too serious, in Remi's opinion. Her conscience almost elbowed her, but she pushed down the irritating internal dialogue. "Most people do two weeks."

Maya shrugged and continued testing the soda gun pressure. "I guess I'm not most people."

Remi didn't even try to hide her irritation. Granted, when she started, she was totally inexperienced, but Gabriella wouldn't even let her make a drink for six months. Every single thing about this entire effed-up situation was totally unfair. She felt like she lost the competition before it even started.

The hostess snapped the blinds shut, the festive music in the background fired up, and the magic of the night began. Now it was Remi's turn. "All right, we've each got our spots. Normally, I cover the right, and you cover the left. No splitting tips, but let's not be jerks. If we step away and one of our bar seats needs something, grab it. But for now, you follow me, learn how the bar operates, grab me things when I need it, and try not to get in my way."

Okay *fine*, that was rude. But Maya's spicy, honeysuckle scent was having some sort of fix on her, and Remi needed to counteract the effects.

"Understood."

"Good luck today," Remi said with a straight face.

"I don't need luck," Maya responded with a smirk.

FOUR

DRINK SPECIAL: NERVOUS ORANGE NECTAR COCKTAIL WITH ABSOLUTELY NO CHERRIES

Did I really just say "I don't need luck"? Who was this alter ego? Maya kind of liked her. She needed to polish, protect, and possibly even name this personality, so it won't leave. Normally, day one on a job would be terrifying. She thought back to all her dry-mouthed, sweaty-handed, first days of the past—college, her bar job in Minnesota, meeting her roommate. She could've used this fierce personality during any of those times.

Remi had walked into Nueve's with a Mount Rainier–size boulder on her shoulder an hour ago but finally seemed to warm up. And then Maya said "I don't need luck" like some arrogant ass, and even though it felt good at the moment, it wasn't who she was, and her stomach turned sour.

Truth was, the hell she didn't. She studied these recipes as hard as she studied for her final exams last semester, committed to doing the best job she could. When Gabriella emailed the notes last week, Maya recorded herself reading the steps and ingredients and replayed the audio during her morning jogs. She took pictures and printouts of the ordering screen and completed at least a hundred fake entries at home, trying to build fingertip muscle memory. And now her mind blanked.

She followed Remi out to the floor, where Gabriella wiped chairs in the corner.

"Maya!" Gabriella draped the towel over her shoulder and scooted over. "Day one. Are you ready?"

Absolutely not. She gave one firm nod. "Sure am."

"Good. I'll be on the floor for most of the night checking on tables, but I'll come by and make sure you two are staying out of trouble." She grinned but flashed a narrowed-eye glance to Remi.

"I'll be on my best behavior." Remi grunted—or chuckled.

Maya couldn't quite tell.

"So will I!" Maya said with way too much exclamation and exhaled as Gabriella walked away.

Two women pulled up to the bar, and in an instant, Remi transformed—an effortless smile, sparkly eyes, and relaxed shoulders. She laid out napkins. "Ladies, welcome in. What can I get started for you?"

Her already deeply sexy raspy voice now sounded like someone lathering their lover's back with a warm honey-sugar scrub. Maya bit her lip to expunge this thought. She'd been going through a serious dry spell lately since her last breakup, but *come on.* The first time she spent any amount of time with another woman, and she salivated? Seriously unprofessional.

"We've never been here before. What's good?" one woman asked, with the tiniest air of elitism funneling through her tone. She hooked her large designer purse on the back of the chair and pressed her bob flat.

Remi eyed the women, with the faintest, flirtiest smirk.

Like her eyes contained some sort of elitist-kryptonite, the women settled back in their stools, disarmed in a snap.

"You look like a blackberry mojito with mint. And you..." Remi strummed her fingertips on the bar and cocked her head toward the other woman. "You look like you live a bit more on the edge."

The woman threw her head back with a satisfied giggle. "That's true. I do."

Impressive, Ms. Soft Pout.

"I suggest instead of a blackberry mojito, how about a sweetened jalapeno one?" Remi leaned in. "I'll kick up the sweetness just a touch to offset the spice."

"Perfect!"

Who was this woman? In a second, Remi went from a salty —albeit sultry—task master with a shitty attitude, to Ms. Charming. Captivating, even.

Remi pulled the ingredients together and built the drink. After giving the mint a hell of a smack to release the oil—with one woman yelling "whoop!"—she tossed the herb into the strainer with the blackberries, ice, and vodka. She gripped the wooden muddler and thrust it repeatedly into the shaker.

Maya stared at the flex of Remi's muscular forearm while she worked the liquid.

"You good over there?" Remi asked with the slightest raised eyebrow.

Maya cleared her throat. "Yes, absolutely. Just love the smell of fresh mint."

So dumb.

Over the following several hours, Maya paid her dues. She retrieved buckets of ice from the back, stacked napkins, and refilled juices. When the tap beer spouted like a choked-up sprinkler hose, she ran back to the kitchen and changed the keg. She filled glasses of water, wiped counters, and cleared dirty glasses from the bar. All these duties were par for the course, but she itched to bartend. During training, all tips went to the trainer, and Maya was desperate to earn more than her hourly wage.

More patrons trickled in through the evening, and Maya watched Remi with a bit of awe as Remi chatted with customers.

"Hey, Chad," she said to a gorgeous blond man and reached for a dark rum. She added pineapple juice, cream, and five cherries, then slid it back to him. "How's the pup feeling?"

The man reached into his pocket for his phone and held it up to Remi as he swiped through photos. "Look at those stitches. But she's better, thank you. Had a bit of a scare." He set the phone on the counter and eyed Maya. "Do we have a new bartender in the house?"

Remi wiped the bottle and tipped up her head. "Yep. Maya. She's not as scary as she looks."

Chad chuckled.

Maya didn't know if she should scowl or smile. "Or maybe I'm scarier than I look."

Later in the evening, a middle-aged man with droopy eyelids slouched down on the barstool. He didn't say a word, and neither did Remi. Instead, she dug out the stepstool and reached for a top-shelf white rum.

And no, Maya did *not* just accidentally check out Remi's curves as she stretched for the bottle, because that'd be extraordinarily unprofessional and crappy, and she was better than that. *Obviously.*

Remi put a double shot in a shaker, added half a shot of sugared lime juice to the ice, shook, and double-strained, and handed it back to the guy without speaking.

Maya leaned into Remi's ear. "Are you sure we should serve him? He looks intoxicated."

Remi glanced at the man. "Nah. He just has a permanent RDF."

"RDF?"

"Resting Drunk Face. He's good. He'll have two, then leave."

The hum of rotating customers continued, and one thing was clear—Remi was good. Great, actually. Her speed was almost two-to-one of what Maya could usually do. And the customers *loved* her. She asked one about their soccer league. Talked about stocks with the other one. Chatted about binge-watching the latest Netflix zombie show with yet another.

Maya's lower back beaded with sweat. She ran back and forth to the kitchen for pineapples, shoved toothpicks in oranges and cherries to top Remi's drinks, and cleaned up spills. The crowd increased and Maya's spirits skyrocketed. If Nueve's was this busy on a Tuesday, weekends she could earn some serious cash. Maybe her dreams of returning to school in the fall would become reality.

"Can you grab maraschinos from the pantry?" Remi asked over her shoulder as she poured a shot of blanco tequila into a glass and stuck a cinnamon and sugar-crusted orange slice on the edge.

"Yep." The kitchen was filled with a symphony of trays thumping against the prep counters, dirty dishes being stacked onto racks, and the sharp clank of silverware getting tossed into bins. Servers scrambled through the kitchen, scooping sides of sour cream and sauces, and calling out to line cooks over the grill.

She weaved her way through the kitchen and scanned the pantry shelf. Rows of olives, sugars, paper items, honey, and syrup lined the shelf. But no cherries. Her heartbeat kicked up a notch, and she ran her fingers across the items to slow herself down. Nope, definitely no cherries. "Do you know where the cherries are?" she asked a line cook.

"Pantry," he said without looking up as he arranged food on a plate.

She ran back to the pantry. Maybe she missed it? She shuffled boxes and looked behind the napkins. "Hey, do you know where the cherries are? They're not in the pantry," she asked another server.

The server popped the tray on her hip. "Try the fridge."

Maya ran to the fridge and opened the massive door. *Jesus.*

Where should she start? Rows layered with fruits and veggies, what seemed like a thousand pineapples, cheeses, and dough lined the cooler. Boxes were stacked in the corner, and she reviewed labels. After sliding them over, re-stacking, and pulling, she finally found it. Thank God she was in the fridge because her heightened pulse and moving two dozen boxes had her forehead prickling with sweat. She pulled the box down, grabbed a cutter, and finally retrieved the jar of cherries.

She speed-walked back to the bar where Gabriella was filling up a line of shot glasses. "Been gone a while."

There was nothing inherently awful about her words, but Maya's stomach twisted all the same. "Sorry, had a little trouble locating the cherries."

"Was the tour earlier not enough?" Gabriella set the bottles back on the rail and added the shot glasses to a tray. "You sounded confident you knew where everything was."

Shit. She'd known Gabriella since she was a child. Gabriella was an aunt-like figure. But this was Business Gabriella, with a totally different voice, and all the warm fuzzies she felt as a kid from her vanished. Maya's face grew warm and her palms cold. "I'm okay now." She pushed fake confidence through her voice when everything in her body wanted to hide under the bar until Gabriella left. *Straight shoulders, head high. Straight shoulders, head high.*

"Good. I'm going back to visiting with our guests. Remi, great job."

The corner of Remi's lips curved up, and Maya wanted to wipe her smirk off with the dirty rag. And then she saw it, tucked under the bar ledge by the soda gun. A nearly full jar of cherries.

Her chest blazed.

Remi followed her gaze and shrugged her shoulders. "Turns out there was an extra one in this baby right here." She tapped the front of the mini cooler with the tip of her toe. "Good thing, 'cause that took you forever."

She wouldn't have... would she?

Maya ground her molars. Remi absolutely did that to make her look bad. And even though Maya wouldn't say anything—today was her first day, after all—karma was a tenacious little thing.

Remi would totally get what was coming.

In between lulls of customers and orders, Maya bobbed like a fighter in the ring when Remi rapid-fire quizzed her on the house staples.

"Coquito," Remi said as she filled up a glass with club soda.

"House-made base, white rum, vanilla, cinnamon, and nutmeg."

Remi cocked her eyebrow.

"Vanilla vodka," Maya quickly interjected, and turned to refill the lemons. "I just misspoke." She hated that her nerves were showing.

"The Amore."

"Dark rum, mango puree, fresh ginger zest, lime juice. Shaken."

Remi squeezed a lime into her soda and sipped. "Good."

Damn. That one word felt better than it should have. Even though she thought she just wanted Gabriella's validation, turns out that she wanted Remi's as well. Maybe her ex's accusation that Maya was a glutton for approval was true. She sipped on pineapple and cranberry juice while checking and rechecking the bottles, napkin supply, and garnishes. After cherry-gate, she had to ace everything. No room for error existed.

Last call was served, and the hostess locked the front door. Maya rolled her neck and pulled out the industrial-size plastic wrap for the condiments.

Remi drained the bar top rubber mat filled with splashed liquid into the sink. "So, how do you know Gabriella?"

"She and my mom are friends. They met when Gabriella first arrived in Seattle from Puerto Rico. They even lived together for a bit before my mom and dad got married." *Dad.* Maya swallowed and hoped Remi couldn't see her face. Nine years had flown by since he passed, but talking about him randomly almost always stirred emotions.

Remi reached for the hose. "Wait. Is your mom Laney?"

Maya blinked multiple times. "You know my mom?"

"Yes. I mean, no." Remi sprayed the mat and cleaned the edges. "I've never actually met her, but Gabriella's talked about her before."

Maya nodded but said nothing and instead focused on sanitizing the bar top. Talking about her family always made her uncomfortable. She held them so fiercely close to her heart, like they were a magical, endangered entity, and if she talked about them, she'd ruin their power.

She wrapped up the leftover lemons and limes, stuffed them in the mini-cooler, and poured hot water over the ice bin until it drained. Back in the kitchen, she retrieved the last of the clean glasses and lined them across the shelf when Remi strolled up to her and handed her a fistful of cash.

Maya squinted. "What's this for?"

"The cash tips from today."

Everyone knew trainees didn't get a cut of the tips. Gabriella even reminded her before her shift. "Trainees don't get tips."

Remi tucked a chunk of dark, curly hair behind her ear. "Look, I can be a total shit, but I'm not an unfair monster. You busted your ass tonight."

Maya curled her fingers around the cash. She was not prepared for this generosity and had no idea what to say. She stood awkwardly, looking at her hand.

Remi pivoted on her feet and walked toward the exit. "See you tomorrow, Maya."

That was the first time Maya heard Remi say her name. Even though enough irritating moments occurred tonight—and she still fumed that Remi set her up to look bad with the stupid cherries—her name coming across those lips was like warm cinnamon-chocolate sliding into her ear. She hated herself that her belly tingled. "Night." She retrieved her purse from the breakroom locker and stuffed the cash in her wallet. She looked around at the place that would be her home for the summer before she walked outside to wait for the bus.

A half hour later, she eased open the front door to her house, making sure not to wake her mom and sister. She toed her grippy sneakers off on the "Everyone Welcome!" rainbow wicker mat and walked across the hardwood floors to shut off the kitchen light. She stopped when she saw her mom sitting at the kitchen table, scrolling through her phone.

"Hey, pumpkin." Laney Marek looked up at her daughter with familiar, purple-circled eyes and a tired smile.

"Why are you up so late? It's after eleven."

Laney shrugged. "Tough time sleeping. Figured I'd try to make what I used to give you and Harper when you were kids."

Maya sat down and sniffed the bowl. "You made hot Cheerios?"

"Sure did."

When Maya was younger, her mom would pour heated whole milk over the cereal and mush it into an oatmeal-type consistency. She took the spoon her mom held out and tried a bite. "Not bad. I don't remember you topping it with so much maple syrup when I was a kid."

"Busted." Laney grinned. "How was your first official day?"

Terrible. "Great." The last thing her mom needed in her already chaotic life was Maya complaining about her long list of mishaps.

Laney scooped the spoon in the snack. "How did it really go?"

Maya grabbed the spoon and took another bite. The smooth, sweetened comfort food settled her belly. "Not as good as I wanted. I really thought I had it down, you know? I studied all week, mapped out the entire place, ran scenarios in my head. Was sure I knew where everything was, but I didn't."

A warm hand touched Maya's shoulder, and she loosened under the touch.

"You put so much pressure on yourself. My forever over-achiever. It's only your first day."

Maya stood from the chair and scoured the pantry for something salty and terrible. She finally found a bag of chips and a jar of queso. "How was Harper today?"

"Good." Laney stirred her cereal. "Her blood sugar numbers were a little all over the place. Trending better lately, but... you know, I'd just feel better if it was always consistent."

"I know it's tough, but fluctuations are normal. Especially with kids. She'll be good." Maya crunched into her junk-food dinner. She pictured the time when Harper was five and a panicked Laney rushed her to the ER, with Maya jogging at her side. The previous few weeks, Harper was constantly thirsty. At first, it was like a joke—that this child could "drink as much as a horse." But then her weight plummeted, and fatigue took over her tiny body.

It came on quick and out of nowhere, with no family history of diabetes. In the ER, words rushed from the doctor about blood sugar levels, ketoacidosis, and admitting Harper to the intensive care unit. Maya saw right through Laney's brave face. Even though Maya was only sixteen, she hyper-fixated on the doctor's words, and filled a notebook with recommendations on foods, symptoms, and maintenance.

Every free second, she researched type 1 diabetes, from treatment options and insulin pumps versus syringes, to digital monitoring. She pictured her father tipping his head back in approval of her helping the family. Shortly after, she knew what she wanted to do with the rest of her life.

Her mom rolled the spoon in her mouth, then set it down against the bowl. She brushed a piece of lint off Maya's shoulder with her thumb and gave her a soft smile. "I heard you last night."

A heated spark flew up Maya's chest. "Crap, sorry."

"Wanna talk about it?"

Maya shook her head. Being a grown-ass adult who still had nightmares was embarrassing enough without having a conversation about it. A healthy dose of stress normally made it worse. When she moved in with her roommate, Amanda, back in Minnesota, Amanda had busted through her door one night yielding a baseball bat, convinced Maya was being attacked.

Turned out it was just finals week.

"Come here." Laney tapped her fingers together, then opened up her arms.

"Really, Mom? Aren't I too old for this?" She leaned into her mom's warm arms and laid her head on her shoulder.

Her mom rubbed the top of her back, broad circular strokes like she was trying to reiki out the stress. "I'm not asking to tie your shoes or hold your hand to cross the street. I'm just giving you a love squeeze."

Maya sighed and pulled back. "You're a good mama, you know that?"

Laney yawned and stretched her hands high above her head before she rested her palm on top of Maya's. "It's really nice having you home." She set her dish in the dishwasher and walked to the bedroom.

Maya stared at the wall. Tonight was rough. But it was also not as terrible as it could've been. Maybe her mom was right. Besides one incident, she did pretty well. And she'd continue to get better.

She had no other option.

Even though it killed her to admit, Remi was hands down a better bartender. Speedy, accurate, and a hell of a lot more charming. But only one of them could earn the bonus. And Maya had too much to lose. She did not put her entire life on hold to come in second place. A few more days of orientation, and game on.

Besides, Maya had a trick up her sleeve. And she planned on using it to her full advantage.

FIVE

DRINK SPECIAL: SNEAKY SIGNATURE SCOTCH WITH OH SNAP! BEER BACK

Remi rinsed the last of the breakfast dishes and set them in the drying rack. The pink-and-blue bubbles popped as she was spraying the suds down the sink, when her phone rang. She wiped her hands on the towel and her heart lodged in her throat when she saw the name.

"Hello?"

"Hi, this is Ken from Seattle's Financial Services and Home Loans. Just following up on our conversations from a few days ago." His chipper voice simultaneously soothed the twists in her stomach and pinched them a little tighter.

A few weeks ago, she was pretty confident the head bartender job was hers. A few days ago, she was totally confident and in a burst of pre-emptive, naïve celebration, she had called him on her way to work to let him know he'd be hearing from her by the following day. Until Maya came in and ruined everything.

She cleared her throat and hoped if she smiled through the phone, he'd pick up on some phantom confidence and ignore the bullshit undertones about to lace through her voice. "The details of the promotion changed to more of a lump sum payment, but I should know soon. There was a bit of a... delay I wasn't expecting."

She could almost hear him nodding through the phone.

"Okay. I researched a couple of things. I can get you a letter that says that you are close to pre-approval, but I don't know how much weight that'd carry. The market is slowing down, but it's still holding steady overall. I'm not sure a *pre*-pre-approval letter will be much help when competing against other folks."

None of this was news, but it still sucker punched the same way. She sat in the middle of the coffee table and stared at the faded white wall. "It seems really unfair that I know I can make the mortgage payments, but they won't loan me the money."

"I know, but banks need to protect themselves." The sound of shuffling papers came through the phone. "Confirming you do not want to include a co-signer on this, which could elevate your chances?"

She and Ben had talked about that, but she remained steadfast—she wanted to own this home outright. She loved Ben. He was the only family she had, and they planned to live together forever. But *forever* was not guaranteed. Violet, her parents, everyone made that perfectly clear. At some point, Ben was going to want to settle down and then what? She refused to destroy the one relationship she had with a mortgage. "No. I'll be owning this home on my own."

A few moments of silence passed. "All right, then. Let me know when you finalize the new position or get the bonus. You said you found the dream home, right?"

"Yep. It goes on market in twenty-seven days."

"Excellent. Since the market is slowing down, we'll hopefully have some wiggle room. Real estate agents are giving folks about a week or two to get in offers. Definitely more than the forty-eight hours like a few years ago." A lighthearted chuckle bounced through the phone, like the intention was to make her feel better.

It failed. *Agents are giving folks more than a few days? Great, thanks.* No pressure.

She hung up and stared at her apartment. This place, at one time, had been a saving grace. Aging out of foster care at eighteen, she'd needed something cheap and available. Ben's abuelita had a loving but extraordinarily strict and stifling home, and Ben wanted to leave at the same time. So, they chose this place because they could afford it, and the building held a certain sort of charm. Okay, maybe *charm* wasn't the right word, but it became a bit of a sanctuary and she'd grown emotionally attached. The apartment was the first place that was hers—really hers—and she loved it for so many years.

But now, the '70s décor and mildewy vapor rising from the cheap carpeting, combined with the clanking radiator and screaming neighbors, no longer held the escapee appeal it once did. She was officially ready to let it go.

She snatched her keys off the hook and made her way to her car. Flipping her hoodie over her head, careful not to crush her curls, of course, she speed-walked to the parking lot. After slamming her door, she turned the volume up high on her favorite grunge band and started the drive to work. Cruising along, she breathed out and recited the timeline in her head. Thirty days. She had thirty days to convince Gabriella she was worthy of the bonus.

Maya had killed it these last few days, except for the cherry scavenger hunt she went on day one. Sure, it worked in Remi's favor that the day bartender didn't put all the products away. And that Remi found back-up cherries buried in the mini-cooler after Maya had left. When Gabriella caught Remi at that moment, balancing twenty different orders between her own bar seats and servers' orders, she had huffed a heavy breath through a scrunched nose and dove in to help.

But Gabriella would for sure cut Maya some slack because the incident occurred on her first day. But today was day four, training was officially over, and that slack Gabriella gave Maya better be chopped in half with a jagged machete.

As Remi pulled into the parking lot with the rain tapdancing on her car roof, she closed her eyes and took in a heaping lungful of air. After a swipe of lip balm, a popped-in mint, and a good crack of the neck, she put on her game face.

Inside, she hung her items in the locker and slammed the locker door when the alley entrance opened, letting in a cool breeze that offset the sticky kitchen.

Maya marched in, her posture so sharp and straight that Remi was sure she had a permanent stick shoved up her—

"Buenos días, Maya. Ven aquí, please." Gabriella motioned her forward with happy, open arms, her tone like a sweet aunt greeting her visiting niece.

Puke. When Remi got home tonight, she was shooting a bleach-filled syringe directly in her ear canal to get rid of the sap.

Maya followed Gabriella's request. Soon, a chorus of hushed whispers and soft smiles leaked like a saccharine-laced, venomous vapor. Remi's neck warmed. Day four and Maya and Gabriella were already a secret society of sisterhood. She moved to the kitchen door and caught Gabriella's tapered gaze.

Was Maya seriously tattling on her like a baby? Okay, *fine,* maybe Remi went a tad hard on her the last couple of days, but *come on!* Remi had been at this gig for four years, and Snow Princess showed up like she expected to be coddled. It wasn't like Remi had hazed her or anything. She was simply... less than charming.

The heat grew from her neck to her scalp. Enough of the favoritism and quasi-nepotism. She needed to call them both out, dispel whatever lies Maya spewed, and play damage control. She grabbed a towel off the pile and pivoted sharply. "Can we have a sit-down?"

Maya's head snapped up as quickly as Gabriella's.

Remi's boots clapped heavily against the concrete kitchen floor.

Maya stepped to the side and held out her arm like she was inviting Remi to join her and Gabriella.

Dammit. Why did Maya have to smell so good? She didn't smell the way she looked—like money and elitism. She smelled like a woman with a little edge, and it was getting to her. Now Remi was all spicy-warm-vanilla distracted, and it was totally unfair. She probably did this on purpose to throw Remi off her game.

From here on out, they needed to implement a no-perfume policy.

Remi twisted the towel in her hand, then dangled it from her pocket. "Look, I might have been a little hard on you for the first couple of days, but seriously? Is this really necessary?"

Remi was met with two cocked heads and blank stares.

"I'm just making sure you can do the job," she continued after neither of the women bothered to respond. "Nueve's means a lot to me and if I was pushing you too hard, I'm not sure you'll be able to handle it tonight with fifty people yelling at you and some drunk schmuck at closing time—"

"Remi. Silencio." Gabriella snapped her fingers a few inches from Remi's face. "Maya said you've been great."

Ah, so Maya's playing the angel role? Cool, cool, cool. So could she. "Oh, good." Remi curled the side of her lip. "Because she's been amazing. Already like a member of the team."

Gabriella's dead-pan stare gave away that her internal bull-shit barometer hit red.

A cook walked past them, his gaze bouncing between the three women, before he rounded the corner.

Remi's tunnel vision widened. The kitchen staff all stared in their direction, probably waiting for some juicy gossip they could use for fodder to get them through their shift. She leaned toward Gabriella. "Can I talk to you privately?"

"Of course. Office." She jutted her chin toward the door.

Maya left without another word.

Inside the office, Gabriella folded her arms across her chest. "You playing nice?"

Remi closed the door. "I'm always nice."

"Baloney."

Truth was, she was mostly always nice—to kitchen staff, customers, or anyone who wasn't trying to rip a promotion from her hands. She gripped the back of the chair. "Look, I just think, well... I am not sure how this... I just—"

"Just spit it out, niña."

"Fine. I think it's really freaking unfair that I've worked so hard for this job for years. Never once have I called in sick. I don't take time off. I bring in twice as much as any other bartender, and you might give Maya this bonus over me because you're friends with her mom. It's crap."

Gabriella stepped back with an expressionless face. One, two, then three full seconds passed before she said anything. "Do you actually think that I'd jeopardize my reputation, and go back on *my word*, for a favor to my friend?"

Remi buckled under the fire in Gabriella's tone and softened her grip on the chair. "I'm sorry."

Gabriella held her hand up like she was physically blocking any more words from leaving Remi's mouth. The silence in the air grew as heavy as the boulder pushing on Remi's chest. *Yikes.* Okay, Remi's words were really insulting. Maybe she should have thought that one through before she spouted off. "Am I not good enough?" The crack in her voice surprised her, and she quickly cleared her throat.

Gabriella's gaze widened. "Your skills behind the bar are top-notch."

Remi's insides settled. Gabriella was stingy with compliments, preferring a tough-love approach with her employees. She always said if she handed them out too often, they'd lose their power. So, Remi pocketed and stored them in her emotional savings bank for the times she needed. "How are you judging us for the bonus? Sales?" *Please say sales.*

"If it was sales, there'd be no competition. You'd always win." Gabriella spun her chair around, sat, and rested her elbows on her desk. "You appreciate honesty. So, I'm going to give it to you."

Oh no.

She folded her hands and straightened her chest. "You're fantastic in your craft. One of the best. Speedy, innovative. I never have complaints about the drinks. And most customers love you."

Remi tugged on the edge of the towel. "I love most customers."

"You pick and choose. And when you don't like someone, there's an issue. The incident that happened last year—"

"Was isolated."

Gabriella remained so still and unblinking that Remi almost checked to see if she somehow slipped into a coma.

"No," Gabriella said through gritted teeth. "It wasn't."

Gabriella bringing this up was unfair on every level. Some dickhead customer would not leave the hostess—who was like a day over sixteen—alone, and she was too timid to stand up for herself. What was Remi supposed to do?

Gabriella pushed her flattened hands into the desk. "We're lucky he didn't file charges."

A rock formed in Remi's throat, but she refused to swallow. She shrugged instead. "It was an accident."

"An elbow to the jaw is *not* an accident."

A nonverbal standoff ensued as the heat of Gabriella's gaze finally cracked Remi, and she stared at her feet.

"I'm not saying he didn't deserve it," Gabriella said in a softer tone. "And you know, had I been there, I would've taken care of it."

But she *wasn't* there. The hostess was in tears, the staff scrambled in the flash grenade of f-bombs, raised fists, and kicked-over chairs. She had no choice. Nueve's wasn't the type of place that had security at the door, and everyone else ran for cover. "I've never once gotten physical with a customer besides him."

"But you've verbally attacked a few."

"Yeah, but only the assholes."

"See, Remi-lita!" Gabriella clapped, and the chair squeaked in response. "This is exactly what I'm talking about."

Gabriella was making this a way bigger deal than needed. Remi had actively tried to soften her language these past few months. And no matter what Gabriella thought, the people she spouted off to deserved to be put in their place. She could smell disrespect or perpetrator cologne from a mile away. And she could put up with a lot. She had tough skin. But when they started messing with staff... all she saw was red.

Remi checked her watch. She needed to head out to the floor and monitor Maya to make sure she did nothing sneaky, like rearrange her garnishes or loosen the tops to her bottles. "I need to know how you're scoring us. If not sales, then what?"

Gabriella rolled her chair under her desk and smoothed down her skirt. "Everything. Sales is a factor, of course. But I'm also looking at customer satisfaction and being diplomatic. With both guests *and* co-workers."

Remi's face grew warm.

"I like all your... fuego. Your feistiness. Just not in front of customers." She laid a gentle hand on her shoulder.

Remi hated how quickly it disarmed her.

Gabriella inched her face closer to Remi's.

The urge to crumble, hug her, and run away under her stare swirled in Remi.

"Be nice. Stay in your lane, and I'll decide by the end of June."

The house would go on the market in less than thirty days. She needed the money by then.

Gabriella popped her bifocals on her face, a clear indication she was done talking to Remi, and grabbed a notebook on her desk.

Remi left for the bar floor. Gabriella had always been stern, but fair. Remi had no choice but to up her game. She exhaled an unsteady breath and pushed through the swinging doors.

The crowd was typical for 3:00 p.m. on a Friday. A few scattered tables finishing a late lunch, a couple of people in their work outfits getting a head start on their weekend, an older couple in the corner enjoying an early dinner.

Maya wiped down the bar, her body softly swaying with each swipe. Remi shook her head, refusing to indulge in those long, lean legs and focused on politely, subtly, kicking her ass on the bar floor.

Picking up a vodka bottle from the rail, Remi checked its contents. "I just spoke to Gabriella." She placed the quarter-full bottle back on the rail and squatted down to reach for the backup on the lower shelf. "Thought you should know. Sales is going to be a huge factor in determining who gets the bonus."

Huge might be a stretch.

Maya looked at her with an expressionless face. Or maybe there was an expression there, and Remi couldn't read her well enough to interpret it. Her mouth was flatlined and her eyes were absent of any sort of smile.

Maybe Remi didn't need to be such a jerk. Today was Maya's first real day behind the bar since training ended last night, and she was most likely nervous enough already. Remi should save the sabotage ammunition for a different day. "Look, you're going to do fine." She picked up the next bottle. "I've been here for a long time and by default will be quicker than you. But it doesn't mean that you're not gonna do great. You're already getting the hang of it."

Maya stood all straight back and straight hair and straight arms like an emotionless, beautiful robot. But soon, a slow smirk grew on flawless skin. "Sure."

Sure? Maybe Remi didn't need to sabotage her, Maya would do it all by herself. The customers weren't going to like someone like her, especially the ones that came here solo. They wanted personality, the idea of an hour-long friendship, or therapist, to soothe them while nursing their drink.

A couple approached Maya's side of the bar and settled into the stools.

Maya placed napkins in front of them. "Hey there, what can I get for you?"

How did the ice queen flip it on like that? In a snap, she was relaxed and smiling. Her posture was still straight, but less militant now and more pageant-like.

Game on.

Within the next two hours, the place picked up. The hostess shut the blinds, and a palpable energy kicked through Remi's veins. The music thumped under her toes, and she was in her zone. Sounds of ice clanking against martini shakers, the hum of conversation, and servers marching through the doors filled the room. Splashes of rum and vodka landed on her mat with a soft plop. Conversation buzzed in the air.

Remi peeked at Maya, who was smiling and filling orders. When Maya made a drink, Remi made two. Not that she was counting. The relief flooding through her that Maya was slower settled in her stomach and released a tension antidote. But still, Maya was damn good. Day one and she was not trailing nearly enough to make Remi relax.

Another hour in, and things didn't feel so odd. They seamlessly moved between each other, like dancers doing a bar waltz. When Remi had a stack of orders and Maya didn't, she garnished for her without a word. When Maya's customer knocked over their drink, Remi flew over, scooped the ice into her hand, and wiped down Maya's area.

"Hey, you guys!" Remi waved at Ben's bestie, Charlie, who walked up to the bar holding her girlfriend Mack's hand.

"Hey!" the women said in unison, and pulled up barstools.

"You two want a cucumber spritzer?" Remi asked, already prepping the non-alcoholic but deeply satisfying drink. The women had ordered the same drink each time they visited for the last year. "Mack, you back already from the book tour? I thought Ben said it was going through to the end of the month."

Mack lived a life that was totally foreign to Remi. She was a thriller writer—a famous one no less—and sometimes traveled the country to promote her books. But she was always a little shy, and Charlie was bubblier.

"I have to go back." Mack frowned. "But my agent gave me a break, so I'm home for a week, then gone the rest of the month. I just landed a few hours ago."

"And this was your first stop? I'm honored." Remi laid out the drinks in front of them and watched them practically tear their clasped hands apart.

"We needed some empanadas." Mack grinned.

Charlie tugged a rubber band in her dark red curls and took a healthy sip of the fizzy drink. "Hey, haven't seen you at Sugar Mugs all week. I almost called the authorities."

Remi grinned. Ben used to work with Charlie at her coffee shop, Sugar Mugs, until last year. She was pretty sure that he still missed being a barista. After he took the job at the hospital, he went through solid Charlie-withdrawals and almost quit the hospital to be back with her daily.

"I know. Terrible. But I've been putting in extra time

training this one." She tilted her head to Maya, who was shaking a martini.

Charlie cocked an eyebrow at Remi.

"What?" Remi lifted her shoulder. Perhaps her gaze had lingered. *Perhaps.* But she wasn't checking Maya out. She was sizing up her competition.

Charlie and Mack exchanged a quick glance and sipped on their drinks.

"Hey, ladies, your table's ready." The hostess gripped the menus against her chest.

"Sounds good." Charlie stood and interlocked her fingers in Mack's. "Give Ben a hug tonight when he gets home. He texted me earlier, he's having a crappy day. Apparently, a doctor yelled at him."

"Yelled? Or gently guided him in a different direction that he didn't want to take?" Remi gathered their napkins and tossed them in the trash.

Charlie giggled. "Good point."

"All right, I'll be nice to him." It would take Maya months to build up this type of rapport with the customers. *Months.* The customers knew Remi. They'd inherently like her better, and if Gabriella used this as a metric to measure them—along with sales—the bonus would be hers.

The air turned a little sweeter, the smell of maraschino cherries and fresh-squeezed lemon overtaking the burn-off from the vodka. She waved at another regular and her chest lifted. Damn near soared.

She needed to stop worrying. If Gabriella was deciding within the next few weeks, Maya would never have time to catch up. Things would be just—

What the hell was that? Remi's head snapped in Maya's direction and dissected the scene—a group of women cheering and the flash of bottles in the air.

Maya glanced at Remi with the dirtiest smirk Remi had

seen in forever and did it again. Flipped the bottles in the air like a flamethrower and caught them like her fingertips were made of glue.

Snow Princess can juggle.

I'm totally fucked.

SIX

DRINK SPECIAL: VIGOROUSLY SHAKEN, EXTRA-DIRTY MARTINI WITH SALTED ATTITUDES

Remi's first full week with Maya continued to spiral into a colossal crap-alanche, as the cherub-faced but devil-blooded Maya gained traction. Her speed might not be to the level of Remi's, but it barely mattered when she brought juggling to the table.

Maya was a smart cookie. She saved the flashiest flipping tricks for the pineapple piña colada served inside the fruit—the most expensive drink on the menu. The one advantage Remi had was her speed, and thus sales. But with Maya creating so many pineapple specials, their numbers almost matched.

A couple approached the bar and ordered the pineapple piña colada. Maya's long fingers clasped the bottles and tossed.

Remi indulged in the fantasy of coating them in castor oil. Not having one bottle plunge to its death went against the law of physics. How many months, maybe years, of practice did it take her to learn how to do this so seamlessly? She must have magic hands. And fingers. Long, beautiful fingers—nope.

What the hell's wrong with me?

Remi desperately needed some sleep. That explained why this odd mashup of fascination and irritation with Maya bubbled up in the most inopportune times. Others rarely impressed her, and putting in these extra hours this week was clearly making her soft.

"If you ever want me to teach you how to do this, I could," Maya said as she stacked the bottles back into the rail. It wasn't an altruistic offer. Her tone and smirk battled each other for the title of Queen Arrogance.

"I'm a professional. I don't do party tricks," Remi snapped back.

Maya's smirk dropped. And the playing field was evened, for now.

"Remi. A customer sent this back." A server set down a glass with a thud. "Said it tasted bad."

"What?" In just over four years, no one had ever returned a drink. She lifted the drink to her nose and flinched at the overpowering fresh pine scent—for a Cuba Libre. A classic cocktail with rum, lime, and Coke that she'd made no less than a thousand times in her tenure. "*Shit.*"

Maya inched toward her and reached for a lime. "Professional, huh? I'll keep trying to learn from you."

Remi glared, then tossed the drink in the sink and remade the order. How in the hell did she swap gin with rum? Sure, they're next to each other on the rack, but she was like a bartender Olympian, her muscle memory so astute she could make this drink in her sleep.

She glanced at the rail and, *dammit*—the bottles were swapped. A flare ripped through her chest. Yeah, Remi made a Long Island Iced Tea a few minutes prior and grabbed multiple bottles at once, but she never returned them to the rack in the improper order.

She wouldn't have, right? Did Maya swap the bottles to mess with her?

Maya's grin told Remi everything she needed to know.

This meant war.

The hustle of the night continued. Remi cashed out tables, popped open beer bottles, and shoved straws into a hundred drinks. Servers lined up at the bar, stacking their trays with freshly made mojitos and shots.

Remi tossed an empty bottle in recycling and reached for a new one when a man pulled up a seat.

She laid out a napkin. "What can I get you?"

He tapped his heavily ringed fingers on the cherry wood. "Ya got something local?"

"Sure do." She listed out the types and the breweries who produced the beer. She shoved the mug under the locally brewed barrel-aged porter spout and pulled the lever. The keg sputtered and her shirt absorbed the splashes. Occupational hazard, of course, but she didn't love that the rest of the night she'd be carrying around a hop-infused aroma on her chest. "Sorry, we're out. Something else?"

More people trickled in, and the noise grew. Remi dashed around the bar, fully in her zone—her happy place—as energy filled the room. Friends laughing, people saying "salud!" and "cheers!", and chairs squeaking across the smooth, hardwood floor.

Remi shook vodka, pomegranate juice, and lime in a martini shaker, and listened for the ice to crack *just enough* to let her know the drink was ready. After double-straining the layered martini, she wiped down the sticky bar for the hundredth time —and planned a hearty revenge on Snow Princess, who clearly sabotaged her earlier.

A loud "whoop!" echoed from across the bar as Maya tossed two bottles in the air and a small crowd gathered to watch her work. A regular clapped and whistled. "Hey, Remi, never seen you do that!"

Remi gritted her teeth and faked a smile.

The rest of the night continued in an endless loop of micro-screwups. Remi fumbled. Lime instead of lemon, sugar rim instead of salt, a knocked-over cup of ice where the cubes scattered like beads. An over-the-top angry customer complained loudly when Remi rang her up wrong, and she had to fix the bill —time that took away from building drinks. Maya crept closer to her sales record, and with her acrobatic skills, she'd surpass her soon enough.

Finally, the hostess locked the door, and Remi began closing duties. She stomped into the kitchen to grab towels and sanitizer. When she returned, she stumbled on the rubber mat and caught herself on the edge of the bar. Her knuckles turned white as her cheeks flamed red. No less than ten thousand times in the last four years had she walked on that mat and never once tripped. "What did you do to the mat?"

Maya moved past her and dumped ice into the bin. "I didn't touch your mat."

"Right. Just like you didn't switch the vodka and gin on me." Remi sprayed the bar with cleaner and scrubbed it like it was an operating room. Ten days after this blond demon came into her life, everything was screwed up.

Enough was enough. She needed a sit-down with Gabriella. The idea of quitting crossed her mind but made her stomach flare. She didn't want to quit. Nueve's was her home, her ticket to a better life. She'd have to start back at the beginning at a different bar, give up her growth, and everything she'd known over the last four years. She refused to be pushed out of her home. Metaphorically speaking or not, she'd never let that happen again. "Did you ask Gabriella if you could juggle?"

Maya ripped open a case of domestics and stocked the cooler. "No, why would I? She knows I juggle. I assumed that was part of why she hired me."

"We're not really that type of bar. People who come here expect a certain level of... class." Did she really just say *class* like some sort of elitist snob? Whatever. War was war.

"You know..." Maya said. "Some people get sick of the same thing over and over and like to change things up a bit."

Her face was stone-cold, and her voice held zero rattle. Calm as always, like this wasn't her life, her job, her *everything*.

"Seems to me they were looking for fresh talent."

She didn't. The words hit with the intended uppercut power punch. Maya just called Remi washed-up. Past her prime. Fire shot to every cell in her body. "Why don't you shove your diva back into your gold-encrusted Gucci purse and go somewhere else?"

Maya lowered the bottle into the cooler and faced Remi. "Seriously, what's your problem? Gabriella reached out to *me*. Not the other way around. If there is an issue, take it up with her and leave me the hell out of it."

Damn if there was not something sexy as hell seeing Maya's typical impassive, unaffected face morph pink and fire ignite in her eyes. "You want to do this? Fine!" Remi balled a towel and threw it into the empty bucket next to Maya.

Oops. At least she thought it was empty, but a heaping splash of gunky, dirty, sudsy water flew out and landed on Maya's chest.

The air was sucked out of the room. Maya looked down at her soaked shirt, slowly lifted her head, and the mother of all stare-downs began.

"I didn't mean—" A handful of ice cubes thrown at Remi's shoulder cut off any other words.

Did she seriously just throw ice at Remi like a ten-year-old? This was not happening. They were in a place of business. They were adults!

Maya crossed her arms and twisted her mouth.

Her eyes narrowed and blazed so fiercely that Remi felt the beginning of a hole being burned through her irises. A standoff ensued. *My-ah* was not getting away with disrespecting Remi in her home. A lemon slice provided the perfection ammunition.

Remi whipped it at Maya, who threw her arm up to block. The forearm failed to stop the airborne citrus, and it landed on the side of her head. The lemon hung on like a yellow, squashed bug that crashed into a windshield before it slipped on the blond glassiness and landed in a plop on the floor.

In a split second, both women grabbed their soda gun and pointed at each other. Fingers twitched, like two cowboys drawing their sugar guns at dusk. No sound existed except for Remi's pulse in her ears. Her gaze zoomed back and forth between Maya's fingers and eyes, zeroing on her micro-movements. She almost *wanted* her to do it.

Remi was unclear who made the first move. But, in a matter of seconds, everything was wet. Swear words were flung.

Blood was shed.

SEVEN

DRINK SPECIAL: MOMENTARY TRUCE MOJITO WITH A DOUBLE SHOT OF BRUISED EGO

"Oh my God, are you okay?" Maya dropped to her knees next to a sprawled-out Remi on the cement bar floor.

Remi blinked up and squinted her eyes. "Yeah... I..."

Everything happened so fast—a sticky mat, wet floors, and the edge of the cooler that must've had the perfect sharp edge that latched on to Remi's skin as she fell.

A moment prior, she and Remi were standing behind the bar, closing up shop after the last customer left, and pointing soda guns at each other like idiots. Maya knew better. Remi knew better. And now someone actually got hurt. Ten days into her job, and Maya was officially part of a workplace accident. A workplace on purpose. A workplace *whatever-the-hell-this-dumb-shit-was*. She was better than this, and her insides raged that she let her ego get the best of her.

Fresh towels on the side of the bar caught Maya's eyes. She grabbed one from the middle of the stack, quickly inspected to see how deep the wound was, and wrapped it around Remi's forearm. "Here, come on. Let's get this on there, nice and snug." She gripped the wrapping and gently raised Remi's arm above her heart.

A curiously quiet Remi sat up and peered down at her bloodied arm. Her face shifted from rosy to white, and her body swayed.

Maya gripped her shoulders and guided her upright. "You're turning a little green." She snugged the towel tighter around Remi. "Let's just set you back against the cooler. There ya go." She popped up, shoved a few ice cubes in a towel, and held it behind Remi's neck.

How in the hell did she let this happen? Sure, the bar was Remi's turf. But liquid on the floor and a slippery surface was Safety 101. She was damn lucky Remi didn't hit her head on the way down. After getting her master's, she'd formally take her Nursing Oath, but she should still try to uphold some level of ethics in the interim. Which, at the bare minimum, was probably not purposely creating an unsafe environment.

Remi looked down again at her arm and winced. "Christ, this hurts." She swallowed hard. "There's... so much blood." Her voice was a hoarse whisper. A gagging sound erupted from the back of her throat.

"Hey, it's okay." Maya rested a supportive hand on Remi's back. She never had a problem with blood. There was something endearing about seeing this strong, powerful, resilient woman get a little ghost-faced at the sight of the substance. "I know it hurts, but you're tough. You got this." She filled her tone with reassurance but wasn't sure if it landed.

Blood fascinated Maya. Harper's life was ruled by the maintenance of its sugars. The hematology courses in her early undergrad unlocked its magic. Diagnosis, cures, genetics were all contained in this liquid.

But Remi clearly didn't share that same sentiment. She flinched as she sat on the hard, concrete floor, and Maya applied more pressure. The color on Remi's cheeks remained pale. Maya clocked the time. She'd give it another minute to see if her cheeks returned to a healthy color. If not, she'd make Remi drink some orange juice.

Maya itched to clean the wound, to stave off any sort of infection. "Come on, let's go into the kitchen so we don't need to call hazmat to clear this murder scene." Maya unwrapped the towel. *Oh no.* The cut was not closing as quickly as it should. She smiled at Remi and outstretched her hand. "Ready?"

A few "ahs!" and various cuss words later, Remi clasped on to Maya's hand as she stood on wobbly legs.

"You gonna pass out?" She teased but glued herself to Remi's side as they walked into the kitchen.

"No." The words squeaked out. "I'm good."

Maya pushed open the door with one arm, to a wave of cleaning supplies and lingering fried pork from earlier in the night.

Remi gagged and covered her mouth.

The kitchen staff glanced up with uninterested eyes and returned to cleaning. As part of the bar pit crew, they'd seen it all. By this time of night, unless someone had chopped off a pinkie with the electric onion slicer, the only thing the team wanted to do was finish their shift and go home.

Maya snaked her foot around the leg of a rolling chair and kicked it over to the stainless-steel sanitizing sink. She wasn't risking dropping her hands from Remi and having her nosedive on the kitchen floor. "Sit."

Remi obliged immediately.

Careful not to pry the towel that might be stuck to Remi's tender skin, Maya slowly unwrapped the fabric above the sink. She crossed her fingers that the first aid kit resting right above the cracked metal-framed mirror contained more than just bandages. "This might hurt a little." She positioned Remi's arm under the water.

"Shit!" Remi yanked away her arm.

Maya eased her back under the water.

Remi turned her head toward the wall, seeming to find any spot to stare at besides her arm.

Maya sifted through the first aid kit and breathed a sigh of relief that the kit contained fresh supplies. "I'm gonna grab some gloves. Keep your arm here."

An apology settled on Maya's tongue. She felt like a dumb kid egged on by some older kids to do something stupid and then did it without consideration. Like in high school when she forged her mom's name, wrote a note to the school office that she had a doctor appointment, and then skipped class with some girls to go to the mall. In the moment, the naughty high was delicious. But five minutes after leaving campus, her stomach had turned rancid, and she cried in a Target dressing room.

When did she become this person? Her life revolved around order, compliance, and stability. Crossing every T, dotting every I, showcasing calm and ease in every situation, was her drug of choice. And yet, she literally just sprayed her co-worker with juice like a toddler. She plucked the sticky, wet shirt away from her skin, and grabbed a towel off the rack to wipe herself before she washed her hands and pulled on the gloves. She gently twisted Remi's arm and inspected it. "Good news. I don't think you need stitches."

Remi sighed. "That's a relief."

Maya turned the water off and dried Remi's arm. She held the antiseptic and took a breath. "Sorry. This is gonna burn like hell."

"Fuuuuu..." Remi sucked in a sharp breath between her teeth and clasped her hand over her mouth.

Maya ripped open the bandages package and avoided Remi's eyes. "I'm really sorry. I shouldn't—"

"Stop. I was being an idiot," Remi said. "We're good."

The tightness in Maya's chest lifted. After securing the last bandage, she clipped the edge and snapped off her gloves.

Remi rotated her bandaged arm. "So, I take it this means I won?" A quick smile appeared before she winced again. Her eyes dropped to Maya's lips and then darted back up to her eyes, and then back to the wall.

Was that a look? That was definitely a look. Nope, what was wrong with her? Maya must have misread the expression in the same way as when someone waves to someone behind you and you mistakenly think they are waving to you. *Embarrassing.*

Remi tucked a chunk of curls behind her ear. "You look like you know what you're doing."

"Oh, yeah?" Maya gathered the wrappers and tossed them into the trash. "That's good to hear. I just graduated with my undergrad in nursing. I'm going to school in the fall to get my master's."

Remi's head flew back. "Wait, you're in school? For nursing?"

Maya nodded.

"You go to UW?"

"No. I go to the University of Minnesota. I'm off until the end of September." Maya plucked two more gloves from the box and grabbed the sanitizing spray and paper towels. People don't go into nursing for the cleaning portion of the job. Maya wanted to give back, serve, and teach people like her sister how to manage diabetes properly. But ever since returning to Seattle, she felt disconnected from her passion. Cleaning the basin textbook style brought back the rush of her profession.

Remi pushed herself from the sink but stayed sitting in the rolling chair. "You're going back to Minnesota?"

Spritz, spritz, swipe. "Yes."

"Then why are you here?"

Maya bristled at the tone. She and Remi may have had a moment, but she didn't need to justify anything. Now was not the time to talk about how Maya had maxed out her student loans and couldn't afford her grad school tuition without this position and bonus. Never mind that she still hadn't come clean to her own mom about why she was back in town. "Because I need the money."

Remi sucked in the side of her cheek. "Why do you need it so bad?"

Maya stared at her hands before she hardened her shoulders. "Why do you?"

All lightness, albeit filled with gagging and blood, left, replaced by a heaviness in the air. Truth was, Remi owed Maya as much of an explanation as Maya owed Remi, which was to say none. Their momentary truce dissolved.

"Thanks for wrapping me up." Remi dragged the chair back to the corner.

Maya nodded. "You can go home, and I'll clean everything up."

"You don't have to do that. It was my blood," Remi said, but the relief was clear in her voice.

Maya shrugged. "I don't want Gabriella to get fined from the health department if it's not done right." She meant it like a joke, but it came out stale.

Remi walked away, muttering, "Thanks."

EIGHT

DRINK SPECIAL: REMINISCING RUM WITH SALTED MEMORIES

For a week, Maya avoided Remi as much as one human could avoid another while working eight feet apart. Their conversations consisted solely of asking for the other to grab back stock when heading into the kitchen or passing lemon slices. And each night, Maya would go home and take the longest, hottest shower her body could handle while tallying everything she could improve on, chastising herself for careless mistakes like forgetting a straw, and replaying drink recipes in her mind. After scrubbing off caked-on corn syrup and liquor residue from the evening, she'd launch herself into bed.

Sunday morning, Maya's alarm buzzed at 8:00 a.m. A sliver of clouded light funneled through the blinds, and she tapped the phone until it silenced. She hoisted herself from the bed and squinted at her phone, praying that Gabriella had messaged that she changed her mind about the assignment.

She reread the group text sent to her and Remi the previous evening.

> Gabriella: Sunday, work at 10. You two don't leave the kitchen until you've come up with a fall drink menu.

Jeezus. She missed Auntie Gabby, not boss Gabriella. But maybe, *just maybe,* she and Remi deserved the irritation. Gabriella gave the cocktail recipe development job to her and Remi last week, but they just bickered and left every night without creating a single one.

Her phone buzzed with a new notification and her heart skipped, then dropped. The text was from her former classmate Erica, sending a selfie in her scrubs outside of a hospital.

> Erica: First day, bitches! Let's get dirty and do some healing.

An unfamiliar sound escaped Maya's lips. Not laughter at the goofy message, not a cry. More of a choke-whimper. Screw this bartending gig, screw insecurities, screw everything! She didn't want to be a year behind her classmates. She'd hated that after maxing out her grant and student loans by sophomore year, she had to cut her credit load and work full time at the bar to pay for school. Being in the field, checking on patients, celebrating discharges, crying with families, that was what she wanted. Not fighting over a bonus.

After tossing on her leggings and sweatshirt, she grabbed her headphones and went into the kitchen.

Harper stood at the counter with her floppy blond bun, fuzzy slippers, and strawberry fleece pajamas.

"What's up, kiddo?" Maya reached into the fridge for vanilla yogurt. "How are your numbers today?"

Harper swiped the smartphone against the sensor attached to her arm for a digital glucose reading. "I'll tell ya in a second."

Thank God for modern technology and her mom's incredible health insurance. Gone were the days of finger pricks on a test strip shoved into a glucose reader and multiple injections through the belly. Replaced by a scanner on Harper's arm, and an adjustable insulin pump on her hip. Not that it was easy.

Harper's life would forever revolve around monitoring her blood sugar and carb intake.

Harper waved the phone in front of Maya's face. "110. Which means I get chocolate!"

"Harper... no. You shouldn't do that. It's not good for you. Even if your numbers are within range, you really need to start out with protein and complex carbs."

She stuck out her tongue. "You're home for like a second and already sound like Mom." She grabbed a jar of overnight oats from the fridge. "Besides, I'm just kidding. *Duh.* I'm not a child."

But she *was* a child. Sure, Harper was twelve going on thirty, but since Maya moved out when Harper was so young, a part of Maya's mind stunted Harper at seven.

"I'm having oatmeal. With chocolate frosting." Harper grinned.

Maya groaned and bumped her hip against Harper's.

Harper giggled, then added a heaping scoop of peanut butter to her jar before she sat down and pulled up her phone. A soothing voice sounded over the video.

"What are you watching?" Maya grabbed a banana from the basket and sliced it on top of the yogurt.

"Neil deGrasse Tyson."

Of all the content online, her sister chose to learn about outer space. Being back in Seattle wasn't *all* bad, and now Maya got the opportunity to reconnect with Harper and rebuild their relationship. She added a handful of granola into the bowl and stirred. This breakfast used to be a favorite of her dad's, although he'd pour gobs of honey on top and pinkie swear with Maya not to tell Mom. She closed her eyes, and a faded, pixilated mirage danced in her brain of sitting with him at this kitchen table, eating before school. She squeezed her eyelids tighter to grasp a crisper image, but the images fragmented and disappeared.

She dug around the cabinet for a cup and stopped on the University of Minnesota Gophers mug. Her father had played basketball there and stuffed their house with gold-and-maroon memorabilia. Maya remembered snuggling on the couch with her dad sharing a Great Dane–size bowl of buttered popcorn, toy whistles around their necks, and screaming out fouls when the refs missed a violation.

The next few years after he passed, everything in the house had reminded her of her dad—his pictures on the mantel, his dusty collection of baseball caps, his hiking boots in the closet. But then her mom removed the photos, donated the caps, and tossed the boots. Even the pictures of Maya propped on his shoulders wearing his alma mater's onesie were swapped with more recent ones that didn't include him. She ached to feel a connection. Soon, Minnesota reminded her more of him than the house did.

After high school, Maya struggled between chasing his memory at the U of M or staying with her mom and Harper in Seattle. Since she was little, he always talked about where she'd go to college. He said he'd come visit her in the dorms, show her how to pontoon on Lake Minnetonka, skip rocks in the Mississippi River, and discover the best cheese-infused burgers in town.

Maya peeked out the blinds to see if the rain had let up and sunk her teeth into her creamy, crunchy breakfast. She skimmed the back of the chair with her hand—her dad's sitting spot—and thought if he were here, he'd have peeked at the rain and said, "Well, at least the trees are happy."

She pulled orange juice from the fridge and heard footsteps approach.

"Not too much." Laney grabbed the coffee carafe from the burner and filled it with water. "That's Harper's emergency stash."

Maya stopped pouring. "Oh shit, sorry."

"Language." Laney put her finger to her lips.

She pressed her hand over her mouth. "Oops." Living with a kid again was taking some getting used to.

Laney pulled her in for a side hug and then scooped the crushed coffee beans into the filter. She glanced at Maya's outfit. "You jogging today?"

"Yeah, around Green Lake. Then I have to head over to Nueve's." Maya dumped the juice back into the jug.

"On a Sunday?"

"Yep. Pretty sure it's punishment from Gabriella. No tips, only an hourly wage. She wants me and Remi to create a drink menu."

Laney started the coffeepot, and soon the nutty, earthy aroma of brewed grounds cut through the air. "Why punishment?"

Ugh, why did she use those words? Now her mom would worry all day along with the million other things she'd worry about as a single mom. Maya shrugged and attempted a deflecting grin.

Besides, she didn't want to share the details of her immaturity with her mom. Every shift, Gabriella asked Maya and Remi how they were getting along, and both gave Gabriella the same "fine" clipped response. Gabriella probably expected her two senior bartenders to work together with a little more grace.

Laney wiped up a water spill on the counter. "I've been meaning to tell you..."

Oh no. Maya knew exactly where this was heading.

"There's this really sweet guy who started in our office—"

"Mom, no. Absolutely not." *For so many reasons.*

Laney threw a hand on her hip. "Come on! Smart, cute, graduated last year from—"

"Mom. No. Not interested." She stirred her breakfast.

"Okay." Laney poured herself a cup of coffee and blew into

the top of the Mount Rainier mug. "So... I was talking to Suzanne and her daughter's visiting here from Bellingham—"

"It's not the gender." She took a last bite of yogurt and stacked the bowl in the dishwasher. "I can't date anyone right now. Man, woman, enby, effing zebra—"

"Maya," Laney hissed. "Language."

"*Sorry.*" She filled up a water bottle from the refrigerator filter. "Dating's a hard, fat pass." She'd be gone from Seattle at the end of the summer. The only thing she wanted to do was spend every second she could with her family, help her mom, and earn tuition money. No way would she get into any sort of relationship—wouldn't be fair to her or the person.

Not that she couldn't go for a solid shag because... *damn.* She'd burned through a bulk package of batteries on her vibrating companion these last few months. But she was pretty sure Laney wouldn't appreciate it if Maya reached out to Suzanne's daughter and asked if she'd be down for a hookup.

Laney took a small sip. "Well, I'd like to be a grandma at some point in my life."

"Good God. I'm twenty-three. Trust me, I have time." She twisted the cap on her bottle and attached it to her fanny pack. "Be back soon."

Her mom lived a few blocks from Green Lake, which was the perfect warm-up to the two-and-a-half-mile lake loop. Maya tugged her ponytail tighter and stretched her hamstrings on the front porch. The air smelled wet and clean, the gray from the clouds and soft mist providing the ideal jogging weather. She snugged her hoodie over her head and started down the driveway.

The cracked pavement was hard against her feet, and before she reached the end of the block, she almost turned back. But soon, her tendons warmed, and she welcomed the cement massage. Her lungs began the slow-fire release, and her body filled with relief. Down the street, she waved at the cars who stopped for her in the crosswalk and started the trek around the lake.

Her heart thumped, matching the beat to the '80s pop music that had become her running bestie. The trees buzzed by as she weaved in between moms and dads with strollers, folks walking, and a couple of rollerbladers. The mist hit her face, a delicate, refreshing relief as her lungs stretched and sweat beads formed.

"On your left!" a bike rider called out, and the dinging of a bell cut through her music.

She shuffled to the right, picked up speed, and inventoried the things she failed on last week that she needed to correct. When a customer ordered the classic cocktail Sidecar, she had to ask Remi how to make it and nearly choked from embarrassment. How could she possibly forget the ingredients? Bartending 101, first week in, you learned all the classics— Manhattans, Cosmos, daiquiris, and Sidecars. And two nights ago, she tossed a horchata martini because she made it with regular vodka, not the vanilla infused. She shook her head. *You've got to do better.*

After she completed a lap, the tension she carried all week finally dissipated. The ducks quacked, the pavement turned smooth, and her muscles fully heated. Her mind was free, juxtaposing images of her in scrubs, studying at a coffee shop, and working at the bar in Minnesota.

She hurdled a shallow puddle and glanced at her watch. She needed to get ready for work, but she felt *so good.* The best she'd felt in weeks, and one more lap wouldn't hurt. She'd just sprint home, take a quick shower, and hop on the metro. She lifted her sweatshirt and wiped the rain and sweat mix from her face and continued.

A smattering of ducks and geese dipped into the lake water. Clam chowder and coffee bean scents surrounded her from the local eateries and trailed her until she reached the other side of the lake. With every step, her memories faded. Crying at her dad's funeral—gone. The shame of withdrawing from a pharma-cotherapeutics course because she failed to earn a proper A—gone. Her ex pounding on her door, begging her to open as she covered her ears with a pillow—gone.

The endorphins kicked into high gear at the start of lap two. Flashes of Remi's face popped into her thoughts. Was her skin as smooth as it looked? Was her tongue as soft as her lips appeared to be? "Christ," she muttered, and shook her head. Maybe she'd call Suzanne's daughter after all. Something to stop all these recurring Remi thoughts—*who she didn't even like* —from badgering her mind.

Lap two complete. Her lungs expelled fire, the fog of breath caught in the mist. Leg muscles ached, and her rib cage verged on exploding. But she didn't want to stop. She peeked at her watch. Dammit. If she didn't hurry, she'd be late for recipe testing.

Just one more lap. She double-timed her speed. Her diaphragm rose and shrunk with every hot exhale and finally, as she finished, she slowed her body, then polished off a water bottle.

The wet grass squished beneath her feet as she cut through the park to jog home. An hour later, she hopped on the metro to Nueve's. Today better be different than this past week with Remi. If not, Maya knew exactly what she would do to change the course.

NINE

DRINK SPECIAL: WARM SUGAR TEA INFUSED WITH BONDING BOOZE

The bus dropped off Maya a block from work, and the walk to Nueve's was treacherous. Without a proper stretching, her leg muscles raged, and she was eternally grateful she wouldn't be on her feet today.

Maya reached for the door and froze. Exhaling through her nose, she counted to five, pushed a smile on her face, and opened the door.

The kitchen was quiet, the Sunday crew most likely nursing a Saturday night hangover. The prep cooks stirred in silence and the staff stacked dishes like they were stuck in sludge. Maya chatted with the day bartender and was pouring herself a glass of water when the doors swung open and Remi walked through.

Holy hell. Remi's fullness and curves overflowed in ripped jeans and a tight white-and-red flannel. Seeing her outside of a work uniform did something tingly to Maya, and she hated it as much as she *didn't* hate it. Maya was always skinny like her dad, and—even though she tried to fight it—a little insecurity gremlin popped up now and then about not having full boobs and ass.

"Hey." Remi filled a glass with club soda. "I thought of some ideas for the menu last night."

"Cool, so did I." *Lies.* She spent the evening playing Monopoly with Harper and crashed early after Harper talked for an hour about the possibility of human life on Mars.

Remi handed her a tray. "We're gonna sit in the booth over there." She jutted a finger to a tucked away corner. "Can you get juice, garnishes, and whatever you think we'll need, and I'll bring over the booze?"

Maya filled glasses with cranberry, orange, pineapple, and tomato juices. She added olives, lemons, limes, and cherries to a bowl. *Come on, come on, think.* She needed a knockout drink, one that would prove to Remi that she could hold her own in recipe development. The menu at her former bar was an Irish pub featuring mostly beers, basic mixed drinks, and Irish coffee. Nothing that could work for Nueve's fall menu.

She followed Remi to the table, where the light from the sun didn't quite reach them. Maya sunk into the U-shaped leather booth and lined up the glasses. Remi leaned over and set the pens and pads of paper down and dammit, nope—Maya did *not* just look at her cleavage that was so beautifully *right there.* She peeled away her eyes and scolded herself for acting like a horny teenager.

"Let's do this." Remi rubbed her palms together.

Sitting in a booth with Remi, who was so casual and effortlessly sexy, seemed oddly intimate. Maya's cheeks warmed in response. She cleared her throat and scooched over a few inches. "Did you have a good night last night?" Something needed to break this ice—heat—whatever element that lingered in the air.

"Yeah." Remi propped her elbows on the table and twirled the pen. "All right, fall menu. We need to think warm. Cinnamon, nutmeg, almond. I was thinking we could do a spin-off of a spicy hot chocolate, using chili powder and coconut milk instead."

Damn. All business. Made things easier, probably. Maya

didn't even know why she had this weird urge to make Remi her friend. It was like Remi was the cool girl in high school Maya would follow in the hall and try to get them to notice her. "I like that idea." She refocused on the condiments and spices. "What if we made homemade cinnamon-and-brown-sugar whipped cream? Or added chocolate and hazelnut shavings on top?"

Remi raised an eyebrow along with the corner of her lip. "Not bad. I'll jot a note to ask the kitchen about the cost of making the whipped cream, and how long it keeps fresh."

"What would we name it? Fuego? Sugar con Amore? Remi Special?"

This suggestion produced a tiny dimple on Remi's lower cheek. "What if we made the base with horchata instead of milk?"

Maya tucked her leg under her butt and ignored the chiropractor's voice inside her head, yelling at her to fix her posture. "And a shot of amaretto with the rum?"

"Perfect." Remi looked around at their table filled with every mixer except what they needed. "I'll grab the horchata. Be back in a sec."

Five minutes later, Remi pushed open the kitchen door with her foot, holding two mugs of piping hot chocolate. "I added the horchata. Let me know if it needs more."

The warm, creamy drink traveled down Maya's throat, and she smacked her lips. "It's good. Nutty, sweet, warm. Let's add a touch more cinnamon and brown sugar syrup on top of the whipped cream."

"Agreed." Remi shook the cannister and sprayed, then added the toppings. She took a tentative sip, then swiped the cream from the corner of her mouth with her thumb and licked it off.

Maya stared at the drink and 100 percent, for sure, absolutely nothing else. "I say one shot white rum, and a half shot of amaretto."

Remi cocked her head. "Not dark rum?"

"I think the overtones would be too deep and take away from the other flavors."

Remi nibbled on her bottom lip for a moment, then nodded. "You're right."

Man, if she could hear those words a few more times, her life may be complete. Maya added the shots to the drinks and stirred. "Mmm... smell this."

Remi filled her lungs. "Smells good. I think the amaretto was a great call."

"Cheers." Maya tipped the mug against Remi's and lifted the cup to her lips. The burn descended her throat, then jumped to her head. "I could have this for breakfast. It's that delicious." She took one more sip and pushed the mug to the side. She rarely drank, always worried a hangover would mess with her studies, and was too tired after her shifts. Getting sloshed at her place of business, especially while competing for the bonus, was probably not the best call, either. She glanced at Remi's untouched mug. "Wait—aren't you gonna try the drink?"

Remi scribbled in the notebook. "I don't drink."

She looked so solemn with her flatlined lips and hard stare that Maya laughed. Remi was a bartender, a damn good one, and was clearly messing with Maya.

A blotch of red shot through Remi's neck and she narrowed her eyes.

Maya cleared her throat to muffle the giggles. "Whoa. You're serious?"

"There a problem with that?" Remi crossed her arms.

Now Maya's cheeks blushed, and she hoped an earthquake would crack through the restaurant and suck her into the base-ment. "No... of course not." The information shouldn't surprise her, but it was a little peculiar. Most bartenders drank. In fact, she couldn't think of a single bartender she worked with over the years that didn't throw down. She clamped her tongue between her teeth to hold back the *why?* begging for release. "Ah. Cool. Well, I'll be the tipsy guinea pig. But promise me if I ask to do karaoke, you'll cut me off."

Remi's shoulders relaxed, and she sipped a soda. "Karaoke, huh? What's your go-to song?"

"'Baby Got Back.' Obviously."

A glorious, husky giggle escaped Remi's mouth. "I can honestly say I didn't see that one coming."

The sun shifted and cracked through the windows, casting a warm ray across Remi and picking up a sprinkle of golden high-lights in her dark brown eyes. Maya had never noticed until now the faded smattering of freckles on the top of her nose, or the tiny curve in the corners of her lips. She shook her head and realigned the bottles to see if an idea sparked.

Remi closed her eyes and inhaled lemon, basil, mint, cinnamon, chocolate. After several hefty sniffs, she smelled coffee and tried a different combo.

"Niñas." Gabriella poked her head around the corner. "You two got everything you need?"

"Yep," Maya said at the same time as Remi.

"Good." She planted her palms on the table, her fire-engine red nails and multiple silver stacked rings clicking against the cherry wood. "Mark told me he can come up with a better menu than you two by the end of the day."

Remi rolled her eyes at the name of the talented, yet arrogant, head chef. "Mark? Really?"

"He bet me twenty bucks." She leaned in. "Do *not* make me lose that money." She squeezed each woman on the shoulder and walked away.

"Oh, hell no." Remi straightened her back. "We're not letting him come up with a menu. He'll never let us live it down. Three summers ago, a group of us went bowling, and he had the highest score. Literally didn't shut up about it for months."

Maya sipped water. "I don't know him that well, but he seems like—"

"A dick. He's a total dick."

Maya giggled. "He does have the best arroz con gandules I've ever had, though."

"Yeah, but he knows how good his food is." Remi's eyes trailed over Maya's face, and her lip tugged up. "Truce? Today, our sole mission is taking down Mark."

Maya extended her hand. When Remi shook it—warm, firm, and totally different from the death grip when they first met—heat traveled up her arm. She dropped her hand and focused on her drink.

For the next hour, Maya jotted down notes on various combinations. After Remi tasted the base and squeezed the tiniest additions until she achieved perfection, Maya would sip the finished product. She googled alcohol, herbs, and spices while Remi went to the kitchen and returned with items like ghost peppers, chili powder, and sage.

Maya tapped her fingers against the glass. "What about a honey lemon tea with blackberry vodka?"

Remi tilted her head. "That could work. Or dark rum. We could also do a ginger-infused vodka."

"Maybe add raw sugar too it?"

"Perfect. I'll go get the tea." Remi stood and stretched her arms.

The bottom of her shirt lifted, and Maya caught a sliver of a smooth belly. She zipped her gaze back to her pen and doodled in the notebook.

Tucked in a quiet corner booth, Maya barely noticed the restaurant doors had opened, until a muffled hum of customers and servers shuffled around. Soon, her limbs loosened, and cheeks flushed with the heat of alcohol. The stiffness she felt earlier from not stretching after a six-mile run disappeared.

"Here we go. Honey lemon tea." Remi placed the mug in front of Maya, then took a sip. "Needs a bit more lemon."

A shot of rogue juice hit Maya in the face. "Hey!" She laughed and wiped it with the back of her palm.

Remi giggled and handed over a napkin. "Oh God, sorry. Crap, that didn't go in your eye, right?"

Maya tossed the towel to the side. "No, no, I'm good."

Remi swiped up the splatters on the table. "Sometimes I think with all the liquids and things flying around, it's like tap dancing in shark-infested waters. You never know when something is going to up and bite you."

"Like lemon shrapnel."

Remi chuckled. "Exactly."

Maya took another sip of the tea. This cocktail she didn't want to toss in the bucket yet. The warm honey and lemon, combined with blackberry vodka, was a light, sweet comfort drink. "Is this the only bar you've ever worked at?"

"Yeah." Remi added mango puree, basil, and a sprinkle of dill into a cup, and sampled. "Gross. Dill. What was I thinking?"

"I like that you try random combinations. We'll never know otherwise."

Remi pinched lavender sugar into a capful of lemon juice and rolled it in her mouth. She swallowed and scribbled on the notebook. "What about you?"

She rubbed her thumb into the back of her neck. "I've worked at two different ones. A sports bar for a hot minute, and an Irish pub."

Remi grabbed a raw sugar packet and slapped it against her palm. "How did you start bartending when you were eighteen?"

"That's the legal age in Minnesota. It's funny—before I

turned twenty-one, I wasn't allowed in the bar unless I was working."

"Interesting." Remi eyed the bottles on the table. She dashed almond liqueur into a shot glass, palmed a few hazelnuts, then trailed both beneath her nose. "My first job was in this weird-ass factory in SoDo making plastic bird feeders when I was fifteen. The place barely had electricity. Pretty sure some industrial electric cords they stole from a neighboring building ran it. We only had a couple of lamps and some fans in the summer. But they paid me cash. I ended up staying for almost a year."

Maya indulged in one more sip of tea. "A year? Did you like it?"

Remi's shoulders softened. "Yeah. It was a constant in my life when so many things then were... inconsistent."

Maya opened her mouth to speak, then closed it.

"The place had been around forever. I worked next to this dude, Lou, who started there after he retired. At first it made me kind of sad, you know, this guy at that age working in a dumpy, cold factory. Turns out, he had a big-ass house on Mercer Island. Used to be a crab fisherman and just wanted to be down by the pier. Plus, he said couldn't stand being around his wife." Remi grinned. "He'd bring me cappuccinos and make me practice long-form math."

Something flashed behind Remi's eyes that Maya couldn't read. Sadness? Maybe nostalgia? Maya pictured a young Remi with an attitude as big as her hair, standing next to a bunch of middle-aged retired fishermen swearing like sailors and swapping stories.

She wanted to pry, ask why she'd work there at such a young age, or where her parents were, but clamped her lips. Maya hated when people asked about her dad. "So, whatever happened to Lou? He still working there?"

Remi's gaze fell for a half second to the table and her back stiffened. "What about rose-and-vanilla-creamed tequila with coffee?"

Maya slumped in her seat. She tried not to dwell on the abrupt shift in Remi's attitude and focused on making the drink. She sipped, and the burn was instant. "No. It's missing something. Probably cream and sugar."

"What if we tried it with condensed milk?" Remi stood without waiting for a response. "I'll grab some."

Maya sipped while she waited. The booze heated her insides. She tossed her hair into a bun on top of her head and fanned her face with a cocktail menu. When Remi returned, Maya added the milk. The vanilla-tequila-coffee concoction slid down her throat. "Perfection. We could even do a heated version with chili liqueur."

"Oh smart." Remi poised the pen over the notepad. "Let's come up with some names. Hot as the Devil?"

Maya scrunched her nose. "That's a terrible name."

"Very true." Remi tucked a piece of hair behind her ear.

Cute, petite ear lobes. How had she never noticed them before? The next several minutes, she tossed out different names, each one worse than the last. *Caffeinated Heat. Corazon Spice. Hot Tamale.* Finally, Café de Cataño—named after Gabriella's birth city in Puerto Rico—won.

"Oh!" Maya fanned her fingers across Remi's forearm. "I know! When I was a kid, my parents gave me hot buttered rum."

Remi glanced at Maya's fingers wrapped on her arm and didn't flinch like Maya's fingertips were spikes. It took Maya a moment to realize she was touching Remi. And another moment to remove her hand.

"Your parents gave you hot buttered rum?" Remi lifted an eyebrow. "And I thought I had an effed-up childhood."

"No, no." Maya's tongue felt thick, and her brain slowed. A picture flashed through her mind of her dad carrying a mug to her while she sat cross-legged under the Christmas tree. "I mean, they didn't have the rum in mine, *obviously*, just the base. I think it'll take us too long to make today, though."

Remi drummed her fingers against the table. "Agreed. But let's add it to the list just in case. And we should serve it with a brown-sugar-crusted rim."

"Ooh, that sounds good!" Everything right now sounded good. So much time had passed since Maya had been at a happy hour. Not that *this* was a happy hour. But the environment felt more festive than work—savory fried calamari, chickpea soup, and beef mofongo scents surrounded her as the Sunday bartender slung drinks for the crowd. "I have an idea. Hold, please." She filled a short glass with white rum, brown sugar, squeezed orange, and a dash of pineapple juice. She stirred with the large metal spoon and held it under Remi's nose.

Remi slow nodded. "Nice."

"Right?" Maya sampled, then shook her head. "No, not quite there." She added a trace of dark rum to go with the light. "Yep, much better."

Remi squeezed lime into her club soda and tipped it back. "How are you going to make that into a warm drink?"

Maya slapped her palm against her forehead and laughed. "Oops, I was just thinking of things that'd taste good." She indulged in one more sip. "And that is really damn good."

The place grew louder with customers. Servers revolved through the kitchen doors carrying trays of water, and the bartender busied himself making the socially acceptable drink of choice on Sunday mornings—Bloody Mary. It always struck Maya as goofy that some people would frown on a patron downing a shot of vodka at eleven on a Sunday, but if tomato juice was added, it was perfectly fine.

The burn in Maya's mouth stopped a while ago, and her tongue and brain lubricated. "We used to have this guy at my old place in Minnesota." She took one more sip, then poured the rest in the dump bucket. "He was like taste deficient, I swear. He'd come up with the most terrible ideas. Like he'd thought he'd sweeten up the Bloody Mary with orange juice."

Remi winced. "He didn't."

"Yep. Sure did. So gross." Maya's limbs buzzed. The music had kicked in, quieter but still with that festive thump she'd grown to love. She had an urge to take a shot, pull Remi with her, and go explore the city. Or dance. Or sing. Something. *Anything.*

Jesus, she needed to get out more. She smacked her hands against her thighs. "What about black-spiced rum, eggnog, and chocolate shavings?"

"I like it." Remi flicked the pen against the table. "Vanilla-infused vodka with espresso and a shot of cream?"

"Or peppermint liqueur and chocolate vodka."

"We could add shaved chocolate. Like, *good* shaved chocolate." Remi bit her lip and lifted herself from the booth. Her gaze dashed around the restaurant. "I'm gonna dig out some from Gabriella's secret stash."

Maya's eyes widened. "She has a secret stash? Where?"

Remi leaned close with a deep grin. "If you bust me, I swear to God, Maya—snitches end up in ditches."

Maya. Only the second time she heard her name leaving Remi's lips, and her ears tickled with the sound. She refrained from asking Remi to repeat it.

"Come on. Don't be suspicious." Remi waved her from the table.

Maya saluted her like a boat captain and slid out of the booth.

"Shhh." Remi peeked above the counter and held her finger to her mouth. "Follow me."

The entire situation was ridiculous, but Maya's adrenaline spiked. In high school, Sophie begged her to call in sick at work or sneak out at night to go to Alki Beach and drink around a fire, and she never would. Sneaking into her boss's office for chocolate was the bottom of the barrel for rebellious acts, but the rush was almost the same as she planned a heist.

She tiptoed next to Remi, not *not* noticing each time their hips brushed, and followed her into the kitchen. A familiar soundtrack of cooks barking out orders, boiling pots of stews, and searing meats played.

"Wait, stop." Remi pushed her back with a gentle arm and flattened Maya against the wall.

Maya sucked in her breath, stumbling with clunky, uncoordinated feet. Remi held her arm against Maya and a whiff of something meadowy, sage-y, and sexy-as-hell reached her nose. She inhaled Remi's heavenly scent and her thighs warmed.

"Okay, clear." Remi jutted her chin toward Gabriella's office.

Maya's head was clouded, thick in a fog of surreal and real.

Remi held the door and waved her in. "Stand guard."

A drumbeat pulsed in Maya's ear. She peeked around the corner to nothing but a sea of white chef jackets and sizzling platters. "We're clear."

Remi yanked on a desk drawer and pulled out a chocolate bar. She ripped open the bag as she scurried back to Maya. After breaking off a chunk, she handed a piece over and popped the other one in her mouth.

A mix of salted caramel and chocolate melted on Maya's tongue. "Yum-freaking-o, why is this so good?"

Remi swiped the corner of her lip with her pinkie. "I know, right? Gabriella has it shipped in from San Juan."

"It's like a chocolate heaven exploded in my mouth." A throaty giggle escaped Maya.

"Hey!" Remi grasped her hand. "That's what we should call

the drink. Exploding Chocolate Heaven." She squinted at the ceiling, then brought them back to Maya's face. "Okay, maybe not the exploding part. Just the chocolate heaven part." She split off another piece and handed it over.

Maya savored the sugar burst. "Or just Heaven in My Mouth."

Remi's smile dropped before she laughed, deep in her gut. "Everything about that is *not* what this establishment is about."

Maya's cheeks blazed. "Don't be a perv. That's not what I meant! I meant that—"

The rapid clapping of heavy heels against the cement floor advanced towards them, and Remi stuffed the bar in her pocket.

A small piece of chocolate evidence remained on Remi's bottom lip. Maya swiped her thumb across the soft surface without thinking. Remi stared at her with *a look*. A definite look that Maya couldn't grasp on to, but it made her belly tighten and other places sparkle.

Gabriella stepped into the room and narrowed her eyes. "What are you doing in my office?"

Remi cleared her throat. "We wanted to let you know that Maya and I came up with a couple of good ideas and um..."

"Yes, a, ah, a spin-off of a classic." Maya shoved her hands in her pockets, took them out, then shoved them back in. "Eh, we should do a caramel coffee, maybe with butterscotch liqueur and—"

"Cut the shit." Gabriella marched to her desk. "Remi, you grabbed my chocolate again, didn't you?"

The corner of Remi's lip lifted, and she tossed up her hands. "No idea what you mean."

Gabriella shooed the women away. "Back to work." The bifocals dangling on her neck now covered her eyes. "Go. I don't pay you two to stand around." The words were harsh, but the tone was so sweet that Maya said a quick gratitude prayer that Auntie Gabby still existed under the businesswoman shell.

"Yes, ma'am." Remi grabbed Maya's hand and led her toward the door.

Grabbed her hand.

Remi dropped it like it was on fire and went back to the booth.

But not before a cozy imprint branded into Maya's palm.

TEN

DRINK SPECIAL: FERMENTED FAMILY FUN
LAYERED WITH POSSIBILITIES

This is not good.

Maya could clearly not hold her booze. Not that Remi could compare since she held no booze, but the smile normally plastered on Maya's frozen plastic lips was softer. Her words, freer. Her eyes, glazier.

For the past three hours, Remi sat with Maya recipe testing for their fall drink menu and realized Maya had not eaten a single thing in between sips. "I'm starving. Gonna have the line cook fry us up some empanadas. Want something else? Coconut rice? Fried plantain?"

Maya sipped water from a straw, her shoulders rocking like she was dancing to the background music. "Nah, I'm good."

Remi wasn't starving. In fact, her stomach had just settled after she and Ben went to a local breakfast joint boasting a twelve-egg omelet and all-you-can-eat hash browns. Not that they got the eggs, but she ordered an extra side of buttery hash browns and cleared her plate. But the princess here was looking loopier than she should, meaning Remi couldn't trust her decisions on the drinks because of muted taste buds. They'd be forced to come back next weekend to keep working on the menu.

Which somehow sounded less terrible than when she arrived today.

She stepped behind the bar and typed an order onto the digital screen when a hand gripped her shoulder.

"Looks like you two are getting along better." Gabriella climbed the stepstool and reached for a top-shelf coconut rum housed in a crystal bottle.

Remi shrugged. She refused to show that no matter how many distractions she dove into—extra cleaning, remodeling shows, realtor websites—she'd gone home every shift and thought about Maya. "She's less annoying than when she started."

"Huh. She's been here what..." She flipped her wrist. "...a little over two weeks. Might be a record for you warming up." She patted her on the hand. "You're doing good. Keep it up."

Remi turned so Gabriella wouldn't catch a sweep of blush that was surely spreading across her cheeks. She moved to the kitchen to wait for the food and stared at the pantry, trying to think of any random combination. Adding anchovy paste to Bloody Marys? Maybe smoked paprika and chili, or blue-cheese-stuffed olives?

"You two comin' up with anything? Or just gossiping like cackling chickens?" Mark—aka Skunk Nut—called out over the frier.

God, she hated him. "Cackling chickens? You have to dig deep into your playground-bully thesaurus to come up with that one?" She stared him down. "I'll have you know we're kicking your ass in the recipe department. Stick to food. We'll stick to the drinks."

He puffed through his nose and tossed a plate of empanadas on the warmer. "Food's ready. Better get some solids into your beauty queen girlfriend before she gets all sloppy."

"She's not—" She didn't know if the insinuation of Maya being a beauty queen, her girlfriend, or being sloppy made her chest flare the most. But she had the deep desire to defend Maya's honor while landing a firm uppercut to Mark's kidney. "Maya's killing it, just so you know."

She grabbed the food and stormed out of the kitchen. Her patience threshold had reached max capacity. One more word from him, and she'd unleash a verbal tirade that would do nothing more than make him laugh and get her written up for inappropriate behavior. The bonus decision was closing in—two weeks and counting. Even Mark would not screw this up for her, no matter how satisfying it would be to take him down.

She set the plate on the table and slid in opposite Maya.

"Oh, yum." Maya cracked open the fried dough, and pork scent seeped out with the steam. She blew on it and crunched into a bite. "I thought of another one while you were in there. A spin-off of an apple cider, but layer in the teeniest anise liqueur."

Remi grabbed an empanada and poked at it so Maya wouldn't feel alone in eating. "Hmm. Black licorice flavor is so potent."

"You mean so good."

Remi scrunched her nose. "You're one of those, huh?"

"Sure am." She shimmied her shoulders.

Oh no. An actual shoulder shimmy, like they were two friends having drinks. Not professional bartenders working on a Sunday to develop a menu while competing against the other for a life-changing cash bonus. Which meant Maya officially passed Buzz Level 1 and was heading down the booze-pike for Buzz Level 2.

Maya's flushed cheeks, glassy eyes, and denser word pronunciation were a clear sign she needed to slow down. Not to mention, for the last two hours, she'd not been a pain in the ass and was even borderline charming.

Not that Remi cared, of course.

Maya took another bite of the appetizer—*thank God*—and mixed a shot of apple and anise liqueur. Her jaw worked in a circle before she swallowed. She cocked her head and frowned. "Hmm. Can you grab me the honey and apple juice? Something's not working here."

Remi reached for the items.

Maya layered and sipped. "Much better." She scribbled in the notebook and doodled a star. With bunny ears.

What was happening here? Ms. Stick Up Her Ass was drawing cartoon animals in their recipe book. And Remi was taking way more pleasure in seeing this side of Maya than she should.

"Oh, poop." Maya slammed the pencil on the table. "Did you notice the ratio? I wasn't paying attention."

Remi chewed on her lip to stop smiling.

"What?" Maya tossed up her wrists.

"You said *poop*. I just... didn't expect that word from your mouth."

Maya leaned forward with a grin. "You wouldn't believe some of the dirty things that come from my mouth."

And whoa, why did that do something to Remi's belly? She squished herself all the way back into the booth and watched Maya with a bit of wonderment. First, this woman came in and ruined her life within the first few minutes. Then juggled like a pro. But then she showed this beautiful, nurturing side of herself when Remi got cut. When Maya took care of Remi—like *really* took care of her—it uncovered a layer that Remi didn't know existed, and she wanted to unravel more.

Remi pointed at the glass. "How's the drink?"

"Good. But sadly, the anise must die. A sad, slow, miserable death. Sorry, buddy." She rubbed the side of the glass like one would pet an animal. "I've gotta shuck ya into the chuck bucket. Thanks for playing." She tossed the cocktail into the discard container with a giggle. "Shuck in the chuck bucket! I didn't even try to rhyme."

Oh, dear God. Remi circled the bottom of the empty glass on the table. "What if we added coconut cream to the top and drizzle with caramel?"

"Perfect. I'll redo it, minus the anise." Maya not-so-carefully measured out a shot of apple bourbon into the cider, plus the other ingredients, and tipped the mug to her lips. "Mmmm. Yep. That's the stuff right there. Let's add this one to the menu." She drew a heart with an arrow through it in the notebook. "I don't know why, but this drink reminds me of my old boyfriend. He loved black licorice."

Something hot and uncomfortable tore through Remi's insides and fell into a ball in the pit of her stomach. "Ex-boyfriend, huh?" *Stop fishing. None of your damn business.* Besides, digging for intel felt unethical when Maya clearly had too much to drink. "Recent breakup?"

Maya whirled the foam on her cocktail with a straw. "With Tate? No."

"I knew it!" Remi slammed down her hand.

Maya squinted at Remi. "You knew what?"

"It's so dumb. I can't believe I'm even saying this." She wiped up condensation on the table with the sleeve of her flannel. "I pictured you having a boyfriend named Tate."

Maya cocked her head. "That's super random. Why would you think I had a boyfriend named Tate?" She chewed on a chunk of crispy dough. "Anyway, he was really sweet. An artist, actually. Super sensitive and kind."

Huh.

"What?" Maya asked.

"I kicked a guy out of here last year and his name was Tate. So, I just assumed every Tate was a jerkhole deserving of a kick in the throat."

Maya's eyebrows scrunched. "That's pretty judgmental."

Remi chuckled. "Definitely."

Ben had told her that more than once. Remi thought her ability to sense the worst in people or pick up micro-movements that could be threatening was her genius. Like, one day the CIA would recruit her to study body language and report on who were the potential criminals. But over the years, it wasn't lost on her that this superpower was also her weakness, and she'd misjudged a person or two.

So, Maya had an ex-boyfriend named Tate. How long were they together? Why did they break up? Why did she care?

She didn't care.

Did she care?

Remi propped her elbows up on the table. "So, did you and Tate date a long time?"

Okay, she cared. But only the tiniest bit. Or maybe it wasn't about caring, per se, but more about passing the time with a co-worker as they trudged through the afternoon of recipe making.

Shrugging, Maya dipped the empanada into the cilantro lime sauce. "I don't even remember. A few months? We were kids, like in the eighth grade, before I realized I was queer as fuck."

Zip! The needle flew across a record with a deafening scratch. The music stopped. All conversations halted.

Snow Princess was queer? Remi's head swirled. In Seattle, a two-degree separation of queer existed. In a room full of people, often there was more LGBTQ+ representation than hetero. So, this news shouldn't be giving Remi a freckling of warm, swimming shivers. When did Remi become this person who took one look at someone else and drew all conclusions on their identity? She'd be returning her gaydar for a full queer refund and checking her biases in the damn corner.

"Eighth grade, huh?" Remi said. "I came out of the womb wearing a pride flag."

Maya laughed, and a blush swept across her cheeks and *damn*. Remi committed that look to memory.

For the next hour, they continued, with Remi making the base and Maya sampling. Tossed liquid landed in the bucket, dinner menus were sprawled on the table, and websites were visited for inspiration.

Maya hummed and swayed to the background music.

At least Remi hoped she was swaying to the music, and not from the multiple liquors sloshing through her brain. "Hey, I think we need to call it." She gathered a few bottles. "Not sure we can trust your judgment anymore."

"Maybe we can't trust yours." She giggled and tapped Remi on the cheek.

Buzz Level 2 passed and Maya was in the fast lane for Buzz Level 3. Remi refused to pay any attention to the flitter in her stomach and instead grabbed a tray from the servers' station to clear their table.

"Wait!" Maya slapped her palm on the seat. "Did we beat Mark? That dude's such a butt-nugget. Totally part of the certified asshole association."

Remi dipped her head and the multiple glasses in her hands clanked together. "Whoa."

Maya joined Remi in cleaning. "What?"

"Such feisty words from such a... proper lady."

Maya put her mouth up to Remi's ear. "I'm not that proper."

Warm breath tickled Remi, and little hairs flashed upright on the side of her neck. She stood completely still, then piled glasses on a tray.

Do not engage. "So, I agree Mark's an asshat. And we came up with eight solid drinks. We totally beat him." Remi slid Maya's water closer. "How about you take a seat and drink some water? I'll go clock us out, so Gabriella doesn't get fined for having a drunk employee."

"I am soooo not drunk." She hiccupped.

"You were saying?" Remi brought the tray into the kitchen and stacked the empties on the dishwasher rack. After clocking both her and Maya out, the sound of a door closing cracked behind her.

Gabriella fanned her face with a menu. "How did it go?"

"Good. I'll type this up tonight and email it to you with rough estimates of what we can charge. I'll pull comps from other restaurants, too." Remi looked over her shoulder and lowered her voice. "Tell Mark to shove it. We came up with some great ideas."

Gabriella clasped her hands in front of her chest. "I knew my girls wouldn't let me down."

Normally, the "my girls" comment would've sprung a pinprick of jealousy in Remi. But today, the phrase made her smile.

Ready to call it a day, she pushed the doors to grab her cross-body and keys. She and Ben had plans to hit the gym later tonight, and HGTV was calling her name. But once she turned to the booth, she stopped.

Maya was doodling in the notebook. She glanced up, her face beaming, and waved Remi over.

HGTV can wait.

Maya patted the seat. "I'm off the clock now. Guess what that means?"

Remi followed Maya's invite and slid next to her. "What's that?"

"I can drink the whole damn thing." She sucked through the straw, the motion highlighting her apple cheekbones. "Ah. So good. Here, smell this."

Remi sniffed the citrus-infused cocktail held beneath her nose. "Delicious. What is it?"

"I kept the base out for you." She bounced on the seat like a kid waiting to open gifts. "Guess!"

Remi indulged in the playfulness of Maya's voice for a few long seconds before scolding herself. Maya was intoxicated. Sure, she was a happy drunk—much better than an angry or depressed one—but she wasn't being herself and would no doubt revert to being a pain in the ass by tomorrow.

Remi inhaled. "Lemon and lime." She sniffed again. "Pineapple juice. And..."

Maya tapped her fingers on top of Remi's. "Come on, you can do it."

The soft fingertips pressing into her skin left a warm imprint, and Remi contemplated not moving to elongate the sensation. She brought the glass back and a hint of a sweet burn filled her nose. "Ginger."

"Yes!" Maya clapped, giddy like Remi performed a circus trick.

It was kind of adorable.

"And mine has tequila and orange liqueur," Maya said. "And I'm drinking the whole thing because I'm not working anymore, and ooooh... it's really good."

Nueve's customers had thinned out, and Gabriella sent a few servers home for the afternoon. Remi leaned over the booth and peeked outside. The clouds parted, allowing a sliver of the late afternoon to funnel through the window. Remi sent Ben a text that she'd be late and reminded him to take out the garbage.

Maya untied her ponytail band, and let the blond strands fall to her shoulders. She tucked her hair behind her ears. "Why don't you drink?" she asked before she slid the straw between her lips.

Normally Remi would prickle at that question, but Maya's tone was curious, not judgmental. "Control issues." No matter how decent, even pleasant, of a day she'd been having with Maya, she didn't want to dive into the fact that she had no one to fall back on except Ben. She'd been taking care of herself since she was eight and always kept herself sharp. If something happened and Ben wasn't there, she didn't have anyone to call.

"Probably doesn't look like it..." Maya waved her hand above the cocktail. "...but I hardly ever drink. There's just so much sometimes, you know? Studying and pressure and pushing and pulling. I'm so freaking over it. So today, tequila's my best friend." She swallowed a hefty amount.

A phone rang in her purse. She dug around and pulled it out. "Hey, Mom." Her smile dropped and her cheeks turned from pink to white. "Yeah, sure. No, I think we're done. I can head home. Yeah, no, I'm good, I'm good." She checked her watch. "The bus should be here shortly, or I can grab an Uber. Yep, it's totally fine. Seriously, don't worry about it. See you soon." She tossed the phone down and gulped back an entire glass of water. "I, uh, have to go home. My mom... she got called into work and my little sister needs me to watch me, er, um, my little sister needs *me* to watch *her*."

Sweet Jesus.

She stood, wobbled, and braced herself against the table. "I, um, I think I ran too much this morning and didn't eat enough..."

Remi couldn't just send her out into the world like this, right? Tipsy, slurry, and butterfingery. How would Maya watch a minor? *Don't do it, Remi. Not your monkey, not your circus.* Her mind flashed to Maya wrapping her arm last week and cleaning Remi's DNA after she'd been a total butt to her for two weeks.

Oh, for hell's sake. "I'm taking you home."

ELEVEN

DRINK SPECIAL: REGRET-FILLED RUM WITH A DOLLOP OF DISAPPOINTMENT

Ten minutes after her mom called and asked Maya to come home and watch Harper, Maya drove with Remi down I-5, gulping back water in a sad attempt to sober up. How in the hell did she let this happen? She knew better. She knew *way* better. Everything about this moment was completely unbecoming of who she was. She had failed. After this, her mom wouldn't trust her with Harper's care. And Maya wouldn't even blame her. The whole point of her moving home for the summer was to help her mom before she returned to school. And now... she was a dirty, sloppy drunk who deserved disappointed and disgusted glances.

All the lightness, comradery, and actual fun she had this afternoon crashed down and landed hard. Her belly twisted, hot and sticky, and her eyes brimmed with tears. "Why did I have that last drink? I just... the alcohol hit me harder than what I thought... and I ran so much this morning, like over six miles, and we had so many samples and..." She sniffled and swiped her sleeve across her nose.

Remi shifted in her seat, her face scrunched in a totally

unreadable expression. Probably worried Maya would puke in her car.

"You good?" Remi asked.

Maya's clothes clung to her sticky skin, and she fanned the top of her shirt. She moved the vents to cool her chest and swallowed back an acidic bubble. "I don't want my sister to see me like this. I'm supposed to set a *good* example. My mom should be able to rely on me and I'm stupid slurry and I don't even know and…" And now she *really* started crying. The tear floodgate opened, a word vomit erupted, and the pressure of the last year burst out like hot lava. She rambled about getting a D on a pharmacology test, her love of buttered popcorn, and that she shared a forty of gross domestic beer with her best friend when she was a freshman. The randomness even baffled Maya. "I'm the worst, and I mean it, Remi, *the worst* older sister of all time. I'm all garbled and jumbled."

"Hey, you're not that bad."

Her voice was gentle, and she reached over like she was going to pat Maya's leg but retreated before making contact.

"Maybe not as pretentious as you normally sound, but not horrible." She nudged her with her elbow.

Maya wiped her eyes with the back of her hand. "I snotted all over the place. Do you have tissues?"

Remi looked at the GPS on her phone and switched lanes. "Yep, in the glove box."

Maya blew her nose.

A hearty laughter erupted from Remi. "How do you look like a porcelain doll but you blow your nose like a three hundred pound over-the-road trucker?"

Maya smacked her on the arm. "That's so mean. And totally true." She blew one more time. "Wait, you think I look like a porcelain doll? Like one of those creepy, unblinking ones with weird bangs that sits in an attic, but secretly stalks you at night?"

The corner of Remi's lips twitched. "Something like that." She glanced at the GPS.

"Over there, to the right." Maya pointed out the window. "The white-and-blue one with all the lawn ornaments." Taking a deep breath, she wrapped her arm around her belly as she felt her neck grow blotchy. Maybe her mom and Harper wouldn't notice she was the most terrible, worst, mistrustful sister to cross the planet.

"Wow. Your family likes gnomes, huh?" Remi eased the car to the sidewalk.

"Ya think? And plants, obviously. My mom is like super delayed in planting them this summer. The hanging pots are just dangling all sad, with nothing in them."

Remi shrugged. "I don't know. It has a certain charm with the swinging bench on your porch. Like they're hopeful or something."

The seatbelt refused to unlatch after multiple attempts, and finally Maya removed it. "Thanks for the ride."

Remi tapped her fingers against the steering wheel as her gaze dashed between the house, Maya, and the house again. "Here, let me walk with you. The last thing I need on my conscience is you face planting on the cement while I drive away."

"I'm not gonna—okay, thank you."

Remi looped the car and held out her hand.

If Maya wasn't mustering all her strength to sober up in the next ninety seconds, she would've enjoyed the sweet, chivalrous act. The surrounding environment looked smudged, like oil coated her eyes, making the house and ornaments blur and ripple. She choked back bile and linked her arm with Remi's. The mossy ground and wet, cracked pavement on the driveway seemed extra slippery today, and she pushed her toes into the earth to keep from sliding.

Remi guided her up the weathered, white, paint-chipped stairs.

"I'm good, I'm good." She hit the doorknob a few times when it opened.

Laney flew out, her short blond pixie not as cleanly styled as usual, and deep worry lines creased her forehead. "Thank God you're home. I've got to run." She shrugged the laptop bag over her shoulder and stuck her hand out to Remi. "Hi, Maya's friend."

"Remi."

"Laney. Nice to meet you. We'll have to do proper intros later. So sorry. I'm just totally frazzled. This unexpected work thing... There's some food in the Crock-Pot and—" She froze and focused on Maya's face.

Maya gulped.

Laney narrowed her eyes. "Maya, are you... have you been drinking?"

A searing heat from her gut to her chest doused Maya, and she wanted the earth to open and swallow her whole. She squeezed her linked arm tighter around Remi. No chance would her mom see her wobble. "No, I just, I mean a little, we had drink sampling and..."

Laney exhaled, checked her watch, and looked at the house with a face that screamed "Now what do I do?" "I don't... shoot. It's okay. You've been working so hard. Okay, okay. Let me think." She drummed her fingers on her bag. "I'll call the neighbor. Or maybe Sophie? Not sure if she has plans." Laney's gaze flashed back and forth on the grass like she was reviewing a Rolodex of options. "Or, you know, I guess I can take Harper. She can bring screens and sit in the office..."

Hot tears sprung in Maya's eyes. *Irresponsible. Unreliable. Failure.* Her mom contemplated people she could call over in her time of need because she couldn't trust Maya, and maybe she was right.

"I can stay." Remi awkwardly raised her hand. "I haven't been drinking."

Laney glanced between Maya and Remi, her low heels tapping against the wooden porch in a *thump, thump, thump*. "I, ah…"

"Mom, we're good." Maya straightened her back. "Go."

Laney checked her watch again and frowned. "Okay, going. Thank you. Remi, help yourself to anything. Soda in the fridge, chips in the pantry, casserole in the Crock-Pot."

The heavy oak door squeaked open, and Maya led the way into the house.

Remi toed her shoes off on the woven wicker mat and stood in the corner.

The pattering of footsteps approached from around the hallway. "Who are you?" Harper looked at Remi and tugged on her ponytail.

"You can say hi first, Harps." Maya tossed her bag against the chair and pulled in Harper for a side hug. "This is my, um, friend. Remi, meet my little sister, Harper."

"Hey." Remi held up her hand in a half wave.

"Hi." Harper dropped her arm from Maya's embrace and wrinkled her nose. "You smell disgusting."

Maya felt her face turn pink. "Rude. Didn't Mom teach you to be nice?"

"She also taught me not to lie." She plopped on the corner of the couch and tucked her unicorn-slippered feet underneath herself.

Maya glanced at a grinning Remi. An acidic bubble burst in her stomach and she leaned against the wall, sweat verging on exploding from her pores. She pushed her palm into her forehead. "I'm not feeling all that great. I'm gonna hop in the shower. Have you eaten?"

Harper burrowed herself underneath her favorite knitted

blanket and kicked a few magazines on the coffee table to the side. "Yep."

"What are your numbers at?"

"They're *fine*." Harper pointed the remote at the TV. "I told you I just ate."

Maya stood in front of the screen and willed her legs to stand firm.

Her sister stared back and crossed her arms.

Remi's gaze flashed between the two siblings, a slow smirk spreading across her face.

"Ugh. You are aggressively annoying, know that?" Harper swiped the cell under her arm, then shook the phone in the air. "One-forty. Satisfied?"

"Very much so." Maya glanced at Remi. "Harper got type one diabetes when she was five because we weren't giving her enough attention."

"Hey!" Harper launched a couch pillow.

Maya snatched it midair and thanked the heavens that her reflexes were still intact, even if her brain was mush.

"We already know I'm the favorite," Harper said. "I didn't need this dumb disease to prove it."

Maya stuffed the pillow next to Harper. "You're not wrong."

"Ewww. You're really stinky." Harper covered her mouth and nose with her hand. "Like crazy amount of stank."

Normally, Maya would be embarrassed that Harper called her out, but today she didn't care. Alcohol reeked to a kid. In her profession, she was so used to it, she was almost immune. "Okay, I get it. Fine. You win as always." She winked at her sister, then motioned Remi to follow her.

In her bedroom, Maya tossed her purse onto the bed. The closet provided leverage for balance, and she tugged off her shoes. She glanced at Remi, who was unusually quiet as she scratched the back of her neck and scanned the room. *Remi's in my bedroom.* Now everything felt pasty and hot and strangely cozy. Yesterday, she was cursing Remi's name while also having a hell of a dream about her. And today Remi leaned against the doorway in her bedroom and stared at her pink fluffy pillows and haphazardly hung posters.

"I have so many questions about your decorations." Remi nudged her chin to the wall.

The room felt warmer and smaller than it did this morning. Maya pushed the shades to the side and cracked open a window. "My mom hasn't changed anything in here since I moved out. And I haven't changed anything since I was a freshman in high school."

Remi peeked at the posters. "So, we've got Lady Gaga, Green Day, Foo Fighters, and two posters of Robert De Niro."

Maya opened the closet door and tossed her shoes inside. "And behind the door is RuPaul. 'Cause, obviously."

Remi grinned. "All solid choices."

The alcohol and sugars burned off her skin, and Maya fanned her face. Her mouth felt tacky and wet all at once, and none of the sensations were welcome. She tugged off her sweater and threw it on the bed. "I think a shower will make me feel better."

It took Maya a moment to follow Remi's eyes as they traveled up her jeans and snug white tank and *damn.* Buzzed or not, Maya felt that look to her toes.

Remi turned and focused hard on the nearest De Niro poster.

Remi is rude. Repeat. Remi is rude. Maya needed to repeat this mantra and not focus on the fact that she had discovered that Remi was so much more than her competition. "With Harper, if she seems off, or droopy, or lethargic at all, come get me immediately. Even if you think it's a false alarm." And the shame that had dissipated for a few moments came back and slapped her in the face. Tears welled, and she pushed a knuckle into the corner of her eye. "I can't believe I did this."

Remi frowned and stepped forward. She stroked Maya's shoulder for only a second when she dropped her hands and tapped her fingers against the doorframe. "It's seriously all good. You're not even that bad. You seem like you sobered up since we left."

Maya plucked off her socks. "But I shouldn't have drunk. They depend on me."

Remi sighed. "Stop beating yourself up. I do stupid shit all the time."

Maya's face fell.

"Not that this is stupid." Remi's phone vibrated. She declined it without looking at the screen and shoved it in her back pocket. "Lots of people have a few drinks after work. You're good. I got you, okay?"

Those words hit hard in an unfamiliar place. "Okay." Hazy, Maya unlatched her belt buckle, and tossed it to the side. She popped open the button on her jeans and froze. *I'm undressing with Remi in my room.* She didn't drop her hands, but she didn't continue either. Her gaze locked on Remi's face, and she watched a subtle, yet undeniable, motion of Remi biting the corner of her lip and swallowing.

The room heated about ten degrees. Yes, the alcohol fuzzed Maya's brain and her cheeks felt abnormally warm, but she saw the shift in Remi's demeanor.

Remi turned her back and stepped out of the room. "I'll, ah, be out here." She shut the door behind her without waiting for a response, and her footsteps faded as she walked down the hall.

TWELVE

DRINK SPECIAL: POSSIBILITY PEAR LIQUEUR
SERVED WITH MIXED EMOTIONS

Remi exhaled a trapped breath after leaving a very buzzed, partially disrobed, totally personable Maya in her bedroom. When Remi arrived at work this morning for recipe testing, she would've never predicted she'd end the night standing outside of Maya's door, picturing her in various stages of undress.

She shook her head. She was just confused, that was all. Minus one instantly regrettable one-night stand with a regular at the bar—which led to an understandable ass-chewing from Gabriella—she hadn't been with anyone since Violet. The lack of sex had clearly messed with her brain cells.

She moved down the hallway and stood under the arched wall separating the living room and took in her surroundings. The home vaguely reminded her of foster home number four—her favorite. This house smelled like hearty stew, a vapor of beef and carrots simmering in some sort of onion liquid. Plants, tiny figurines, books, or pictures filled every nook. It felt complete, not cluttered, like every item had its place.

Like most homes built in Seattle in the '60s, the tiny kitchen was tucked in a corner away from the main living area. The home had a perfect mixture of modern and original—soft gray pallet flooring, red-brick fireplace, a large bay window, and over-stuffed couches and chairs next to a built-in bookshelf.

Remi took another step into the space.

Harper sat curled up under a blanket, watching the TV, and didn't look up.

Remi was never good with kids. Especially ones who lived in homes like this—loving family, blood-related, probably a fat cat nestling itself under a bedspread. Unless they were trauma sharing, or planning some great foster home escape, she did not know what to say. She spun her keychain around her index finger and cleared her throat. "How's it going?"

Harper returned an uninterested nod.

The sound of shower water started in the background. Remi contemplated if she should stand guard and watch over this annoyed preteen, or sit next to her and stare at the screen. She crossed the room to the bookshelf and looked at pictures—Maya and Harper in front of a campfire sticking out tongues, Maya onstage with a graduation gown, a selfie of Maya, Harper, and Laney in front of the ocean.

She leaned in and focused on a picture of a preteen Maya holding a baby with hospital monitors in the background. She faced Harper. "What are you watching?"

"Neil deGrasse Tyson." Harper scooched her feet back and pointed to the edge of the couch with her slippered foot. "You can sit."

Oh man, she and Ben seriously needed a sofa upgrade. Her body melted into the overstuffed couch. She glanced at Harper, who didn't remove her eyes from the screen. "How old are you?"

"Twelve. How old are you?"

"Twenty-five." She flicked her fingers against her thigh, then cracked her thumb.

Harper changed the channel. A narrator spoke about the James Webb telescope and the ability to see into the past—

which Remi tried to comprehend and finally gave up. "Do most kids like studying about planets and stars?"

Harper shrugged. She grabbed a box of cheesy crackers from the coffee table, popped a couple in her mouth, and offered some to Remi. "Did you know that the Milky Way has over two hundred billion stars?"

Remi chewed on the salted cracker. "No. I didn't know that."

Harper nodded. "Did you know the sun is so big that it would take over a million earths to fill it?"

Remi reached into the box for a few more crackers. "A million earths, huh? Hard to wrap my brain around that fact."

"Yep." Harper propped her elbow on the armrest of the couch.

She stared at Remi for several long moments, her head cocked to the side. Probably wondering why this stranger was sitting with her, while her sister was sick in the bathroom.

"You have pretty hair," Harper finally said.

Growing up, she hated her curls. A huge head of thick, dark brown curls she had no idea how to style made the perfect runway for junior high bullies. Thank God for Ben, who sat her down at fourteen and introduced her to the magic of curl cream and a proper diffuser. "Thank you."

Harper released her messy bun and re-wrapped it in a bright pink scrunchie. "My hair's stupid boring. I always wished I had curls."

"Funny you say that. I used to always want mine straight."

Harper scratched the top of her arm. "Why is Maya sick?"

Because no matter how good it tasted—or how little she thought she had—having tequila, chocolate, vodka, pineapple juice, and apple bourbon on an empty stomach after a jog would make anyone feel like crap. "I think she just had some bad food or something."

Harper slanted her mouth like she knew Remi was feeding her a line of bull but didn't call her out.

The pictures on the wall, Laney's clear decoration of choice, captured Remi's gaze. Only three non-family related pictures were present—a photo of Seattle's skyline with a sunset, and two framed drawings. One, butterflies with Harper's name written diagonally across the front. And one of pink and purple flowers with Maya's name scribbled inside a heart. Even behind the plexiglass, the flower had clear crinkles in the corner. Remi pictured a young Maya bursting through the front door, getting hit with the smell of buttery cookies browning in the oven, and beaming with pride while gripping the corner of her flower picture saying, "Look, Mommy! Look what I made!"

"Why do you look sad?"

Harper's voice broke through the haze of her thoughts. Remi jolted back to reality. "Do I?" She had no desire to tell a kid that sometimes thinking about what a *normal* family looked like tugged on some dormant heart strings. "Must just be my face."

Harper slid lower and rested her neck against the back of the couch. She grabbed a pillow and handed it over.

"What's this for?" Remi asked.

Harper shrugged. "Sometimes it's nice to hug something, you know?"

Remi wrapped her arms around the pillow and decided she'd just met a twelve-year-old Yoda. The shower water was still going in the background, although it was hard to hear over the narrator talking about Saturn and Jupiter. She tried to ignore the savory scents wafting from the kitchen. Even though Laney said to help herself, it felt weird to grab a plate and dig into the gloriousness simmering away in a Crock-Pot. Foster family number three—the one with the patient mom who taught a nearly feral Remi basic manners—had this on her top five list: never interfere in another person's kitchen.

Harper crisscrossed her legs under her bottom. "Did you know sea turtles can't tuck themselves into their shell like a regular turtle?"

Remi shook her head. "I did not know that."

"Have you ever had grape pop?"

Remi smiled. "Actually, that's my favorite."

Harper's eyes widened. "Will you sneak me one sometime? My mom doesn't let me have any pop because of the sugar and it's seriously unfair. She legit treats me like a child."

Remi raised her eyebrow. This perception of age must really irritate Harper, since it was the second time she mentioned it in the short time of being at their place. Meeting Laney for exactly ninety seconds left an impression that she bubble-wrapped Harper on the daily. Remi supposed Harper would not love a lecture on how good she had it that her mom cared enough to withhold these things for her safety. "That sucks. In all fairness, grape pop has a weird aftertaste. You ever go to the dentist and have cherry or banana fluoride and the flavor just sort of sticks to the roof of your mouth? Same. Maybe your mom's on to something."

Harper rolled her eyes. She shifted her focus to the screen for several long moments before looking at Remi. "Do you have a girlfriend?"

Remi shook her head. "No."

"Do you have a boyfriend?"

"No."

Harper poked her fingers through the fuzzy-edged knitted holes on her lap blanket. "Good, 'cause boys are dumb."

Remi scooted sideways to face Harper. "Why would you say that? My roommate, Ben, is a boy, and he's like the coolest person in the world."

Harper shrugged. "There's this guy in my school named Gavin McJerkface and he says the meanest, rudest stuff to me.

And on Friday he hit me in the arm." She pushed up her T-shirt to reveal a small purple ring on her upper arm.

Remi made a mental note to get Gavin's actual last name and put the fear of God into him for laying a hand on anyone, much less this wickedly cool girl. "Kids your age are the worst. It's like they don't even know how not to be crappy."

"Hey!"

Remi chuckled. "Sorry, I didn't mean you. Just most preteens suck. It'll be way better in high school." Remi grabbed another handful of white cheddar-dusted crackers from the box resting between them. "Did you tell someone?"

"I told the gym teacher, but Gavin said it was an accident. Like, how do you accidentally wind up and punch someone in the arm, I said to the teacher. So, she sent him to the principal's office but pulled me aside and said that Gavin probably hit me because he likes me."

Remi's mouth popped open. "That's the dumbest fuc— um, the dumbest freaking thing I've heard." Were schools still teaching young kids these archaic lessons that if someone hits you on the playground that they *like* them? Remi added a note to her list to find out that gym teacher's name and give them a verbal lashing alongside this Gavin kid. "I'd never hit someone I like. I'd only hit someone I don't like."

Harper's eyes widened. "Have you ever hit anyone?"

Remi stayed silent. A few scuffles as a rowdy teen no longer held the cool factor she thought it did back then. Not that the boys who got a taste of her right cross didn't deserve it. They were terrorizing her foster brother in the hallways—bodychecking him into lockers, tripping him in the cafeteria, ganging up on him at the bus stop. But her bruteness used to be bragging rights, a badge she held with pride, and she feasted off daring people to mess with her.

Now, looking at these innocent green eyes, wondering if she caused anyone physical pain curdled her stomach. "Well, you should never hit anyone, right? Basic human decency and all that." She waited for Harper to nod in acknowledgment. "But I can show you a few things to help you defend yourself."

Harper dropped her legs to the floor and clicked off the TV. "Like right now?" She leaped up and tossed the blankets to the side.

Remi joined her and pushed the coffee table against the couch to create more space. "I'm gonna show you how to block a punch, and how to throw one. Promise me you'll only use this for good, not evil, okay? That's rule number one."

"I promise! Jeez. You've been hanging out with my mom and sister too much. Fist bump swear." She knocked her knuckles against Remi's, then firmed her arms and legs so tightly she looked robotic.

Remi bit back a smile. "All right, we've gotta get in a boxing stance, okay? Loosen up a bit. Even though we might think being all rigged and tight will make us harder to knock over, it's the opposite." Remi bounced on her toes, rolled her shoulders, and pushed a palm into her neck until a gratifying pop released.

Harper mimicked her movements.

"Have you ever skateboarded?" Remi asked.

Harper continued, rolling her head. "Only a couple times when I was super little."

"And I suppose you never surfed?"

Harper shook her head.

"Okay, no worries. Loosen the legs and stand with your legs aligned so you don't lose your balance, like this." Remi pointed at her bent legs, shifting her weight between her hips.

Harper wobbled as she shifted her feet.

Remi crouched and tapped her ankles into the right position. "Good. Move forward with your left foot. Back with your right. Like you're dancing."

"I used to take ballet when I was a kid."

"Perfect. So, you know how dancers pivot, right? We're gonna do that."

Harper shuffled and gritted her teeth.

"Damn. Your game face alone might intimidate enough. Okay, slow down so you don't lose your breath. Remember, breathing is super important. So much of the power comes from your air. Got it?"

"Got it." She kicked off her fuzzy slippers, and they slapped the wall with a thud.

Facing Remi, Harper's eyes focused so intently that it seemed she wasn't blinking. Something moved inside Remi. A spark ignited, a feeling probably like the sensation a teacher might have when entering a classroom for the first time. "Let's make a fist. A *proper* fist. Protect your fingers. If you don't have a decent fist, you could break your fingers. And then what happens?"

Harper paused for several seconds. "Um, you'd cry?"

"Yes, you'd probably cry. But also, you won't be able to hit again. Just in case you need to." Remi tucked her fingers. "See this?" She tapped her knuckles. "Keep it flat. This is the part you want to hit your target with."

Harper's brow furrowed as she followed Remi's instructions and curled her fingers. When she finally got her thumb properly wrapped around the index and middle finger, she held up her hand. "This right?"

Remi inspected the grip. "Sure is. You're doing good. Listen to me carefully. Rule one, good, not evil. Rule two, breathe. Three, protect your fingers. What's four?"

Tiny fists dropped to Harper's side. "Um, protect your face?"

"Yes! You're a quick learner. Gotta protect your face, always. So, tuck your chin down."

Harper pushed her chin against her chest.

Remi laughed. "Not quite that far. Up a little. Good. Now

elbows, tuck 'em into your sides. This'll help protect your rib cage and get you ready for the proper stance."

Harper drew back in her fists and checked the tops of them. "Can I hit now?"

"Not quite." Remi rolled up the sleeves on her flannel. "Let's get the feet going. Move forward with your left. Now back with your right."

Harper followed the movements exactly, her cheeks growing rosy.

"Dude. You're a natural. You're doing great."

Harper tightened her ponytail and resumed the position. "Ready to punch now?"

"Jesus. Should I be worried?" Remi grinned. "Give me rule number one."

Harper groaned. "Only use my newfound superhuman punching powers for good and not evil."

She was snarky, and Remi loved it. Remi secured her elbows tight against her ribs. "Now that you're tucked and protected, I'm gonna show you a basic jab. Make sure you exhale on the hit. Remember, breath is power. Your body is the weapon, and your breath is your ammo. Watch." Remi's fists angled next to her face, a familiar, comforting motion she used so many times to destress. "You said ballet, right? Watch how I twist and pivot here. In a one-two motion." She swung her hips, exhaled, and threw her arms. "Your turn. You try."

Harper twisted at an awkward angle, and her bare feet tangled. "Dang it. It shouldn't be this hard, but there's like a million things I keep thinking about."

"It's okay." Remi dropped her hands to her hips. "All the power starts in your feet, then travels up like—"

"Like a snake?"

"Sure. Like a snake. But the most powerful, precise snake ever to slither across the earth. It starts at the feet, then shoots up, travels to your hip, through your arms, and then BAM! Out through your fists." Remi backed up a step and motioned Harper forward. "Show me what you got."

Harper twisted, overexaggerated.

Remi alternated between standing in front of Harper and lining hip-to-hip so she could see Harper from every angle. "Breathe, remember to breathe. No breath means no power."

Grunts and deep exhales left Harper's mouth and she jabbed into the air.

Remi slapped her palm. "Right here. Punch this right here."

Harper's wide eyes filled with concern. "Am I going to hurt you?"

"Maybe." Remi laughed, then shook her head. "No, you're good. Come on, show me what you got."

Fingers tucked, hips aligned, and Harper swung.

"Great! Look at that form. Keep going. Bring your hands back to cover your head."

Fists struck Remi's palm, each one more precise than the last, and she nodded in approval. She thought back to her first time with a punching bag, in foster home number two. Remi had been there a few days when the fear of a new home wore off and anger seeped in. She vaguely remembered screaming at the foster parents and using all seventy pounds of her strength to throw a chair into the kitchen wall. The dad had bear-hugged her and took her into the garage as she kicked and shrieked against his ear.

He'd plopped her in front of a red faded bag dangling from the ceiling in their tiny, one-stall garage. "I know you're angry, Remi. You got every right to be. But instead of hitting stuff in the house, hit here." He had slapped the bag, tucked her fingers, and she whaled on it.

Over and over she hit until she collapsed and her body shook from crying. He had handed her a cream soda and popped one open for himself, and they sat there in silence, shoulder to shoulder, as she wiped dirty sweat and tears from her face. The bag became her saving grace, sparring became her outlet. This cylindrical block of vinyl became her magical entity, an object that dulled the pain and released the rage.

"Water break." Remi made a T with her hands.

Harper flopped on the couch, sipped on water, and popped crackers into her mouth. She lifted her phone and scanned her arm. "Blood sugar's fine, so don't ask."

Remi tossed up her hands. "Wasn't going to." *Lies.* She was totally going to make Harper check her glucose numbers. She'd never been around a diabetic kid before and had no plans to have her fade on her watch. "Boxing is about form, but you know what else it's about?"

Harper crunched on a cracker. "What?"

"You gotta psych out your opponent."

"Like trash-talk them?"

"More like silent eyeball them." Remi threw back some water and fanned her shirt. "Before you go in, flick the side of your nose with your thumb, and give them a grin. It'll throw them off their game."

Harper swiped her hand across her nose like she had a severe case of seasonal allergies.

Remi laughed. "Not quite so... intense. More like this." Remi demonstrated the thumb-to-nose flick.

Harper popped off the couch and repeated the motion.

"Yes!" Remi joined her and put her palms back in the air. "Tuck your elbows. Tighter. Okay, strike!"

Harper hit her opened hands.

"Good." Remi bent at the waist to meet her at eye level. "Show me a tough face. Scrunch your nose and grit your teeth."

Harper twisted her mouth. "Grrr?"

"Grrr is not a question. Don't show weakness. Come on, tougher! Growl. Show 'em who's in charge."

"Grrrr!"

Remi clapped. "Yes, more!"

"GRRRRRRRRRRR!"

Harper roared so loud that Remi dropped her hands and laughed, deep within her gut, so much that unfamiliar, fresh laugh tears sprang to her eyes. Her belly quivered as Harper laughed, too. They both sank onto the couch.

Motion in the room's corner caught her eye, and Remi's focus snapped. A fresh-faced, makeup-less, soft smiling Maya stood in flannel pajamas, slippers, and a white T-shirt, scrunching her hair in a towel.

The air ripped from Remi's lungs. *Dammit, she's beautiful.*

Maya's gaze bounced between Remi and Harper. "Do I even want to know what's going on here?"

The playfulness in Maya's voice warmed Remi's insides. She straightened to a sitting position, the laugh fading but the grin remaining.

Harper grabbed a water bottle from the table. "Remi's showing me how to throw a punch."

Note to self, Maya's little sister cannot keep a secret.

Maya lowered the towel from her hair and stepped into the room. "Oh really? Is this becoming of a young lady?"

Harper shook her head. "Nope."

"Perfect." She walked toward the kitchen. "Harper, are you hungry?"

"No, I'm good."

Remi pulled the coffee table back into place.

"Thanks for showing me that stuff." Harper reached for the remote. "I feel like a badass."

Remi inched toward Harper. "Are you allowed to say that word?"

She put her index finger to her lip. "If you don't say anything, I won't tell Maya you almost said the F word in front of a sweet, innocent, impressionable sixth grader."

"I did no— okay, deal." Remi shook Harper's hand.

A moment later, Maya emerged with two heaping bowls of

some beefy, noodley, creamy concoction that smelled like comfort and sodium. She handed one to Remi without checking if Remi was hungry.

And Remi loved it.

"Harpoon—can you go grab Remi and me a glass of water?" Maya asked as she settled into the couch.

Harper rolled her eyes. "Sure."

Maya kicked off her slippers and crisscrossed her legs on the couch, pink toenails peeking out from under her knees. She set the plate on her lap and took a healthy bite. "Thanks for all of this. Really, like above and beyond."

Remi shrugged and dug into her food. God, it tasted as amazing as it looked. Like something a grandma might make on a winter day after the kids came in with rain boots and wet clothes. "It's all good. Your sister's pretty cool for a kid." She twirled the noodles on the fork and took another bite. "How are you feeling?"

"Like dog poo." Maya pointed at her plate. "Hoping this food will soak up some of the alcohol. The shower helped, though."

Remi dipped a chunk of roast beef into the cream sauce. "God, this is so good," she said between bites. "I never have home-cooked meals."

"Oh, yeah?"

"Yeah. Me and my roommate normally just get takeout, or I eat at work. The most I can make is decent scrambled eggs and toast."

Harper bounced into the room with a popsicle stuck in her mouth and two glasses of water. She handed them over, snuggled in the middle of the women, and flipped to a documentary on sea animals. "Did you know in Antarctica there are seals called elephant seals and they weigh like five thousand pounds? That's like more than Mom's Honda Civic."

Remi washed down the salted food with water. "Huh.

Nope, didn't know that one either. You keep working on your punches and you could totally take that seal on in a fight."

Harper giggled, then returned her focus to the TV.

Remi glanced above Harper's head, and her eyes locked with Maya's.

Maya's lips tugged at the corner, and she mouthed, *Thank you.*

Remi felt that smile from her toes to her scalp. She studied the sharp line of Maya's cheekbone, the softness of her posture, the way she was sitting, comfortable, no nerves, no pretentiousness. The house, the sister, the freaking cushy couch that was cradling her ass like a baby felt so natural, like she'd been here before.

An alert popped up on her phone. She clicked it off and tossed it upside down. For the first time in a year, she didn't care she was missing open houses. She laid her empty plate on the coffee table and rested her head on the back of the couch. "Seriously so good. I'm going to have to thank your mom."

In a twenty-four-hour period, Remi felt like everything she'd known these last couple of weeks flipped. Maya was sweet. Her sister was hella cool. Their mom seemed super... mom-ish. Never in her life would she have thought sitting in a cozy living room with a kid in the middle, Maya in pajamas, and her belly filled with casserole, would make her this comfortable, feel this natural, this quick.

Maya set down her plate and spread the blanket across their laps. She uncrossed her legs and laid her head back on the couch so they were facing each other from across the sofa. "My mom is the queen of comfort food. She always says the best way to show love is through food."

"That's a good mantra."

Maya tucked the blanket around herself and smiled. "I'm going to miss this so much when I go back to school."

Every warm, light feeling Remi had this entire afternoon

zapped from her like a lightning bolt reached into her chest and ripped it out. She tossed the half-eaten bowl of noodles on the coffee table, crossed her arms, and stared at the wall behind the TV.

Maya's leaving. Going back to school—*in a different state.*

How the hell did she forget?

THIRTEEN

DRINK SPECIAL: COLD SHOULDER COLADA

Hangovers are for chumps.

And apparently Maya was the reigning Queen Chump, of Chump Island. The near scalding shower water beat down. She leaned her head against the tiled wall and prayed the steam would remove whatever alcohol remained in her system from yesterday's recipe testing debacle. Sickly-sweet jasmine conditioner swirled in the air, and she gagged. Her lubricated tongue from yesterday now felt raw and shredded. She ran her fingers through her hair to rinse and promised the booze gods if they took away her pain, she'd never overdo it on drinks again.

She squeezed body wash on her loofah and scrubbed in a circular motion, as thoughts of Remi distracted her from achieving the optimal exfoliation. When Remi stayed for hours last night until Maya's mom came home, laughed a real, genuine laugh, and boxed with Harper, a barrier broke. She peeked through her tough exterior, like a cotton blouse under a steel-studded leather jacket. Although toward the end of the night, Remi got quiet, and when Laney came home, she bolted.

After drying off, her phone buzzed on the countertop with a group message to her and Remi.

> Gabriella: Shift bartender called in sick. A bank is bringing in the entire staff for happy hour. Can you two cover? Let me know ASAP or I'll see if the day bartender will work a double.

The only thing Maya wanted to do was stay in her leggings all day, go to lunch with Sophie, and spend the evening binge watching crappy reality TV with her mom and Harper.

> Remi: Sure, I'll be there.

> Maya: Me too!

Heck no, would Maya let Remi one-up her. Like it or not, even with a small reprieve yesterday, she was still competing for the bonus. She swooshed the towel across her legs to dry when her phone vibrated.

> Remi: If you're not feeling up for it, I can handle on my own.

Maya reread the message more times than necessary. Was Remi being snarky? Genuinely helping? Hard to tell. Yesterday, they bonded over the recipe-creation goal. But after Remi's abrupt departure from Maya's house last night, it felt like they were back to being rivals.

> Maya: Feeling great! See you there.

> Maya: Thanks again for yesterday. Hope you made it home ok.

Maya wiped the steam from the mirror with her hand and grabbed her toothbrush. She glanced at the phone, then spit into the sink. Her eyes traveled back to the screen, then she grabbed lotion. Before she fully slathered, she peeked at the phone again. Her foot tapped against the floor, and she started blow-drying her hair.

She hit send, right? She scrolled back to the message to confirm. *Whatever.* The statement itself did not require a response. She didn't even add a question mark to the end. But they had a moment, right? More than one. Her mind may have been a bit fuzzy, but she knew what she felt yesterday. An energy shifted between them and—

"Ouch!" She whipped the blow-dryer away from her head and fanned off the burning spot on her scalp. Her phone buzzed, and she snatched it from the counter with lightning speed and opened the message.

Remi: NP

NP? That's it? Her stomach pinched like she was sucker punched, which was illogical. Her arch-nemesis did one nice thing, and now Maya was all buttery and warm? Enough with this nonsense. She had to refocus—earn the bonus, get the tuition money, go back to school.

She lugged herself into her room and pulled up a few nursing articles. With a three-month break from school, she needed to stay sharp. Only fifteen minutes into reading, she shut off the laptop, popped two Tylenol, and waited for Sophie to pick her up for their lunch date.

An hour later, Maya and Sophie sat down for dim sum in the International District. She tentatively sipped congee and pressed a thumb into her temple, ignoring the other food.

Sophie eyed her suspiciously. "If you don't dig into these soup dumplings, I'm gonna eat them all. Fair warning, onetime only offer."

Maya swallowed the creamy rice porridge. "I think I might just stick with congee today."

"What's happening here?" Sophie twirled the chopsticks in the air.

"I'm dying," she groaned.

"That's a lot of drama for a Monday afternoon." Sophie poked a hole into the wonton, releasing a soup-base steam cloud. "What happened?"

The restaurant was quiet enough, but even the murmur of chatting customers and swinging doors sounded like a freight train being sliced with a table saw. "Recipe testing with Remi yesterday."

"Ah, crap, was it torture?" She added vinegar base to the spoon and set a wonton on top. "Is she still a pill?"

Maya stirred the soup with her spoon and shrugged. She maintained focus on her bowl, hiding her face behind the steam so Sophie couldn't read her swirling emotions. "No. I mean yes, no. I don't know. She's manageable. I just, she came over last night and we hung out with Harper, and you know—"

"Wait." Chopsticks smacked against the plate. "Remi came to your place and met Harper? I'm so confused."

Me too. "Mom got called into work, and I couldn't fully watch Harper. Not my finest moment, trust me. I went from running around Green Lake to day-drinking on an empty belly."

Sophie bit into the seaweed-and-cucumber salad. "You could've called me. I would've watched the Discovery Channel with her for the afternoon."

Maya added a dash of soy sauce to her bowl. "How did you know that's what we did?"

"Come on." Sophie crunched into a potsticker. "I've learned more about our solar system from Harper in the last few years than I did in my entire education. She's gonna take over the world someday."

Maya grinned through a squeeze in her chest. Sophie was in the hospital waiting room with Maya when her mom delivered Harper. She loved holding her, giving her bottles, and saving up babysitting money to buy Green Day and Aerosmith T-shirts for the waddling toddler. Junior year, Maya and Sophie even fought over Harper, when Maya accused Sophie of wanting to hang out with her sister more than her. Sophie's explanation of how she hated being an only child didn't make a difference until Maya realized she was a total butt, and they hugged it out.

But when she left for college, Maya was deeply grateful that Sophie stayed close to her family. But she'd be lying if she said Sophie and Harper's tight relationship didn't bother her a little. Maya pushed the soup aside and reached for the water. "I just kind of hate everything right now."

"You thinking about school?"

Yes, but also no. She wasn't ready to tell her bestie what... er, *who...* currently occupied her mind. "How's work?"

"Don't think I didn't notice you changing the subject." Sophie added soy sauce to her side dish of stringed ginger and stirred. "But since you asked... incredible. I have a call this afternoon with the manager. They might send me to Vegas this summer for a convention. Like business class and everything."

"Vegas? God, that'd be fun. Convention during the day, naked acrobatics at night. Maybe even someone can drag you out club-hopping."

Sophia scrunched her face. "Hell no. I'd rather eat my way through a movie-theater-size popcorn bucket of stale edibles before I went clubbing."

Maya giggled. "When did we become these people?" She finished her water and waved to the server for more.

"The novelty of clubbing died by my twenty-second birthday." Sophie ordered a red bean sticky-rice wrap. She turned her attention back to Maya. "You're doing amazing, too."

The congee couldn't fix whatever monstrosity was happening on her insides, and she pushed the bowl to the side. Amazing was not the word Maya would describe her life with. *Lost,* maybe. *Failing,* maybe. *Uncertain,* maybe. But definitely not amazing.

Sophie stopped all chewing and leaned back against the

chair. Her rings tapped against the table. "What's going on with you? This seems more than you being hungover. You good?"

No. Maya sighed. "I just really wish that school started this summer, you know? Waiting for the fall feels like forever."

"It's not like your life has to stop. Live for the now, you know? Life doesn't start after school. And no one knows how short it is and if you'll die tomorrow." Sophie slapped her hand over her mouth. "I didn't... mean..."

No doubt Sophie didn't mean to say something that would make Maya want to cry. But there she was, asking for the check while blinking back tears. Memories flashed through her—she and her dad screaming while sliding down a twirly water slide in eastern Washington, a ghost-stories and marshmallow-fueled camping trip on Whidbey Island, fighting back the heat and mosquitos to bring back a walleye during a Minnesota fishing trip.

During the quiet car ride to work, Sophie maneuvered through Seattle afternoon downtown traffic and squeezed Maya's hand.

Maya rested her head on her shoulder. She loved Sophie for knowing when she needed quiet time. The grief waves of her dad's death were temperamental and unpredictable. She could go months and, out of the blue, giggle at a memory. And like she stepped into an invisible electric fence, the smallest thing would jolt her to reality—the scent of his favorite cologne at the mall, a floating red balloon, or the taste of her mom's peanut butter bars. Maya pointed at the corner. "You can drop me off in the back, by the alley."

Sophie pulled over the car and killed the engine.

Maya leaned her head against the back of the seat and removed the seatbelt.

"You gonna be okay?"

"I just need a minute." Maya bit at the corner of her pinkie. "My headache's gone, thank God. The power of congee."

"And here I thought it was from our stimulating conversation." Sophie held out her arms.

Maya leaned into the warm hug and inhaled Sophie's lavender scent. "That, too." She sighed and reached for the door handle. "Love you. Thanks for the ride."

"You too. Call you later."

Maya slammed the door and glanced up to Remi's heated gaze. Her feet felt like they got stuck in the pavement. When did Remi pull up? And what expression was that on her face? She couldn't fully decode it, but it wasn't happy.

Without a word, Remi pivoted sharply and marched to the door.

Maya scampered to catch up. "Hey."

Remi lifted her head in a nod. "You don't look nearly like the shit I thought you would."

"Um, thanks?" Maya followed her into the steamy kitchen and fumbled to open her locker. *Breathe.* "My sister thought you were pretty cool. I tried to tell her otherwise, but she wouldn't listen to me."

Remi shoved her sweatshirt into the locker. "Smart kid." Her grin dropped as quick as it appeared. "Gonna check the stock and make sure we're good. Want to double-check the kegs?" She slammed the locker shut and walked away without waiting for a response.

Maya's cheeks flamed. She trailed a few steps behind, feeling like the girl stood up at prom. Laying her flattened palm against the swinging door, she exhaled and forced up her chin.

Remi grabbed a towel from the pile at the end of the bar and shoved the corner through her belt loop.

Maya tested the soda gun nozzles and tried to ignore the pinching in her belly. "Crazy we both got called in on a Monday. I can close tonight when it slows down."

Remi held up the glasses into the light, her eyes narrowing in as she rotated the glass. "Whatever works."

Forget a cold shoulder, Remi's body was like an embalmed corpse. Last night ended up being a pretty decent night—at least, she'd thought so. They'd chatted on the couch, watched boring shows, and laughed with Harper. *Bonded*, for God's sake. Maybe she misread the signals, and Remi was simply being nice. She gulped back a full glass of water, blaming it on hangover dehydration and not her body feeling like an internal sauna. Even her ears were hot. She continued setting up her station for the evening—checking the bottles, inventorying the garnishes, validating the juice and soda levels in their holding boxes.

Remi did the same without a single word. She topped off an already full ice bin, wiped the bar down twice, and moved to the back, where she turned each top-shelf bottle to have the labels facing outwards.

Which Maya had never seen her do.

"I had congee for lunch. Best hangover cure in the world." Maya stared at the back of Remi's neck and waited for a response. "You know the soup with the rice? So good."

"Yeah, I know what it is."

Jesus, that tone, like Maya just said the most annoying thing in the world.

Remi moved to the furthest corner and swiped her towel against the cabinet door like she thought a health inspector would storm through at any moment. She scraped at a phantom stain for so long that Maya was sure the wood would splinter.

The air was heavy like molded fog, and Maya gnawed on her lip. Should she apologize? *Nope.* No, she was not apologizing anymore. She thanked Remi and apologized enough for her slipup yesterday. And even though a nagging, internal voice chipped away at her conscience for failing so spectacularly, she elbowed the chatter down deep. "Did I do something?" It wasn't *exactly* an apology. But the itch to know if someone was mad at her superseded her internal promise to ease up on her people-pleasing tendencies.

"What?" Remi squinted, then shook her head and returned to cleaning.

"You seem super pissed." *And this is why I should never ask a favor from anyone, ever.* "Is this about yesterday and being at my house?"

Remi's shoulders stiffened. Her mouth opened and clamped shut. And without another word, she stormed from the bar area and slammed through the kitchen doors.

Maya's cheeks burned, and she swallowed a lodged, sticky ball. It didn't take a super sleuth mastermind to deduce that Remi was seriously irritated. She had a conflicting urge to snap her towel against the stainless-steel cooler or climb inside and hide among the bottles.

A man and a woman with either the world's worst or best timing approached the bar.

Maya laid out a few napkins. "Hey there, what can I get started for you?"

"I had a hell of a day." The woman pushed heavy brown bangs away from her eyes and climbed into the seat. "What do you suggest?"

"Hell of a day, huh?" She could relate. "I think that calls for a crisis-martini. Some people like to call it an *F-this-day martini.*"

The woman laughed. "Perfect."

Maya grabbed the ingredients and glanced at the closed kitchen door. *Fine.* If Remi wanted to play the silent game, she could do it, too. Honestly, it'd be easier. Why did she think they were becoming friends? One stupid look passing between them when she was four drinks in, and she got all soft? Painful, truly.

Whatever the fleeting moment was, Maya was done. Two could play this game.

. . .

My God, bankers could drink. The happy hour Remi and Maya got called in for turned into a close-to-a-Friday-night crowd. Maya had never seen so many people in business suits and ties drinking from pineapples with umbrellas. The servers scrambled to keep up with orders, and it took Maya over an hour to get into her groove. But once she did, the heat of competition pulsed in her fingertips. She tossed bottles, juggled a few lemons, and spun the shaker in her palm. A small crowd gathered near her to watch.

A dusty-blond-haired man, maybe in his early thirties, with a loosened tie, rolled sleeves, and popped-open top button on his shirt approached.

She wiped her hands on the towel, then dangled it from her back pocket. "What can I get for you?"

"Whiskey neat. Maker's."

She reached for the top-shelf whiskey. "Looks like you and your buddies already have a tab going with the server. Should I add this to your open ticket?"

"Nah, I'll pay cash." He scratched at the scruff on his chin. "You got some pretty sick moves. Where did you learn to juggle like that?"

She filled the short glass and slid it over to him. "Would you believe me if I said I ran away as a teenager and joined the circus?"

He removed a large bill from his gold-plated money clip. "I'd believe just about anything you'd say."

His voice dropped an octave from earlier and now had a growl like he was trying to be bedroom sexy. *Gross.* She had a fleeting moment of wanting to tell him that his efforts were completely wasted on her for more reasons than one.

She laid his change on the bar.

"Keep it." He winked and walked away.

The sickly feeling of accepting an overly generous tip popped up, but cash was cash. Tuition would sneak up soon enough, and if she wanted to return to school in the fall, she'd have to choke back a little pride.

Within an hour, the hostess pushed together tables in the center of the room, and Gabriella dashed around cleaning tables. She peeked at Remi, who was smiling widely with a man as she lined up ten shot glasses and filled them with tequila. Remi said something to the customer with a smirk, and the man shook his head and laughed.

Maya's stomach clenched. Remi hadn't smiled at her once the entire evening, and originally, she thought Remi was just having an off day. Yet, watching her now, Remi's husky laugh and dimples were clear from ten feet away.

Mojitos, pineapples, and alcohol-filled horchatas flew off the shelf. The bar runner rushed to restock their drink glasses. Gabriella was a ghost, flying between tables and the kitchen, playing the role of hostess, server, and stocker.

The generous tipper from earlier returned. "I'll take another whiskey neat."

Maya poured. "Is your server ignoring you?" She forced a grin. "You shouldn't have to come up here and grab your drink. I can let him know to give your table extra attention."

"Nah. I just like the view better from here." He wiggled his scraggly eyebrows and leaned in.

She gagged on the smell of freshly doused cologne. "Can I get you anything else?"

He dug out a wad of cash. "Yeah. Your number."

"Never heard that one before." Her voice teetered on snark, but she hoped he was a few drinks in and couldn't unmask the cringe. Did lines like that ever actually work? Doubtful. Getting flirted with was an occupational hazard, but most people were being goofy, or interested in having her as their therapist for the evening. Half the time she thought if someone would come up and say something original, like she had sexy elbows or cute pinkies, she'd give them a second glance. But this dude had creep factor written all over him, and the hair stood up on the back of her neck.

Another generous tip, and she swallowed.

The man lingered, and she ran her towel down the bar. She could turn down a tip, but depending on the fragility of his ego and the amount of alcohol consumed, it could create a tense situation. She shook out her arms, added ice to the bin, and smiled at Gabriella.

"Niñas!" she called over her shoulder, balancing a good dozen glasses and scurrying past Maya and Remi. "Good?"

"Yep!" Maya said in unison with Remi.

No chance would she flag Sir Creeperton and give Gabriella any opportunity to think she couldn't handle herself. Being in the bar business for five years made her tougher than when she started. And so many customers were great. They just wanted to let loose, hang with friends, relax after work. But it also gave her a heightened awareness, and Maya learned long ago to listen to the flags in her body—which currently flashed a fire-red alarm bell.

She glanced at Remi—who she had effectively ignored all night—to gauge her expression, but Remi had her back to her. If any other bartender were on shift, she would've engaged them in the common drink-slinger dance: a look, a nod, a whisper, and when the offender approached, the other person would take over. But no chance would she ever ask Remi for help again.

The rush slowed and the crowd of intoxicated bankers drifted out of the bar, leaving Maya and Remi with nothing in between them but a wall of silence. Maya poured herself a cranberry and pineapple juice and rolled her neck.

A gaggle of hefty laughs from the group of men at a corner table erupted. Mr. Whiskey Neat gave his friend a hard slap on the back and strolled up to the bar.

She reached for the bottle as he approached. "Same as earlier?"

He strummed his meaty fingers against the bar, and the chunky, gold, graduation-style pinkie ring clicked against the wood. "Still as beautiful as last time."

She held up the bottle. "Another whiskey neat?"

"Why don't you toss this one? I feel left out. You're not doing any tricks for me." He gave her an overexaggerated frown.

At least she hoped it was overexaggerated. A drop of sweat beaded below the base of her spine. "I'm not taking a chance on breaking a top-shelf on the floor." *Not exactly the truth.* She hadn't dropped a bottle once in almost five years.

"I'll pay for the bottle if you drop it." His gaze lowered to everything but her eyes. "I've been watching your fingers all night. I think the whiskey is in very, *very* good hands."

The coil in her belly surpassed her gut and shot to her lungs and chest. For once in her life, she wished he were just a touch more intoxicated, and she could cut him off. "You want the same, or can I get you something else?" She didn't even try to be charming. Their interaction was a business transaction from here on out.

He swiped his hands across the bar like he was clearing a space. "How about a date?"

She'd rather eat her own toenails. "Man, you're a persistent one, huh?" She stabbed the metal scooper into the ice, the cracks and crunches releasing the tightness in her chest. "If you don't need anything, I've got to get to the other orders."

"Yeah, yeah." He put up his hands. "I'll take another." He plunked down on the stool and stared.

Most often, when people sat and watched while chatting with their friends or scrolling through their phone, it felt nice. Like she was a sparkle in their otherwise gray day. But this felt voyeuristic, her tongue felt sticky, and even if someone ordered the pineapple colada, she wasn't tossing bottles until he left. She filled orders, wiped the counter, and glanced at Remi, who drizzled chocolate into a martini glass.

He twirled the drink in his hands. "How long have you worked here?"

She sighed. "A few weeks now."

He took a long pull from his glass. "Sure wish I would've known that. I used to come to this place, but it's been a few months. Had no idea what I was missing out on."

The condiments looked low. And maybe the napkins needed to be topped off. And... and... was there a keg that needed changing? She crouched down to grab cherries from the mini-cooler and fanned the coolness at her face.

He tapped the coaster against the bar with a *tick, tick, tick.* "You sure are a pretty thing. But I bet you know that. Girls like you always know that kind of stuff." His voice sounded joking. If someone were to record this conversation and play it back, they'd say whatever reaction she was having was an over-reaction.

But she was over it. She refused to respond and scooped out more olives for the condiment tray. The heat of his eyes bored into her, and she pretended it didn't make saliva coagulate in the back of her throat. She fled to the kitchen and leaned against the wall. *Breathe. Exhale, inhale.* What a weird freaking twenty-four hours. Right now, she wanted to fake an illness—which really wasn't all that fake at this point—clock out, and return tomorrow. But Gabriella was marking sales as a metric to see who'd get the bonus, and she couldn't afford to run away.

She loved her job. If nursing wasn't her true passion, she could see herself opening a bar specializing in bar tricks. She could train the bartender to toss bottles, the same way she learned all those years ago. Maybe even bring in talent once a quarter, like a cross between an acrobatic show and a performance.

But tonight, she hated it. Remi had not said a word. Gabriella was totally distracted, and she was drowning in annoying juice. When she returned to the front, the dude tapped his glass against the bar like an attention-seeking child.

"Come on now, I'm serious. I've tipped you like a hundred bucks. What do I have to do to get your number?"

And there it is. This deep-rooted, misogynistic idea that she now owed him something because he'd dropped some cash. "Not gonna happen." She felt her cheeks betray her attempt at confidence. She gripped the towel to hide her trembling fingers.

The man stood in a huff, the heavy chair screeching against the floor. "Why you gotta be such a bitch?"

Her mouth dropped, and her tongue froze.

"Say it again." The sharp but even-keeled voice sounded behind Maya.

Maya turned, and *holy shit*, was she glad she wasn't on the receiving end of Remi's glare. She'd vaporize first and ask questions later. She had no idea that Remi's dark eyes could get any darker, and yet, here she was with midnight-black irises. Remi held her stare so long that Maya didn't understand how her eyeballs hadn't popped out.

The man's head flung back, and he gripped the bar. "Excuse me?"

Remi stepped in front of Maya. "Say. It. Again."

Remi was not out of control. In fact, she was freakishly calm. No red face, no heavy breathing, no shaking. And something warm and gooey filled Maya's chest.

The dude opened his mouth.

Remi inched forward and squared her shoulders. Confident. Strong. Controlled. Everything that Maya wasn't in that moment, and everything she needed.

The man's nostrils flared, and Maya felt like she was watching some horror show tennis match. Her body threw all sorts of conflicting signals—a clenched stomach, weak knees, hot chest, an arid mouth. A several second visual standoff ensued, and Maya's accelerated pulse throbbed in her ears.

Did Remi blink yet? Remi was a good three inches shorter than Maya but seemed like a giant.

Finally, like an omega to an alpha, the man backed away.

"Fuck this." He threw some cash on the table and stormed off.

Remi stood motionless and watched him until he reached the front door. When he was on the sidewalk, her shoulders softened. She spun towards the kitchen, leaving Maya alone on the floor with nothing but the chairs sliding across the floor as folks exited.

Everything in Maya wanted to follow Remi, collapse into those seriously strong arms, and let Remi take care of her. She lifted a shaky glass of juice to her lips, then put his money in the till.

Fifteen minutes later, the hostess locked the front door.

Remi popped off the keg toppers and filled a bucket with cleaning solution. She didn't seem to be actively avoiding Maya as much as she was simply not engaging. The coolness from earlier had dissolved, but the silence remained.

Maya packed up the leftover garnishes in the fridge and tried to gather her words. She had to say something. Conflicting feelings or not, her co-worker had her back tonight. "Thanks for that earlier." The words sounded gurgled, and she cleared her throat. "Been a long time since that happened, and I just froze."

Splashes of liquid from the mat Remi was draining landed in the sink. She grabbed the hose and sprayed the residue. "Yeah, he was a dick."

"I bet his name was Tate."

Remi stopped spraying and laughed—a full, raspy, hearty laugh.

And Maya felt that tone to her core. She didn't know what the hell came over her. Blame it on the adrenaline of the evening, or an unexpected feeling of being protected, but Remi's laugh was the hottest sound she'd heard in forever. Her thighs tingled, and her chest turned warm. She grabbed the condiments and walked to the kitchen. The walk-in refrigerator was heaven, evaporating the heat of the evening. She shoved the container on the metal shelf next to the boxes of pineapple and oranges and let her body cool.

The door swung open, and Remi marched in, empty-handed.

Maya's gaze locked with Remi's. *Really* locked. The door closed with a soft click that somehow still seemed to echo in the tiny space. The soft, amber-toned inside light illuminated Remi's dark hair and cast a golden glow over her pale skin.

Remi stood motionless, her eyes narrowed, her cheeks flushed.

Maya crept forward and stopped, refusing to break eye contact. Her breath hitched, and she took two more steps. The energy was palpable, heavy, filled with uncertainty and intention.

Remi's eyes were soft but determined. She dropped her gaze to Maya's lips and lingered, glazed, almost like she was intoxicated. She bit the side of her lip and trailed Maya's face until she made eye contact again.

Every unholy place imaginable in Maya grew warm. Another step closer. She tried to ignore what her insides were screaming at her to do but failed. She hooked an index finger in Remi's pants loop and tugged. As if her finger carried the strength of an army, Remi floated to her without hesitation. Maya rested herself against the wall for support because she was about to collapse from overdosing on pheromones.

Remi reached near the sides of Maya's head and flattened her palms against the wall.

Being caged inside Remi's arms made her pulse surge. A delicious scent of citrus and sage floated to Maya's nose, and that definitely needed to be bottled up and sold as an aphrodisiac.

"What are we doing?" Remi whispered.

A chill erupted on Maya's neck from the soft words. She couldn't speak, and her body melted. Her heartbeat throbbed through her chest and in her ears, and she was sure Remi must hear it. Thank God they were in the cooler, because the air was sauna-like. Her breath caught in her mouth, and she swallowed.

Actions like this were against Gabriella's rules, but it didn't matter. Rules didn't matter. Air didn't matter. Nothing outside of this area, at this moment, mattered. Maya lowered her other hand, snagged her finger in Remi's second loop, and pulled. They were not touching, nothing was touching, yet Maya could feel Remi's body. The energy zapped between them. Maya forgot to breathe, but she didn't care. She didn't need air.

Remi's chest lifted with a heavy breath, and their breasts touched in a whisper.

Sinking deeper against the wall, she pulled Remi against her. The soft, pouty lips that she'd wanted to taste since meeting her were there, inches away. She felt Remi's chest rise and lower, but Remi wasn't moving anything else, wasn't angling her head, wasn't licking her lips. And *damn*, Maya wanted Remi to move, to do something, protect her, *touch* her. Anything. Her body craved and ached, and yet... Remi stood still.

Maya dragged her gaze off Remi's soft mouth and brought it back to her eyes.

Remi's lips parted. She stared at Maya's mouth and took a sharp inhale.

"Dude! Give me a second," a voice outside the door yelled. "Let me put this away first."

Remi pushed herself off the wall and left without another word.

And Maya used the last of her strength to lift herself from the wall and leave.

FOURTEEN

DRINK SPECIAL: TENTATIVE TEA WITH A DOUBLE SHOT OF ROOMIE RUM

The pounding of knuckles—or a freaking boulder breaking off in a mudslide and crashing into her bedroom door—jolted Remi from the bed. Her heart leap-dove in her throat and she squinted the room into focus.

"Remi! You up?" Ben's voice sounded from behind the wall.

She peeked with one eye at her clock. 7:02 am. Seriously? After the cooler incident with Maya last night, Remi's subconscious gave her a gift this morning, and she was right in the middle of a hot-as-hell dream that was so realistic it was essentially the most action she'd seen in a year. And Ben ruined it. "You better be dying, I swear to God, or I'm gonna kick you in the liver."

He flung the door open, shirtless and barefoot. "Good. You're up."

His wide grin indicated he was, in fact, not dying. Which now meant she was gonna strangle him with used dental floss. She chucked a pillow at his head and sagged back on the bed.

He tugged his hospital-scrub shirt over his chiseled abs and bounced on the end of the mattress like a toddler. "Before you rage all over me, you're never going to believe who's coming into town today."

She pulled the covers over her head. "It better be Satan himself."

"You are the grouchiest person alive. No, Mama Butter Nips!"

Remi ripped the covers off and bolted upright. "What?" She dug her knuckle in her eye. "Are you serious? I thought her tour wasn't coming in until next month."

"Check your phone. He texted us both." Ben bounced from the room. "I've got to call Charlie. She'll totally freak out."

Mama Butter Nips—or Darius Williams, offstage—was one of the few shining lights in Remi's dark youth. The person who offered a fifteen-year-old Remi a safe place to crash when she needed a break from her foster home and had nowhere else to go. Mama was a bit of a local celebrity, as the 1997, 1998, *and* 1999 winner of a national drag competition crowned in New York City.

Remi met Darius through Ben, who met him through the vibrant Seattle Capitol Hill queer scene. Sometimes she'd sit for hours watching how a man that looked like a taller, skinnier, hairless Jamie Foxx transformed himself into a spitting image of Tina Turner. Once the makeup, wig, and dress were on, Darius became Mama Butter Nips, who became one of the most iconic singers in our history. He even strutted like her, powerful arms, spectacular legs, amazing growl. She'd go with Ben to Darius's apartment above a tattoo parlor on Broadway to watch him perfect a routine while complaining that dancing in heels as a forty-plus-year-old killed his hips.

Remi picked up her phone and read the group text.

Mama BN: Last min changes of plans. Gonna be in Seattle tonight and tomorrow instead of Portland. I'm too pretty to comprehend the details. Effin' queens. We're all over the place. You two gonna be around?

She tossed the phone next to her pillow and stared at the popcorn ceiling. It'd been over two years since Remi saw Darius. He moved to California for a job transfer, his "real job" —a data analyst—at the beginning of Remi's senior year. Although he came back and watched her walk across the stage in her graduation uniform.

Slowly, her brain shifted from Darius to Maya. She drummed her fingers across her chest as the events of yesterday traveled through her mind. Not that it was any of her damn business, but Maya got dropped off at work by a seriously beautiful soft butch with a shaved head, multiple piercings, and deep red lipstick. And she hated that she had stared at them for so long that she remembered all those details.

Her fingers twitched. *Don't do it.* Dammit. The urge for intel superseded any rational thought, and she pulled up Maya's socials. She and this woman—Sophie, per the tagged photo— were clearly close with the way they hugged and laughed in multiple photos. A tightness pulled in Remi's chest.

What the hell was she thinking anyway, chasing after Maya yesterday in the cooler? After the whole McDickerton situation with the dude at the bar, she was simply making sure Maya wasn't too freaked out. She would've done that for any co-worker. Right? Probably?

But then Maya tugged her in and *damn.* Every ounce of willpower housed in Remi's body was used to overcome her ferocious desire to taste her perfect, full, bubblegum lips. She tossed her arm across her forehead and closed her eyes. *Enough.* These... feelings... thoughts, whatever, were impractical. She didn't even *like* Maya that much. Sure, she might have realized that she wasn't a totally terrible human being. And being in her home with her sister and eating casserole on a couch was the best Sunday she had in months. And the gut-wrenching need to protect her from the guy last night shocked even herself. But really, Maya was the one standing in the way of the bonus money. And she was *leaving*, heading back to Minnesota. And then what? Remi had a lifetime of getting close to people and having them split. She had no desire for a replay.

Besides, Gabriella would fire them both on the spot if they broke the no-dating policy.

She schlepped out of bed and followed the scent of frying eggs. "You better be doubling that batch since you almost killed me this morning." She poured a cup of coffee and moved to the couch.

Ben reached into the fridge for more eggs. "Of course, my little dark princess of the night." The pan sizzled with the freshly cracked egg, and he tossed a pinch of salt on top. "God, I'm so excited to see Darius. I texted him and told him to meet me after work at Nueve's."

She sipped the dark, Colombian roast, and her brain fog lifted. "Perfect. What time?"

"I get off at eight." He piled the plates full of eggs and buttered toast and slid next to her. "I mean, I get off all the time."

She groaned. "It's too early for your immature jokes."

"Is it, though?" He handed her the pepper shaker and stabbed his fork into his breakfast. He scrolled through his phone, then leaned back into the couch. "So, my supervisor talked to me yesterday about moving to the pediatric unit."

Remi coughed on a chunk of egg. "You hate kids."

"Not true." He swallowed his food with coffee. "Okay, it's kind of true. But after I shadowed that unit a few weeks ago and did that puppet show, something hit me. I may hate kids in general, but oddly, turns out I don't hate sick kids." His phone buzzed, and he frowned and tossed it on the counter.

"Was that—"

"No," he snapped.

Ben had been part of a throuple for the last few months. Even though he claimed it was all about the sex, Remi saw him come home a few times with an enamored look on his face. He seemed genuinely heartbroken when they all split last month.

"I'm done with relationships."

"Uh-huh." She raised an eyebrow. "That'll last until next week."

He soaked up the runny yolk with his bread and shrugged. "I think I need a break, for real. I'm getting too old for this shit."

Remi scraped butter across the toast. Ben was normally positive and joking. And cranky and pissy, of course, but in general had a smile to his voice. But his dejected tone gave her pause. "There's someone out there for you. You and I aren't meant to be single forever. We'll find a soulmate at some point."

Ben's jaw slowed in a chew.

She glared. "What?"

He wagged his finger. "No. *Hell no.* What did you do with my roommate?"

"What do you mean?"

"This is the basis of our relationship. After a breakup, I go over to Charlie's and cry. She hugs me and tells me that true love is around the corner and makes me rub one of her jade crystals and hoses me down with sage smoke. Then I come home to you, where we agree that love sucks and is overrated, and being single is the best and only way to live. We have a routine."

Remi pushed the food to the side of her mouth. "I just think..." Maybe something *was* out there, waiting for her. What if the timing wasn't right before, or her heart wasn't in the right spot, and now, if she would just let herself... She swallowed.

"You know, you're right. I don't know what the hell I'm thinking. I watched a short video on some love crap and the algo-
rithm sucked me in. I'm inundated with fluff. Don't worry,
tomorrow I'll be back to my salty-ass self."

Ben resumed his chewing and let the subject drop.

Thank God. Because she had no idea what to do with this
odd swimming sensation in her belly. Her phone buzzed with
an alert for an open house. She clicked it off.

"You going to an open house today?" He stood and rinsed
off his plate.

"Nah. Not today." She joined him at the sink and dried the
dishes.

"You feeling all right? You haven't gone for like a week."

She pushed the clean coffee mug onto the shelf and leaned
against the counter. "No reason to look at anything else. I found
the house in the U District."

"Ah." He sprayed the soap from the last dish and handed it
over. "All right. Gonna head out. I'll pinch your bootie later
upon my return."

She rolled her eyes. "There's something seriously wrong
with you."

He chuckled and snatched the keys from the hook.

The door closed, leaving Remi with nothing but her clam-
oring thoughts. Moments later, she threw on gym clothes and
flew out the door.

After a solid workout with her gloves and the bag, a solo
sexual release, and a hot shower, Remi sat on her bed as she
typed out and erased her third text message to Maya. She tossed
the phone on the dresser, paced the room, then picked it up
again. Her fingernails scraped against the back of her neck as
she stared at the screen. One deep inhale later, her thumbs flew
across the screen.

Remi: hey, I'm running errands in your
neighborhood. Need a ride to work?

Exhale. After a minute without a response, she buried the phone under her pillow and folded a pile of laundry. Picking at the corner of her thumb cuticle, she left the phone in the room and moved to the kitchen. Lingering egg scent filled the room, and she cracked open the window to fan out the space. She checked her watch and paced again.

In one more minute, she'd look. If Maya didn't respond, that'd be the worst because Remi wouldn't know if she didn't get the text, or if she got the message and ignored it. If she responded and said no thanks, Remi would feel like an idiot but could totally save face. But if she responded and said yes...

She pumped a few drops of lotion in her hand, smoothed it up her arm, and tiptoed into the bedroom.

Her locked screen showed a message.

> Maya: Not sure how'd I'd feel about missing the metro and all its special smells.

> Maya: I'd love a ride. Thank you.

> Maya: What errands are you running in my neighborhood?

Remi bit the grin on her lip.

> Remi: I needed condoms.

> Maya: Dying! You do you.

> Remi: pick you up in an hour

Remi googled spots near Maya's house in case she asked what errands she completed. She finally found an independent skateboard store that could work as an excuse.

The next thirty minutes were filled with anxiety sweeping and dusting until her stomach loosened. She grabbed her keys, jogged down the stairs, and shielded her eyes from the sun cracking through the sky. Lavender scent from a bush outside their space mixed with the skunky marijuana smell from her neighbor. She waved at a vaping man leaning against a car and pulled out of the lot.

The traffic whizzed by, and she tapped her fingers on the steering wheel. She turned on the radio, turned it off, then back on again. A few blocks away from Maya's house, she stopped at a light, flipped the mirror down, and checked her teeth.

After a primo parallel parking job, if she said so herself, she skipped a small puddle at the end of the driveway, swiped her palms down her thigh, and took one more breath before ringing the doorbell.

Harper opened the door with a wide smile. "Hey, Remi! Come in. Maya's in the kitchen cleaning up our disaster station."

"I'll be out in a second!" Maya's voice yelled between the walls.

Melted butter and warm chocolate wafted to Remi's nose. "Hey, you. Why aren't you in school?"

"It got out yesterday."

She slid her shoes off on the mat. "Ah. Have you done anything special with your time?"

Harper put her hands on her hips. "Yep. Do you ever look at the sun sometimes when you have to sneeze but it won't come out?"

Remi chuckled. "I have done that. What does that have to do with doing something special?"

"Becaaaaaause... I found out the reason." Harper closed the door behind Remi. "Or at least a theory. Turns out that some brains think the pupil closing up so quick confuses the motion with nose funk, and then you sneeze."

Was that actually true? "That's pretty cool info. And now I know what to say if it ever comes up during a bar trivia night."

Harper grabbed Remi's arm and tugged her toward the kitchen. "Maya and I made you something. Come on!"

The kitchen looked like a flour tornado hit it, with white dust covering the better part of the countertops, floors, and even the basil plants on the window sill. Chocolate chips scattered the counter, and bowls stacked high in the sink. "Whoa. What happened here?"

Light reached through the kitchen window and sprawled across Maya's smile. And shone down Maya's bare leg in her shorts and T-shirt, and no, *absolutely not*, was Remi salivating at the unexpected sight of smooth skin on top of long, lean, muscular legs. "The bag of flour jumped to its death after we burned the first three batches." She scooped the contents into the dustpan and tossed them in the trash. "Harper and I thought we'd bake earlier today."

Harper peeled a cookie from the parchment paper and handed it to Remi. "Look what I made you."

Remi studied the distorted chocolate smear. "Is that a... smiley face?"

"I told you she'd know what it was." Maya popped the dustpan on the back of the broom and set it in the broom closet.

Harper bit into a cookie.

"Harper." Maya's mom-voice released. "No more. You're already over the limit."

"I've had one. One!" Harper snapped back. "Jeez-us, you need to let up. Seriously. You are like in my butt all the time since you moved back home."

"In your butt? Not sure that is the right phrase." She whipped open the drawer and grabbed a pair of tongs. "But I'll get your butt." Maya snapped them like a shark, giggling, and chased her from the room.

Harper squealed and ran.

Something stirred in Remi, and she couldn't quite define the feeling. But she didn't want to leave this space to toss drinks for Seattleites. She crunched through the rough, burnt bottom of the cookie. And even though the treat was pretty bad, it was also the best cookie she'd ever had.

Maya returned, her smile shifting from sisterly to warm, and her cheeks blushed with a pink hue. "Hey."

"Hey." Remi didn't know what to do with her hands, needing to shove them somewhere far and deep because of the intense urge to hug Maya. She crossed them and leaned against the wall.

A quietness filled the air as Maya washed her hands. "Get your errands done?"

Busted. "Um. Yep."

Maya dried her hands and handed her a bag of cookies. "These are for you. Look, a pink, ultra-sparkly ribbon that I thought you'd love."

"How'd you know this was my favorite color?" She sniffed the bag. "They smell delicious. Thank you. How did you do all this so quick? I only asked you if you needed a ride like an hour ago."

Maya nibbled on the corner of her lip. "I made those earlier."

Everything in Remi crashed to a halt. *Earlier?* Too many things to review now, but a smattering of thoughts crammed into her head. Remi was not a baker. She had no idea what to do with a recipe that wasn't alcohol-laced, but she assumed baking took a few hours. And the cookies in her hand were cool. Which meant Maya must've made these this morning, which meant Maya thought about her *all damn day.* Remi needed to go into the next room to process.

The front door opening and closing sounded, and a moment later, Laney rushed in. "Remi! I'm so glad you're here." She set multiple grocery bags down on the counter and enveloped Remi in her arms.

Remi froze and melted in the span of one second, the sensation in her belly the same as when Gabriella hugged her.

"Mom." Maya clapped her hands twice. "Boundaries. You know, the whole my body, my choice? Get consent before you do that kind of stuff."

"Sorry, sorry." Laney dropped her arms.

Remi almost reached back up for more.

"I never got to properly thank you when you were here the other day for watching over *both* my girls." Laney nudged Maya. "I got you a little something. Maya said you liked coffee. I was going to send it with her to give to you at work, but since you're here..." She dug around in her purse and pulled out a gift card.

"What? You didn't have to do this." And Maya told her mom that she liked coffee? Did this mean Maya talked about her with her mom?

Laney ran her fingers through her pixie cut and patted her bangs. "Happy to do it. I really appreciated you the other night. I was in such a jam."

Remi tapped the card against her palm. "Harper was no problem at all. It was this one here that I struggled with." She jutted her head at Maya.

Maya rolled her eyes, then faced her mom. "Did you get everything you needed?"

"Yes." Laney reached into her canvas tote bag and pulled out grocery items. "I think I bought enough food for an army for the week."

Maya checked her watch. "Crap. I still have to change for work. Be back in a sec."

Remi added the gift card to her back pocket. "You headed somewhere?"

"Harper and I are going to Port Townsend for the next week." Laney set a carton of milk in the fridge and closed the door.

"Port Townsend? I haven't been there for years." Remi took another bite of the cookie, thinking about the quaint Washington town on the water. "It's so beautiful there. When I was younger, I stayed for a few days at Fort Worden."

Laney stuffed the shopping bags inside each other and rolled them together. "Oh yeah? Did your parents bring you there?"

Dammit. She walked right into that one. It wasn't her folks. It was a *special* program for *special* kids in *special* homes, where a local philanthropist paid for a weekend trip for Remi and other Seattle kids like her to go to the ocean. She stared at her hands. "Ah, more like a field trip, camp type of situation."

Like she had some sort of superhuman power and picked up on what Remi wasn't saying, Laney rested her palm on Remi's shoulder and gave her a sympathetic smile. She patted her arm twice, then dropped her hand. "Hey, real quick, before Maya gets back, I just wanted to say thanks for everything."

Remi polished off the cookie and dusted the crumbs from her hand. "Seriously, Harper was pretty fun to hang out with. I remember being twelve and I had nowhere near the cool factor she does. Learned some stuff about the solar system I never knew."

Laney huffed a chuckle. "That girl and her documentaries. But, no, I'm talking about Maya and everything you've done since she started at Gabriella's place."

Remi's face heated. Everything she'd done? Remi had been an ass to Maya for the first two weeks. Her plans on outright sabotaging her had faded once she realized she couldn't be *that* mean, but she certainly hadn't made Maya's time easy.

"Maya was so nervous to work there, terrified she wouldn't do a good job. Coming back here, leaving Minnesota, being in the house again after everything with her dad..." She twirled the bags in the air like that completed her thought. "Well, anyway, I just really appreciate you taking her under your wing. She talks about how good you've been."

Remi didn't know which path to digest first. What happened with her dad? Maya, the queen of cool and collected, was nervous? And she said Remi had been good to her? Too many pieces of intel blasted at her, and her tongue turned to lead. "Yeah, uh, of course. She's been a, ah, great partner."

"Time to go!" Maya called as she entered the kitchen, flattening her palms against her head to smooth her hair into a ponytail. "Have fun at the cabin. Take lots of pictures so I can get really jealous and cry that I'm not there with you."

Laney pulled her in for a hug and patted her on the back. "We'll have a s'more in your honor. Love you. See you in a week."

Remi followed Maya to say goodbye to Harper, then hopped in the car. Besides the sound of the tires clanking against the pavement, the car ride was fairly quiet. Remi peeked over at Maya a few times and swore she moved closer. The typical driving stance with her elbow propped against her window's edge was changed for sitting upright, as the gravitational pull to be close to Maya intensified.

She turned on her blinker and pulled down the street to Nueve's.

"What errands did you do in my neighborhood?" Maya asked.

Remi's thigh muscles tensed. "I, uh, didn't have any errands in your neighborhood." Well, she said it. No taking it back now. She could probably follow up with some snarky comment, or say she was kidding and tell her about the skateboarding place.

Maya stared at her hands with a soft grin. "I was hoping you were going to say that."

FIFTEEN

DAILY SPECIAL: BLUSHED WHITE WINE

An hour into her shift, Maya's body finally slowed from being in the car with Remi. Sure, she'd been in Remi's car on Sunday when they recipe tested, but Maya was too buzzed and numb to feel *this*. And man, *this* was scary.

But also kind of fun.

"Mr. Thompson. Been thinking of you." Remi smiled warmly at an elderly gentleman as he propped his wooden cane against the chair. "You know, not in a weird, creepy sort of way, of course. Been awhile since I've seen you."

The man chuckled and tipped his US Army Veteran hat toward her. "Edith went into the hospital a few weeks back."

Remi poured brandy into a glass. "Oh no. Sorry to hear that. Is she doing better?" She circled a sliced orange around the rim and slid the cocktail to the man.

"Yeah. Too good." He gripped the glass. "Now she's all back in my hair and told me to get out of the house so her book club could come over and gossip."

She put a few cherries into a shot glass and handed it over. "Gossip? Maybe they're talking about the books."

"Pfft." He nibbled on a cherry. "Been married to her for

over fifty years and the only book I've ever seen her read is the Betty Crocker cookbook."

Remi patted his hand and moved back to the station. "Well, I'm glad things are back to normal. Good having you back. You catch the Mariners game last night?"

He shook his head. "I missed the last inning. *Family Feud* was on and Edith wanted to have popcorn and watch that instead." He motioned her forward. "You know I wouldn't have it any other way."

Remi grinned. "I do know this."

The genuine warmth coming from Remi filled Maya. Remi hid her sort of grizzly-turned-panda-bear side. But Maya saw through the uncaring, prickly monster facade with the way she interacted with Harper, chatted with customers, and how she stood up for her yesterday.

The hostess closed the blinds. Servers danced by carrying steaming plates of corn fritters, fried calamari, and garlic-crusted mahi-mahi. A large table in the corner cheered "Happy birthday!" and raised their glasses in celebration. Soon the symphony of clanking silverware, ice tumbling in glasses, and plates filled the air.

"Niñas! Bueno?" Gabriella called over her shoulder, balancing an arm full of empties as she scurried to the kitchen.

"We're good!" Maya said while making a spiced rum piña colada. She popped a topper in a fresh bottle of dark rum when she felt a hand touch her arm. A swoosh flew up to her earlobes and back down.

"Grabbing pineapples in the back. Need anything?"

Never had Remi asked if she needed something in the back. And definitely never had she touched her while asking.

"I, ah, no, I'm good." Was this an invitation? Maybe she wanted to re-create the cooler scene from yesterday. Maybe this would be Maya's opportunity to fist her fingers through Remi's plush hair. But the crowd was too big for them to have any sort of moment. Remi hurried away and came back a short while later with a box of pineapples and lined them in the cooler.

Maya needed to stop questioning every word, tone, and gesture from Remi. But God, that handprint was like gourmet chocolate—one sample and she craved more. In a daze, she watched Remi shake the martini shaker, ice clanking and cracking against the tin, her muscles acute and firmed. Maya needed an excuse to get closer. Just one little touch would carry her through for the night. Maybe she could reach into her bin and steal some ice, or grab some olives, or...

Knuckles thumped against the bar. "Excuse me."

The heavy exasperation in the voice would have normally irritated Maya, but she had no idea how long she was staring off into Remi-wonderland.

"Did you catch that?"

Maya stuffed her towel in her back pocket. "Sorry, again, please."

An exasperated sigh left thin lips. "Two pineapple piña coladas."

Maya tossed the rum bottle in the air. She folded a cherry into an orange slice and was sticking it in on the side of the pineapple, when two seriously good-looking men approached the bar.

Remi's chest lifted, and a smile broke through with the type of sunshine Maya didn't know Remi carried. Remi flew out from behind the bar. She wrapped her arms around the older one, a beautiful, middle-aged, thin, bald Black man, who must've been at least 6'3", and probably had Maya's same dress size. Maya had never seen Remi hug anyone like this—a full-court press with a firm embrace.

"Well, damn. Look at you." The man held Remi's arms out like he was inspecting her, the way a grandmother would inspect a child to see if they'd grown. "Your hair is longer. Still not wearing any makeup. Still strong as hell." He laughed and squeezed her shoulders. "How ya doing, kid? Good to see you."

Remi's face beamed. "I'm good. And I refuse to give in to the patriarchy and wear color on my eyelids."

Ouch. Maya loved makeup. She instinctively swiped a pinkie under her eye to catch any rogue mascara flakes.

Remi glanced at Maya. "Just kidding. I actually wear it sometimes. I just can't let him know that he still has influence over me."

The men pulled up a seat and tossed their phones on the bar. The younger one's smile highlighted his deep dimples. "So, you're the newbie Remi keeps talking about."

Remi bunched a napkin and chucked it at his face. Her mouth dropped and snapped shut before she opened it again. "I don't talk about you, it's just... casual conver— whatever. Ben, meet Maya. Maya—Ben, my roommate."

Maya's chest flushed. Remi mentioned her to Ben? Was the conversation like *She's a pain in the ass co-worker that's ruining my life*, or more *She's the woman I think too much about when I go to bed at night*? "Nice to meet you."

Remi flashed her arm to the other man. "And this is Darius. My... ah... Darius."

Maya's curiosity piqued. Friends? A family member? "Well, hey there, Remi's Darius." She shook his hand.

Darius's long, lean fingers wrapped around Maya's, and he firmed his grip. "Tonight, I'm Darius. Tomorrow, I'm Mama Butter Nips onstage. You've probably heard of me. I'm sort of a big deal around here." He wiggled his eyebrows, but his tone was joking.

Maya filled a cup with pineapple juice and sipped. "Mama Butter Nips?"

"He... she... Darius is a drag queen." Remi laid out napkins in front of the men.

"Not just *any* old drag queen..." Darius swung his arms wide. "I've been playing this gig for thirty years."

Wow. Thirty years in a profession was some serious dedication to the craft. "Well, it's great to meet you." Maya added napkins to the holder, cocking her head at Remi's unusually soft smile.

"You guys want the usual?" Remi reached for vodka and pomegranate liqueur. A minute later, she set two Cosmopolitans in front of the men.

Darius clicked his cocktail against Ben's. "You still have the perfect ratios." He tapped his multi-ringed fingers against the top of the bar. "Get into any bar fights lately?"

Remi grinned. "Not this month."

He stopped strumming his fingers, leaned back, and studied Remi's face. "How ya doing, kid? For real. Ya look good. Much better than the last time I saw you."

Now Maya *really* wanted to know what happened the last time they saw each other. Remi either was not concerned with Maya's reaction or purposely avoided her gaze as she stared straight ahead.

Remi rinsed the martini shaker and scowled. "Thanks for bringing that up the first time you see me after all this time."

Darius chuckled, and Maya officially felt like she was encroaching on a family reunion. She eased back and worked on customer orders as Remi chatted to the men in between making drinks. A good hour passed when Darius excused himself to go to the bathroom.

Ben slid his chair to Maya's side of the bar and rested his arms on the wood. "How do you like working for Gabriella?"

Remi scooted nearly shoulder to shoulder with Maya. "Careful. Ben is Gabriella's nephew. He'll absolutely report back if you talk shit."

Every lightbulb in the city blinked on. "Wait, you're *Ben*?" The puzzle piece slowly joined, and the picture finally turned clear how Remi was connected to Gabriella and Ben. "I've heard about you! I'm Laney's daughter."

His eyes narrowed, then flew wide open. "Laney's daughter? Wait... Oh my God, *Laney's daughter Maya*." He slammed his hands down on the bar. "What the hell, Rem? How did you never tell me about this before? Maya is Laney's kid?"

Remi shrugged and wiped her hands on a towel. "Not my place to be spreading people's business. I don't know how private Maya is about her family."

A small pinprick of something stabbed Maya. Not jealousy. Not sadness... more of a yearning. She couldn't put her finger on it, but it didn't feel good that Remi kept her identity hidden from her roommate and also felt *really good* that Remi was respectful.

"Gabriella's talked about you before, but I haven't seen Laney in years. And honestly, I haven't seen Gabriella in months." He shook his empty drink at Remi. "Speaking of, where is she?"

Remi tossed ice in the shaker and added vodka. "She had to run an errand. Should be back in about an hour."

"Perfect. I'll duck out before then. She's going to leave a bite mark on my ass for ignoring her calls. But man... she can talk, you know? She doesn't understand I'm a working man now." He lifted the newly poured drink to his lips. "So, Maya. You've got one hell of an arm. Where did you learn to juggle like that?"

"I was born behind the stage at a Cirque du Soleil show and a performer took pity on me." She rarely shared with anyone where and how she learned how to juggle. Explaining that would lead to why she left home five years ago, and she kept that type of conversation in a vault.

"Remi tells me you're a superb pain in the ass." He said it with as much of a twinkle in his eyes as in his voice.

"Jesus Christ, dude, really?" Remi flicked his arm, then faced Maya. "No, I didn't. Ben likes to tell stories."

The acid from the lemons and limes burrowed into Maya's skin and she rinsed her stinging skin next to Remi's station. "Funny, and here I thought we were best friends." She nearly ached to suck up any sort of intel from Ben. What *exactly* had Remi said? Did he think Remi thought about her the way she thought about Remi?

The barback rushed through the door carrying a case of domestic beer. Remi grabbed the box from him and stacked the cooler. "Don't pay attention to Ben. His sole purpose in life is to get me riled up. He succeeds like ninety percent of the time."

Darius returned and whispered something to Ben, and both men laughed so hard that Maya thought they'd knock over a glass. She leaned into Remi's ear. "How long have you two been roommates?"

"Seven years."

Maya's mouth dropped. "Seven years? You must actually really like each other."

She glanced at Ben, who was doing some form of a snake dance with his arms.

Remi cracked up. "I guess he's all right."

Maya had so many questions. Remi lived with Ben since she was eighteen. She and Darius were obviously close. But did she have siblings? Did she always grow up in Seattle? Did she have an animal? Were her rounded shoulders and arms as strong as they looked? She shook her head and focused on the parade of order tickets. Mojitos, piña coladas, rum and Cokes flew from her fingertips.

Finally, a lull in orders. She popped a few nuts in her mouth and moved towards Darius. "Life on the stage. Is it as glamourous as it looks?"

Darius tipped back his drink. "You know, back in the '90s, I owned those clubs. Drag shows then were still a little taboo and underground. Queens weren't as... plentiful as we are now, so they gave us the respect we deserved." He dragged out his words with a chuckle. "But now every damn person wants to be a queen, and the competition is fierce. And the young ones nowadays, up there doing flips and tricks that never existed. It used to be about the art and now it's about shaking asses."

Remi dashed a side-eye at Ben. "Darius, do you hear yourself? You sound like your dad."

"This is a shame." Ben tsked. "Never in my life would I have thought I'd hear Mama Butter Nips talk about too much bootie shaking onstage."

Darius released a deep, throaty chuckle. "You both are terrible children who belong in an attic."

Remi giggled and waved at an approaching customer.

"For what it's worth," Maya said as she broke down the box for recycling, "I've always appreciated the art form behind the transformation and impersonation."

Ben lifted an eyebrow. "And I've always appreciated the booties."

Darius waved his finger at Ben. "From here on out, I'm only speaking to Maya, thank you very much."

The night carried on, and Maya used every free moment to watch Remi interact with Darius and Ben. The men were like a key who unlocked this playful side of Remi, which drew Maya in like a magnet. Hell, she was drawn to almost any side of Remi at this point—snarky, salty, serious—but this was diving into a different side.

And Maya really, *really* liked this side.

The crowed thinned out, and orders slowed. Maya gripped the edge of the bar and twisted out a knot in her back.

"So, Maya." Darius draped his arm over Ben's vacant chair, who left for the restroom. "Someday you're going to have to have Remi show you pictures of my finest moment."

Maya squeezed lemon into her water. "What moment was that?"

"Junior prom," he said. "The day I transformed Remi into a sparkly debutante."

Remi stacked a tray with empties and glared at Darius. "Oh God, really? We do not have to relive that day."

Maya propped her elbow on the bar and rested her chin on her palm. "I have to know more. Remi in a dress?"

"Oh, honey. Not just any dress. *The* dress. I gave her one of mine and tailored it to damn perfection. Red, sequins, halter, open back, hair up, makeup on point, of course." He laughed. "She was a princess that night."

Remi pushed the tray to the end of the bar. "Darius and Ben were like mother hens that day. I'm still blinded by how many pictures they took."

Maya giggled at the visual of an irate Remi being forced to smile and twirl in a gown. "My mom was the same way. Like it was my wedding. In reality, it was just my best friend, Sophie, and me. It was stupid hot that day, so we only stayed for like an hour, then went down to Lake Sammamish and waded in our dresses."

Remi winced. "I bet she was pissed."

"*So* pissed," Maya agreed.

Darius dropped his arm and folded his hands. "Although the shoes..."

Remi grabbed the cutting board and sliced an orange. "Do we really need to talk about this?"

Maya lifted the straw to her lips and nodded. "Yes, yes we do."

Ben returned to the bar and his eyes dashed back and forth between all of them. "What are we talking about?"

"Remi's prom." Maya pulled an order slip for a server and grabbed the espresso liqueur.

"You remember this, Ben?" Darius shook the ice cubes in the glass. "Poor thing just could not figure out how to walk in heels. She looked like a damn baby goat getting its walking legs."

Ben scooted his chair forward. "Oh God, she was so cute. Darius and I'd practice with her in the apartment like a runway, but sadly, we all had to give up the dream."

"I hate every single one of you." Remi laughed. "Heels were made by sadists. I'll die on my sword saying that."

Darius's phone rang, and he stepped away to take the call.

Remi tapped her watch next to Ben's face. "Look at the time. Don't you have to go to bed for your shift tomorrow?" She moved her attention to a customer who pulled up a stool.

Ben shooed her as she walked away. "Ah. The patients can take care of themselves."

Maya's head snapped up. "Patients? Where do you work?"

"I'm an RN at Pacific Northwest Hospital," he said.

Maya's heart skipped a beat. Ben was a Registered Nurse at the hospital? Remi's roommate was living her dream. She straightened her spine, her mind jumbling with a gazillion questions. "Which unit?"

He tilted his head. "Right now, in the general surgery aftercare area. But I just told Remi that I did a shift a few weeks back in pediatrics and I'm going to job shadow there and see what I think."

"I love it." She lined the drinks up for the server. "Pediatrics would be amazing. Are you thinking NICU, epidemiology, cardiology, endocrinology?"

He paused, his eyes narrowing. "I'm leaning toward immunology but would have to go back for more studies, and not sure that is in my game plan right now." He leaned back and drummed his fingers under the barstool. "How the hell do you know about these things?"

She grinned. "I just graduated with my four-year and going back in the fall for my master's in nursing. I'm doing endocrinology because my sister has diabetes. The program adds on another twenty credits, but it's totally worth it."

"Endocrinology is fascinating. They're coming up with some really cool stuff that I think is going to change the way they treat type one diabetes soon." Ben pushed his drink to the side. "I just read a *Seattle Times* article about some new learnings coming out of a UW study."

Maya barely acknowledged the approaching customer and was grateful Remi took over and served her group. She missed everything about healthcare, except for the long study nights. Nope, wait. She actually missed that, too. When she fully grasped the concepts, or read about newly funded groundbreaking research, she was filled with so much hope.

Darius returned to the bar and slapped a hand on Ben's back. "I have to get going. Practice and sound check tomorrow." He shook Maya's hand. "You and Remi have to come see me perform tomorrow night. It'll be a little quieter cause it's a weeknight, and I need all the hype-people I can get."

The idea of hanging out with Remi outside of work made Maya's belly flutter. She tried to read Remi's straight-lipped but soft-eyed reaction to Darius's invite. *Why wasn't she saying anything?* Maya wiggled her toes and shifted her hips from side to side. "Oh, um, I don't know. We're both on shift, and I feel like maybe this is a thing for you three. I can cover Remi here tomorrow and call in a closer so she can leave early or something?"

"I won't take no for an answer." Darius smacked his long, delicate fingers on the bar. "I'm only in town performing once a year. Trust me, I can be persuasive. Remi—do I give up when I want something?"

Remi's face cracked with a grin. "Well, Maya, looks like we're going to watch Darius tomorrow after work."

Maya's gaze followed Remi and the men as she walked them to the door and hugged them in the lobby. She snatched the sanitizing spray from the hook and whistled as she cleaned.

An hour later, after the hostess locked the doors for the evening and cleaning duties were over, Remi threw her cross-body around her shoulder. "Want a ride home?"

Maya's chest lifted. "You're going to spoil me. You probably live in the totally opposite direction."

"I do, actually." Remi closed the locker door. "But I don't mind at all."

Following Remi to the parking lot, her pulse reacted with skipped, unsteady beats. The car was warm and spilled alcohol fumed from their clothes. Maya cracked open a window and breathed in the summer breeze. "I can't believe your roommate is Gabriella's nephew. How have none of you ever said this to me?"

Remi crossed lanes and sped past a bus. "How have you two not met before now?"

Maya shrugged. "How often do you hang out with your mom's friends' nieces and nephews, though, you know?"

Remi's body tightened, and she clamped her lips.

Maya's belly turned with the sudden shift in the air. She didn't know what she said wrong, but the question obviously struck a nerve. The blur of cars flashed by, and she tapped her fingertips on her leg. "Anyway, it was nice meeting both. They seem great."

Remi nodded. "They are."

"Is Darius a friend of Ben's or something?"

The only sound was a few rocks being crushed under the tires as Remi exited Aurora and navigated into Maya's neigh-borhood. Maya twisted her hands in her lap.

Finally, after what felt like a gazillion and one seconds, Remi sighed. "Yeah... something like that."

Maya needed to let this conversation drop but was desperate to unlock more of the Remi mystery-package. Remi's personal or family life really wasn't any of her business, but Remi kept opening and closing her mouth like she wanted to say something. No... no, she should definitely let this drop. "Want to tell me about how you know each other?" *Too late.*

The silent response was thunderous. Why did she do that? She should have said nothing at all, considering the Olympic Mountain–sized brick wall Remi just assembled.

Remi eased through Maya's neighborhood and pulled over in front of her house.

Should she apologize? Say anything? She unbuckled her seatbelt and put her hand on the door handle when a hand touched hers.

"It's... a really long story." Remi kept her eyes on their hands. "How much time do you have?"

If Maya didn't know any better, she'd say Remi's voice was demure, almost fragile.

"I have all night."

Remi didn't move her hand from Maya's.

Maya held her breath and waited for Remi to say something else. Finally, she put her other hand on top of Remi's. "Want to come in?"

A soft uptick in Remi's lips occurred. She opened the car door and got out.

SIXTEEN

DRINK SPECIAL: CHERRY COSMO WITH TWO SHOTS OF VULNERABILITY

What am I doing? All sorts of awful, uncomfortable, itch-inducing emotions filled Remi. Emotions in general were terrible, but these were supervillain level of terrible. A sweat bead developed beneath her temple, and her mouth was so dry she couldn't speak. She followed Maya up the gnome-laden path to her house and contemplated sprinting back to her car and peeling down the road.

She stepped into the home and another overwhelming emotion engulfed her, but this one she couldn't name. The lingering smell of the cookies from the morning, the pictures and plants, the over-sized couch with hand-knitted blankets, felt like a hug. If her mornings could start with this feeling, she'd probably be a better person.

"Hungry? My mom made a ton of leftovers." Maya walked to the kitchen and rummaged through a stack of containers in the fridge. "We've got lasagna, tuna casserole, and..." She popped open a lid and sniffed. "Sloppy Joe mix."

Any other day, Remi would've devoured all of them and asked for more. But today, her stomach clenched so tight she wasn't sure she'd ever eat again. "I'm good."

"I'll make some tea." She filled the kettle with water and pulled out two mugs. "I think my mom forgets I lived without her for the last five years. I feel bad she's making me this food when she's gone, like I wouldn't know how to do it without her."

Remi sifted through the assorted tea packets and grabbed the peppermint. "Maybe she just likes doing it and doesn't see it as a chore?"

"I think she loves it. Like this biological need to make sure her kids are being fed." She pulled honey from the cabinet. "Do you mind if I throw my pj's on and you watch the water?"

"Sure."

Remi's throat tightened as she scanned the fridge—Star Student Award Certificate with Harper's name, a dozen magnets from Mount Rainier, photos of Maya and Harper, and an insulin dosage schedule.

The kettle screeched. She filled the mugs, tucked the honey in the crook of her arm, and moved to the living room. After finding coasters under a few magazines, she settled into the couch when Maya stepped into the room. Why did the sight of her in a messy bun and a two-piece button-up, cherry-decorated pajamas send a zap through Remi? She focused on dipping her tea bag and not the flutter in her chest.

Maya pulled a leg underneath herself and squeezed honey into her mug. Her spoon clanked against the ceramic. She licked it off and set it to the side. She seemed to be waiting for Remi to say something as she sat there, testing the water temperature.

Remi's chest felt like weighted sandbags were stacked on top of her and the only way to remove them was to shed pieces of her past. But those sandbags also protected her. If she opened up, Maya would probably give her some version of "poor Remi," or "such a shame," or some other disgusting phrase that would make her cringe first, become irate second.

"I met Ben in foster care." The words stumbled out before

she could snatch them and shove them back down. If she saw pity, she wouldn't be able to handle it. She despised those expressions—the ones she used to get as a kid—a sort of weird half smile, half frown.

"Okay." Maya blew into her mug and took a tentative sip.

Her face contained no pity or sympathy. She looked almost like she was reading a grocery list. Remi exhaled. "I was thirteen and Ben was fifteen." She removed the tea bag and set it on a plate. "We sort of hated each other for the first few days. He wasn't there long... his grandma left Puerto Rico when she found out about his situation and moved up here to take custody."

Maya added another drop of honey to the drink and stirred. "How long were you there?"

"That home? I think like a year or so." She wrapped her hands around the near burning mug, the sensation a welcome change from the chill running up her neck. "It's hard to remember. I just remember their number. This house was home number three."

Maya's face still didn't show any emotion except curiosity. "Were there a lot of homes?"

Remi chuckled, even though it wasn't funny. She used to name them when she was younger. The Blue House home. The Orange Tabby Cat home. Ice Cream for Dessert home. But after the third one, she resorted to calling them by number. "Yeah. I think none of them knew how to handle all this." Remi waved to her chest with a smirk.

Maya didn't smile. But she didn't do a sympathy frown, either.

"Did you have a favorite one?"

Remi tucked herself in the corner of the couch. "I was lucky. They were all good in their own way. Home number one taught me how to floss. Home number two introduced me to boxing. Home number three showed me how to do laundry and

I met Ben there. So yeah, they each had their, I guess, special thing."

Maya drained her tea bag and laid it on her plate. "Was Darius a foster parent?"

Remi shook her head. "Not technically. Ben introduced me to him, and Darius was sort of like a fire station. A safe haven. My foster home at the time was pretty lenient. Or I irritated them enough and maybe they needed a break, but they used to let me crash over there a lot." She scraped her fingernail against her mug, remembering when Darius depleted an entire box of pancake mix with the patience of a patron saint until she learned how to cook them without burning the edges. "His couch always had fresh sheets when I'd show up, almost like he was expecting me. He gave me a space to breathe, you know? I could swear, be angry, I could just... I don't know... just *be* without judgment. His rules were don't be an asshole, no drugs, and stay in school, and other than that, he was super flexible. It was the first time I felt safe. Not like physically safe. More... safe to be me."

Oh shit. That was a lot of words, a lot of honesty, a lot of *bleh*, in a short amount of time. She sipped as much tea as she could handle, but the liquid did not quench her thirst. The back of her neck itched, her arm itched, her entire body felt like it had fire ants burrowing into her skin.

Maya recrossed her legs and propped her elbows on her knee. "Where are your parents?"

The Space Needle on the mug caught her attention and she traced it with her fingertip. "Part of the Seattle opioid crisis."

Maya nodded. She sat for several long moments before she stood and walked to the kitchen. Remi almost flinched. Was it too much? She hadn't talked about this stuff for years. And here she just trauma-barfed all over Maya. Stickiness gathered in her throat.

A moment later, Maya returned with a plate of cookies. "I

think tea and cookies make the best combo."

Remi's chest relaxed, and she grabbed a cookie. Thank God Maya didn't talk about how heroic Remi was. Or, say something like "Look at you breaking the cycle!", or "Look how well you've done despite everything" like her life was a consolation prize. The beginning of a vulnerability hangover crept in, and her muscles twitched to jump rope or hit a bag. She bit into the chocolate and sunk into the couch.

"My dad died." Maya nibbled at the cookie. "Got a diagnosis, got super sick, and died in like four weeks."

Whoa. Remi had noticed all the photos in this home were of a single parent but hadn't thought too much about it. Maya chewed on her lip, her face contorted in a way that showed much more pain than what her cavalier tone produced. "Shit."

"Yeah. Pancreatic cancer is an evil bitch that needs to die." Maya wiped the cookie crumbles that fell on the top of her knee. "When he died, it's like everything just stopped. The world... it just didn't move."

Remi set down the mug and shoved her hands under her legs to refrain from touching Maya.

"Is Ben your person?"

Remi nodded. "He's my only family."

Maya pulled a pillow into her lap and ran her fingers through the shaggy threads. "My dad was my person. You would've loved him—he had a wicked sense of humor. But my God, when he thought he'd stumbled upon a teachable moment, no one could get him to shut up." A soft smile passed her lips as she twisted the fabric on her finger. "After Harper was born, we got super close. My mom was taking care of a baby, and I understand how much work that was, but she and I grew apart. And my dad became my everything. Does that sound awful?"

Remi shook her head. "Not at all."

Maya crunched into the cookie. "He's the one who taught me how to juggle."

The wistfulness in her voice tugged at Remi. She knew longing well and could spot the knitted eyebrows as Maya unraveled the thread. "I wondered where you learned how to do that."

Maya set her mug on the coffee table and smiled. "My dad grew up in Minnesota and told me when he was younger, they had long winters and no internet. So, him and his brothers taught themselves to juggle. After he died, when I'd really miss him, I'd pick up a few objects and toss them, like I was channeling him or something. It probably sounds really dumb, but when I juggled, I felt close to him. And I became a little obsessed with it."

"It doesn't sound dumb at all." Remi's hands now almost needed to grip the cushion underneath her to refrain from scooping Maya in her arms. But Maya showed her mad respect by maintaining her boundary earlier, and she needed to leverage all restraint and give Maya the same regard. Remi understood parental loss. What she didn't understand was missing a parent you actually loved. When she went into foster care, she was angry, of course, but she was also relieved. Maya's situation was totally different. "How do you even start juggling?"

"First you do scarves or something super lightweight that floats. After you master that, you move up to a tennis balls, and so on. I didn't even mean to juggle bottles. I was tossing lemons one night and my manager loved it and had me work with the bottles."

"Did your dad teach Harper how to juggle?"

Maya wrapped her arms around her leg and rested her chin on her knee. She shook her head. "Harper was only three when our dad passed. She barely remembers him. But I was fifteen... and I remember." Her chin trembled, and she inhaled a shaking breath.

Remi's stomach fell, and the back of her throat got wet. She wanted to hold Maya's face in her hands and tell her how sorry she was for her loss. "I can't even imagine how hard that must've been for all of you. How did your mom take it?"

"My mom was thrown into single motherhood, paying bills, burying her husband, potty-training Harper, and teaching me to drive all at one time. She tried to protect Harper from feeling any sort of pain and sort of left me to fend emotionally for myself. Not that I blamed her. She had an energetic toddler that needed attention, and I wanted to be alone." She flicked at the back of the pillow. "The grief consumed me, and isolation comforted me."

Maya's words should not have been as profound as they were, but something heavy sunk to the depths of Remi's core. Although it wasn't logical, Remi always believed if someone grew up in a loving house, they were exempt from pain. She wanted to shake her head at the ridiculous notion. "So, your dad was from Minnesota..." The connection to the state became clear. "Is that why you went to school there?"

"Yeah. The college became a sort of emblem for me and my dad's history. He always wanted me to go there. And when Harper got sick, the school's power increased and became not just a way to connect with my dad but to learn everything I could about diabetes." A fat tear rolled down her cheek, and she swiped at it with the back of her hand. "I was so desperate to stay connected to him, you know? I just couldn't..."

Remi's insides coiled and burst, and she wanted to do anything she could do to alleviate those tears. She had no idea what to say, because all her words would be sympathy-induced and she couldn't do that to Maya.

Maya ran the corner of her sleeve over her nose. "I went to Minnesota and chased his ghost, you know? And I was living out his dream. Every place on campus reminded me of him, and since he died, it was the closest to him I felt. But then..."

Remi pulled out her hands and rested them on top of

Maya's. "Then what?"

The quiver in Maya's chin deepened. "I love my mom and Harper so much, but they're not the only reason I moved back home. They think they are, and I'm such a horrible daughter for lying to them."

Years had passed since she had this level of conversation. Even with Violet, nothing came close to hearing this crack in Maya's voice as her body seemed to curl into itself. She hated prying. People's business was their own business. But yet... Maya *seemed* like she wanted to say more. "Why did you move back?"

Maya released a heavy sigh and petted the pillow in her lap like a comfort animal. She bit her trembling lip.

"He started fading. The images of him in my mind... it was like trying to capture steam in a bucket. I couldn't *see* him anymore. And I thought moving back home, he'd come back into focus." She choked out a dry sob. "God, I'm a mess. You must think I'm the most emotional person ever."

Emotional, yes. But not in the negative connotation way that Maya meant. More like the love she had for her family overflowed, and she tossed her pain, sorrow, and heart on the table. "I think you are deeply... human."

A low-pitched, guttural cry released, and Maya buried her face into her hands.

The sounds burrowed into Remi, like a pain-filled corkscrew that stabbed her in the chest and twisted. She exhaled, waiting for confirmation of life. The need to maintain boundaries crumbled. She scooped Maya into her arms.

Maya shook against her. "I just miss him so much."

Remi rubbed her back and stroked her hair. Her neck and shirt absorbed the moisture from Maya's tears. Remi squeezed tighter, the rawness of Maya's sobs making Remi's throat tight. She wanted to absorb these tears, put them on herself, then throw them away. And as she sat there, feeling Maya's cries like they were her own, she begged whatever God that may exist to take away Maya's hurt.

Maya clung on to Remi like she was drowning, and Remi was a lifejacket. Remi didn't know how long they sat like that—minutes, hours—as Maya's tears dried and her tremors slowed. But Maya remained, her head against Remi's chest, her fingers absentmindedly playing with the clasp on Remi's watch. Remi dared not move, dared not shatter whatever this moment was.

The moon cracked through the windows, a slice of hope cutting through the dark room. Quiet talk filled the space, stories about the chaos when Harper first got sick, the stress of midterms, and fishing off a dock in the Mississippi River.

Positions were switched. Remi swiped her thumb on Maya's shoulder, as she talked about social workers, the mom from foster home number two who made Spam meatloaf, which sounded gross but was really delicious, and an art teacher she loved who was the only reason she didn't skip school. Maya outlined Remi's palm with her fingertip and rested her head on Remi's shoulder and talked about walking out of her first bartending job when the owner got handsy, not learning to whistle until she was a teenager, and seeing the northern lights in Minnesota. The moon arched over the living room skylight, filling the room with a glow. A fit of giggles broke out when Remi talked about the mother of all awkward birds-and-bees conversation with Ben's abuelita when she thought she and Ben were sleeping together, and Remi finally just said, "I like boobs."

A blanket was spread across their laps. Yawns, sluggish words, and sleepy breaths filled the room. A kink in Remi's neck nudged her awake, and she looked at a tousle of blond hair spread on her chest. She shifted and when Maya squirmed, Remi stiffened until Maya's sleepy breathing pattern returned. She dipped her chin, kissed Maya on the top of her head, and closed her eyes.

SEVENTEEN

DRINK SPECIAL: SHAKEN NOT STIRRED LUST MARTINI

Maya did something she hadn't done in years.

Slept through the night.

She peeked out the window as Remi made her way down the driveway. The morning overcast leaked through the living room blinds. As the crunching gravel sound of a car driving away echoed through the room, the space felt too big now without Remi. She stumbled down to her bedroom and squiggled under the covers. 7:00 a.m. after a full night of tears and laughs was way too early to function. She threw her arm over her sawdust eyes as her body ached with fatigue.

But she also ached with something else.

She flipped the pillow under her head and tried to go back to sleep, but she couldn't. What happened last night? How did they talk that much about so many things? The honesty and openness from Remi shocked Maya, but soon after, everything felt like they'd braved their hearts a million times before. She told Remi some of her deepest secrets she hadn't even told Sophie or her family. As Maya's chest lifted and her heart soared, she saw a shift in Remi. And waking up with pretzeled legs and tangled arms was more than she could've imagined.

She tugged the blanket over her head, but it was useless. A nagging voice she'd had for the last few weeks turned screaming, almost menacing, and then, finally, comforting. She whipped the blankets off and dug out her laptop. After firing it up, she took a shaky but cleansing breath. She knew what exactly she had to do and was only upset she had waited so long to do it. Her fingers hovered over the screen for only a moment. Exhaling, she typed. "Dear Admissions Office..."

Later that afternoon, after a several-hour long nap, a short jog, and a hot shower, Maya wrapped a bathrobe around herself and dialed Sophie.

"What's up, sugar pie?" Sophie asked.

So many things. Feelings, thoughts, revelations. Everything she *thought* to be true was wrong, and everything she *felt* to be true was right. She wanted to talk and didn't want to talk and wanted to run and cry and sing, all at the same time. "Remi spent the night last night."

"Whaaaaa," Sophie squeaked. "Oh, hell no. Hold. You do not drop a bomb like that without FaceTiming so I can thoroughly evaluate every single face movement and count how many times you chew the corner of your pinkie."

Maya dropped her pinkie gripped between her teeth and answered Sophie's FaceTime call.

Sophie cocked her head, and her gaze dashed around the screen. "You don't look happy. But you don't look sad. You don't look in love and you don't look like you're regretting the hell out of your actions. My powers are useless. I'm sending them back to the universe in shame. You're gonna just have to tell me what happened."

Maya lay on her side and propped the phone on the bed. "It wasn't like that. Can't two women spend the night, without, you know... *spending the night?*"

Sophie's mouth pursed. "Well, sure, but I mean you've kind of been crushing on her since you met, so..."

"What?" Maya popped up. "That's totally untrue. Pretty sure I've hardly said that many nice things about her."

"Exactly." Sophie grinned. "I've never heard you complain about someone in so much excruciating, seriously boring detail in all my life. You know, I painted my entire bathroom during your last vent session."

Maya rolled her eyes. "You're such a liar."

"Okay, fair. But I could have." The phone shook as Sophie made her way from the kitchen into her bedroom. She set the phone up on the desk and held up various shirts against her chest as she glanced in her full-length mirror. "So, did you just call me to tell me that, or is there more to this?"

"No. Yes. No. I don't know." Maya tugged the pillow between her legs to release a pinch in her lower back. "It's like everything I thought about Remi is thrown out the window. She's actually a really decent person, you know? Smart, kind, sweet. Last night... I told her about my dad."

Sophie lowered the shirt. "That's a pretty big deal."

The significance in talking about her dad, and his death, and the impact to her, wasn't lost on Maya. Until last night, Sophie was the only one who knew all the details besides her family. Maya gripped her headboard and twisted her hips until she felt a crack. "I just don't know what to think. Maybe I'm overthinking, maybe I'm underthinking. Maybe I should stop thinking..."

Sophie pulled the phone so close to her face Maya could practically see pores.

"And maybe you should just enjoy a sliver of happiness, whatever that looks like. We don't know what's in store for us."

Maya sighed. Of course no one knew what was in store for them. Two months prior to her dad's death, he'd ordered a special, NASA-grade insulated tent that was on back order. She and her dad were going to brave winter camping over the holidays, and that was the first of their purchases.

The tent arrived a week after his funeral.

Sophie resumed evaluating her outfit. "What's the worst that could happen if you just went for it?"

Maya shrugged. "I lose my self-respect and dignity. Jump into a flaming pile of rejection, flail until fall semester, and potentially lose my job."

Sophie lifted an eyebrow. "Anything else."

Maya swallowed back the lump in her throat. "I could get my heart broken."

So many moments followed that Maya wasn't even sure if they were still on the call.

Sophie sat on the edge of her bed and pulled the phone to her face. "Or... your heart could heal."

Tears burned Maya's eyes. She pushed her fist into her forehead and exhaled. "I love you."

Sophie smiled. "I love you, too."

Maya rolled on her side and set the phone on the pillow. "Oh, Soph, one more thing."

"What's that?"

"The second shirt you held up, the canary-yellow one. Hideous. Seriously, burn it."

"God, you're a jerk." She giggled and held it up next to her chest. "Fine, you're right—on this one only."

Maya hung up and let the words simmer. What did happiness look like in the *now*, not after graduation—not when life settled—not when she "had time." What did it look like even temporarily? Was temporary happiness worth potential heartache? Too many questions and not enough answers, and all she wanted to do was focus on this floating sensation she'd had all day.

She dug into her closet, looking for an outfit to change into after work for Mama Butter Nips's performance. After tossing perfume and a few cosmetics into her bag, she changed into her work outfit when her phone buzzed.

> Remi: I have more errands to run in your neighborhood today. Need a ride to work?

Maya's chest flushed. She had wanted to reach out to Remi this morning but wasn't sure if Remi was feeling as emotionally raw as she was after their conversation.

> Maya: Another errand? My lucky day. You know, you keep spoiling me with rides and I'm going to start depending on you.

Bubbles popped up and disappeared. And popped up again and disappeared. Finally, her phone beeped.

> Remi: that's the goal 😉

Oh God, she left a winking face. Maya's belly fluttered in response.

An hour later, a knock on the door and the flutters that tickled earlier in her belly were now high kicking. She opened the door and faced an oversized cup of coffee held out in front of a grinning Remi. Seeing Remi on her doorstep, relaxed, her rich, dark curls haloing her head, reassured Maya in a way that she didn't know she needed.

Maya tapped the edge of the cup and sipped. "Oh yum. What is this?"

"I stopped by Sugar Mugs. It's one of Charlie's specialties—Blackberry Honey Latte. Not sure if you're as hella tired as me, but I needed a caffeine jolt." Her dimples appeared, and she clicked her cup against Maya's. "All set?"

"Yep." The sweetness of the latte traveled down Maya's throat. She patted her bag. "Clothes for tonight." She followed Remi down the driveway to the street.

Remi popped the trunk and took Maya's bag for her. "Darius doesn't hit the stage until after 10:00 p.m. so we'll only miss a little of the show."

Maya clicked her seatbelt and cracked the window. "I'm so excited. I haven't been to a drag show for over a year. Minneapolis has some iconic performers, but with work and school... I just never got the chance."

Remi drove down the block. "I don't get out enough, either. Sometimes I get so wrapped up in routine that I forget to just enjoy life, you know? This'll be good for me." She pushed her thumb into the back of her neck and rubbed in a circle as she winced.

"Did you pinch your neck last night with the, ah, sleeping arrangements?" She wanted to roll down the windows. The pheromones weren't bursting as much this time, but the air felt heavy.

"I did." Remi stopped at a red light and her gaze locked on Maya's. She reached over, put a gentle hand on top of Maya's, and squeezed. "And it was totally worth it."

The arm on the bar clock inched across the minutes like it was stuck in taffy. Closing time couldn't come fast enough. The entire evening, Maya made any excuse possible to brush up against Remi. Using her ice, whispering about a customer, reaching over and grabbing napkins from her bin. And Remi's soft smiles, fingertips grazing her arm, and long looks with blush-swept cheeks made Maya's skin sparkle. As exciting as all the touches were, all Maya really wanted to do was to climb on top of Remi and taste her mouth. "Can you believe that guy proposed to his girlfriend here tonight? I could see him shaking from here."

Remi tipped a glass under the beer tap. "For real. Probably one of the sweetest things I've seen in a long time." She set the glass down and started the next one. "Kind of strange. Stuff like that would've irritated me in the past."

Maya piled trays of empties. "Really? Proposing?"

"Not that exactly. Like all that gushy love stuff. I just didn't want to see it." She set the third glass under the spout. "I guess I'm maturing in my old age."

"Guess so." Maya grinned.

Remi leaned in next to Maya's ear. "Or maybe it's not *all* about getting older."

The buttery tone made Maya melt. "Maybe it's—"

"Niñas!"

Maya jolted upright.

Remi overfilled her glass and cleared her throat.

Gabriella dashed her gaze between the two of them and frowned. "Venid aquí!" She motioned them toward her.

No way could Gabriella have picked up on that exchange, even with her superhuman sleuthing skills, right? Maya and Remi were simply two co-workers sharing a sweet moment. Maya's stomach twisted, and she made her way to Gabriella.

Remi rang up her customer and dashed over to the women. "What's up?"

Gabriella blew her bangs away from her face. "Just got an email from the coordinator for Thursday. The news station is coming down to film!"

Oh damn, that just upped the pressure. Last week, Gabriella asked Maya to join Remi and a few other staff in a charity bartending and serving competition on Thursday morning. It sounded both fun and an under-the-radar way to spend a little more time with Remi. But she didn't think cameras would be in her face.

"You two know what this means, right?" Gabriella wiggled her fingers.

Remi tilted her head. "No swearing, no fighting, and wear some lipstick."

Gabriella snapped her heels against the hard floor and moved behind the bar. "I don't give two shits about what you put on your face." She filled a glass with pineapple juice. "Best behavior. *Both of you.* Our goal is taking down la diabla. On the TV."

"I thought the goal was raising money for charity?" Remi smirked.

"Gah! Silencio! En boca cerrada no entran moscas..." Gabriella slammed her juice and stormed off, muttering words that Maya couldn't translate.

"She's going to hate you forever now." Maya drained the alcohol runoffs from her rubber mat. "Who's the she-devil?"

Remi cracked open a fresh bottle of vodka and tossed the empty into the recycling. "A woman who owns a Latin-inspired restaurant downtown. Pretty cool actually, serves dishes from all over—Mexico, South America, Colombia, Puerto Rico..."

"Oh no."

Remi glanced over her shoulder. "Yep. Gabriella is convinced she stole her flan recipe from like ten years ago. Her restaurant competes every year at this event, and it's the one time Gabriella gets to stick it to her."

Maya patted the mat dry. "Ah. She's normally not like this... until she is."

"So true." Remi chuckled.

The servers warned of last call to their tables and the music lowered. With fewer customers than normal—thank the sweet holy gay gods—Maya flew around the bar, stocking, wiping, and covering condiments.

Remi practically sprinted in the back for back stock and carried up two cases at a time. *And yes*, Maya absolutely noticed the definition in Remi's forearm when she lifted them on top of the cooler.

In record time, the till was closed, Maya waved goodnight to Gabriella, and the bar was cleaned.

"We good?" Remi asked while wiping the top of her glistening brow.

Maya scooped the last of the towels for the laundry. "Yep, I'm gonna go change in the bathroom."

Remi flipped off the bar light. "I'll go in Gabriella's office. Meet you in back."

Maya dropped the dirty rags in the laundry bin and grabbed her items from her locker. Ripped clothes off, dress slipped on, low heels attached to feet, and she looked in the bathroom mirror. *Grrr.* Her makeup looked like it melted through a night of sweat-inducing work. She readjusted the eyeliner, added a swipe of gloss, and walked under one spritz of perfume. She backed up and gave herself a once-over. The straps of her halter dress accentuated her collarbones if she said so herself, and she hadn't worn an all-black dress in forever. *Not bad...*

She stuffed her clothes into the duffel bag and scurried into the kitchen area, past a couple of line cooks who did a double take. The dishwasher hummed in the background and the scraping sound of a steel sponge being dragged across pans floated in the back. The door was still closed to Gabriella's office, and she knocked a few times. "Hey, you almost ready?"

"One sec." Remi stepped out of the room with ripped black skinny jeans, perfectly applied wing-tipped eyeliner, and a sleeveless black crew neck bodysuit.

Maya was sure her mouth fell to the floor. Christ, her arms. Her hair. Her full, round hips hugged in the denim. Remi was... mouthwatering.

The look Remi gave Maya mirrored what Maya was feeling —like she wanted to have Maya for dessert.

Remi nibbled on the corner of her lip. "You look... amazing."

Maya swallowed and smoothed down the front of her dress. "I, ah, was going to say the same about you." She locked her gaze with Remi's until the loud clank of something sharp and high-pitched hit the floor. Her head snapped to the cooks, who'd apparently swapped cleaning duties with staring at her and Remi.

Remi shook her head with a grin. "Come on!"

Maya slung her bag over her shoulder and followed Remi to her car.

On the drive to the show, Remi blasted club music. She navigated through the Seattle traffic and tapped her hand against the steering wheel. "This is my version of pre-funking." At a red light, she checked her phone. "Ben texted. He's saving us some spots."

"Perfect." Maya pulled down the vanity mirror and tucked a loose strand of hair behind her ear. "Did he bring Charlie and her girlfriend?"

"No. Charlie has to get up like stupid early because of the coffee shop."

Maya flipped the mirror back up and settled back. "Do you ever get jealous of their relationship?"

"Charlie and Ben's? Nah. She's super nice and can put up with way more shit than I can."

The car slowed. Remi parked old-school-style, with her arm wrapped around the back of the seat, no back-up camera, and eased into the spot. *Sexy as hell.* From the way Maya's legs tingled, she might ask to watch Remi change a tire someday. Maya stepped out of the car.

Remi nudged out her elbow. "I'd hate to see you fall with heels on."

Maya's cheeks burned as she linked her arm with Remi's. Everything about this moment felt date-*ish*, and she pressed her tongue in between her teeth to keep from yelping. "Contrary to *your* experience, I do, in fact, know how to walk in heels. But I'll take your arm, anyway."

The June evening was perfect. Warm air replaced the chill of the previous week, the smell of wet pavement replaced the cherry blossoms of the spring. The crushed purple rocks imbedded into the concrete sparkled with the glow from the surrounding light posts. Vendors roasted hot dogs, the music leaked outdoors from the various clubs, traffic and pedestrians surrounded them.

It had been forever since Maya had been at a nightclub. In Minneapolis, she and some classmates busted out one night after finals, taking in a superb drag show at the iconic Gay 90s. Queens in roller skates and miniskirts, artists performing as P!nk, Whitney Houston, Lady Gaga, and Beyoncé filled the stage, combining fresh new talent with seasoned veterans.

Remi tightened her grip as they crossed the rainbow sidewalk to a line waiting outside of a velvet rope. "I gotta chat with the bouncer. One second."

She placed her fingertips on Maya's arm as she turned to talk to the bouncer. Maybe to make sure Maya didn't feel alone, or abandoned, but safe. Whatever the reasoning was, Maya felt like she could melt directly into the sidewalk and still land softly.

Wallflower was not a word she'd normally consider calling herself. As Remi chatted with the bouncer, with straightened shoulders—amazing, round, thick shoulders—and the man lifted the velvet rope and waved her through, she felt totally out of her league. And she kind of loved it.

Maya wasn't sure who did it first, but as they moved through the doors, their fingers intertwined like gravity pulled them together. Bass thumped below her feet. Cyndi Lauper's "Girls Just Want To Have Fun," combined with cheers and whistles, filled the air. The artist onstage shook her hips and lip-synced to perfection while wearing a leopard print leotard with what Maya swore were six-inch heels. She leaned into Remi's ear. "I'll give you twenty bucks to try those shoes on."

Remi laughed. "You suck, you know that? I'll send you the bill for me breaking my thigh bone." She weaved through the crowd as the MC popped onstage with an oversized neon-magenta feather boa—and a sequined thong—and dropped some amazingly raunchy jokes about worshiping the latest performer on their knees.

"I didn't know you rolled VIP style for these types of things," Maya said as she kept her fingers glued to Remi's.

Remi strained her neck and pointed to Ben cheering from a table. "I think Mama Butter Nips just wants me to see that she's still got it. More about her than me."

They weaved between the animated crowd, with someone bumping into them as they fist-pumped into the air. Remi firmed her grip.

"Hey!" Ben reached over and hugged Maya, then tapped his elbow on Remi's. "Damn, you both clean up nice. Remi, are you wearing actual eyeliner?"

She rolled her eyes and pulled out a chair for Maya. "Yes. I know how to get ready for a night out."

"You look incredible, Maya. Dress, heels, makeup, everything's on point." He waved to a server. "You two made good time."

"We flew out of there." Remi settled back into her chair. "Has Mama been on yet?"

He shook his head. "No, but she should be next."

Maya dug in her purse and laid a stack of ones on the table. "Look what I brought. What better use of our tips than giving back?"

"No way! I did the same." Remi pulled out a wad of cash from her pocket with a grin. "Gabriella's gonna wonder what the hell happened when her till has no ones."

A server stopped to chat with Ben, who pointed at Remi and Maya. "You two want anything?"

Maya shook her head.

Remi lifted a brow. "No more tequila coffees or amaretto chocolates?"

Maya playfully gagged. "Nope. I drank enough for a year. Just soda and lime from here until I die."

The server plopped two candies on the table. "My sober lovers get free lollipops." He blew a kiss and floated away.

Remi popped the sucker in her mouth. Her lips wrapped around the candy as she clapped and cheered with the MC. She tugged the candy in and out of her mouth and Maya couldn't push away the seriously un-saintly thoughts traveling through her system. Club lights flickered and stage lights zeroed in on the MC. Maya wiggled and clapped in her seat, her heart racing as a performer took the stage. Sure, they were impersonators—that was the nature of the job. But it was almost as thrilling as seeing the real singer live.

"Ladies and gents!" The MC shouted into the microphone. "Enbys, pans, trans, queers, and queens... put your gloriously dirty hands together for a local legend, Mama Butter Nips!"

The drumbeat boomed. Remi hooked her thumb and index finger in her mouth and blew a crystal-shattering whistle as Mama Butter Nips took the stage.

"Yes!" Ben screamed, and clapped.

In the heat of the dark club, with the lights pulsating as glow-stick laden servers shimmied through the crowd, everyone amped up. Mama owned that stage, strutting and shaking in her dress, perfection in her lip-syncing and spot-on impersonation of Tina Turner. Remi grabbed Maya and Ben and yanked them to the stage, and fanned Mama with cash.

After Mama exited, Maya followed Remi and Ben back to the seat and gulped soda water. "I seriously don't understand how Darius transformed like that."

"I know, right?" Ben pulled the straw into his mouth. "There's such an art to it. Rem and I used to watch him for hours. He'd study her face from every angle, watch video after video, contour the hell out of his face. It was intense."

The show continued, and Maya sat back and watched

performers grace the stage. Remi looked alive, almost... *whole*, with her screaming and whistling. Maya wanted to sit back and watch how this woman transformed into this sphere of energy.

Dollar bills whittled away as Ben cracked jokes about how he was willing to sell his body to the hottest person in the club to replenish their funds. He waved at a person in the corner and excused himself from the table.

Maya's cheeks were on fire from all the grinning. She sipped from her tart soda and caught Remi's eye.

Remi stared at her, a soft grin lifting from the corner of her lips. She popped up from her seat and held out her hand. "Come on."

Maya lowered the straw stuck from her lips. "What?"

"Let's dance."

Maya tossed her hands. "No. Absolutely not. I don't dance."

"Why not?"

"Because I may look like a graceful ballerina, but let me tell you, I am not. I've got two left feet and ten right toes."

A sly grin spread on Remi. "I call bullshit. Someone who handles bottles the way you do, I bet is *very* in tune with her body."

The salted-sugar tone cut through any self-doubt. Remi could ask her to skydive off the Space Needle right now and she'd agree. Maya interlaced her fingers with Remi's and followed her to the dance floor, through the swarm of flickering lights and gyrating bodies. The music pulsed beneath her toes, a club beat with bass thumping so hard she felt it in her chest. After several moments—but not nearly as long as she expected —Maya's body turned fluid.

Holy cannoli, Remi had moves. She danced the way she acted off the floor—smooth, confident, completely sure of herself. Just daring people to mess with her—and taunting Maya to not fall for her. A few elbows, legs, and various body parts nudged into Maya.

Remi brought her mouth to Maya's ear. "Over there, closer to the wall."

Something about the magic of a vibrating dark club combined with the way her heart swelled for the last few weeks, Maya would've followed Remi into a cyclone. The DJ dropped heavy, thumping beats and her body swayed. Her fists pounded the air along with the pulsation in the room. She closed her eyes, the music so thick, so soothing, she lost herself. She was in a sea of sweaty bodies and expensive cologne, surrounded by people kissing on the dance floor and music that made her feel alive.

Each beat lifted her and ascended her into heaven. Damn, it felt good. Remi was bouncing, unchained. *Hot as fuck*. The crowds packed in, a human love buffet, everyone celebrating joy and love. Gender didn't matter. Identities were only a piece of who you were, not the entire part of you. The theme was love.

The waves continued, the electric music seamlessly morphing '80s pop with current pop, and her brain couldn't handle the sensations. She floated, dazzled by the lights and the endorphins. Remi looked like she was in a different world. Her black curls sprung as her beautiful full, feminine body bounced with each step.

Maya moved closer. She wanted Remi's energy to seize her, jump-start whatever dormant piece of her existed. She needed to let go, be free. To *live*. An inch closer, another inch. Her heart pounded, and she swiped her fingertips down Remi's arm and held her breath for Remi's reaction.

A sly smile appeared on Remi, and she didn't stop moving. Body heat filled the room like air waves, like if she squinted enough, she could see steam rise off people. Sweat glistened on the top of Remi's shoulders, and Maya salivated. Her hands ached to reach over and fill themselves with Remi. She brushed against Remi again, and her skin sizzled, electrified.

The music continued, and she faced the stage, taking in the

DJ and dancers. She felt Remi behind her. The meadowy, salty scent that she had woken up thinking of since the moment in the cooler reached and touched her nose. She inhaled and leaned back. For a moment, she refused to exhale, letting her ass meet Remi's front, and waited to see if she recoiled.

She didn't.

Remi's body pressed into hers, and the softest touch, a whisper of thumb, swiped down her hip. *My God*, that single touch was one of the sexiest things Maya had ever felt. Her knees buckled.

The heavy bass pounded at the same rate as her heart. She pushed herself further into Remi and waited for a hint of a hesitation. Fingertips pressed against her outer thigh, and shivers crept down her spine. She locked her fingers around Remi's and guided her hand up her leg, slow and steady—giving permission, asking for permission. She dropped her hand, and Remi's grip continued to glide higher. Remi rested a hand on Maya's waist, and Maya swore she would melt into the floor.

Was Remi having the same thoughts? Maya wanted this— wanted her—wanted nothing more than to take Remi's full body and strong hips and soft mouth into the bathroom and explore. She wanted to talk like they did last night, and not say a word, and stare at her, and feel her. Swaying and breathing, the music loud and rhythmic. The pulse on the floor matched the ones in her chest. A flattened hand against her stomach tugged her back, firm, strong. The heat of Remi's breath on Maya's neck, Remi's breasts pressing into her back, made Maya's knees crumble under the intensity.

Maya needed to see Remi's eyes—confirm they were thinking the same. She whipped around to look at Remi, and like Remi didn't want to lose the connection, she pulled Maya into her and pressed her thigh in between Maya's legs.

Maya's breath caught in her throat.

"Is this okay?" Remi whispered.

Maya could only nod as she fought against crumbling at the sensation and the urgency to create more friction. She locked eyes with Remi, the deep, dark eyes that gnawed at her soul. She saw the character, the spirit, *the heart*, underneath those eyes, and she wanted it all. The room no longer existed. The crowd didn't exist. The only thing with her was Remi and the music. Maya ran her fingertip across Remi's lower lip.

A delicate swipe of Remi's tongue against Maya's finger and her breath hitched. Maya trailed her moistened finger across Remi's lip and her heart pounded so hard that it reached her ears.

Remi clasped a hand behind Maya's neck and pulled her forward with her mouth parted but stopped before she made contact. Her eyes were so dark and wide, and the flickering club lights illuminated her thoughts, like she was asking, maybe pleading, for permission.

Maya closed the gap and *damn*. Remi's mouth was on hers. Firm, smooth lips. Confident, yet exploring. Maya wrapped her arms around Remi's neck, her heartbeat triangulating between her chest, ears, and head. She pushed the tip of her tongue into Remi's and wanted more. Remi's lips tasted like pomegranate lip balm and cherry lollipops, and her thighs clenched.

They were alone. The only people in this place who existed. Maya pulled back, her body weak with anticipation. She pressed her mouth against Remi's ear. "Want to go back to my place?"

EIGHTEEN

DRINK SPECIAL: RAINBOW COCKTAILS FILLED WITH SPARKLES

Remi couldn't concentrate on the road. Cars zoomed by at the same rate as Maya's hands zoomed up her thighs—simultaneously the best and worst car ride of her life. Twenty minutes ago, at the nightclub after Maya invited her back to her house, Remi was pretty sure she'd never flown off a dance floor that quickly. She'd run to say goodbye to Ben, tell Mama Butter Nips she'd talk to her later, and bolted out the door.

Remi parked the car, stumbled into Maya's house, and kicked off her shoes at the door. She reached behind and locked the door with one hand without removing her lips from Maya's. Her mouth was perfect, soft yet skilled, hungry. Maya reached for her like she was on fire and Remi was a hydrant.

The house was dark. Maya slapped at the wall until a flicker of light popped. "Oh my God, that's so bright."

Remi took a breath and scanned the room. "Your mom and Harper didn't come back home, right?"

Maya shook her head. "No. I mean, I would know... ugh, now I'm paranoid. Hold. Do not move. I'm serious. I'll check." She dashed down the hall.

Holy hell. What an evening. She brushed her thumb

against her lip that throbbed in the best way possible and tasted like lime and mint from Maya's mouth. Her lips, her scent... *dammit*, if it wasn't everything Remi thought it would be.

Too many seconds passed, and Remi's body calmed, and her head raced. As her heart slowed, she glanced around the room. She was in Maya's *family* home. And she was pretty sure they verged on doing exactly what she'd wanted to do since day one. But their conversation, their time together... Maya knew everything. Maya knew *her*. Sex had always been separate from conversation and intimacy. If Remi had one, it meant the other didn't exist. Those worlds didn't collide. And now everything barreled on a collision course, and Remi knew what it would mean if they slept together. And she wasn't braced for the heartache aftermath.

"We're good." Maya leaned against the wall, barefoot. Her fingers tugged at her dress, her *effing dress* that Remi ached to know what was under. She stepped toward her. Shy shades of pink swept Maya's cheeks and Remi paused. She wanted this. *Of course* she wanted this. But *this* was more than what she thought. Her mind flashed to Violet—the closest she had to *this* —which was still not the same. Maya knew pieces of her she'd never shared with anyone.

Remi focused on the floor and inhaled.

"Oh no." Maya put a hand on her arm. "Are we good?"

Remi nodded. "Yeah, for sure. I'm just... I don't know." Jesus, what was she doing? She was in this home, with a smart, incredible, talented woman, and Remi got performance anxiety? This was her lane. Sure, it'd been a while since she last slept with someone, but never once had thoughts impeded the bedroom.

"You in your head?" Maya flopped on the couch and rested her chin in her hands.

Remi officially killed the buzz. She slumped next to her.

"Me too." Maya's voice was gentle, and the tigress who'd unleashed at the club and in the car vanished.

So many words piped through Remi. But if she said them out loud, then she'd be exposed. Sex and feelings and communication were new, uncharted, uncomfortable territory. *Dammit.* Maya might not feel the same. Maybe oversharing last night made Remi trauma-bond to Maya, and she was confusing those signals. Did Maya go to bed thinking of her the way Remi thought of her? Or make excuses to see her? Did Maya picture Remi in a house, sitting in *their* living room, making breakfast in *their* kitchen? Probably not.

Remi might just be a friend Maya wanted to fuck, and Remi had to decide if getting laid by someone who was more than a friend to her was worth it. As she clenched her thighs and tried to breathe away the arousal, the answer was probably no. Tonight, she had the cover of a nightclub and atmosphere and music and couples dancing around them in a love fest, and that cover was blown. They were back to reality, in Maya's house, surrounded by family items and cushy couches and oversized pillows. And Christ, this sucked so hard, but maintaining a friendship was too important to ruin with sex.

Remi eased off the couch. "I should go." Never had words felt like sandpaper tearing across her throat in all her life.

Maya's wide, confused eyes dashed across Remi's face. "Go?"

Stay strong. Ben had been her family for so many years. Her person. But spending time with Maya, understanding her, was too real, and her friendship too valuable. She nodded and took a step back.

Maya sucked in a breath and blew it out. Her eyes narrowed, and she pointed to the couch. "Sit."

The couch collected Remi as her body followed the command before her mind caught up.

Maya's fingers tugged at her dress. Inch by inch, she hiked

up the fabric, showing glimpses of creamy, exposed thighs. She gripped Remi by the shoulder, straddled her body, and lowered herself into Remi's lap.

Remi's eyes were directly at Maya's breasts, and she closed them, not knowing where to look. Her hands grasped the couch cushion. Warm hands pressed against her cheeks and pulled her face up, as Maya's body lowered further into her lap. Remi opened her eyes and met Maya's.

"Do you really want to leave?" Maya's voice was commanding and soothing, and Remi wasn't sure she actually asked a question.

Even though Maya lowered herself, she didn't move as her gaze dashed between Remi's eyes.

Did Remi want to leave? *Hell no.* Everything in her being wanted to stay here forever, with Maya's warm vanilla scent filling her nose, and her body pressing against hers. She wanted to close her eyes and imagine what a life could be like, imagine what *this* could be like. "No. I don't want to leave."

Maya hovered her lips above Remi's until Maya's exhales were Remi's inhales. Remi's hand planted onto the couch, and she soaked in Maya's warm palms branding into her cheeks.

"Then why aren't you touching me?"

Maya's raspy whisper sent a shiver down Remi's spine, and she shoved her hand under her thighs to keep from picking Maya up and throwing her underneath her. Maya's expression was hard to decode, but she looked warm-faced, vulnerable, and filled with lust. "I can't," Remi whispered.

"Why?"

Because she knew what would happen if they did this. The one-night stands, the women at the bar, Violet, every other ex in the world, hadn't felt like this. Her heart was on the verge of exploding, her mind zipped with thoughts, and her body teetered between protection mode and hunger. This was the line, and if she crossed it, she knew what would happen. And she wasn't sure she could let her heart go there.

Maya dropped her hands from Remi's face and curled into Remi. "I'm not going anywhere. Even if I leave, I'm not going anywhere."

The words held the weight of a million anchors, and Remi felt Maya's message to her core. College, Minnesota, the bar, here, everything. Even if Maya left, she'd still be here. Even if everyone in Remi's life had left, she wouldn't abandon her. Yes, it was fast and sudden, and Maya'd only been in her life for a month, but nothing had ever felt so... stable.

No words formed in Remi's mouth. She wrapped her arms around Maya and squeezed. Time passed, maybe five minutes, maybe ten, where Maya's breaths warmed Remi's neck, her body filled Remi's lap.

Maya's lips pressed into Remi's neck, so softly that Remi swore Maya was telling her skin a secret. Remi lowered her arms to Maya's lower back and pulled her closer. Lips brushed Remi's neck, to behind her ear, to the crook between her collarbones. Tingles flew up and down Remi's flesh, reaching her toes and back up again. Her heart increased, a steady *thump, thump, thump* as Maya continued, grazing Remi's jawbone, her cheek, and hovering her mouth over Remi's.

Remi's skin flamed, every pore on fire. She shifted her head to meet Maya's mouth and froze. No lips touched. The only sound was jagged breaths and heartbeats, and soon Remi didn't know whose pulse was louder. The glow from the lamp made Maya's eyes glisten, a sea of jade and turquoise that Remi wanted to swim in, lose herself, forget her past, see her future.

Dropping her gaze to Maya's mouth, Remi knew what would happen if she moved. Did she want this? More than anything, she was almost sure. Her nervous system screamed, but her heart pushed back, fighting like an exhausted boxer in the ninth round. Remi closed the gap, her mouth meeting

Maya's. She parted Maya's lips open with her mouth and accepted Maya's exploring tongue. Maya's wrapped thighs tightened, and Remi slid her hands across her skin. "Is this okay?"

"Mmmm, yes," Maya murmured into her mouth, and slowly rotated her hips.

Gliding her palms across Maya's silky-satin skin, her resolve crumbled as her fingertips traveled. She slid higher, then hesitated as she reached Maya's upper thigh.

"Don't stop," Maya breathed into her ear.

Remi cupped her ass and pulled her firmer onto her lap. Oh God, her skin, her ass, her *everything* was soft, sweet, perfect.

Maya locked her hands behind Remi's neck. Her mouth moved from frantic to soft, swipes of her tongue pulsing between the sucking of her lips. "You don't like anything... you stop me..."

"Same," Remi said, through a heavy breath. "Tap me, pull back, anything, okay? We'll stop."

Remi kept one hand locked on Maya's ass and moved the other to Maya's head to expose her neck. She licked the salty, sweet skin and sucked on her earlobe as Maya moaned and pushed herself tighter into Remi. Every moan was a drug, feeding an addiction, and Remi would crave that sound for eternity. Her skin sparkled, her core clenched. She was almost trembling, and they hadn't even removed a single piece of clothing.

"You smell so good," Remi whispered as she twirled Maya's hair into a hold and traveled her mouth across Maya's nape.

Maya's hands flattened against Remi's waist and tugged. And tugged again. She looked down. "Freaking bodysuits."

Giggles filled the room.

"Wait! Hang on." Remi shifted Maya back, reached into her jeans, and unsnapped the bodysuit. The action wasn't sexy—she was sure of it—but Remi hardly cared at this moment. "At least they're snaps."

"Invented by someone with a vagina, thank God." Maya clasped on to the fabric and ripped off Remi's bodysuit. She threw the suit and the metal clasps hit the wall with a ping.

Maya leaned back and her eyes traveled from Remi's chest to mouth to eyes to chest again. "You're so beautiful, Remi."

Regular sweetness and higher-pitched tone swapped with musk and honey, and the sound alone made Remi shiver. Topless and exposed, Remi shifted between feeling vulnerable and sexy.

Maya's finger grazed the top of the black lace bra, then hovered. "Can I..." Maya pulled her lip between her teeth.

That sentence could've finished with anything, *literally anything*, and Remi would've agreed. "Oh, God yes. Everything, you can do everything."

"Same. I'm... I'm just so ready." Maya fisted Remi's hair and moved her mouth to meet hers.

Remi wanted to pinch herself, tell her this was a dream and not reality and to please not wake up. She returned the kiss and ran her flattened hands against Maya's legs, eating up the goose bumps erupting beneath her touch.

Maya cupped Remi's breast in her hand and waved her thumbs across her fabric-covered nipples. Even with the layer between their skin touching, Remi moaned and licked the side of Maya's neck.

She scooped Remi's breasts from under the bra, freeing them. "Seriously, I can't..."

Maya filled her hands, massaging, pinching, rubbing, until Remi nearly screamed. Remi's mouth fit against Maya's as she unbuttoned the halter on Maya's dress and tugged to lower. When Maya pulled back, Remi froze, not moving again until she got approval. "Is something wrong?"

"I'm not... as... full as you."

The crack in Maya's voice, like she was worried *she* was not enough, inadequate, anything less than utter perfection, made

Remi want to cry. She gently lowered the dress while scanning Maya's eyes, waiting for any hesitation. "You still okay? Can I keep doing this?"

Maya nodded. "Yes."

The dress dropped. Remi unclasped the pink lace bra and tossed it to the side. She was exquisite. "Maya. You are *perfect*."

The tension in Maya's body softened. Remi brought her lips to Maya's chest, kissing across her collarbone, the dip in her cleavage, around her breasts. She pulled a nipple into her mouth, her tongue exploring, relishing, savoring. Every internal sense moved. Her heart sang, her core clenched, her brain relaxed. She moved her tongue, mouth, sucking and filling herself as her moans matched Maya's, and the hip twirling turned to gyrating.

"Take off your pants," Maya commanded.

Holy shit. Remi's pulse spiked, and she had never shimmied out of anything so quickly. She kicked the jeans to the corner and scooted back on the couch.

Maya dropped her dress to the floor and swung herself back onto Remi's lap. Her chest rose and fell with heavy breaths, and her eyes locked with Remi's.

No words needed to be said. Maya's eyes said enough. Remi saw her future, a real future, making cookies in the kitchen, a rescue dog in the backyard, Friday movie nights with family and friends.

Maya licked Remi's lips, slowly, deliberately, before she leaned back, exposed and open. Maya reached down, cupped Remi into her hands, and latched her mouth onto Remi's nipple. The delicious pulling and suction, all nerve endings meeting in one place, and Remi nearly lost control. She pushed herself into the couch and lost all senses. Her hands couldn't focus, her mind couldn't focus, nothing could focus on anything but Maya's lips wrapped around her. She moved her hips against Maya's straddled legs, pleading for more friction. "Oh God, Maya, I can't..."

Maya's tongue danced in between her breasts, to the corner of her neck, to her earlobe. "You can't... what?" Teasing layered her tone, and if Maya wanted Remi to come on breast play alone, she was dangerously close. Remi needed this night to continue. She could not, under any circumstances, tap out early.

She lifted Maya's face to meet hers and devoured her mouth, gripped her back, held her bottom lip in her teeth for a split second as Maya moaned and stirred.

Pulling back, Maya pressed a hand into Remi's heart. "Your heart is pounding." She pushed Remi's hand into her own heart. "Just like mine."

"Yeah." Remi's breaths inflated her chest, and she paused. "But it's more than..." She struggled with the rest of the words and Maya kissed her fingertips.

"It's more for me, too."

Did this mean what Remi thought it meant? This was not about Maya's body, or a pending release. Tonight was about *them*, the connection, this stirring feeling like home and heaven collided, and Remi didn't know what to do with it all.

The couch was soft beneath her bare back, the mid-June evening warmer than normal and sweat beads gathered on her neck. Maya pulled Remi's hand up to her mouth. She kissed every fingertip, then every knuckle, then her palm. She rotated her wrists, kissed the inside, then the outside. Then Maya took Remi's index finger and licked it. Upside down, on the side, and she grinned, and *ohhh*, her smile made Remi's heart spring into her throat, and she nearly strangled on anticipation and want.

Maya guided Remi's index finger, down her neck, down her chest, past her belly button. She hovered Remi's finger over the waistband of her panties.

The motion was the sign, and encouragement, Remi

needed. She wanted to feel her. *Needed* to feel her. She tugged Maya's waistband and Maya lifted herself. Remi flipped her wrist upside down for a better angle and dipped her finger into Maya.

Maya crumbled against her shoulder. "Rem... yes..."

Remi pushed into her, gliding, her silkiness wrapping around her finger, and Remi nearly collapsed with the sensation. She moved, twirled, and pulsed to the dreamy motions.

"More," Maya whispered in Remi's ear, her voice heavy and wet. *Dreamy.*

Remi slipped in a second finger, her bare breasts pressing into Maya's as she steadied Maya against her. Maya's moans and whispers of *"don't stop"* as she circled and moved made Remi want to collapse. Being so close to Maya, touching her, feeling her, the sensation was so deep. She felt like she *knew* her. And as scary as it was, she also felt safe, secure, alive.

Maya rocked against Remi's touch, her hands losing all grip like they wanted to hold on to Remi but didn't have the strength. She tipped her body back, and Remi increased the motion. She added her thumb to Maya's outside and circled. Gliding in, gliding out, she was honored to know Maya on this level. "Oooh, Remi... I'm gonna..."

"Yes. Good. Do it." Power filled Remi, a hunger to watch Maya collapse in front of her, proud her fingertips carried the ability to coax these sounds from Maya.

Maya stopped in the middle and pulled herself away.

"Wait, are you okay?"

"Yes, yes. I just... I need..."

She hopped off the couch and dropped to her knees. Her breaths were heavy, and Remi felt Maya's heartbeat against her legs. Maya hooked her fingers on Remi's panties and paused. "Can I?"

Remi couldn't properly think or form words. "Yes... yes, oh my fu— yes."

Maya lowered Remi's garment to the side. Her tongue traveled, slow at first. Starting at Remi's knees. A calm swipe of the tongue followed by the rush of her knuckles routing their way up her leg. Higher and higher, Maya's mouth hiked. She scooped her hair to the side, and her moans matched Remi's.

Closer and closer, Maya's lips moved past the knee, past the upper thigh, closer, closer, and so close... there. A soft pink light engulfed Remi as she held Maya's hair. Maya's tongue swirled, her breath on her, her mouth vibrating on her core, tasting her. Remi had no air. She lay back, her body soft and tense, her core engaged and lax, her heart full. Sinking into the couch, she rotated against Maya's mouth heaven, her body turning lucid. She was in a dream, floating.

She was so close, but she couldn't do it. Maya needed to be first. From here on out, all she wanted to do was worship the shrine of Maya. She gently lifted Maya's face up towards her. "We need to move this to the bedroom."

Maya kissed her center and slid back. "Agreed."

NINETEEN

DRINK SPECIAL: COMPETITION COGNAC

Clap, clap, clap! Maya's ears perked at the impressive decibel of Gabriella's palms smacking together, and her equally impressive shrill whistle. She stepped back to protect her fragile organ that was about to crack if she stood closer. She snuck a peek at Remi, who, if she said so herself, had the same glow she did as last night—and this morning.

After Remi left Maya's house earlier today to rush home and get ready, Maya almost refused to shower to keep Remi's lingering scent on her skin. And a quick make-out session in the car a block away from the hotel where the bartending competition was being held only whetted Maya's hunger for more. She needed a little time to process everything that took place last night, from the nightclub to the couch... to the bedroom, shower, and bedroom again. Every part of her body ached with exhaustion in the most delicious way.

But she'd have to process later, because today was the annual Seattle Cocktail Wars charity event, and Gabriella was *not* in the mood as her frustrated claps and whistles sounded like she was herding cats. Sadly, Gabriella's attempts failed to compete with the coordinators with Secret Service–style earpieces hurrying to set up competition stations.

"Venid, venid, venid!"

Gabriella waved over a handful of her scattered, top-performing employees. Everyone halted their conversation and stood straight for the kitchen drill sergeant.

"No horse playing." Gabriella, who clearly came ready to compete with a rare black power suit and fresh blow-out, tossed a stern gaze to each employee. "Got it? Do not make me look bad. We're on camera today."

Maya glanced at Remi, who pulled in her lips and gave her an exaggerated wide eye. She stifled a giggle and cleared her throat. She looked back at Gabriella like she was a kid talking at the back of the class, about to get scolded by the teacher. Maya peeked at Remi again—she couldn't help it. Everything about last night was more than she ever expected. Amazing, hot, exciting. But also—*more*. A connection that she had never experienced. Her core blushed with emotion.

After Gabriella dismissed the group, Maya followed Remi to set up their station. "My God, she is *not* playing around today." She organized the bottles the same as Nueve's.

Remi glanced over her shoulder and stacked glasses. "She gets super tense every year, but this is the worst I've seen her. She must be feeling—"

"Niñas!" Gabriella screeched.

Damn. This was supposed to be a fun, festive event, and Gabriella looked more frazzled than during a Saturday night rush.

Gabriella stomped over to Maya and Remi and shoved her phone in the air. "Oh, I'm so angry, Dios mío. La diabla. Look! I know she does this to mess with me before this competition. You know what she did? I swear to... She stole my camarón recipe! First the flan and now mis camarónes!"

Remi studied the picture of a platter of shrimp. "A lot of people serve shrimp. We live in Seattle—"

"No, Remi-lita! No one serves with the avocado, cilantro, and serrano juice but me."

Her voice sounded like a crack of a whip, and her cheeks turned a fiery red. She paced, pivoted, and paced again with a deep scowl and stopped.

"If you two win, you get the weekend off. With pay. Plus tips."

Whoa. Gabriella must be serious about winning. Maya couldn't remember the last time she had a weekend off. Paid weekend? Never.

Remi nodded once. "Done."

Gabriella stomped away.

Maya waited until she turned the corner and she and Remi looked at each other and laughed. She wrapped an apron around herself, then picked up each bottle to confirm the weight. "A weekend off with pay sounds incredible."

The words hung in the air. After their night, she assumed Remi would want to hang out. But why should she assume that —because they slept together and bonded on the couch? Maybe Remi just wanted to relax or hang out with Ben. Maybe she didn't have this swirling sensation in her stomach that was so intense that she either wanted to scream or laugh or run a marathon. She could ask Remi what she was thinking. Or was that too pushy? Definitely too pushy. She exhaled and moved her eyes to the bottles, gently tossing each one to confirm her grip. After shoving napkins in the container, she felt Remi hook her pinkie finger around hers.

"I know exactly what I want to do this weekend if we win."

Remi's breathy whisper sent a tingle down Maya's spine, and she felt the heat of a blush roar through her cheeks. She put her mouth up to Remi's ear. "Me too."

Remi grinned and stared at Maya's lips for several seconds

too long. She shook her head and popped toppers into the bottles. "Did we decide on plan number one or two?"

What plan? The one where they denied anything in case Gabriella sniffed out any behavior, knowing damn well what happened last night was grounds for firing? Or the plan that Maya wanted to find any sort of open room and pull Remi on top of her or... "What plan is that?"

"You do quality, me quantity. You pull out the biggest flip shots while I make the drinks. Or plan two, we both focus on quantity."

"I was hoping this had something to do with finding a vacant room."

Remi set the bottle on the rack and raised an eyebrow. "Don't do this to me. You cannot distract me while we're competing. After, you can distract me for hours."

The blush from her cheeks now spread to every single other nerve ending in her body. "Fine, *okay*—no distractions. Honestly, anything that will get us the weekend off. Let's decide when they give us the official rules."

Maya focused on their station, testing gun pressure, checking the weight of the martini shakers, the size of the lemons, the order of the condiments. She moved around Remi seamlessly and watched the staff set up orange cones, velvet ropes, and white linen-topped tables. Folks from other bars set their stations, every glass clink, snappy voice, and chatter booming in the massive open ballroom.

A camera crew and producer from the news station wandered the space, spanning the camera across the room. The producer waved the crew toward Maya and Remi, and Maya swallowed hard.

"Excuse me," the man said, looking more at his clipboard than the women. "We're hoping to get a couple pre-shots before the competition starts of you both mixing some drinks."

"Sure." Remi tossed the towel on the table, with absolutely

no sense of nerves like she'd been on camera a million times before. "Anything special you'd like?"

Gabriella marched over, pressing her hands down her suit. "These are my two head bartenders at Nueve's, located downtown near Pike Place. Remi is the quickest in the business. Lightning speed. And Maya does a little something special—you're gonna want to keep your eyes on her."

Gabriella—God bless her, never wasting an opportunity to plug Nueve's.

The man nodded and made a note. "Great. We'll do a couple takes of each of you." He moved and directed the staff to swarm the bar area.

She wanted this weekend off. Needed this weekend off. And the nerves rarely kicked in like this. But having a camera shoved in her face made her feel like she underwent a lobotomy. She crossed her fingers they wouldn't ask for an interview.

"You're gonna do great." Remi kept her voice low. "Just pretend we're back at the bar filling orders, okay? The cameras don't exist. It's just us, got it?"

It was like Remi could read her thoughts. Her chest lifted, and she nodded. Maya flexed her fingers and waited for the producer to yell "action!"

At go time, Remi yanked the bottles so fast that Maya couldn't understand how she didn't break a sweat. She stacked shot glasses, filled the shaker, tossed ice, and drained the liquid in a blur.

When the producer turned the camera to Maya, she focused. She spun the martini shaker on her wrist and slammed it down on the mat. After juggling six lemons, she popped each off her forearm and caught with her other hand and lined them up on the counter. She mixed the drink, tossed straws in the glasses, and set them on the bar.

"This is amazing." The producer smiled and took off his

headphones. "Great shots, friends. We'll be filming throughout the day and might get a quote or two after the setup."

"Thanks, sounds good," Remi said. When they were out of earshot, she wiped a spot near Maya. "I've probably never told you this 'cause I suck at compliments. But you're really incredible. I'm sure you know that, but in case you didn't."

"You mean with juggling?"

A soft grin, followed by Remi's dimples. "With everything."

Every fiber tingled. The comment wasn't said with a sexy tone, or low whisper. Her voice was genuine and warm, and the urge to hug Remi filled Maya.

The screeching echo of microphone feedback jolted Maya from la-la land, and she focused on the stage.

"Hey, everyone! Oops. Haha. Is this thing on? Apparently, yes. Hi, hi. Welcome, thank you." A woman with shaky hands and an even shakier voice stood at the judges' podium. "Sorry about that unpleasant sound. Let's try this again. Hello. Welcome to the Tenth Annual Seattle Cocktail Wars! Such a fun opportunity for local bars and restaurants to share their skills, for fans to taste some incredible food and drink, and, of course, for us to raise some funds for epilepsy research. We'd like to thank so many of our generous donors, including George and Claire Northwood, who paid for this space for the tenth year in a row." She waved her arm across the ballroom and a round of applause followed. She flipped her page on the clipboard. "Let's go over the quick logistics. The doors open at noon, and we have sold out this year in record time! That means a thousand of your biggest fans will be here, watching the magic."

"A thousand?" Stickiness built in Maya's mouth.

"Don't worry." Remi leaned against the bar and crossed her arms. "Once you get in the groove, you won't notice. Plus, it's not like they'll stare only at us. There's like twenty other bars we're competing against."

Maya swiped her brow with her palm and felt fingertips graze hers.

"You got this. *We* got this, okay?"

Maya definitely did not have this. But she nodded anyway.

"This year we'll be scoring on speed, agility, and taste," the producer continued. "And for an exciting twist, we added originality as a metric. Many of you are probably thinking, what does this mean? Well, the judges wanted the ability to use some discretion in scoring based on some amazing things we've seen. We all remember the origami napkins from last year, am I right? This will be a five percent bonus attached to your scores. All right, let me go over the rules..."

The ballroom soon filled with the smell of food, competition, and music. Bystanders filed in, filling the space around the cloth-covered tables and bleacher-style seating. Staff scurried around carrying silver platters of cheese, crostinis, mini-ravioli, and gourmet grilled cheese sandwiches.

Maya folded and refolded a few towels at the edge of the bar. "Plan one."

Remi grabbed a towel and attached it to her belt. "Huh?"

"You stick with speed. I'll stick with the tricks." She grinned. "We're going to nail this."

Gabriella gathered the team. "Final pep talk. Don't screw this up. You are the best of the best. Make me proud or find a different job." She laughed and hugged each staff member.

Maya joined Remi in the corner to cheer on the waitstaff as the first event kicked off. "Come on! Yes! You're killing it!" she screamed as the servers ran figure-eight style between cones holding trays stacked with non-breakable wine glasses. Three judges positioned themselves at the end, one with a clipboard, one with an old-school timer wrapped around his neck, and one monitoring the other two.

"Time's up!" one judge yelled, and raced over with the ruler to measure the amount of spillage. The judges spoke in whispers, checked and rechecked measurements, and made notes.

Maya swallowed.

The following two hours flashed—a blur of tossed bottles, stacked shot glasses, flung fruit, and the thunderous booms of cheering. Maya pumped her muscles, increased her speed to max capacity, and downed glasses of water in between sessions. She swiped her brow as Remi threw her hair up into a rare bun. The sweat glistened from Remi's neck and Maya was almost too tired to notice the moist skin. *Almost.*

"Intermission!" the coordinator called into the microphone. "The staff will take a thirty-minute break. Please, everyone, look at ballroom two, where we have some fabulous silent auction items."

The crowd dispersed, and Gabriella hustled over with a large plate of food. "Eat." She pointed at the food and hurried away.

Maya popped a crostini in her mouth and chugged a glass of water.

Remi rubbed her shoulder and rotated her arm.

"You getting sore already?" Maya grinned and dipped her toast into hummus.

Remi narrowed her eyes and smirked. "I would've been fine had I not spent the night using every one of my muscles."

A blush skyrocketed to her cheeks. "Can we take a break in the backseat of your car?"

Remi opened her mouth but closed it when Gabriella approached.

"We are in the top three, niñas, with Oceana de Azul, and Pete's Steakhouse. Good. But not good enough. Step up the game. Maya, more flips. Remi, more speed."

Remi set down her water. "I'm going as fast as I can."

"A weekend off, Remi-lita." Gabriella tugged at her blazer.

"I'll step it up."

The next hour was a teamwork of agility and strength as Maya pushed her body and skill to the limits, flipping, tossing, and catching bottles behind her back. Her breath and body felt like she was on the last mile of a half-marathon where if she stopped, she'd collapse.

The final round. Remi fanned her face. She rolled her neck and bounced on her feet, then clapped her hands, hovering over the glasses. "Let's do this," she said from the corner of her mouth.

Maya wrung her sweating palms in the towel and tossed it to the side. She hadn't dropped a bottle in five years, and no way in hell would she do it now. The news crew chose her and Remi to film at this moment, and the camera was so close she could hear the buzz of electricity. Her head swirled, and her heartbeat kicked in her chest.

"Can you all take a step or two back?" Remi asked, her voice as authoritative as sweet.

Maya mouthed, *Thank you*, to Remi, exhaled, and flexed her fingers. She glanced at the board with the timer. The crowd chanted, "Ten, nine, eight, seven..." Her heart thumped in her ears and cut with the shrieking sound of a whistle. Five lemons circled and flew. She stabbed each airborne citrus with knives and lined them up on the counter. Tins catapulted into the air, gravity containing the liquid. Fruit and glasses danced against each other as her peripheral caught Remi's arms moving so fast Maya wasn't even convinced they were attached to her body. The sounds of her teammates cheering and a howling crowd buzzed around her until the deafening buzzer rang and she slammed down the glasses.

The waitstaff and Gabriella screamed and clapped, and she and Remi high-fived. She exhaled a jumbo-jet lung filled with air and gripped the edge of the bar as her smile stretched her cheeks.

"Damn. We did good. Even if we didn't win, we killed it." Remi tapped her water glass against Maya's.

"I had no idea you could go any faster."

"And I had no idea you could stab fruit like that. Remind me to never get in a dark alley with you." Remi pulled the straw between her lips. "Wait, on second thought..."

Maya laughed and glanced around, making sure no one could hear them. Thankfully, the chatter of the crowd drowned out their voices.

The judges huddled on the podium, multiple iPads and clipboards scattered on the table. They stood and Maya's chest gripped tighter. She and Remi did amazing. They busted their butts tonight. Gabriella beamed with pride. Remi's rosy face and red chest transformed back to white.

"Everyone, come, come." Gabriella waved in the staff. "So proud of you. You all did great. Whatever happens, I know you put your heart into this."

The coordinator approached the microphone, and Maya joined the staff in a circle. They squeezed hands and Gabriella looked like she stopped breathing.

"Thank you, everyone, for coming today. Such a fierce competition and fun afternoon. We appreciate all the guests who attended, and the staff who brought their skills to this event. We want to thank..."

Jesus, lady, come on! All Maya wanted to know was if she got the weekend off, and this woman was rattling off the list of sponsorships.

"With no more delays, it is time to announce the winner!"

Gabriella gripped Maya's hand, and a server linked his arm with hers. She shifted the weight between her feet and watched as Remi's mouth flatlined and stood frozen in the corner.

"And the winner is... Nueve's!"

Gabriella screamed, her gold bangles clanking against themselves as she clapped. She pulled Maya into a death grip hug and rocked.

Remi's ear-piercing whistle outbid everyone for airspace. Teammates joined Maya in jumping and yelling. Remi scooped her up in celebration and set her back down. Clapping deafened her ears as she hugged the other teammates. Her chest soared and her skin prickled, and she felt like she was a million feet tall.

The producer trotted over with the camera crew, a trail of cords and lights lagging them. He shoved a microphone into Maya's face. "Congratulations to Nueve's! You all pulled out no stops. Speed. Accuracy. A professional juggler. You performed brilliantly at the end to really combine what looks like your two skills. How long have you two worked together?"

Maya glanced at Remi and prayed that her surely rosy cheeks could be mistaken for celebration and not being called out how seamlessly she and Remi clicked. "Uh, almost a month."

"A month?" He dashed his gaze between her and Remi. "You two look like you've been a team for a lifetime. Gabriella, you must be proud of your staff."

Gabriella put her hands on her cheeks, her breath labored and smile wide. "We're a family at Nueve's. La familia. My kids here did me proud."

"How does victory taste?" the producer asked.

"Like un dulce." Gabriella chuckled.

The producer yelled, "Cut!" and the camera team packed up. He jotted down a few notes and tapped his pen against the notebook. "In about twenty minutes, we'd like to interview you. The history of your restaurant and recipes, a bit about your background, those types of things."

"Yes, absolutely." Gabriella beamed and waved as he walked away. She turned to Maya and Remi. "I make good on my promises. Go, go, go. Don't come back until Wednesday for your shifts. Mis niñas. Good job. You two can leave. The other staff will clean. Consider your vacation starting this second."

Vacation! Maya's heartbeat kicked up a notch, and she fought back the urge to do a pirouette on the way to grab her purse. If she didn't rush out of the building, she might implode on the spot.

Remi had already grabbed her keys and wallet before Maya took a step. She jutted her head to the door and Maya affirmed with her eyes and a lift of a smile. Swarms of voices, crews taking down tables, teams cleaning their stations surrounded her as she weaved through the crowd. She maintained a treacherous several feet distance from Remi. Could anyone tell that her insides were ready to burst through her pores and land flat on the ballroom floor?

"Great job!"

"You guys were incredible. We're gonna come see you soon."

"Nueve's in the house!"

Voices merged. Maya nodded and smiled and hoped to God no one would stop them for a conversation. She bounced through the crowd, following Remi, who bulldozed through with a smile and nods of thanks.

At the elevator, Maya shoved her hands in her pockets and stared at the buttons like she was studying an exam. She shot a glance at a silent Remi, who looked as awkward as she felt, her arms rigid and fingers tapping against her thigh.

Inside, she stared at the ceiling until the doors shut.

Like a force, Remi gripped Maya behind the neck and pressed her lips against hers. The frenetic energy made Maya's legs tremble, but Remi held her, steadied her with her hand. She gripped Remi's waist, cupped her ass, and her pulse thickened.

Ding!

"Damn," Remi murmured. She stood straight.

Maya forgot every word in the English language. She tiptoed next to Remi, trying to catch her breath. The fresh, warm, summer-scented air hit her, and she squeezed Remi's arm. "I can't believe we did it!"

Remi glanced over her shoulder and quickly kissed her hand as they made their way to the car. "We nailed it. Seriously. And you are phenomenal."

"Me? Jesus, I had no idea you could move that fast. It was like watching some sort of superhero movie. I just saw a blur." Maya slid into her seat and unclenched her stomach. What a day. She'd experienced adrenaline before, the rush of pushing herself to the limit for an outcome. But until now, it was typically scholastic-related. She didn't realize the same rush of getting an A on a final existed with the possibility of spending some time with someone special. She tucked her hair behind her ears and blew out a heavy breath. Once Remi pulled out of the parking lot, she stroked her knee.

Remi brushed her thumb across Maya's skin and exhaled.

Maya dug out her buzzing purse with Sophie's name flashing across the screen. "Scrappy!" She giggled into her phone. "You should've seen us. Remi and I knocked it out of the damn park."

"Well hello to you, too," Sophie said with a smile in her voice. "I'm surprised you picked up. I didn't think you'd be done with the competition so soon."

"Then why did you call me?"

"A girl's gotta try, right?" Sophie laughed. "You'll never guess who I just ran into on the ferry today. Don't even try to guess. Mr. Olson!"

"What? Shut up. Our old math teacher?" Mr. Olson was the only human alive who could make math cool. She remembered actually lining up with other kids to join his math club freshman year.

"Yep. And get this. Same purple polka-dotted bowtie as he had in high school."

The visual cracked Maya up. "Did he have an alligator logo on his chest?"

"Ha! You know it."

Maya glanced at Remi, who now had both hands on the steering wheel, a flatlined mouth, and her body stiffer than it was a minute ago. She wasn't even sure when Remi dropped her hand, but her skin felt cool without the presence of her touch. She reached back and put her hand on Remi's knee. "Hey, I've gotta run. I'm in the car with Remi."

Sophie coughed. "When do I get to meet her?"

"Soon. I promise. Luvs."

"Luvs, too."

She clicked off the phone. "Sorry about that. Sophie normally texts, so I just wanted to make sure everything was okay."

Remi stopped at a red light. "All good?"

"Yeah, just childhood memory stuff."

Remi lifted a brow and nodded. She pulled back into traffic and slowed for a merging bus. "So... five days off. Beautiful weekend. Got any plans?"

Maya knew what she wanted to do since the moment Gabriella dangled this fermented weekend-off carrot. But she was unsure if Remi would want what she wanted. She nibbled on the corner of her pinkie, then dropped it in her hand. "I'm a little nervous, honestly, to ask because I don't want you to feel obligated. We haven't even really talked about last night, and if you don't want to..."

A slow grin spread. Remi dropped her hand to cover Maya's. "Whatever it is, I'm game."

Maya exhaled. "Good. Then, I have an idea."

TWENTY

DRINK SPECIAL: SPIKED SIGNATURE SALTWATER

Remi flew into her apartment. She leaned against the door and inhaled. She needed to slow her heart, slow her mind, slow freaking everything, and just process the last twenty-four hours. Maya's house. The competition. *Maya's suggestion for the next several days.*

Admittedly, she thought Maya would say they should have a clothing-optional weekend filled with takeout food and sex after winning the bartending competition. So, when she said, "How would you like to go camping with my mom and Harper in Port Townsend," Remi clammed up. She didn't respond for a what seemed a million minutes until Maya apologized about moving too fast, and Remi wanted to kick herself for making Maya feel self-conscious.

She pushed herself from the door and stumbled into the shower. The scorching water washed away the sweat from the competition, and the nerves from the upcoming weekend. Camping—with a family. A *real* family. Her mind flashed to several places, some dark, some light, some scary. After feeling what she felt last night, a connection she'd never experienced with anyone where she trembled for nearly an hour after Maya fell asleep, pulling into the family-fast lane was as terrifying as enticing.

And yes, camping with Maya's family wasn't naked marathon sessions, but it sounded, although obviously differently, almost as fun. S'mores, campfire, and beachy sand... years had passed since she'd enjoyed any of those things. After drying off and getting dressed, she packed a duffel bag.

Her phone rang, and her heart leaped. On the screen showed Ken, Home Loan Officer. Her heart dropped.

"Hey there, Remi. Just checking in. I saw the U District house came up for sale. I hope you don't mind, but I made a few phone calls. They won't look at any offers for at least two weeks, so you have a bit of breathing room. I already have all your information, so once you get that bonus you mentioned to bulk up your deposit, I'll expedite the pre-approval letter for you."

This phone call should make her jump up and down, not twist her stomach.

"You're still interested in the property, yes?"

She swallowed. "Ah... no, yes, I mean, thanks for the heads-up. I... um... should find out about the bonus soon, and I'll let you know." After hanging up, she pushed her thumbs into her forehead and stared at the wall.

The house had seemed like everything she needed. *Before.* This fairy-tale, three-bedroom entity that held the brass skeleton key to happiness behind its brick walls and original hardwood floors. The place that would give her the closure and stability she craved, and the beginning she needed. House don't leave people—people leave houses. The comfort in that reality ran deep.

And sure, she wanted to get out of her hellhole apartment with its funky carpet smells and random 2:00 a.m. banging noises that were either an old radiator, or the ghosts of past residents. But at what cost?

What if the house wasn't the answer to her problems. What if she needed more than just a structure?

She wrapped her hair on top of her head and fanned the stickiness off her neck with a book. After downing two glasses of water, she dug into a box of crackers to settle the sickly sensation. Her phone buzzed against the countertop. She clapped the crumbs from her hand and read the message.

> Maya: Here's a question. What type of underwear do I wear? I know we just, "~you know~", so I want to keep it sexy. However, we'll be sleeping in a cold tent and cotton ones feel better.

Remi grinned. She walked down the hall and flopped onto her bed.

> Remi: you could wear old man boxers and still be the sexiest woman alive

The blushing emoji followed by a peach emoji sent an energy spike through Remi. She tapped her hand against the bed, willing the time to move faster. The front door banged shut and keys clanked against the counter.

"Rem?" Ben called as his footsteps thumped down the hall.

"In here!"

He knocked once on the door and poked his head inside. "I'm tired AF. Stayed up way too late last night. Work was hyped. One of the pregnant nurses went into pre-term labor. Can you believe it?" He gripped the top of the doorway and stretched. "Tell me I'm still sexy, even with bags under my eyes and sweat seeping through my scrubs." He pulled off his shirt and dropped down to his boxer briefs.

She rolled her eyes. "Is it weird that I'm not fazed by you stripping off your clothes to have a conversation?"

He bunched up the scrubs into a ball and tossed them down

the hall toward his room. "How did the charity thing go today? Was Gabriella all up your ass, or not too bad?"

"Nah, she was good. We won. Gave me the weekend off—with pay."

"Damn, she must be super happy." He tugged off his socks and added them to the discarded clothes pile. "So, you and Maya rushed off last night. And I didn't hear your chainsaw-style snoring last night, which means..."

God dang her smile. She shoved the pillow over her face and screamed. A half-naked Ben ripped off the pillow and hovered with wide eyes.

"You better spill every single glorious detail. I'm dead serious. Shy and timid? She as flexible as she looks? Any light spanking involved?"

She pushed his arm with a chuckle. "I'm not telling you shit, dude."

He poked her shoulder. "Come on, you're killing me. One tiny little morsel to get me through this dry spell."

"You really want to picture me doing it?"

He shuddered. "Okay, fair point."

She laid her arm on her forehead, stared at the ceiling, and sighed.

"Whoa. You like her. Like you really, *really* like her." He grabbed a robe from her closet and wrapped it around himself. "Slide over."

"You're totally washing that." She scooted over. He lay next to her, and a faint smell of antiseptic wafted to her nose. The water spot on her ceiling drew her in, and she thought about how much that spot intrigued her for years. The first year here, she convinced herself the ceiling would collapse when she was sleeping. After that fear wore off, she'd try to figure out where it came from—did something shoot from her room back in the day, or leak from above? Odd how something that freaked her out at first ended up bringing her so much comfort.

He crossed his arms and tapped his fingers on his biceps. "She seems pretty great."

She sighed. "She *is* great. I just..."

He shifted to his side. "Oh no. Your voice is way too soft for just getting a paid weekend off. What's going on?"

She couldn't articulate every thought because she couldn't grasp herself how all this... stuff... happened after only knowing someone a short time. But yet, her mind filled with images of talking on Maya's couch, Maya wrapping her arm after falling, the way she was with her mom and sister, and the love of her dad. "I told her everything."

She glanced up at Ben's furrowed brow.

"What do you mean... everything?"

She stared back at the water spot and cracked her thumb knuckle. "Like everything, everything. The foster homes, meeting you, Darius, my parents."

He stayed motionless. "Damn. You never even told Violet that stuff, right?"

She shook her head. "And she shared stuff, too, and God, it's just a lot. Like it's intense but also super comfortable. Does that even make sense? And last night..." She wiped the grin off her face. "Don't even ask. You get no details. But it was different, you know? Like more, I don't even know—"

"Intimate?" he asked, softly.

"Yeah." *Oof*, that word was hard to hear and even harder to admit. Intimacy—true intimacy—opened the door for the type of heartache she wasn't sure she could endure. She spent a lifetime protecting herself from loss. Armoring herself and braving this new world made her want to bury her head under the covers. "Honestly, I don't know what to do. She's leaving at the end of the summer to go back to Minnesota, and all I'm doing is setting myself up for an ass-kicking, right?"

He plucked at the fuzzies on the robe. "I don't know. I mean, she's going there for her master's, right? So, if she buckles down, she'll be out of there in eighteen months. Maybe she'll come home for holidays and breaks. I don't think it's a deal-breaker."

Maybe it was, maybe it wasn't. "I'm kinda freaked out."

"I get that." He shimmied down on the bed and pressed his head against her shoulders. "You've had a lot of change in your life and not a lot of foundation. It's probably pretty normal to feel janky about this whole situation."

She scratched at the blanket and inhaled. "I wasn't freaked out with Violet, or the other women."

"Of course you weren't. Those were women you liked and had sex with. You weren't in love with them."

She bolted upright. "I never said I was in love with Maya."

"You didn't have to," he whispered. He rolled off the bed and adjusted the robe on his shoulders. "You deserve to be happy, Rem. Never forget that."

God, sometimes he said things that nailed her directly in the heart. She wasn't convinced she didn't deserve happiness—she was a decent-enough person who tried not to be a complete asshole most days. But she wasn't sure happiness was in the cards for someone like her. Solitude equaled comfort. Expectation equaled heartbreak.

The phone buzzed on her nightstand, and she rolled over to read the message.

> Maya: I'll be ready in less than an hour. Last chance to back out of giving up your first paid vacation to hang with an annoying sister, overbearing mom, and me. Speak now, or forever hold your peace.

Her heart filled. Nothing existed she wanted to do more.

> Remi: Your words don't scare me. Leaving now.

TWENTY-ONE

DRINK SPECIAL: BURNT CAMPFIRE BOURBON
WITH A TRIPLE SHOT OF FAMILY TIME

The city of Port Townsend was exactly as Remi remembered. A small-town feel shaken and stirred with a historic coastal city, with sweeping, beautiful views of the Pacific Ocean. As a cranky thirteen-year-old, she probably didn't appreciate the scenery. But driving to the campsite with Maya's head resting on her shoulder, bare feet on the dash, and the smell of salt and greenery streaming through the windows, hit differently.

Fort Worden, an old military base turned historic park, welcomed Remi and Maya. Large captain quarters and bunkers turned into cabins, lush green yards, and a lighthouse overlooking the ocean. The sun had lowered already, a tiny sliver of the remaining golden-magenta sunset slicing through the horizon. Remi navigated the car down the windy road to the camping area, her stomach flipping as they approached the site.

Maya stretched her arms against the roof. "My mom is really excited to get to know you a little better. I just hope she doesn't chase you around the fire asking a gazillion invasive questions."

Remi slammed her hand over her mouth. "Oh, my God! Your mom. Gabriella. Does she know she can't say anything to her? How the hell did I seriously just think of this now? We've officially broken every single one of Gabriella's policies."

"Multiple times," Maya said with a husk to her voice.

She chortled, then her chest grew hot. Her stomach tightened and twisted, and she lost track of where she was driving. "I'm serious, Maya. My job is really important. I can't... we have to figure out a way to tell her or something. I don't know. She just can't find out from your mom."

Maya gripped her knee. "Hey. We're good. I told my mom. And yes, of course she loves Gabriella, but my mom would lay down for her family. She promised she wouldn't say a word."

Slowly, Remi's stomach unclenched, and she drove past campers gathered around campfires. She followed Maya's direction to the eastern end of the campground.

Maya wrapped her hair in a bun. "I feel like we need a code word in case it gets to be too much being here with Harper and my mom. What about 'mayday'?"

"Hmm. Mayday feels wrong, since we are at a former military base." Remi pulled down another tiny road and passed a couple swinging in a hammock. "What about 'pineapple'?"

"Why is everyone's safe word a pineapple? Where did that term even start?"

Remi giggled. "Wait, do you have a safe word? Have you done... that?"

"There's lots of things I've done," Maya said with a sly grin and ran her hand up Remi's thigh.

She would never, ever get sick of the flock of tingles. "You're killing me. I'm seriously turning this car around and finding an empty spot for us to take advantage of."

Maya bit the corner of her lip. "Aren't you tired from... ahem... earlier."

Remi lifted her brow. "I will never tire."

The tires crunched over gravel. She eased down the path to a waving Harper and Laney standing by a fire and a small pop-up camper. Remi hopped out, the rich scent of salted ocean water engulfing her nose. Harper rushed over, her floppy blond ponytail bouncing, wearing an oversized sweatshirt that said IT's URANUS. NOT YOUR ANUS. GROW UP.

And the case was officially closed—Harper was the coolest kid on the planet.

"Remi!" Harper wrapped her arms around Remi's waist. "I can't believe you actually came. Mom said you guys were gonna come down, but I didn't think you would. It's going to be super clear tonight. We should walk down by the water and look at the stars. Mars will be out, but sometimes it's hard to know if it's Mars or a satellite. Oh! There's a chance for northern lights, but honestly, I don't think that we'll be able to see them from here. Maybe if we go to a higher altitude—"

"Harper, let Remi breathe." Laney wiped her hands on a towel, then embraced Remi. "Hi there. You guys made good time. Light traffic?"

Remi melted into the hug. "Not too bad once we got out of Seattle."

"Perfect. Harper and I set up a small tent for you two." Laney pointed.

A tiny two-sleeper tent rested on the edge of the lot. "Nice, thanks. I thought we'd have to do that in the dark." She rubbed her hands together. "Thanks for letting me come down. I'm really excited to spend some time with you two."

"Seriously, you guys? I'm right freaking here." Maya raised her arms.

Laney laughed and scooped in Maya. "Yes, my love, we are very happy to see you, too." She kissed Maya's temple. "Harper and I were just about to roast hot dogs and banana boats. You two hungry? Thirsty?"

Remi tossed her bag over her shoulder. "What's a banana boat?"

"Best things ever." Harper bounced on her feet. "It's a

banana that you gut like a fish, stuff with marshmallows and M&Ms, wrap in foil, and put on the fire."

"Oh, that sounds really good. But the whole gut like a fish thing sounds off. Should I be worried?" Remi kicked a rock out of the way as she followed Harper to the tent.

"Nah." Harper grabbed a light from the picnic table. "Be back in a bit. Going to the bathroom."

The sound of the trunk slamming sounded behind her. Maya walked towards her, tugging a sweatshirt over her head. It was just a sweatshirt and leggings, but Remi was sure she'd never seen anything so beautiful in her life.

After digging out their sleeping bags and pillows and shoving them in the tent, Remi followed Maya to the fire. The crackle of twigs and burning-wood scent drifted, and Remi's shoulders relaxed. She watched Harper climb on top of the picnic table, lie on her back, and cock her head at the sky.

Laney motioned to a chair set around the fire. "You must be hungry. Do you eat hot dogs? We also have lots of fruit and veggies, some macaroni salad from the grocery store. Chips?"

Remi sunk into the canvas-wrapped seat. Laney's love language was clearly food, and Remi didn't know until now how good it felt to have someone so worried about her caloric intake. "Man, I might start demanding these kinds of options. Seriously, so generous. Hot dogs are perfect."

Laney ripped open the package and added a hot dog to the metal stick. "The true test. What do you take with your hot dog? Ketchup, mustard, or relish?"

Maya pulled her chair next to Remi. "Don't fall for this. It's a trick question. And if you get it wrong, she'll never let you live it down."

Remi's gaze flashed between Maya and Laney. "None, of course. I take it with cream cheese and fried onions."

"Oh, that's my girl." Laney clasped her hand on her chest.

Every part of Remi filled with something warm and

wonderful. Laney handed Remi the stick, and she stuck it into the flames. The breeze from the water made her shiver, and before she rotated the hot dog, Laney wrapped a blanket around her shoulders.

"Maya said you guys won the competition?" Laney passed Remi the cream cheese and a plastic knife. "Gabriella talked about this event before. She gets a little—"

"Over-the-top?" Maya said, as she reached into a bag of kettle popcorn. "Amped to the nth degree? Possibly possessed by some sort of supernatural bartender creature who feasts on the souls of young children?"

"*Passionate*, Maya. She gets passionate." Laney wrinkled her brows. "How was it having the news station there?"

"That was bizarre," Remi said, keeping an eye on her simmering dinner. "I honestly don't know how reality stars live with cameras in their faces."

Maya cracked open a soda. "I thought you were going to punch the one camera guy in the throat during the close-up shot."

Remi chuckled. "I mean, I would've... but this was a timed competition, so..."

"When are they doing the segment?" Laney added a bun to a plate and set it next to Remi.

"Probably in the next few days. I think they're going to Nueve's for some internal shots." The hot dog sizzled against the flame and Remi's mouth watered. "We'll have to check it out when we get back. Maya and I made a no-cellphone-and-internet pact while we're up here."

Maya pulled the basket of branches next to her and tossed twigs into the fire. Like she was in another world, her face looked soft and unaffected as the glow from the fire highlighted her hair. If they weren't sitting in front of her mom, Remi would've scooped Maya into her arms and kissed those delicious lips.

The hot dog popped and burst. Remi wrapped it in the bun and sunk her teeth into the food. The salty burst of flavor in her mouth almost made her moan, and she scarfed it down in record time.

After multiple downed s'mores, sticky fingers, and Harper's explanation of constellations, Remi felt like she could happily live in this campground. The faint sounds of zipping tents, lapping water, and country music from a different campsite funneled in the air, and with a full belly and sunken chair, Remi's eyelids were heavy. And her heart, full.

Maya yawned and stretched. "I think I'm going to head to bed."

"Me too." Remi collapsed the chair and set it under the camper awning.

"Do you girls have everything you need? Bug spray, extra blankets, flashlights?" Laney asked while adding the pop cans to recycling.

"Yep, we're good." Maya dumped food scraps into the compost bin and snapped it closed.

Harper hopped over to Remi, fisted her hands, and air jabbed. "Hey, do you think we can do some boxing while you're here? Practice a little bit?"

Ambitious. Harper might be a lightweight champion of the year someday. Remi grinned and ducked under the jabs. "Yeah, we can totally do that if that's okay with your mom."

Maya wrapped her arm around Harper and gave her a hip bump. "Don't you have, I don't know, like a planet to discover or something?"

"Ugh. So rude." Harper scrunched her face. She skipped to Laney, who dumped a bucket of water at the fire.

At the tent, Maya unzipped it and crawled in. Remi did not feel bad for one second for checking out her ass in the moonlight's glimmer. She zipped up the tent and helped spread out the sleeping bags and blankets. Maya lay down, pulled Remi on top of her, and brought her mouth to hers.

Remi sunk lower onto her, Maya's mouth an intoxicating combination of marshmallow flavor and firmness. "Your mom! Harper. They're like right outside," she whispered, and kissed the slope of her neck. "We shouldn't do this until we get back to Seattle."

"If you think there's any chance I'm waiting five days, you're insane." Maya glided her fingertips down Remi's back-side and gripped her ass. With herculean strength, she hooked her leg underneath Remi's and flipped her flat on her back.

Her breath caught in her throat. "Oh, damn. That's hot."

Maya tugged up Remi's shirt. She swiped her tongue across Remi's lips, moved to her collarbone, and grazed her fingertip down her belly.

A fleshy trail of protruding goose bumps formed down Remi's arm and up her neck, and her stomach quivered under the sensation. Her pulse thudded in her chest and reached her ears as she moved in hushed whispers and swirled underneath Maya's touch. Gripping her hips, Remi pulled her in tighter to her body, needing to feel Maya's weight on her body.

"Maya!" Harper's voice and the sound of cracking twigs under feet advanced on the tent. "Do you guys want to go into town with us in the morning? Mom said we need a couple of things."

Remi froze and dropped her hands.

Maya collapsed onto her in a fit of giggles. "God, she's a cockblock."

"Terrible, terrible thing to say about your sister."

"I think we're going to sleep in tomorrow. Thanks anyway," Maya called out.

Remi tugged down her shirt and tried to lower her heart rate. She rested her arm across Maya's pillow.

Maya snuggled into Remi's chest and intertwined her legs with Remi's. "I love this so much."

"Pretzel legs?"

"Pretzel legs? This?" She wiggled her toes against Remi's calves. "Yes, I love that. But I mean, all this. The air. Family, food. Time with you."

Remi pulled her against her and kissed her forehead. "Hey, what did you tell your mom about us?"

Maya pulled the blankets up to her chin, and lay on Remi's chest. "I told her the truth."

"Which is?"

She put her mouth up to Remi's ear. "I told her you were my woman."

Remi's insides heated, and she kissed Maya on the top of her head. Her body was tired, but her brain shot multiple messages and she couldn't sleep. Once Maya's breathing turned heavy and her body stilled, Remi unraveled herself and slipped out of the tent. She tiptoed to the car and grabbed her phone from the glove box. After leaning back to confirm Maya hadn't emerged from the tent, she powered on the cell.

With shaky thumbs, she typed an overdue message.

TWENTY-TWO

DRINK SPECIAL: EVERYTHING IS PERFECT
PEACH MARTINI

"Hurry up, Maya! Pretty sure Grandma could beat you by now. Seriously, you walk like you're stuck in taffy or something." Harper, aka Devil Child, yelled from the bottom of the hill. "You know this is *downhill*, right?"

"You know you are not too old for a spanking, right?" Maya glared but couldn't hold back her grin as she caught her breath and took Remi's hand to guide her down the slope.

The last four days had flown by in a blur of campfires, s'mores, cribbage games, and hikes. Maya and Remi explored the forest, the beach, and each other. After her mom and Harper went to sleep, she and Remi talked every night around the campfire, each detail inching her closer to Remi's soul. She thought she knew everything about Remi, and each night something new popped up. Like how Remi could legit carry one hell of a tune, after she made some side comment about paying for rent one month with earnings from a karaoke contest. Maya forced her to belt out Fleetwood Mac's "Silver Springs" and she was sure the campground turned silent to listen to the sugar rasp in her falsetto.

At night when they connected, every muffled moan, every

time she tasted Remi, every sensation of when she slipped inside of her, they grew closer. Remi whispered to her, feeding her, filling her, and Maya bit into a pillow to not wake up the neighborhood. They played charades by the fire, skipped rocks, and lay on the beach at night with Harper as she pointed out Orion and the Big Dipper.

"Careful." Remi clasped firm hands around Maya's waist and steered her down the slope.

Maya would melt forever under that touch. She sat down on a washed-up tree trunk and stuck her tongue out at Harper's irritated face. "I'm taking a break. You two go look for your glass."

"Cool!" Harper grabbed Remi's hand and dragged her several yards to a pile of rocks that had washed ashore.

Truth was, she wasn't tired. But she didn't know how much her heart would soar watching Remi interact with her family. A few nights ago, Laney showed Remi how to make homemade burgers. After, Laney and Remi took a long walk. Maya teared at the sight of her mom strolling with Remi as she kept her hands in her pockets and casually kicked a few pebbles while they walked. Within a minute, Remi laughed from deep in her belly, no doubt at some painfully embarrassing childhood memory of Maya. And Maya felt her soul fill.

Maya heard Remi laugh more than she ever thought possible, especially while playing terrible games of frisbee. She still couldn't understand how Remi—who was so athletic—could miss nearly every single catch like she had ghost-hands.

The salted air fanned Maya's face, and a honking shipping barge sounded faintly in the background. She bunched her sweatshirt under her bottom, repositioned herself on the log, and closed her eyes, begging her brain not to lose any of the memories from this magical week.

Yesterday, she took Remi into town, and strolled hand-in-hand to admire the art galleries and independent bookstores.

After dragging Remi away from a senior dog rescue event, she kissed Remi as she choked up talking about a sweet golden lab at foster home number four. Remi vowed that when she got a house with a yard, her first order of business was to adopt a dog.

In the afternoons, Remi trained Harper like Mickey trained Rocky—within the confines of what a twelve-year-old diabetic child could handle. While they were ducking and jabbing and doing whatever boxers do, Maya and her mom bonded.

Last night after dinner, Maya stayed back as Remi and Harper looked for sea glass. Maya confessed to her mom about her father, and her conflicting feelings about being in Minnesota vs Seattle.

And then she broke down and told her mom about the phone call she made to Gabriella right before Remi picked her up on Thursday.

Her mom had stared at her with wide eyes and no words.

"Do you think I made the wrong decision?" she had asked, while focusing her gaze on the towel and not on her mother. She cared what her mom thought, of course, but she'd make the same decision again in a second.

Laney had waited several moments before she spoke. "I think you followed your heart. And if that's what your heart told you to do, then you'll never be wrong. What did Gabriella say?"

"She didn't answer, which was probably for the best."

Her mother had squeezed her shoulder and pulled her in for a much-needed hug.

"Hey, you good?" Remi's voice jolted her from her thoughts.

Maya entwined her arms around Remi's. She stood from the log and gave her a kiss. "Yep. Sorry. What were you saying?"

"Ewww. You two are really gross. Anyway, we were *saying* that I want to go where I found the purple sea glass yesterday. So, *come on.*" Harper's sandals flapped against the sand as she tore down the beach.

A soft roll of waves and a few squawking seagulls were the only sounds on the nearly isolated beach. She held Remi's arm, rested her head on her shoulder, and watched as Harper raked her fingers against the sand, digging up pebbles.

Remi leaned back on her flattened palms. The sunlight ricocheted off the deep-amber highlights imbedded against her dark curls. She dug her feet into the ground and funneled the sand through her toes. "It's so beautiful here. I'm thinking of quitting Nueve's and living here out of a tent."

Maya sifted through the ground, looking for sea glass. "We're here on a beautiful weekend in June. No chance you'd say that in February."

"Good call." She glanced at a crouched-over Harper running her palm across the earth. "I need to seriously consider taking more day trips on my days off this summer."

The rhythmic wave sounds lowered Maya's heart rate and her eyes felt heavy. Her life looked so different from when she moved home, and she needed to sit with the changes for a while. Her heart had awakened in a way that she didn't know existed. "How did you ever become a bartender?"

Remi crossed her legs. "Life is strange. My obsession with this profession all began when this dude I hated started bartending in Belltown. He'd talk about all the tips he'd get, that his female co-workers couldn't keep up, that he was the hottest piece in the place, you know the drill. A total jackwad. I craved to crush the cocky spirit in him, so I looked for bartending gigs to beat him."

Nothing about this confession surprised Maya. "You definitely like a challenge, huh?"

"True." Remi threw a stick into the water, her eyes following it as it floated away. "But something happened. The bar became like a home, and Gabriella became like family. She said she saw potential in me, and it just felt good, you know? And the more skilled I got, the better I felt. After a lifetime of doing things wrong, I got hooked on the profession."

Maya's gut sunk with the hint of sadness laced in Remi's tone. Remi was a survivor. But these brief comments, *doing things wrong*, or *they couldn't handle me*, stacked upon each other, had to weigh her down. She pulled Remi's hand into hers and traced her palm.

"Blue!" Harper waved, sand flipping up beneath her feet as she ran towards them. "Holy crap, look how big this is!" She dropped the glass into Maya's hand.

Maya held it to the sun, the light beaming through the translucent cobalt jewel. "Nice, Harps. Those are almost as rare as the purple ones."

Harper snatched it back and rubbed the glass between her moistened fingers. "What if this was part of a shipwreck and the spirit of the boat captain imbedded into the glass and will haunt us forever? You know, there's some seriously fascinating discoveries on paranormal stuff."

Maya nudged Harper with her toe. "You're so morbid."

"What are you going to do with all this sea glass?" Remi asked.

Harper shrugged. "I was thinking of making a mosaic of the Milky Way and using the sea glass as stars."

"Great idea." Maya tugged at her arm. "You almost done here? All this fresh air has made me hungry."

"Nope. Byeeee." Harper pivoted with a hip shimmy and sprinted down the beach.

Remi scooted down and rested her head in Maya's lap.

Maya lightly ran her fingers through her hair—but not enough to ruin the curls as Remi spelled out the treachery of high-maintenance curl care.

"You hit the human jackpot with your family." Remi curled her legs and grasped Maya's thigh. "Do you ever take them for granted?"

Years spent mourning her father, and padding her heart against further devastation, pulled her away from her mom and Harper. "I want to say no. Especially with my dad and everything, I valued them. But honestly, being back has given me a fresh perspective. In my mind, I always have *one more thing*. One more class. After midterms, I'll call more. After spring break when work isn't so intense, I'll FaceTime longer. But I never did."

The breeze picked up and sprayed salted air. She licked her lips and planted a kiss on Remi. She didn't want to go back to reality tomorrow, slinging drinks, or chatting with anyone but her family and Remi. Grabbing a flannel blanket, pillows, and not leaving the beach until the elements evicted them sounded like a better plan.

Time was inconsequential. Touches were euphoric. She swiped her fingers across Remi's jawline, her forehead, down her cheeks, across her eyebrows. She wanted to absorb her through her skin, memorize every tiny freckle, every bump, the smooth, plump lips. Her chest lifted and lowered. With each inhale, she thanked the universe for bringing Remi into her life. With each exhale, she pushed away the fear of loss.

Harper cheered from down the beach at what was surely a new treasure. Sand and rocks flew in a tunnel behind her, reminiscent of a dog digging for a bone.

Remi lifted from Maya's lap and glanced down at the beach.

Her face grew serious, a crumpled brow and frowned lips. Maya couldn't read what was happening behind her eyes. "What are you thinking about?"

Remi gnawed on the corner of her lip and drew her legs to her chest. "It's hard to describe. Being here with you and your family, it feels so surreal. It's like I'm watching a 3-D movie about what life *should* be like, and I'm a participant. I don't know."

Facing Remi, she leaned in. "Wait, do you not feel welcome?"

She waved her hand and gave a soft smile. "Are you kidding? Your mom's amazing. She brings a divided tray for fruit slices while camping for God's sake. She could not be more welcoming." Her smile faded, and she tapped at the sand. "It's just..."

The tone in Remi's voice made her pause. She cupped her cheeks and searched her eyes, but it was useless to interrupt. "What is it?"

Remi's gaze fell, and she released a shaky breath. "It's scary to dream, you know?"

She didn't need to say anything else. Maya knew what she meant. Family. Love. Life. She wrapped Remi in her arms, held her against her chest, and kissed the top of her curls. With Harper in the distance, and the surrounding waves, Maya put her mouth up to Remi's ear. "I love you."

Remi's head snapped back, her gaze dashing back and forth at record speed. Maya could interpret this look—with every twitch of Remi's brow, Maya could see her fear and joy and nerves flash across her face.

Like she was holding her breath, Remi's chest lifted and stopped. "What did you say?"

Time on earth was a scarce, unpredictable resource, and she refused to waste it any longer. Pushing through the skipped heartbeats, clenched stomach, and the voice inside her head that warned her she might scare off Remi, Maya squeezed Remi's hand. "I. Love. You."

TWENTY-THREE

DRINK SPECIAL: BACK TO REALITY RUM WITH BITTER SHOT

The drive back to Seattle felt duller than the drive to Port Townsend. Spending five days in a magical world that Remi didn't know existed released a lifetime of tension and made her feel fulfilled and alive. Heading into the city, the increased traffic and high-rise condos broke the spell and shifted her back into reality mode.

But... Maya loves me.

When Maya first said it, Remi was sure she misheard. She leaned in, needed her to repeat it, and still didn't believe her ears. She had frozen for a good several seconds before softly pressing her lips against Maya, swiping Maya's cheeks with her thumbs, and saying, "I love you, too."

And when Remi said it back, she meant it—*hell yes, she meant it*—but the words didn't flow from the tongue. Her heart had skipped and soared. Yet, the familiar, threatening thoughts crawled up like some love zombie, warning her to not get too comfortable. Because everything felt so good. *Too good.*

And Remi was not accustomed to good.

But then Maya said it again, and again. And Remi said it back. She had to keep saying it, twenty times, thirty times more that day. Every syllable chipped away at the demon, striking down the fear that this wasn't real, that this somehow wasn't deserved.

Remi had only seven weeks left with Maya in town, and she didn't want to think about losing her. She'd use this time to love the hell out of her and figure out the next steps. Yes, Violet left. Yes, her parents left. But Maya was different. Right? *This* was different.

The blinker clicked and she pulled into Maya's block, yawning against her hand. "Why is it I've never had five days off in a row, and now all I want is more?" She killed the engine and shifted to Maya. "I'm legit depressed about going back to work tomorrow."

Maya stretched, her cheeks rosy and soft bags under her eyes. She leaned her head on the seat. "Same." She tugged Remi's hand to her lap. "I had the best week of my life."

"Me too." She leaned over for a kiss and unlocked the door. "Come on. I'll help you unpack."

"Ugh." Maya groaned and removed her seatbelt. "We have so much stuff. Want to do laundry here?"

Remi lifted her brows. "You mean as opposed to walking my hamper next door to the mat by my apartment? That sounds like another vacay."

After gathering sleeping bags, pillows, and dirty clothes, Remi dragged herself up the stairs and yawned into the blankets. The home engulfed her with that same feeling that she could never quite place. A mash-up of a hollowness being filled with a trickle of nerves.

Everything could be taken away in a snap.

Maya tossed the bags on the bed. "We ready to turn on our phones yet?"

Remi shook her head. "Nope. Nothing good can come from it. I already have Ben's number programmed so he could bypass my notifications. Other than that, I don't care."

Maya laughed. "Same with Sophie."

A slight ping with the sound of Sophie's name dug at Remi. It wasn't jealousy—she knew that feeling well, snarling insides and her gut hardening at the sound of someone else's name. She'd experienced it to a debilitating degree with Violet and refused to be that person again. No, this feeling was different. A bit of intrigue, sadness, and curiosity about this person who Maya loved so much. "I'd like to meet Sophie sometime. What do you think?"

"Oh God, she'd love that. We were just talking about arranging something soon. Maybe we can do a lunch before work one day this week. You're gonna love her."

Remi swallowed and started the washer. "Do you think the news show played the episode about the competition?"

Maya shoved the sleeping bags into the hall closet. "Maybe? We should check. I'll grab my laptop."

"Damn, you're really sticking to that no-phone thing, huh?" Remi laughed and lay in Maya's bed, unable to not think of the naughty things they'd done in this room.

Maya dug the computer from her closet and lay shoulder to shoulder with Remi. She hooked her leg around Remi's. "Pretzel legs." She grinned and tapped at the screen. She scrolled through the site and stopped on the article. "Yes! Ready?"

She hit Play.

The video panned the inside of the ballroom as people assembled mini-bars and loaded stacks of liquor, and a newscaster came into focus. "We are here at the Tenth Annual Seattle Cocktail Wars. Nearly a thousand people have lined up to see local bartenders and servers compete against each other..." The camera moved to the crowd outside and resumed to show a flash of the ballroom.

"Look!" Maya pointed to the screen. "Gabriella's in the background."

"We spoke to the coordinator for the event," the journalist continued, "who said an afternoon like this is expected to raise close to three hundred thousand dollars for epilepsy research with a silent auction, specialty cocktails, food, and a fierce competition between the best of the best of the greater Seattle hospitality industry."

The video panned to Remi and Maya, and Remi's body tensed.

Maya paused the show. "Oh my God, they're like right in your face!"

"Jesus. Why do I look so pissed? Is that how I always look?"

"Um..." Maya laughed. "That's your concentration look."

Remi leaned in closer to the screen and groaned. "It literally looks like I'm going to stab someone in the eyeball. I think I need to soften my face."

"I love your face." Maya kissed her on the nose and resumed.

The video showed a long shot of the area and snippets of servers running between orange cones holding trays above their heads, as the journalist narrated. "Nueve's pulled out a surprise and delight with a secret weapon, Maya Marek, who performs flair bartending."

Remi paused the show, unable to hold back how freaking kick-ass Maya looked spinning bottles and stabbing the knife into airborne lemons. "Is that the term?"

"I just call it flipping stuff." She laughed. "Ugh, it's seriously hard to watch yourself on film." The episode continued as Maya paused and pointed out the other bartenders. "Poor Gabriella. She looks like she's embalmed. She's so stiff!"

Remi nodded. "Pretty sure she didn't blink until the event was over."

The video panned back to the anchor. "The competition was intense, narrow, and heated, with less spilled drinks or broken glasses than we thought possible. After a speed and agility round, it came down to the final three, and Nueve's won."

The camera panned again with the winner being announced and closed in on Nueve's team cheering. Remi's chest lifted, the feeling of victory still fresh. The waitstaff yelled and jumped in the chaotic shot, and Remi skimmed the video for her and Maya. On the side of the screen, Remi watched herself pick up Maya and spin her around as Maya grabbed her for a kiss.

Maya sucked a breath. "Oh fu—"

"Oh my God." Remi moved her hand over her mouth. "We kissed? I don't even remember—"

"I don't either." Maya stopped the video and stared at Remi with wide eyes. "It happened so fast and... there was so much cheering and screaming and—"

"And it wasn't like a *kiss* kiss." Remi's neck flamed. "It was a celebration kiss." Her timid voice killed her attempted confidence. She scratched at the side of her neck.

Maya sat up and chewed on her cheek. She replayed the video, scrolling in and out, and finally exhaled. "We're in the corner of the screen. If Gabriella watched this, she might not have seen us. Right?"

Remi's mouth was tacky as the jovial feeling from a few minutes ago crashed. *Gabriella notices everything.* She leaped from the bed and guzzled back half a bottle of water and wiped her mouth with her hand.

Maya's eyes squeezed together, and she put her fist against her forehead.

"Okay, this is salvageable." Remi prayed Maya couldn't hear the shakiness in her voice. She'd figure something out, talk to Gabriella, put the heat on her. "You know, we were in the moment, celebrating. She might not have even noticed."

Maya released a breath. "She's not going to fire us for sharing a quick kiss—that we don't even remember. Right?"

Remi stroked Maya's arm and lifted the corner of her lip. "She's unreasonable but not *that* unreasonable." She pulled Maya against her and kissed her head. "After this, we need to be really, really careful with everything."

"Okay." Maya pressed her lips against Remi. When she pulled back, she grabbed her phone and dangled it in the air. "All right, I'm going in. Firing up the phone."

Remi dug hers from the backpack. Since she knew Ben was okay, the only thing waiting for her might be automatic billing notifications, or a message from a sparring partner.

Multiple messages appeared. Darius letting her know he made it to Portland and wanted to FaceTime her and Ben soon to tell them about someone he'd met at a show. A few messages from a couple of co-workers talking about covering a shift. A notification of an auto-deduction for her car insurance. *Gabriella.*

A group message to her and Maya.

Maya's pale face and blotchy neck looked the way Remi felt.

> Gabriella: Maya and Remi. Both of you report to work an hour before shift. We have a very serious matter to discuss.

"She... used our names," Remi whispered.

Maya put her hand against her chest and lowered herself onto the bed. "What are we going to say?"

That I fell in love and acted a fool and loved it and didn't love it, and I'll take whatever punishment and to leave Maya out of this, and secretly please don't punish me because the idea of not having this job guts me. Or something along those lines. "Exactly what we said. We got caught up in the moment and didn't even remember it happening."

Maya bit the corner of her pinkie, then sat on her hand.

"What if she asks us if there's something going on? I hate lying to her."

Remi tugged Maya's hand from under her legs and kissed her knuckles. "I know you do. But I got you, okay? We'll be careful from here on out."

Maya nodded. "We just need to hang on until the fall."

Remi's stomach knotted. *Fall.* The dirtiest of dirty words, and she had no place for them in her life. "I don't even want to think about it."

Maya crawled into Remi's lap and pressed her hands against Remi's cheeks. Her crystal blue eyes seemed to search hers as they dashed back and forth. "No more talking, okay?" She kissed Remi slow, deep, deliberate. Her tongue swiped against her mouth, her warm body pressed up against her chest.

Tonight, Remi didn't want to do anything but feel Maya against her. Tomorrow, she'd face the consequences.

TWENTY-FOUR

DRINK SPECIAL: CONSEQUENCE COCKTAIL
WITH A WHAT THE HELL MIX

Maya stepped out of Remi's car a block away from work. She was being extra cautious, perhaps paranoid, but she didn't want it to look suspicious if someone saw her and Remi pull into Nueve's parking lot together. Which might actually look suspicious because she'd driven her before. So now it probably looked *super suspicious*, and everything was suspicious, and gah! She straightened her back and marched through the kitchen.

The familiar clanking of pans and fried food scent lingered in the air as she made her way to the locker next to Remi. "Have you seen her?"

Remi shoved her bag in the locker and glanced over her shoulder. "No, not yet. I think we'll be good. A slap on the wrist at most."

How was Remi so calm? Last night something switched in her, and she acted like it was no big deal. Remi had even more to lose than Maya, and she brushed it off like they did a minor infraction. Both knew Gabriella's strict policy, including immediate termination. Granted, they only shared a quick kiss, but Maya couldn't lie. *Wouldn't* lie. She swallowed back a metallic taste. "I'm overthinking this. We were in the background of the shot, which was even a little fuzzy." She followed Remi into the office. "She probably didn't notice."

Oh God. She noticed.

Maya stared at a scowling Gabriella and her cheeks burned. She peeked at Remi, who looked totally unfazed. She sat, confident and casual, on a chair with almost a disinterested look. But Maya could see the back corner of her jaw clench and a small line of white around her neck veins.

If something were to happen, she'd storm out of here, take full blame, and quit. She'd have to think, fast, but maybe she could get hired somewhere else for the rest of summer or return to the Minnesota bar.

"Sit." Gabriella pointed to the chair.

Oh no. No *sentémonos* or *venid* or *niñas*. Sit—in English— with a very sharp tongue.

Maya contemplated bolting under the desk earthquake-drill style, closing her eyes, and covering her ears.

Gabriella's heels pounded the hardwood floor with heavy stomps. She sat down, hard, and leveled her shoulders. She stared, unmoving, unbreathing, for one hundred million seconds before she exhaled. "Well, you two have put me into a hell of a position."

Remi cleared her throat. "Gabriella, this is on me, I—"

"Silencio, Remi." She snapped.

Literally snapped her fingers.

Gabriella dropped her hand. "This is on both of you."

Remi pulled in her lips.

Maya stopped breathing. Remi could not take the fall for their actions. She was the one who planted a fat kiss on her in the first place. She lowered her head under Gabriella's fire-stare. "No, it's not. This was all me."

Gabriella clicked her nails against the desk. "When I hired Maya to join the team, I knew she'd be great. I figured it would light a fire under you, Remi, which it did. And I figured Maya would draw in some folks, which she did. It only took a few days, and the bumps worked out and our sales have never been higher. You two should be proud."

Okay?

She slammed her arms across her chest, pink returning to her cheeks. "Do you not trust me as your leader? Do you not trust me to run my business the way *I* see fit, the way *I* decide?"

Maya dashed a glance at Remi, whose creased brow and squinted eyes looked as confused as she felt.

Remi tilted her head. "What do you mean? Of course we trust you."

"And I don't think you two were in..." She waved her hands like she was grasping at a floating word. "Cahoots together. So now I need to figure out what the hell to do."

Cahoots? Did Gabriella mean to say that word? Was there a Spanish word similar to one which meant *sleeping together while betraying the rules, her trust, and causing a potential toxic workplace environment*? "Can we just explain?"

Gabriella slammed her hands down.

Apparently, no, she couldn't explain.

"I've owned this place for nearly twenty years and have earned the right to make the decisions *my* way." Her heavy rings clacked against the desk, and she aggressively tapped the wood. "Maya, what would your mother think? And, Remi, what are you thinking? I'm both so angry with you two and proud of you, which makes me so goddamn... muy furioso!"

Maya's head spun. Honestly, Gabriella's reaction was over the top. What would her mom think? Why was she proud? None of this made sense. They shared a quick celebration kiss. That was it. End of story.

Remi looked at her from the corner of her eyes. She opened and closed her mouth, then leaned back on the chair. "Is this about what happened at the charity event?"

Gabriella flinched and soon her eyebrows squished together. "The charity event? Unless you cheated and I didn't know, no. This is nothing to do with the charity event."

So, this *wasn't* about the kiss? Maya was officially lost—in the wilderness, blindfolded, and wandering aimlessly. "I'm not understanding. What is this about?"

Gabriella pointed at her, then Remi. "This is about both of you having the... the... *gall* to disrespect my decisions."

Remi huffed. She tapped her foot against the floor and leaned back in the chair. "I'm seriously not tracking with a word you're saying. Can you just tell us what we did?"

Gabriella glared. "You two forfeiting your bonus so the other one could have it."

"What?!" Maya was sure she said this in unison with Remi. She slapped her hand over her mouth and looked at Remi. Her heart lifted with Remi's generosity and sank so quickly she was sure her pulse turned irregular. "You gave up the bonus? Remi, no."

Remi's face turned red, and her wide eyes quickly narrowed. "You forfeited? What the hell, Maya? Why would you do that?"

The sharp tone jolted Maya upright. "Me? Why would *you* do that?"

"Why would I do that?" Remi gripped the arm rest. "Are you serious right now? Why would you give up the money for tuition? You need it for—"

"Enough!" Gabriella smacked her palms together. "Why would both of you do that? Now I'm stuck here trying to figure this shit out. Both of you have put this back on me, rather than accepting the outcome and dealing with it like goddamn adults afterwards. You put this on me so neither of you would look like the bad guy, or the good guy, or whatever... Dios mío, whatever you're trying not to look like. And it's unfair. This was always my decision, and you have stripped that from me."

Maya slumped in her chair, her chest heating from the anger and disappointment in Gabriella's voice. She never intended to be disrespectful or take away her power. When she called and left a message for Gabriella last week before the camping trip, she cried after but only for a moment. Forfeiting was the right thing. Remi was a better bartender than her and deserved the money. She'd worked hard her whole damn life, and Maya refused to stand in the way of her dream. Listening to Remi talk about the original hardwood floors and '80s-style, cotton-candy pink bathroom house in the U District, and what it meant for her to have the stability she'd been chasing for a lifetime, made the decision easy.

At the same time, she wanted to collapse into Remi's arms, kiss her, and tell her she'd never had anyone be willing to give up their dreams for her. She wanted to scream how much she loved her, tell her that she needed—deserved—to have the home, and they would plow through this shitstorm together.

Remi curled her shoulders and exhaled. "So, now what?"

"Now? Now I don't know." Gabriella pressed her palms against her knees. "I have half a mind to take it away from both of you."

Remi leaped from the chair. "Wait, no!"

"You don't have a say anymore," Gabriella growled. "Both of you out until I calm down. Go!"

Maya fled from the office, the back of her eyes stinging with unreleased tears.

Remi jutted her head to the alley door.

The sound of the city muffled around them, as honking cars and weaving traffic muted in the distance. Once they stepped into the alley, Remi gripped her forearm. "What were you thinking?"

It was hard to place her tone. Defeated? Angry? Definitely not happy, for sure.

Maya stepped back, her gaze flashing between Remi's eyes. "Me? What about you?"

Remi sighed. "You need this for school."

"You need this for the house."

The brick building provided leverage for Remi as she rested her forehead against it, then pushed herself off. "Your school is more important. You can change lives."

"And you have the ability to change yours."

Remi shook her head and stared at the hovering clouds. "You deserve it more."

The sincerity in Remi's voice brought Maya's tears to the forefront. No one deserved it more than the other. Forfeiting was simply the right and fair thing to do. The bonus was Remi's chance for a better life. To get out of a crappy apartment that Maya still hadn't seen and give her a fighting chance at a new beginning. But Remi's flared nostrils and rigid fists didn't make sense. "Why are you mad?"

Remi clenched her jaw. "Because," she hissed through gritted teeth. "You shouldn't have done this for me. Stupid fucking decision, Maya."

Maya flinched like she'd been slapped.

"I'm an asshole. And you... you're this angel who gives and helps." She crossed her arms, her eyes darkening. "You did this out of pity, and I don't need your goddamn charity."

And now Maya felt like the slap upgraded to a dropkick. Her chin trembled. "This wasn't charity. Is mine from pity?"

Remi's sharp breaths slowed, and she lowered her head. "No, yours was out of love." She pivoted and stomped back to the bar.

Maya swiped a tear from her cheek. "Same," she whispered into the air.

TWENTY-FIVE

DRINK SPECIAL: CHIVALROUS CRAB APPLE-TINI WITH A BACKFIRED SHOT

The magic of working with Maya disappeared the moment Remi had stepped into Gabriella's office and faced her angry-mom look. The sickness from deceiving Gabriella collided with a gut-wrenching need to save Maya from herself, and she was left with nothing but a burning sensation in her gut.

Remi couldn't grasp why Maya would willingly give up her future, *just like that*. Maya had a chance to do something good with her life. Help her sister, help others. She carelessly tossed her future—a future that Remi couldn't even dream of—aside like it was garbage. Remi could never live with that guilt. She'd made a gazillion mistakes in her life, and she refused to add another to the bucket. The way her heart soared and ached in a weird confusing ball had her wanting to run out of this place.

The flirting, grazing of arms, everything that kept her sparking these last few weeks, dulled in a flash. She and Maya didn't speak for most of the night, and in between order lulls, Remi focused on buffing and shining anything with a non-porous surface.

"Taking a break to call Sophie," Maya muttered a few hours

into her shift. She returned fifteen minutes later with puffy eyes and her shoulders unusually curved.

Remi gripped the inside of her pockets to stop herself from scooping her up and comforting her. She'd have to talk to Maya soon, but she needed to wait until her body cooled so she didn't snap. Maybe she'd beg the owner to leave the gym doors open tonight and hit the bag until her mind cleared. Because right now, she was so in love with Maya she wanted to rip her heart from her chest, and she was so angry at the woman she loved so much for giving up something so substantial.

Gabriella seemed to have calmed down, as she chatted with customers with her customary cackling laugh. Orders filled and the waitstaff tore around while Remi rethought the way she shot Gabriella a jumbled text from the campground on her first night there with Maya, without giving her a chance to respond.

Thinking more, she probably should've been honest with Gabriella since day one. Her original issues with Maya, then falling for her. Gabriella gave her a chance when no one else did. She loved her. She respected her. And she let her down.

The night continued, and the realization of Maya's sacrifice burrowed into Remi. Maya gave up her tuition money, her dream, her school, for Remi. Her mind flashed to Maya wrapping her arm, her mouth on hers, holding her on the beach. The way Remi *almost* cried, and instead of being embarrassed, she felt loved when Maya held her. The blond hair grazing her naked chest as she lay, her legs pretzeling hers at night. How it took almost two full days to release the pinch in her neck when she slept on her couch, but she'd do it every night if it meant she could continue to feel this way forever.

Her arms ached from cleaning, and her fingers burned with sanitizing solution. Slowly, the anger lifted. Dammit, why did she lash out so hard? She dashed a glance at Maya, who was smiling at a customer without her eyes crinkling, and Remi's chest dropped. Maya was willing to walk away from the money for her. *For. Her.* And she all but screamed at her in the alley. What the hell was wrong with her?

How did she deserve to have someone like that in her life? She didn't.

But maybe she could do something to earn her.

She tossed the towel on the bar. "Taking a break."

Maya didn't look up but nodded, and greeted an approaching customer.

Shoulders pulled back and chin lifted, Remi marched through the kitchen and knocked on the office door.

"Pasa."

Thank God. Back to Spanish.

Remi filled her lungs, exhaled, and pushed open the door. Staring at Gabriella's blank face, her shoulders didn't feel as strong as they did a second ago, and she swallowed. "Can we talk?" She stepped into the office. "I'm really sorry. I shouldn't have put you in that position."

Gabriella softened her chest and waved for her to close the door.

A small trickle of bile gurgled behind her throat, and she coughed. She knew what she had to do, but damn, facing this head-on was harder than she thought. "You took a chance on me, in the beginning. Why?"

Gabriella raised her eyebrow. "That's a loaded question." She set down her pen and strummed her fingers against the ledger. "I saw a feisty spark in you. A fighter. You reminded me a bit of me."

Remi's face warmed. That might have been the best compliment of her life. "I did?"

"Yes, por supuesto, you did. You might be a little bit more..."

"Mean than you?"

A smile spread on Gabriella. "Not mean. You're not *mean*, Remi. You have such heart. I was going to say more *guarded* than me. And probably a bigger temper." She spun the rings on her fingers. "But you've mellowed out in your old age and seem to be in a better place. You changed, for the better. Whatever that caused that, I suggest you keep hanging on to it."

The air in the room turned stuffy, and Remi hooked her finger in her shirt collar to loosen. "That's, uh... That's the thing. I think I need to quit."

"No."

That was Gabriella's response. Quick, sharp, like she slapped at a pesky mosquito that landed on her arm.

Remi lowered herself to the chair and firmed her spine. "You've always been honest and upfront with me, and I haven't been truthful. I've been keeping something from you, and I didn't mean to, and um, I feel like it's not anyone's fault really—"

"Enough, Remi-lita." She held her hand up. "Is this about you and Maya being together?"

The stuffy room air now turned non-existent. "You knew?"

Gabriella rolled her eyes. "How dumb do you think I am? You two were gaga over each other the second you met."

Remi shook her head. "That's not true."

"That's one hundred percent true. Do you really think I didn't catch on? The looks between you two. The flirty... *ooh lalala...*" She swirled her hands. "Besides, I have security cameras all over this place. *Even in the cooler.*"

Oh God, the security cameras. The heat in her body catapulted to her cheeks, and if she didn't dive into the ice bin in the next two seconds, she'd liquify on the spot. "Wait, why do you have them in the cooler?"

"In case la diabla sneaks in here and steals more recipes." She chuckled and moved to the window. She peeked out the blinds, letting in a small flicker of light, then leaned against the edge. "I didn't hire Maya for you two to get together. But I'd be lying if I said it wasn't in the back of my mind."

Everything in the universe collided, and she squinted as the room blurred. Gabriella knew? Not only knew, but maybe even hoped for this? None of this made sense. "But this is against your policy."

"This is against my policy for idiots. You two are not idiots." She folded her arms across her chest. "Besides, it's my place and I can change the rules if I want."

Gabriella knew. Remi and Maya weren't losing their jobs. She breathed out the worry she'd been holding this entire time with Maya, the guilt of hiding, the fear of giving up the place she loved as her home. She was safe. *They* were safe. "About the money..."

Gabriella stiffed. "That decision is up to me. I'm still not happy. But also, so damn proud of you both."

"Understood." Remi stood and tugged on her shirt, her heart lifting. "Thank you for everything. I, you, this place, it means, well, you know..."

Gabriella pulled her in for a hug. Remi nearly collapsed against her rose scent and gold bangles scratching her back as Gabriella patted her.

"I'm proud of you, niña. You did good."

Remi returned to the front of the bar, her step so light she almost floated. She and Maya didn't need to hide, and their jobs were safe. No more dropping her off a block away. No more checking behind her back if someone was listening to them whisper. *No more hiding.* Yes, the bonus money was an issue, but she'd figure out something. Even if Gabriella gave her the cash, she could give it back to Maya, and Maya could do nothing to stop her.

The people in the back of the bar could probably see her smile. Her foot tapped against the floor as Maya filled an order. They'd still have to come up with some agreements. PDA was unprofessional, of course, so the idea of lifting her on the bar for a quick make-out session would have to stay as a fantasy. Once the server walked away, she refrained from sprinting to Maya.

"I'm so sorry for the way I acted. Legit getting all pissed like that was not cool. It just surprised me, and I didn't know how to process everything."

Maya tilted her head and exhaled. "Thank you." Her words were soft and timid. "We really need to talk more about this later, though. The money, the bonus. We just need to sit and figure out how to apologize properly to Gabriella and talk about how we reacted."

"Agreed. But I have something amazing to tell you." She leaned forward and put her mouth to her ear, the words tingling her tongue. "I told Gabriella about us."

Maya's head snapped so quickly, their cheeks almost smashed. "You did what?"

"She was seriously so cool!" Remi's heart pattered against her chest. "I can't wait to tell you all about it. She already knew! So damn perceptive, seriously. She said she could tell—"

"I can barely look at you right now," Maya said through clenched teeth.

Remi stepped back and stared at Maya's fiery gaze. Why wasn't she feeling the same sense of relief? She heard her, right? They were *clear*. Good. Great, even. She reached for Maya's hand and her belly sunk when Maya ripped her arm away. "Why are you mad? This is awesome, right? We don't have to hide."

Maya glanced behind her shoulder and clenched her jaw. "Did you ever once consider you should have asked me first? What if she didn't know and fired us on the spot?"

Shit. Getting them fired never crossed her mind. She went in, laser-focused on protecting Maya, and plowed through. She was prepared, ready even, to throw herself on the sword so Maya could keep her job. "I did this for us."

Maya whipped the towel from the bar and scrubbed a nonexistent spot on the cooler. "Without considering me."

Remi placed a gentle hand on hers. "You are *all* I considered."

A group of women approached the bar, and Maya turned her scowl into a smile. "Hey, ladies. Welcome. What can I get for you?"

Remi slumped to her side and stared at the pile of servers' ticket orders. She filled glasses of rum and pineapple, stacked shot glasses, and waved at a regular. And contemplated for the rest of the shift how she could make Maya see her side of the situation.

After the hostess locked the door and the last customer left, Remi stepped to Maya as she stocked the cooler. "Are we going to talk about this?"

Maya lowered the last bottle and broke down the cardboard. "No. Not now. I need some time to think."

Remi chewed the inside of her cheek. "I did this because I didn't want you to take the heat. You see that, right? If she blamed you, I was going to tell her I came on to you."

Maya tossed the recycled box to the corner and slammed the cooler. "I can't believe you made this level of decision for me, like I was incapable. Without even understanding the consequences. It was impulsive, and unfair."

Remi put her hand out to reach her but dropped it. "Maya, listen to me—"

"Stop talking. Please, not another word." She turned her back and yanked the toppers from the bottle.

The only other time she spoke to Remi was when she said she was taking the bus home.

Remi sat in her car and watched Maya at the bus stop until she was safely picked up. Then she rolled into traffic, the stinging behind her eyelids nearly reaching the surface.

TWENTY-SIX

DRINK SPECIAL: FEAR-BASED FRUIT COCKTAIL

Maya woke up groggy, thirsty, and almost sure that she had only a solid hour of actual sleep. She hugged her pillow and tried to distill her feelings methodically and appropriately so she could function as a human being at work tonight.

What Remi did was wrong—that was a fact. She made a decision for Maya, without consulting her. Not only a decision, but a major life decision, something that could've cost her job. Everything was out of order, out of place, and she hated not having control over this situation.

But... her heart filled that Remi was going to sacrifice her job for her—after already sacrificing her bonus. The sweetness behind the action wasn't lost on her, which made her feelings even more difficult. But still, it was not in her plan. And she lived by plans. For the first time since Gabriella brought them into the office, she had a taste of what Gabriella felt when she and Remi stripped her power. It felt awful.

She pulled the blankets up to her chest and flopped her arm over her eyes. She wanted Remi here to talk and hold her. But she also didn't want to see her. Maybe the anger was too much. She loved her—that didn't change. She wanted to be with her—

that also didn't change. But she needed to figure out how to navigate this situation of being so fiercely in love with her, while so intensely angry.

The smell of bacon and eggs filled the air. She stumbled out of bed and followed the savory trail into the kitchen. Harper sat at the kitchen table, her cheek resting in her palm as she played with the food on her plate.

"What's up, Stinks? How did it feel sleeping in a bed last night?" Maya pulled down a mug from the cupboard and filled it with coffee.

Harper yawned and stretched her arms above her head. "Good. I'm still tired, though."

"All that fresh air knocks people out." She added a dash of milk to her drink and bumped the fridge door shut with her hip. "Mom in the shower?"

"Yeah." Harper handed Maya a slice of bacon from her plate and rubbed her eyes with the back of her hand. "I told her I didn't want to go to summer camp today, but she's making me. It's seriously so unfair."

Maya chewed the salted breakfast. "You love summer camp. And it's only, what, like five hours from your day. It's not like you're sharing bunks with some rando."

"It's bullshit."

"Harper! If Mom heard your language, she'd be ticked. You know the house rules."

"Whatever. You're here for like a few weeks and all up in my business, like I'm a stupid kid who can't even think on their own. You don't even *know* me. The last time you even lived with me, I was watching *Sesame Street* with a blankie. Don't you have some studying or something to do?" Harper twirled the eggs on her fork, then pushed it to the side.

"*Jesus.*" Maya winced and her heart sunk. She breathed out the hurt. Being twelve sucked, and she remembered that age well. Hormones, crappy social situations, and teetering between kid and teenager was not fun. Today, she'd give Harper a pass. "Well, I'm glad I am back home now and learning all about how amazing you are."

Harper slumped her face into her hands. "I just need a chill day. Don't you ever have days that you just want to veg out and not talk to anyone?"

More relatable words had never been spoken. Maya understood the need to have quiet to regroup more than anyone. And Harper was probably feeling some of the post-vacation blues coming back from a week at the ocean. She scooped up Harper's barely eaten toast into the yolk and bit into it. "I totally get it. Sometimes people suck."

Another sleepy yawn escaped from Harper, and Maya involuntarily mimicked the motion. She finished breakfast, changed into workout clothes, and left the house, determined to get clarity on her run.

Later that afternoon, the bus dropped off Maya in front of Nueve's. The jog from earlier had helped clear up things. She texted and called Remi, but she didn't respond. She didn't appreciate Remi making this huge decision for her, but it came from a place of love. And that should be enough. *It was enough.* After a lifetime of hyper-control, following timelines, and striving for goals, it shocked her that someone took the reins. After their shift, she'd ask Remi to come over and they could talk everything out.

She tied the apron around her waist and moved to the bar.

Remi added lemons to the condiment container and made exactly zero reaction that she even knew Maya entered the space.

"Hey." Maya crept towards her with a shaky voice. "Let's talk after work, okay?"

A solid three seconds passed before Remi shrugged. "Whatever works." Without looking up, she ripped a napkin package open with one tear and stuffed the container.

Okay, maybe, *just maybe*, she deserved this reaction from the way she acted yesterday. But still... Remi had no right to take matters into her own hands the way she did and tell Gabriella about their relationship—no matter how chivalric she thought she was being.

Remi turned sharply to a couple of guys that took a seat on her side. "Hey, what can I get for you?"

Maya slunk back to her spot and prepped her station.

The following several hours had fewer customers than normal, which made each awkward, silent moment with Remi nearly unbearable. She wanted to talk to her, but they needed to fully flush out a conversation, not stop and start in between the smattering of orders. Maya spent downtime flipping through an old recipe book searching for a hidden drink gem, but the words blurred and she snapped the book shut. She peeked at Remi, who wiped each glass on the bar with a towel, held it to the light, and wiped again.

Maya sucked in a breath. "Are we good?"

Remi lowered the glass and narrowed her eyes. She set the mug down with a heavy hand and flung her wrists. "I don't know, Maya. Are we?"

A prick of white heat flashed up her neck. God, she was pissed. Or maybe hurt. Her voice wasn't angry. It sounded... nonchalant. Which was more terrifying than angry. Maya glanced around the bar to confirm no one was looking and put her hand on Remi's lower back. "We will be. We just need to talk, communicate, okay? I'm not going anywhere. Angry doesn't mean running."

Beneath her fingers, she swore she felt Remi's back relax. She'd never understand what it was like to be a child of abandonment. Yes, her father was gone. But that was a different situation than willingly leaving. She needed to reassure Remi that disagreeing, being angry, being livid even, didn't mean leaving.

Maya moved to the back of the bar for an inventory spot check. She grabbed a notepad and scribbled. *Two vodka, one gin, three white rum.* She moved to the next cabinet. *One pomegranate liqueur, one espresso liqueur, one—*

"Maya. Maya!"

Maya leaped at the shrill in the voice. *What the hell?* "Soph? What are you doing—"

"It's Harper," Sophie spit out in a raspy breath.

Every hair on Maya's arm and neck stood straight up. She threw the pen and pad on the bar and rushed to Sophie. "What happened?"

"Your mom tried calling you, she called me..." She held out her arm like she wanted to pull Maya over the bar. "She was frantic, in the ambulance—"

"The ambulance?" The room ceased to exist. Her heartbeat slammed against her ears.

Fingertips seized her arm. "Go."

Remi's commanding voice snapped her back to reality.

"I got this," Remi said. "Which hospital?"

"Pacific," Sophie said, stepping backwards.

Maya snatched her phone from the cabinet and nearly choked at the ten missed calls. She ran next to Sophie through the restaurant. "Where's your car?"

"Illegally parked out front." Sophie ripped the door open and flew out onto the sidewalk.

Maya strapped her seatbelt on and flung back as Sophie tore into the traffic, whipped an illegal U-turn, and floored the gas. She weaved in and out of traffic as Maya wiped her damp hands across her thighs. "What do you know?"

Sophie yanked the steering wheel down an alley, the car bouncing hard against the potholes. "Not a lot. Harper wasn't feeling well. Her blood sugar. Something happened at camp, and your mom got called. I couldn't understand everything."

Maya pressed her thumbs against her temples. "Oh, God... this morning. I saw it. She was tired, cranky, she gave me her breakfast..." How did she miss this? She was so wrapped up in her ridiculousness with Remi, she missed the classic textbook signs of irregular blood sugars—fatigue, discoloration, lack of appetite, irritability. Her cheeks burned. She cranked the air on max and pointed the vents at her face.

Sophie weaved between the carpool lane and fast lane, riding the cars in front of her, honking. "Do not blame yourself. Not now, not ever. She's gonna be fine." Her voice cracked.

Harper was Sophie's family, too.

The car lobbed over potholes on the exit. Sophie sped through a yellow light and slammed in front of the hospital door.

Maya sprinted through the emergency doors and bolted to the admissions station. If something happened to Harper, she'd never forgive herself.

TWENTY-SEVEN

DRINK SPECIAL: DARK-ROASTED SHOT WITH A TERROR TOP

Remi rang up customers in a haze of darkness, without smiling, without monitoring portions. She strained her neck for Gabriella, but being down to one bartender, the line was fierce and orders backed up. She powered on her cell, breaking Gabriella's firm no-phone policy on the floor, and shoved it in her pocket.

The clock showed Maya had left over thirty minutes ago. She rapidly tapped her foot against the floor, tossed a botched drink down the drain, and thought of Harper lying in a bed. Was she scared? Unconscious? Did she get in an accident, or something happen with her meds? Did she hit her head, or trip, or did an appendix burst? She pulled her phone out and checked for messages.

Dammit. Why did everything have to go down like this? She should've never left things with Maya the way she did. Should've faced it head-on, admitted that it scared the hell out of her when Maya was upset, and then talked to her like a goddamn adult. But no. She had to revert to her rotten-ass ways, make Maya feel bad, and now *this*.

Should she call her? What if she was talking to a doctor?

What if they were in surgery? She pulled the drink order from the screen and had to read it three times before her brain recognized what she needed to make. She pulled out the vodka, slammed it back down, and grabbed the gin instead.

After finishing the orders in record time, she called Maya. The call went straight to voicemail. She shot her a text and paced the floor.

Gabriella walked by, carrying a water pitcher and tray of empties.

"Gabriella!"

She must've seen the look on Remi's face because she set the pitcher down, her eyebrows weaved. "Remi-lita. What's wrong? Where's Maya?"

"There was an accident. I don't know anything. Harper's in the hospital."

"Harper? Oh no, oh no. Laney." She strummed her hand against her chin and glanced around the restaurant. "You—go. Go be with them. I'll cover the bar."

Remi tugged off her apron. "You're down two people then—"

"My place, my rules." She moved behind the bar and put on an apron. "I can handle. I'll bring up a server to help. Family first, always. You call me immediately the second you know something."

Remi ran to the back, grabbed her stuff from the locker, and pulled into the heavy traffic. On the highway, the cars slowed in front of her, and she cut into the forbidden carpool lane as a single rider. She checked her phone a dozen times and called Maya again.

The sluggish rush hour traffic halted her progress, and she slammed her hands against the steering wheel. Shaky exhales left her mouth as visions of a tiny Harper lying with IVs stuck in her arms filled her mind. She was a tough girl, though, right? A twelve-year-old badass that could power through whatever happened. If she just knew *what* happened, she could release her stomach. She just needed to know Harper was going to be okay, that her spunky little self had a minor setback, and they'd be back to boxing in no time.

Finally, her tires squealed to a stop in the parking garage, and she rushed through the doors. The smell of ammonia, bleach, and sickness hit her, and she gagged on a metallic burn in her nose. Her eyes scanned the floor to people in scrubs, folks pushing cleaning carts, and security guards checking bags outside a metal detector. She tossed her keys, wallet, and phone into a bowl and marched through the detector as quickly as she could without seeming like she was running from the cops.

Under the INFORMATION sign stood a line of four people. As the line dragged in slow motion, she balled her fists inside her pockets to keep from body slamming people out of the way. Finally, she reached the front. "Looking for Harper Marek's room."

The woman tapped against the keyboard. "Fifth floor, intensive care. Are you family?"

Remi swallowed. "No."

"Then you'll have to wait in the lobby. We only allow family members to enter the rooms."

Her stomach twisted at the words. How could she explain to a stranger that after spending this last week with Harper and Laney at the beach, she knew what a family could be? And she cared so much that her heart had not slowed since Sophie showed up at the bar. And maybe the timing seemed quick, but for the first time, she *felt* something for someone besides Ben and Gabriella that was wholesome and protective and lovely and terrifying.

She hit the elevator button multiple times and messaged Maya again. On the fifth floor, Remi's fingers tingled like they were falling asleep, and she shook them as she stepped into the lobby.

Every *Grey's Anatomy* episode she'd watched flashed through her mind but didn't prepare her for what the intensive care unit was really like. The space was calmer than she'd thought, quieter somehow. No one was running back and forth, no doctors were screaming "code blue!", no stretchers were being slammed through the operating doors. Instead, sunken-faced, lethargic folks sat in the lobby chairs, some sleeping, some staring into space. A woman mouthed words while her fingers raced across the rosary in her hand. A man near the corner flipped through multiple magazines and slammed each one down. A sobbing couple hugged each other in the corner.

She sat, scratched at her neck, hopped up, sat back down, and finally succumbed to pacing the floor. Each second on the large industrial clock ticked by like it was a minute, and each moment her insides heated a few degrees.

The bubbling from the water cooler caught her attention, and she became hyper-aware of her cotton mouth. Three cups of water barely eased the dryness. She filled water cup number four when the secured doors opened and Maya walked out with a doctor, followed by Sophie and Laney.

Family only rang in her ears.

Remi moved a step in their direction, but her knees wobbled. She froze, watching from the water cooler.

Maya's gaze locked on the doctor as they moved to the nurses' station. The doctor picked up a notepad and pen and handed it to Maya. Her posture was firmer than Remi had ever seen as she furiously scribbled. Sophie's arm was wrapped around Laney, who leaned on her like she'd fall over if Sophie weren't there.

A small grin and a look of relief crossed Maya's face, and Remi's chest lifted. No tears and a smile meant Harper hadn't died. That she'd be okay. That she was *safe*. Maya held Sophie's hand and hugged her mom. She shook the doctor's hand and, when he left, wrapped her arms around both Laney and Sophie, and they took a collective sigh.

Remi saw her future burn. Her heart shattered. She wanted to be there, seeing if Harper was okay, comforting the women, checking on this amazing kid. But this wasn't her family. She didn't belong here, in this world, with them. Maya had everyone she needed. They'd never include Remi in the way Sophie was at this moment. Maya hadn't called or texted, like Remi was an afterthought.

Remi was *always* an afterthought.

This type of life was never meant for her. She was delusional to think otherwise—an imposter, an outsider, shown the good life and trying to fit in. This was *their* family. The way Laney hugged Sophie was how Remi wanted to be hugged. She had to let this go, let them go, to protect herself. No use clinging on to something that wasn't meant to be and dragging a mom and sister along with the mess.

Her chin trembled, and she clenched her jaw so tight to stop the motion, she worried she'd crack a tooth.

She eased backwards, held her breath, and gaped one last time at the family. With a heavy heart, she rounded the corner and hit the down arrow on the elevator.

TWENTY-EIGHT

DRINK SPECIAL: DOUBLE-STRAINED
EVERYTHING LAYERED WITH FATIGUE

Maya glanced at her phone and frowned. Her crappy cell service blocked all her messages from going through as delivered to Remi. She didn't want to leave the intensive care floor yet, as Harper's tiny, sleeping frame looked so frail lying on the hospital bed with wires adhered to her arm. If Maya stopped watching, or missed an update from the doctor that she could help translate for her mom, or failed to notice an obvious sign, *again*, she'd never forgive herself. She glanced at Harper's vitals for the millionth time in the last few hours and shifted in the chair.

But the crisis was over. A sharp blood sugar drop, fainting episode, and a hairline jaw fracture from hitting the side of a table on her way down was enough to freak out anyone. The CT scan didn't show any head trauma, but her blood sugars needed to be heavily monitored after such an unexpected variation. Lab test results still needed to arrive, but for the last twenty minutes, Maya exhaled for the first time in the last four hours.

"Here's a cup of really terrible coffee, powdered milk, and I think some sort of genetically modified sugar." Sophie held out a steaming cup. "Your mom's still at the nurses' station."

"Thanks." Maya sipped the sludge and coughed. "You're not wrong about the coffee."

Sophie ran her hand across Harper's metal safety bar. Tugging at the side of her lip, she peered closer. "Any change?"

"You mean in the last ten minutes since you went to find this mud drink?" Maya grinned. "No. Same. Out like a light."

Sophie sat on the folding chair and blew into her cup. "Poor thing. This has got to be so hard on her little body."

Four years were spent studying, testing, and reviewing case studies. Thousands of pages read, highlighted, and memorized, on glucose, insulin, hyperglycemia, hypoglycemia, and autoimmune diseases. She completed her clinical practicums at a pediatric hospital, learned from the best teachers in the country. But nothing quite prepared her for the helplessness she felt watching her ninety-pound sister laid out with the vitals monitor beeping her heartbeat. The only thing that could make Maya feel better right now was Remi's reassuring voice telling her, "I've got you."

She grabbed the cell and circled the room, scanning the phone from the floor to the ceiling, praying for a single bar to appear so she could message Remi.

"No luck reaching Remi?" Sophie asked.

Maya shook her head. "She's probably worried sick. She and Harper have seriously bonded these last few weeks. No matter how tough she looks, I know she's tearing up." The last forty-eight hours felt like a lifetime. Images blurred of Harper and Remi boxing on the beach, returning from Port Townsend, Gabriella, the bonus, their trivial fight... Maya rubbed her temple.

Sophie dumped the coffee down the sink and washed her hands. "Want me to go outside and call her for you?"

"Thanks for offering, but no." Maya's chest deflated. "I need to call her and give her an update. With everything that happened at work, our fight... I need to tell her I love her."

Sophie's eyebrows shot up. "So, you're saying there's been some developments since we last spoke about the status of your relationship?"

Maya slumped in the chair and pulled her hands down her cheek. "I love this woman. Hard. And I was so hellish to her. I tried to talk to her today, before this all happened, and she just shut down. Like literally shut down. Dead eyes. No feeling. I was a ghost. She might be totally done with me. And I just... I don't know what I would do without her."

Sophie let out a low whistle. "Damn. You really care about her, huh? I've never heard you talk like this before."

Maya wrapped her arms around her legs and bent forward, pulling in breaths. Leaning back, she exhaled. "I really do." She tried to shake off the sickly feeling that she'd ruined their relationship. "She's everything I ever wanted, that I didn't even know that I wanted, if that makes sense. I thought I had it all. And I do, I did. I wasn't unhappy. But now I know what's out there, and I know how it feels to be loved. I can't lose her, and I royally screwed this up."

"Stop being so hard on yourself." Sophie patted her on the knee. "From the little you told me, Remi had a seriously awful past that may bleed into this. You can't take that on." She leaned against the wall and folded her arms. "But it might help explain why she shut down so hard, so quickly. If anyone can help someone through this, you can."

Sophie was being kind, but she missed a key element. It wasn't about *Maya* helping *Remi*. In fact, it was the opposite. Remi was the one who lifted Maya from the fog of her father's death, made her realize more existed in life than school and sorrow, and helped her open her eyes to the phenomenal family she took for granted on the daily. She *needed* Remi.

"Seriously, go outside and call her. Your mom will be back

in like two minutes, and I'll sit next to Harper. I promise I won't take my eyes off her, and if anything happens, I'll steal the intercom and shout into the hospital speakers." Sophie pushed her to the door. "Go."

Maya nearly sprinted down the hall and pushed the elevator button. She checked her watch. The bar was just about at closing time. What if Remi was sticking to the no-phone policy and had her phone on silent?

Or what if Remi never spoke to her again?

TWENTY-NINE

DRINK SPECIAL: THE DARKEST OF BITTER WHISKEY WITH A SIDE OF FLAMING HEARTACHE

The last straggler of the evening left Nueve's, and the hostess locked the door. Remi sprayed sanitizer across the bar and wiped. When she returned less than an hour after she bolted, she told Gabriella they blocked her from seeing Harper. Which wasn't a total lie. Her head spun, her heart was broken, but Harper was like a niece to Gabriella. The last thing Remi wanted was to put any more weight on Gabriella's shoulders as she tried to single-handedly manage the bar, restaurant, and her worry until Remi returned.

"Remi-lita, what a night." A heavy-eyed Gabriella wandered into the bar and put a hand on Remi's arm. "You okay?"

No. Remi nodded but remained silent. Nothing about her was okay. But everything was clear—she knew what she had to do. An ache spread so deep in her chest that her breath constricted. She hooked a finger in her collar and tugged.

Gabriella lifted the garbage bag from the container. "You going back up there tonight?"

Remi shook her head. "You should go home." She opened a case of domestic and stacked bottles. "I got all this."

Gabriella swiped a thumb under her eyes. "You're as worried as me. I stay and help." Her knees cracked when she bent down to grab the plastic wrap for the condiment. She hoisted herself and ripped the wrap.

"Please, go home." Remi pushed out a half-hearted smile. "I honestly just need some quiet. I'm totally fine." Now she was straight-up lying but hoped Gabriella was too fatigued to notice.

She patted Remi on the back. "When you talk to Maya, let her know I've covered her shifts for the rest of the week."

When. Remi had to work with Maya, like it or not, for the next six weeks before she returned to Minnesota. *Left,* for Minnesota. The thought of Maya being in another state made her stomach roll, but would be easier in the long run.

After a while, Remi could forget about her. She'd think back on this summer as a fun fling, remember Harper like her foster sister from home number four, and think of Laney like her foster mom from home number three. Warm, sad memories that only surfaced during certain smells, or random songs. This, she was an expert on. She'd done it before, and she could do it again.

She stacked the last bottle and moved to wipe the beer spouts. With every swipe, she played the game she'd played since she was ten—allowing space for a memory to pop up and picturing herself waving goodbye. And if that memory resurfaced, she'd scold herself, force a shadow to block the image, and find something to distract her until it faded.

She waved goodbye at the image of Maya sitting in Gabriella's office the first day. Gone was the tightness in her chest when she watched Maya toss bottles for the first time. Dancing on the nightclub floor—*poof.*

Her lips trembled, and she chewed on an ice cube to break the action. She piled the recycling in the corner and moved slower than she had when she first started here years ago. Thinking of leaving the bar tonight made her cringe. This spot was her safety shield. Once she stepped foot outside, reality would hit her. Here, she had purpose. Here, she had spouts to clean and glasses to stack and bottles to refill. She was needed, wanted, she provided value. Out there, she had a shitty car, a shittier apartment, and the loneliness of an empty bed.

A vibration in her back pocket snapped her from her trance. She pulled out the phone with Maya's name flashing across the screen. She dashed through the kitchen and out to the alley and caught the call on the fourth ring. "What's up?"

What's up? What was this—casual bro talk time? She sounded like an ass. But the best thing to do now was to make Maya hate her. Years of experience proved that anger was a much easier emotion to tolerate than heartbreak.

"Hey."

God, she sounded exhausted. Was she still at the hospital? Back home? She pictured Maya loosening her blond ponytail and rubbing her head, failing to stop yawns from escaping. Remi leaned against the brick alley wall and closed her eyes. "What's up?" she repeated, and now vowed to stick with the ridiculous greeting.

A long pause followed before Maya cleared her throat. "I just, um, wanted to tell you that Harper's in a stable condition. Scared the hell out of us, though. Her blood sugar numbers crashed, but she's going to be okay."

Remi pressed her palm into her forehead. Whatever God that may or may not exist came through tonight. She'd never been more relieved in all her life to hear the words "stable condition." Was Harper scared? Conscious? How did this happen?

She shook her head. *Stop. No longer my business.* "Cool."

"Cool?" The faint sound of tapping sounded through the phone. "I was so scared, Remi. I wanted you to be there with me."

The crack in her heart spread at a furious pace. "Yeah, well, you had everyone you needed—Sophie and your mom. I would've intruded."

"Intruded? What do you mean? Remi, you're family."

"No, Maya. I'm not." She clenched her jaw. Remi didn't have family. That word was caustic, burning her from the inside out. But, in a sad sort of way, the knowledge also brought comfort. This was a space she knew, where she was comfortable. The quicker she could get back to independence, the better off for everyone involved.

"I mean, not technically, but you are. I know how much you care about Harper. And how much you love me."

Remi scraped her thumbnail against the brick until it got down to the nub and then dug her heel into the pavement. "I don't really know how to tell you this. You're a pretty cool chick, much more than I thought when we started."

"*A cool chick?* What... Why are you talking like this?"

The acid crept from her belly up her chest. "It's my bad, for real. I just got hella confused, you know. Too much work, too little fun. And you were, well, fun." The acid now shot up her throat, and she verged on puking.

"I was... fun? Do you mean like, us? You, me? Remi, I *love* you. And I know you love me."

Her toes dug into the wall, and she kicked at a loose brick. "That's the thing, though. Super uncool of me to do. I shoulda never said that." She pried at the brick, needing to feel it crack, needing her foot to break something. "You're nice. But whoa, seriously slow down. You're just a lot of... reality... for me. Like, you're all thinking of houses and marriage and babies, and I just want to enjoy the rest of my twenties."

"You want to enjoy your twenties?" Her voice cracked. "This isn't how you talk, Remi. Your voice doesn't even sound the same. Are you drunk?"

The brick would not crack. Remi kicked at it, the side of her foot scraping the edge, her toes cramping. "Nah. Only one of us is irresponsible enough to get shit-faced at work." The acid flew up her throat, and she put her phone on mute to cough and spit on the ground. Her cheeks burned.

"Wow." The word was soft.

Knots built and twisted in her belly. Remi ground her knuckles into her thigh. *End this. Be done with this misery. Move on with your life. Let Maya move on with hers.* "I'm glad the kid is good."

"The kid? The kid?" The words were no longer soft. "Okay, I know we had a tough couple of days, but let's just end this conversation now before we say something we really regret."

Too late.

"Let's talk tomorrow after we both get some rest."

Remi pushed herself from the wall and firmed her shoulders. She clamped her cheek in between her teeth and squeezed her eyes shut. "Nah. I'm good."

The seconds ticked by. "What do you mean, you're good?"

Rip the Band-Aid. "I mean, I'm good, Maya. This, all this. It was fun while it lasted. But it's over. You, me, time to move on. Better to do this now before you leave, anyway. Gabriella covered your shifts for the rest of the week, and after that, until you leave permanently, you and I are nothin' but co-workers." She shoved the phone under her chin to stop the quivering.

Yell at me. Scream at me. Tell me I'm a piece of shit and you're better off without me. She pulled the shaky phone back to her ear, praying she'd be met with a tirade of swear words and screaming.

Instead, she was met with silence. For so many excruciating moments, she checked her phone to see if Maya had hung up. And then a guttural sound, like a shrieking wounded animal, cut through the night air, followed by a quiet sob. "Bye, Remi."

The phone went dead, and Remi stared at the blank screen.

Fuck! The trembles started low. In her calf, up her legs, up her arms. Her gut quivered, sick and tacky. The shaking moved to her chest until it reached her chin. She chomped, she bit, she exhaled, but nothing could stop it.

Remi slid down the brick, her back scraping against the rough edges, until she hit the pavement with a thud. She wrapped her arms around her knees and dropped her head.

And for the first time since she was a child, Remi bawled.

THIRTY

DRINK SPECIAL: A SOPHIE & THOMPSON COMBINATION SPIRIT DRIZZLED WITH NOSTALGIA

The following day floated by in a murky, dense fog. Remi didn't remember showering, getting ready, or leaving her apartment. Her body ached from the unfamiliar crying, her dusty eyes burned. Gabriella took one look at her puffy, red face and assured Remi that Harper would be fine. Remi had forced a nod and let Gabriella believe that her demeanor was about her concern for Harper, and not about her sabotaging the sweetest, purest love she'd experienced in her lifetime.

Maya hadn't called, hadn't texted, hadn't shown up at work crying or yelling. Remi had checked her phone. More than a hundred times, she tapped the screen, begging for a message, voicemail, something.

Nothing. Maya was done.

She could normally compartmentalize like a champ, slap on a smile, and shake the hell out of a martini. But tonight, everything hurt—her arms, her cheeks, her chest. Her heart. Tonight, she didn't have it in her to play nice.

Mr. Thompson thudded up to the bar, hung his cane on the back of the chair, and tipped his military hat her way. She nodded at him and filled a low-ball with brandy, slid an orange across the rim, and handed it over without a word.

"No cherries?" he asked.

Snap out of it. "Sorry." She stuffed cherries in a shot glass and set it next to him.

How was she going to do this? Each time she looked at the day bartender who was covering Maya, she flinched, expecting to see blond hair and a perfect smile. Nothing felt right.

Mr. Thompson glanced at the day bartender with a scowl. "Where's your partner in crime?"

Remi focused on scrubbing the corner of the sink with a wire brush. "She, ah, took some personal time off."

"She gonna come back?"

"Who knows?" She wouldn't blame Maya for never returning. The words she said to her last night... *Enough. No more living in the past.* She willed the shadow image to block any more thoughts of Maya.

Mr. Thompson twirled the brandy glass and watched the liquid run from the sides. "You two sure were a fun team to watch. Her with all the flips, you with all your snark." He chuckled. "She's only here for the summer, right?"

She did not want to talk about Maya. She didn't want to talk about anything. The only thing she wanted to do was to get through this miserable shift, bury her head under her comforter, and sleep until she had to come back tomorrow. "Yeah."

He tilted his chin and gazed at his glass.

The place was quieter than normal, an unwelcome lull in her already dull night. If she were slammed, she could focus on orders and not the shame suffocating her. She stomped into the kitchen and returned with a stack of glasses, nearly shattering one as she slammed it on the counter. She pressed her thumbs into her temples and rubbed.

"Edith at book club tonight?" She forced a grin.

He shook his head. "No, she and the ladies went to the

church to help with some bake sale." A tiny uptick of a grin appeared. "God help them if Edith is the one baking. She always burns the bottom. She should set the oven on a lower temperature, but I think she's just always in a hurry. Don't matter much. Even her burnt cookies are the best I've ever had."

A small yelp left Remi's mouth, and she coughed to cover it up. The image of Maya baking, Remi biting into a burnt cookie, and the over-the-top pink sparkly ribbon Maya used to decorate burrowed into her brain. A sting started in the back of her eyes, and she blinked to chase away the tears.

"I can't say nothing bad about my Edith." He dug a cherry from the shot glass and tossed it in his mouth. "She saved my life, ya know?"

Remi's ears perked. She set down the glass and moved to stock napkins. "I didn't know that. How so?"

"My number got called for the draft. I was just a kid—a day over nineteen. Scared shitless. None of us wanted to go, and my buddies were damn near proposing to anyone they could. They wanted to know someone would wait for them, maybe send some postcards and pictures to pass the time."

The nostalgic tone in his voice filled the space. She tossed the empty napkin wrapper in the garbage and leaned closer.

"Edith and I had only been together for a few months. Oh, that girl. Such a firecracker. Different from any girl I'd ever met. Fearless. She'd twirl in her poodle skirt in the rain. Or tuck herself and roll down the hill with little kids. She'd bluff like nobody's business and beat me and the guys at poker, an unlit smoke dangling from her mouth." He chuckled and tapped his glass for Remi to refill. "I loved her immediately."

"Poker, huh? She just upped her cool factor even more." Remi placed the brandy back on the shelf, warming at the story. "What happened?"

"When we got drafted, everyone was chasing their woman. But not me. Edith was a bird that couldn't be caged, and I didn't want to try. Thinking of her worrying about me while I was in a foxhole, going to church praying instead of dancing, crying with her friends instead of stealing her daddy's truck to drive on the country roads... I couldn't do it." His eyes turned misty, and he bit the edge of the orange. "I treated her real mean, said some pretty nasty things, tried to push her away. I wanted her to live for herself, not for me. And I thought things would be easier for me somehow if I weren't always thinking of her."

Remi's heart sunk at the words. She leaned her hip against the bar and wiped her fingers on the towel. "What did you do?"

"Well, she told me in no uncertain terms where I could shove my attitude, she ain't going nowhere, and it was gonna take a lot more than me being a horse's ass to scare her off." He drained the last of his drink. The cane wobbled a bit as he hoisted himself into a different position. "So, I took her with me. In the foxhole, in the barracks, on the ship ride over. She was right here, with me." He tapped his heart. "Getting back to her kept me alive."

All words left Remi's mouth as the sweetness of the story sunk in. For four years, she served Mr. Thompson twice a week, and never once had she heard this type of emotion. She was honored to hear his words. "Thank you for sharing this story with me."

He tugged on his jacket and transferred the cane to his right hand. He laid cash on the table and leaned on his palm. "I sure hope that everything works out for your friend." He pointed to the space where Maya normally worked. "It would be hard to lose someone who helps keep you alive at work." He knocked on the wood and shuffled away.

A dullness invaded Remi's chest. She swallowed away the nausea as her eyes followed him to the door.

What have I done?

.   .   .

Closing time did not come quick enough. After her chat with Mr. Thompson, her head swirled, and she couldn't concentrate on a single order. Thankfully, the day bartender was trying hard to make a name for himself, as he swooped in and covered her slack.

Remi dumped hot water down the ice bin. She did what had to be done, right? Maybe she didn't need to go so hard. But if Maya hated her, she'd avoid her, and Remi could go back to the routine soon enough.

Was Harper still in the hospital? What actually happened, anyway? How long would she be there? Was she—

Knuckles rapping against the front door jolted her upright. Probably some drunk passing by being stupid. She swiped her towel across the rim of the bar and dipped it back in the hot suds. The knock landed again, multiple times, and harder. She released a heavy sigh. Might be a patron who left their wallet or phone in a booth.

She pried open the blinds. "What the f—" Her pulse slammed against her chest. She unlocked the deadbolt and ripped the door open.

Sophie stood on the sidewalk and ran her palm across her buzzed head. She tossed her hand up in a sort of half wave as her cheeks pinked. "Um, hey. Sorry. This is probably really weird—"

"Is everything okay?" Remi halted her breath.

"Oh yeah, totally. Or, well, I mean Harper's still in the hospital." She tugged at her gold lip ring before she dropped her hands and cleared her throat. "Can we talk?"

Remi exhaled and waved her inside. After bolting the deadlocks, she pulled down a chair stacked on top of the bar and pointed to the seat. "Want something to drink?"

"Enough tequila to kill a camel, please." She grinned and laid her purse on the table. "Kidding. Water's good."

Remi slid a water glass across the bar and leaned against the wood. "How's Harper?"

"Not a ton of change since she was admitted." She strummed her fingers against the glass. "She's stable. I think with diabetes, it's super tricky. When it crashes so fast like that, they need to monitor for a few days to make sure it doesn't happen again. And poor thing, she already has a hefty bruise on her jaw from where she landed."

Remi winced. "The jaw hurts like a bitch, too." She thought of a few past scuffles, and a sparring match gone wrong. Harper's determined face and fierce growl flew through her mind. "She might think this makes her look tough."

Sophie chortled. "Probably." She gulped down a few swallows and spun the bottom of the glass. "She's a hell of a kid. Total spitfire. Been that way since she was born. I love that girl like she was my sister."

A flash of something prickly and unpleasant flew through Remi's gut, and she stiffened. Everything about the last several days already felt like a hallucination. A lifetime of moments stuffed into a forty-eight-hour period. Facing this woman who represented everything she'd never be pushed the haziness to full-fledged reality, and Remi's insides couldn't keep up on how they should respond. And the worst part, Sophie seemed genuinely nice, timid almost, as she curled into the seat and glanced around the room like she didn't know what to say. "You just here to give me an update on Harper?"

Sophie plucked a napkin from the bin and rolled the edges between her fingers. After pulling in a heavy breath, she exhaled and kept her eyes on the tissue. "I asked Maya multiple times for us to meet. She was going to set something up for later this week, before... all this happened."

Remi lifted her chin. How everything changes in a snap. She'd been excited, maybe even a little nervous, to meet this woman who held Maya, Harper, and Laney so close to her heart. But seeing the comfortability, hugs, the *family only* in the hospital, killed the dream. And the way she spoke to Maya yesterday, the way she ended it, killed any chances. "Yeah, she mentioned that. It's all good, though. Things change, right?"

"Obviously." Sophie narrowed her eyes. "What you said to Maya yesterday—it wasn't right. She's hurting, which makes me mad. And, well, you suck. There, I said it."

Ouch. Remi pried open a straw box and stuffed them one by one into the holder. "I probably sound like a major asshole, thus proving your point, but what are you doing here?"

Sophie shrugged and wrapped the tightly folded corner of the napkin against the bar. "Even though I'm mad, my best friend is hurting and not thinking clearly, and I want to help. I wanted to come here and, I don't know, just scream at you or something. I might not know you, but I recognize hurt. I see your face. And you're hurting, too." Her eyes softened. "And now I don't want to yell at you."

The final straw refused to be crammed into the holder, and Remi chucked it into the trash.

Sophie's eyes brimmed with tears. "When Laney called 'cause she couldn't get a hold of Maya, I just lost it. I mean, I held it together, but I lost it inside. Seeing Harper like that was so scary. She's so tiny and had all these wires poking into her, and the blood pressure monitor beeping like this weird ticking time bomb and... well, ugh." She swiped a tear from her eye with her thumb. "I just don't think anyone else would understand what this feels like."

Remi's gut dropped. She stared at her hands, blinking, trying to remove the visual. "Why did you think I would understand?"

"Because they're your family, too."

No, they weren't. She saw them together, witnessed what it was like, and it wasn't hers. She was a visitor. An imposter. The bar space was too small. She needed more air than this place provided. She filled a glass of ice water and chugged. "No, they're not," she said flatly, and picked up a towel.

Sophie cocked her head. "Well, I mean as much as they're mine."

"No, they're really not. I don't know why the hell everyone keeps saying that." Remi scrubbed the grooves on the backbar. The dirt was imbedded into it, years of spilled liquid and dust. How had she never noticed it before? She grabbed a toothpick and scraped against the seams. After this, she could clean the floors with a bottle brush. Really get into the cracks and scrub whatever gunk the nighttime facility crew missed. "I went up to the hospital an hour or so after you all left."

"What? You were there?" Sophie's surprised tone traveled across the bar. "We didn't see you."

"I know. I saw you guys from the lobby and bounced. Didn't want to break up the moment." She stopped cleaning the grooves and peeked at Sophie's scrunched eyes.

"I don't understand. Why didn't you grab us?"

Remi shrugged. "They said family only. And, well, I'm not."

Sophie waved that word away with a huff. "That wouldn't have mattered. When we checked in, Maya said I was her sister, and she gave the nurses your name as another sister in case you showed up."

The room blurred and blinked back into focus. Her ears rang. "She... what?" Maya had said she was family? Told the nurses to let her in?

Sophie nodded. "Maya was frantic. We all were. She kept trying to call you, but the service didn't work up there. She knew you'd be freaking out about Harper, and she was freaking out about you. When they brought Harper back for the CT scan, she started bawling and said she wished you were there to tell her you had her back." She unfolded the origami napkin and flattened it out. "I don't know what secret powers you have, but you've changed my best friend. And honestly, for the better.

Since she's been back home, she's let her guard down. She's laughing and less rigid, and less focused—which she needed. And, well, damn. She's wildly in love with you."

Remi's brain came to a screeching halt. Her chest was hot, her brain clouded, her mouth dry. She tossed the blackened toothpick in the garbage. "She *was* wildly in love with me, you mean." No chance that after the words she used did Maya maintain those feelings.

"You heard me right the first time." She strapped the cross-body purse across her chest. "I should probably go."

Remi moved from behind the bar. "I'll grab the door."

Sophie stepped onto the sidewalk and pulled back her shoulders. "Sorry if this was super weird for you." She opened her mouth, then twisted it closed. A moment passed. "Take care, Remi."

Remi swallowed back a cry. "You too."

THIRTY-ONE

DRINK SPECIAL: BEST FRIEND COCONUT CLARITY COSMO

The antiseptic soap stung the inside of Maya's nose. She closed her eyes and lifted her face to the two-degrees-below-scalding water, but her shoulders still shivered. Going on fifty-plus hours of nothing but cat naps and hospital food took its toll.

She swiped the mirror with her forearm and stared at her pale face, red eyes, and dark circles as she toweled off in the hospital bathroom. Thank God the children's unit allowed families to shower so she didn't need to leave Harper's side.

The beeps of Harper's vitals monitor echoed against the linoleum walls and floors, and she cracked the door to peek.

"You're, like, aggressively obsessed," Harper groaned with a groggy voice and half-opened eyes.

"Go back to sleep." Maya grinned. She waited as Harper's eyes fluttered and closed. She clocked the vitals, watched her chest expand, and exhaled when Harper's deep breathing returned. Never again would she let something like this happen to her sister.

Tonight, the pressure, the not-knowing, the chair tight-gripping, eased. Harper passed the forty-eight-hour mark of no new blood sugar fluctuations, and Maya could breathe. Laney had slept, finally, for more than an hour at a time. Maya ate a solid dinner, and Sophie went home.

The pressure of the unknown shifted, replaced by the gaping hole that ripped through her heart from her conversation with Remi two nights ago. After their call, she'd stayed outside, maybe ten, maybe twenty minutes, until her core breathing calmed her, and she returned to the room. Laney had peeked up at her with squinted eyes, and Maya had mumbled something about being worried about Harper.

Which was true, of course. But she was worried about herself. Remi had ended it, carelessly, callously, and Maya didn't deserve the way she was spoken to. But she knew Remi, and the woman on the phone wasn't her. The voice on the other end was not the woman who she fell in love with. It was not the woman who stepped in front of her to protect her from the revolting patron, or boxed with Harper, or made her feel like the most beautiful, irresistible woman in the world when her mouth was on her.

Maybe she was a glutton for punishment. And maybe she had a hero complex, or was a perfectionist, or a control freak, or any of the other terrible things that exes who didn't mean anything to her had said in the past. But the label didn't matter.

She missed Remi.

She scrunched the towel through her hair and flickered her eyelids to stop the tears from unleashing. Her mouth formed a circle and she blew out, until her navel calmed and her chest released. *Head high, shoulders straight.* Her mom did not need to see her cry. Now that Harper's crisis was over, she couldn't blame her tears on her worry.

After snapping on her slip-ons, she eased out of the bathroom. Laney's breathing rattled with a snore and she sprung upright.

"Sorry, Mom. Lie back down."

Laney ran her fingers through her hair and patted it down.

"You look so tired, honey." She patted the seat next to her for Maya to sit.

"I'm good." She peeked at Harper's rising and falling chest and frowned. "Damn kid. Always likes to scare us."

A soft chuckle left Laney. She brushed Maya's hair back from her shoulder. "Don't think I haven't noticed that there's something going on with you."

Maya flinched. "Mom, I—"

"It's okay. You're a grown woman, and you can tell me when you're ready." She stretched her legs, flexing and curling her toes. "I'm so glad you're here with us."

"Me too. I don't know what I would've done if I were in Minnesota."

She hugged her cardigan across her body and gave Maya a soft smile. "I don't want you to take this the wrong way, but we would've been fine without you."

Maya's heart dropped.

"I mean that in the kindest, most wonderful way." Laney sighed. "Harper isn't your father. She's going to be okay. You hovering over her isn't going to change anything. She's tough like you. I raised two amazing, independent, strong-willed girls. But you've got to give me some credit. I'm pretty damn amazing and strong-willed myself."

Of course her mom was the most resolved of any human on the planet. But she needed Maya, right? To alleviate burdens, to smooth things over, to help? She bit the corner of her pinkie. Her mom tugged her hand from her mouth and swiped her thumb across her wrist. "Please, go get some food. Get some rest."

"I really don't want to leave you. Or Harper. What if the doctor comes back and says something that I need to hear, or something changes?"

"Then I'll call you. You need to trust me when I say I've got this. Please, honey. Go home. Don't come back until Harper is discharged."

A heaviness weighed on Maya, and she nodded. She kissed her mom on the forehead, grabbed her things, and made her way down the hall. Maybe a shower at her own place, and a solid sleep would do her some good. By the time she reached the elevator, the heaviness lifted.

Absolutely, her mom had this. She'd *always* had this. Now she could worry about herself, and her next steps. Her stomach growled. But first, food and a cup of coffee.

The freshly fried turkey bacon, eggs, and coffee scent drifted to Maya's nose. The time was barely past 3:00 a.m. and her belly clenched at the thought of having anything too heavy. A coffee stand in the corner of the cafeteria caught her eye. She made her way there, ordered a latte and scone, and opened her phone to look at messages.

None from Remi. Not one single word.

"Maya?"

She snapped up her head, assuming the barista called her name for an order. "Ben?"

Ben set his coffee on the table and held out his arms for a hug. She folded herself into his crisp blue scrubs.

He adjusted the stethoscope around his neck and picked up his coffee. "What are you doing here?"

"My sister was admitted a few nights ago. Blood sugar issues." She grabbed her cup and pastry from the pickup area. "Remi must not have told you." Her body sunk. Remi had officially stopped caring.

He scooted over for a few nurses to pass him. "No, I haven't seen her. Spent the night at Charlie and Mack's the other night and been on day shifts. We keep missing each other." He motioned for Maya to sit at a table. "You okay?"

Tears sprung, and she flicked them away with her fingertips. "I'm just super tired."

"Uh-huh. Tired." He lowered the cup he brought to his mouth. "I get that. I do. But this right here, this is more than sleepy."

"Remi, uh." She cleared her throat. "She broke things off."

He cocked his head. "She did what now?"

The tears streamed again, and she didn't stop it. The wound was so fresh and raw, the fatigue so deep even her bones were lethargic. She swiped her sleeve across her cheeks. "I just don't know what to do. She was so mean... the stuff she said to me. How do I come back from that? And what the hell does that say about me, that I *want* to come back from that? Like I'm some sort of emotional masochist or something."

Ben leaned back on his chair and tapped his fingers under his seat. He stared out in the crowd, a smattering of tired guests and hospital personnel, people on their phone, or closing their eyes for a cat nap. "The person you talked to wasn't Remi," he finally said. "I mean it was her, but not *her* her."

Cryptic messages at 3:00 a.m. and a handful of hours of sleep did not make a good combo. Maya was tired and done, and had no mental brainpower left to decode. "I don't know what that means. And I'm so spent. I don't even know if I care." That was a lie. She *did* care. Too much.

"Do you know one time a social worker arranged a meeting with Remi's parents? She was maybe like thirteen or fourteen. She'd been in the system for years by then. But her parents were clean for a hot second and wanted to reconnect." He pulled the top off the coffee and blew into the cup. "So, she spent the day with them. I remember she had fun. They went to some pawn shops, looked at classic vinyl records maybe. The details are fuzzy. And they were going to visit again, the following weekend."

Maya picked at her scone.

"Remi doesn't get nervous. She's the most confident human alive, always has been. That week, she asked me to teach her how to use curl cream. And she'd saved up money from lawn mowing to buy boxing gloves and shoes but bought a new outfit instead. She was so goddamn excited. We sat at her foster parents' house and stared out the window, waiting for them to arrive. And kept sitting. Twenty minutes late turned into an hour late, turned into two hours late."

Maya stopped picking at her food and bit her lip. She wasn't sure she wanted to hear more details.

"She just stared out the window, Maya. Almost like she didn't believe they weren't coming. Her foster parents brought us food, then pillows and blankets. Finally, had to have been midnight, and I saw her dim, you know. Literally, the light in her just vanished. We never talked about it. But she took on a different personality. She'd pick fights with me, say terrible things, tell me she hated me. But I knew what she was doing. She needed to protect herself. For so many years, she'd been left unprotected. Her personality was her armor. She wanted to see if I would leave her, too. But I stayed. And I fought for our friendship. And, well, now here we are."

The scone crumbled between her fingers and she dusted off her hands. A child-Remi waiting on a couch for parents who never showed cracked Maya's already splintered heart.

"Whatever she said to you, how she treated you, it wasn't right. You have every right to tell her to eff off. She's a grown-ass woman. But her reaction comes from a place of deep trauma. What I do know is that you are the only person I've ever seen bring a flicker of Remi's light back. I thought it was gone from that day. And... you unleashed it."

The thudding in her chest increased and she stared at her fingers. "I didn't know... she told me so much, but I didn't know everything."

"Yeah, she's a tough one to crack." Ben nodded. "Did you call her later?"

Maya shook her head.

"Send a text?"

Her stomach dropped. "No. Nothing."

"It's okay. I don't blame you. She can be difficult. But man, I'll take her saltiness any day to keep her in my life." He tapped his beeping smartwatch. "Sorry, break's over. I've gotta run upstairs." He pushed out his chair and grabbed his drink. "Good luck, with whatever you decide."

Her lips lifted in a whisper of a polite smile, but she could barely make eye contact. Thoughts collided, each one more confusing than the other. She stared at the destroyed scone and her full coffee, as her stomach turned. She wrapped her arms around herself, regret seeping in. *I need to fight for her.*

"Hey, Maya." Ben jogged back over to her, his stethoscope and lanyard rattling against each other. "I have an idea."

THIRTY-TWO

DRINK SPECIAL: HAPPINESS HOP-INFUSED LAGER WITH PRETZELS

Sleep was unattainable. The first crack of daylight seeped through her blinds. Remi squinted at her clock. 5:32 a.m. She'd drifted off a couple of times, but stirred awake with thoughts of Maya, visions of Harper, and picturing Laney's tired eyes and slacked shoulders. And replaying the conversation with Maya.

She rolled to her side and pulled the pillow into her chest. Sleeping alone was miserable. She wanted Maya here, next to her. Wanted to smell the jasmine in her hair, feel her warm body and freakishly cold feet against her skin, hear her peaceful breaths as she drifted to sleep.

She wanted Maya.

But she also wanted to protect her heart. And thus, the circle began again. Everything Mr. Thompson and Sophie said lit an unexpected fire. Maya had said she was family and wanted her at the hospital. Remi forced her away without giving her a chance.

Love was scary as hell. This gripping sensation that made her feel like she couldn't breathe, or was floating, or that she'd crush under the heaviness. She wanted to throw up and fly, all at once.

Family was even scarier. What if she got too close to Harper and Laney, and she and Maya ended their relationship? Then she'd lose *three* people, not just one. And she wasn't sure she could handle that. But Sophie was an ex-girlfriend... and she stayed in their lives. She was at the hospital, comforting Laney, supporting Maya, and she was an *ex*. The question was, could she risk her heart and really do this? Could she wait for Maya to return from Minnesota eighteen months from now after her program finished? Was Maya worth it?

Yes. Absolutely.

Was *Remi* worth it? She exhaled through her nose and flopped on her back, searching for the spot on the ceiling in the dusky room. Was she, herself, worth it? Her parents didn't think so. Violet didn't think so. What if Maya didn't think so? Three strikes on a heart were too many. She wasn't sure if she could take the pain.

She had to grow more. She knew that. So many things existed in the world that she had yet to learn. A few years ago, she thought she knew everything. Genuinely thought through all her experiences in the system, her parents, Ben, Darius, Gabriella, that she knew everything. She saw the best and worst society had to offer. She saw people with grit and resilience and fire, and *she knew it all*. And then she fell in love and realized she knew nothing. How could something hurt, feel so good, and be so terrifying simultaneously?

So, the question remained. *Am I worth it?* Her heart pinched. She blinked at the ceiling. A wave started in her stomach and moved to her chest. She didn't know the answer, not yet anyhow, but a sliver of optimism broke through.

I think I can be.

Her breath shook. Now she had to fight like hell to win back Maya. Try to explain, not justify, why she said what she said. Trusting others was a foreign concept. But Remi would sacrifice her heart and shatter the nine-hundred-foot wall she built around herself, because Maya was worth it.

The squeak of the apartment door opening and keys jangling funneled through the thin walls. Footsteps moved through the apartment, and Remi breathed out. "I'm awake!" she called out to Ben. For once, she wanted to talk to him, get his advice on how to approach Maya, and describe the tingly feeling rushing through her body.

A quiet knock came outside the door.

"Come in." She slid over to the side of the bed. The door cracked open. *Huh?* She bolted up so fast she got dizzy from a head rush. She wiped her eyes with her fist. "Maya?" She squinted at the doorway as the image of blond hair and a timid body took place.

"Hi," she whispered, and stepped into the room. She took a moment and looked around the space. "So, this is your room, huh?"

Remi tugged the blankets to her chest and dashed a glance around the room. "I'm so confused... How did you... You don't know where I live. You've never been here. I'm—what?"

"Can I come in?" She tucked her hair behind her ears.

Remi's eyes adjusted to the dusky light. She saw heavy bags under Maya's eyes, that she was wearing sweatpants and a sweatshirt, and her normally straight and shiny hair was frizzy and unkempt. "Yeah, of course." She shifted over.

Maya took a seat on the edge of the bed.

Words wedged in her throat. *Sorry* seemed so small, so insignificant. Her mouth paralyzed. Remi's words were unforgivable. Maya was scared, hurting, and Remi let her down in her time of need. She'd spend a lifetime making amends.

A tired half grin appeared on Maya. "Do you have any idea how disgusting hospital coffee is? Like, truly, truly awful."

Huh?

She pulled her leg under herself and plucked at the edge of

the bed. "Around three in the morning, I wandered down to the hospital cafeteria to scavenge for something resembling caffeine and ran into Ben."

Ah...

"He was on a break. Long story short, he gave me his keys, you guys' address, and, well, here I am." She rubbed her fingertips together and chewed the side of her cheek. "I told him what happened... with Harper, with, um, our conversation."

Remi gulped, suffocating under the shame of her words. "I'm so unbelievably sorry. The way I talked to you, I just..." Her lips trembled, and she breathed through her nose. "You have every right to hate me."

Please don't hate me.

Maya plucked at her pant seam. "You hurt me, Remi. My sister was sick, and you... you weren't there for me. I needed you, and you just left."

Oh God. *I abandoned her.* Just like her parents, just like Violet, and here Remi did the same thing to someone she loved. She stared at the ceiling. *No, no, no.* She didn't leave *because* of Maya. She left *for* Maya. She protected her, protected herself. Simple as that. Never once did she intend on making Maya feel deserted.

Her brain felt gooey, foggy, as a lifetime of things she thought was true kicked down her internal door and splattered themselves on the floor. No more running, no more avoiding. She needed to unravel her past and come to terms with her childhood. "I can't even begin to tell you how sorry I am. That person on the phone—it wasn't me."

Maya snatched a pillow and eased onto her back, her eyes looking like they weighed a million pounds. "Ben and I talked. I understand that I'll never fully understand the effects of your past." She swallowed. "But I'm willing to try if you are."

Willing to try? She would do anything to keep this woman in her life. Even from a distance. Remi wanted to stroke her hair, hold her hand, wrap her in her arms, but lay motionless. "Are you sure?" She slung an arm over her eyes. The truth would be easier if she didn't have to look at Maya. The back of her throat turned wet. "I'm broken. I don't know if I can be fixed."

Gentle fingers tugged her arm from her face.

"You're incredible." Maya folded her hands on her chest and closed her eyes. She lay so still for so many moments that Remi thought she fell asleep. "I'm so used to controlling everything," she whispered. She pulled Remi's hand onto her stomach and lazily interlaced her fingers. "I thought perfection and order made me feel safe. If I could control things, then everything would be okay. Before my dad died, I was like this. And after, I don't know, perfection became my safe haven. I couldn't stop his dying, but I could control everything else. And now, with Harper, with everything... I realize no matter what I do, things will happen I just can never control. And I have to be okay with that."

The words pushed heavy into Remi. So much existed that she still wanted to learn about Maya. Remi slid her arm off her hip and rested it on the bed. "And I thought by pushing you away, I was protecting you from me, and me from you. I'm so ashamed of disrespecting you. Never again. I promise you, Maya. You could storm out right now, and I will never, ever disrespect you like that. No matter what happens."

Fingertips grazed the top of Remi's hand. Maya's thumb swiped across her skin, sending tiny, reassuring bubbles up her arm. She rolled over and wrapped a leg around Remi's. She lay into her chest.

Remi scooted in closer and nuzzled her face into her hair. She breathed in Maya, feeling her chest rise and fall against hers. Twisting a lock of Maya's silken hair between her fingers, she snugged her body closer. She wanted to hold Maya, have her fall asleep in her arms, be with her—temporary, forever, intermediate, it didn't matter. She'd take anything, whatever that looked like.

"I love you," Maya whispered. "And I don't want to lose you. I want you, all of you. The messy, the disorganized, the imperfect. Any shape, any form, I want to be with you."

Hot tears sprung to Remi's eyes and trickled down her cheeks. Her chest squeezed, and she swiped at her cheek with the back of her hand. "I do, too. And I'll wait for you. It's going to suck when you're gone in Minnesota, but I'm here. We'll figure that out, too. We can FaceTime. I'll take my first plane ride. You can come home on the holidays—"

"I'm not going."

Remi's breath caught in her throat. "What? Why not? This is your dream. You can't give this up."

Maya blinked open her eyes and scooted to sit upright. "I don't want to leave."

Panic seeped in. No doubt would Maya eventually turn resentful for giving up her dream. She searched her eyes for any hesitation, but Maya looked determined with a soft smile. "You can't do this for me."

"I'm not doing this for you. I'm doing this for *me*." She kissed Remi's fingertips. "And Harper, and my mom, and to help me stop running, stop chasing. I said goodbye to my dad. I need to focus on life."

Remi gnawed on her lip. "This is such a huge decision. Do you need time to think?" This could be the tired talk of an emotionally depleted woman who just saw her sister in the hospital. "You might feel different in the morning. And that's okay."

"No, I won't." She crossed her legs and tugged on the blanket. "You know that first night you slept over? And we talked about everything? When you left in the morning, I withdrew my application from Minnesota and reapplied at the University of Washington."

"What?" Remi's mind flashed to that evening weeks ago. "Why didn't you say anything?"

She shrugged. "I didn't want to say anything until I heard from UW. I was a little scared, but I knew it was the right thing to do. I need to be with my family. And I want to be with you."

Remi's stomach stopped twisting. Her chest relaxed. She felt Maya's words to the top of her toes, to the deepest part of her core. Maya loved her. She loved Maya. Maya wasn't leaving. "So... did you get in? What happens next?"

"For once in my life, I don't know, and I'm totally at peace. I haven't heard from the admissions office yet. But if they reject my late entry, then I'll start in the winter, and it will be okay. I'm going to be okay."

Remi eased herself back on the bed. "I love you so much."

Maya snuggled into her chest. "I love you, too," she whispered, her voice groggy and heavy with sleep. She flung her legs across Remi's and hooked them in between her calves. "Pretzel legs?"

Remi kissed the top of her head. Her body filled with warmth and her chest relaxed. Everything was going to be okay. Even if wasn't going to be okay forever, it was okay for now. And that was all she needed.

"Definitely pretzel legs."

EPILOGUE

DRINK SPECIAL: IMPERFECT PERFECT
COCKTAIL MIXED WITH WE GOT THIS VODKA

"Go! Come on, Maya, you got this!"

Remi's eardrum-busting scream and whistle cut through the rowdy, cheering crowd, past the grunts of workers, and over the clinking of bottles.

"Time!" A screeching referee whistle tore through the crowd.

Maya set down the bottles and flexed her hand. She followed the sound of Remi's voice and saw her bouncing curls in the crowd as she cheered and high-fived Harper and Laney.

Harper and her mom both cupped their hands around their mouths, screaming something inaudible against the crowd and their massive smiles.

Vegas was everything Maya thought it would be—an insomniac of a town filled with endless lights, glamour, and noise. The city was alive, bright, and fun—for this week. After that, she'd look forward to going back to her quiet-*ish* life in Seattle.

A whirlwind of the past few months flashed through her as she took a break, twisted her hips to crack her lower back, and gulped water. From an outsider perspective, some might think she was on a downward spiral. The University of Washington rejected her application for fall admission. Her student loans became due because she was no longer enrolled in school. Gabriella awarded Remi the bonus money based on performance and sales.

And yet, she was the happiest she'd ever been. At first, Remi tried to give Maya half the money, and Maya steadfastly refused. She digitally transferred the amount, and Maya transferred it back. She wrote Maya a check, which Maya cracked up at—she had no idea Remi had actual paper checks. Maya refused to cash it. Remi threatened to bury the cash in her mattress, and Maya said she'd break up with her if she did. Even though they both knew she wouldn't.

Remi pleaded and said she no longer felt like she was in the space where she wanted to buy a home and didn't know what to do with the cash. Finally, Remi used the money to put a security deposit on a beautiful, new two-bedroom apartment for her and Ben that was closer to Maya, Harper, and Laney. She even had space in the primary bedroom for a "Maya" nightstand when she stayed over several nights a week.

When a headhunter contacted Maya in late August about a weeklong flair bartending competition filming for a reality show, she contemplated joining. Then he mentioned the grand prize, which would cover her entire tuition, *plus* part of her student loans. Even the third-place prize would cover almost a year of tuition. Bottom line, she jumped at the chance. And now she was here, confident with the summer she spent honing her skills at Gabriella's bar, she would place third at a minimum.

The announcer called the bartenders back up to reveal the results of the competition. The camera crew lights flipped on, and Maya squinted into the crowd. She winked at Remi, who blew a kiss, and took a deep breath.

Everything was perfect.

A LETTER FROM THE AUTHOR

Hey there!

Thanks so much for reading *In Walked Trouble*. Remi and Maya were such fun characters to write, and I hope you loved getting to know their story. I was also *super* excited to bring back Ben, the best sidekick in the world. When I first drafted this story, Remi was supposed to have a different roommate. But I fell in love with Ben so much during *Not in the Plan* (Book 1) that I couldn't imagine him not having a solid role in *In Walked Trouble*.

As I continue to write my sparkly, upbeat romances celebrating queer joy, I'd love to keep you posted about my new releases and bonus content. Please sign up for my newsletter, below. I promise I won't spam you or sell your info.

www.stormpublishing.co/dana-hawkins

I'd be so grateful if you liked this book and wouldn't mind leaving a review. Even a short review can make all the difference in encouraging a reader to discover my books for the first time. Thank you so much!

In Walked Trouble was inspired by my younger days when I learned the tricks of the bartending profession and elbowed to find my place in (at that time) a male-dominated industry. I wanted to bring forth that fighting spirit in Remi and Maya and balance the complexities of working together as a team while competing.

I love exploring the human spirit and how loss affects people differently. It's a delicate balance writing a story dealing with loss and trauma while keeping it fun. Hopefully, I have landed my intention while keeping you entertained.

I consciously choose to write stories where coming out is not an "issue" and being LGBTQ+ is nothing to "overcome." Creating a world where my characters live in a safe, affirming, celebratory space while navigating their relationships and real-life issues fills my heart. I am keenly aware the queer community continues to live in fear and is subject to discrimination, violence, anti-inclusive legislation, and more. I write novels that create a reality I want to be a part of—a hate-free world.

Thanks again for being part of this amazing journey with me! Please stay in touch—I have so many more stories and can't wait to share them with you.

Dana Hawkins

𝕏 x.com/DHawkinsAuthor

⊙ instagram.com/d.hawkinsauthor

ACKNOWLEDGMENTS

I cannot believe I am writing my second batch of acknowledgments for my second book. *Second.* Just a few short years ago, when sitting down to write for the first time, I could have never fathomed this would become my reality.

There are so many people to thank, but I have to start with my spouse (my forever). You have had my back since the moment we met, and your encouragement is limitless. People often don't understand the sacrifices a partner makes when the other is fulfilling their dreams. Household chores, kid duties, carpooling, dog grooming appointments... the list goes on. Not only have you taken over so much so I could do this, but you have done it without one complaint while saying, "Honey, you're amazing!" How did I ever get so lucky to have you? I love you.

To my kids, Tanner, Kianna, and Joey. Since I started this writing journey, you have all shown me so much encouragement and celebration. I love you so much and hope you all know how proud I am of you.

To my parents, Dave and Esther Dusha. It is not lost on me how incredibly privileged I am to have the most supportive, loving parents in the world. You have encouraged your kids to dream big and are always so proud of what we do. Thank you for being in my corner. And Mom, thank you for beta reading! Your eagle-eyed attention to detail is incredible. I love you both so much!

Jennifer Gatewood. My critique partner extraordinaire. I

will shoulder-shimmy with you until the end of time. Thank you, always, for your friendship, guidance, partnership, and mentorship. Your willingness to, book after book, roll up your sleeves and provide kind, thoughtful, and brilliant feedback means so much to me. Your gift of storytelling and plot weaving is inspiring, and I am so grateful to learn from you every day.

Amy Nielsen. Whether we are critiquing work, podcasting, tossing ideas, or talking about the struggles of motherhood, you have been with me since day one. You have supported me, encouraged me, and guided me. Can you believe we did it?! From where we started to where we are—it's pretty darn amazing. Thank you for everything.

Dana Renee Green. You are an inspiration to me and so many others. Your grit and resilience are beyond this world, and I am so grateful to have you in my life. Thank you for joining me on this ride and being a continual, strong supporter. Your beautiful words will move the world, and I cannot wait to see it happen. Thank you for teaching me the power of manifestation! Your teachings help get me here.

S.E. Reed. Thank you for sharing this journey with me, taking me along with yours, and your daily check-ins. I am beyond jealous of your imagination and the world you create in your stories. Thank you for sharing so much knowledge (cut book, flash fiction, words are currency!) and encouragement (don't delete the cut book!). I'm so lucky that you accepted me into your world.

Katharine Bost. Your editing and critique skills are out of this world. Thank you for reading "The Scene" when I was so nervous about sharing it with others! The professionalism and teachings you gave me early on in my writing career guide me to this day. I appreciate you so much.

Emily Gowers. Thank you for being with me on this second book. Working with you this last year has been everything I hoped and more. You embody empathetic leadership, and I am so grateful to have learned from you.

Michael Dolan. Thank you for checking my boxing scene.

Bryn Donovan. Thank you for offering amazing feedback on my first few chapters.

So many more. Amanda (there is a reason you are a reoccurring character), Erica, Dustin, Ryan, Mollie, my Seattle friends who have encouraged me from the beginning, and my Minnesota family who cheers me on. Thank you.

And finally, thank you to Storm Publishing for giving my story a home.

Printed in Great Britain
by Amazon